SECRETS OF CASTLE ROWLEY

MATILDA LOCKWOOD

NIMBLE PIG PRESS

For permissions and inquiries, please contact:
matildalockwoodwrites@gmail.com

Please visit the author at:
matildalockwoodwrites.com

ISBN: 979-8-9892935-1-3
Library of Congress Number: 2023923038

Cover Design: Sarim Shuja
Published by Nimble Pig Press
PO Box 489
Indianola, WA 98342
Printed in the United States of America

First Edition

*To my beloved husband, who has been the anchor in my tempests and the
warmth in my winters.*
Thank you for being my muse and my rock.

CONTENTS

Chapter One

A Fresh Start

As Annabel attempted to summon up enough courage to knock on the imposing castle door, a wave of apprehension washed over her—yet, as she hesitated, the thought of retreat seemed equally daunting.

Therefore, she extended her fingers to grasp the frigid door knocker with a trembling hand, hesitating briefly before giving it a gentle rap against the stone. Her heart seemed to pound more rapidly in her chest, a whirlwind of fear and anticipation coursing through her veins as the sound echoed and reverberated through the desolate courtyard.

As she waited, a gust of wind rustled the leaves of the nearby trees, making her shiver involuntarily. Beside Annabel, her mother, Arva, sighed, rhythmically tapping her long fingers against the knuckles of her other hand. Annabel's stomach churned. She took a deep breath, steeling herself, and knocked again, this time with more force.

Finally, with an agonizing creak, the door swung open, revealing an older man with a languid, long face, like a horse with hooded eyes.

"Welcome to Castle Rowley," he intoned monotonously. "Who are you here to see?"

"She's here to be married," Arva wasted no time introducing herself and her eldest daughter. "I'm Arva Barlow, and this is Annabel. We're due in the castle chapel within the hour."

Their greeter let out a gloomy sigh and gestured for them to enter.

Both women gasped in awe as they stepped inside, exchanging astonished glances. Gold-painted plasterwork cherubs adorned the ceiling, while intricate tapestries draped the walls. The plush rug beneath their feet felt as luxurious as a sheep's fleece. A roaring fireplace filled the air with comforting warmth while the stern gazes of painted ancestors seemed to scrutinize Annabel's every move.

The man introduced himself as Leif, the castle's butler, and instructed them to wait. Annabel felt excitement and anticipation intertwining with her nerves as she exhaled a shuddering breath.

Glimpsing her reflection in a grand glass mirror, she offered a small, startled smile and eased the tension in her shoulders that had held them rigidly near her neck.

Rubbing her hands together nervously, her mind drifted to the day that had brought her to be married in this castle.

Months earlier, Arva had burst excitedly through the kitchen door, her words tumbling out urgently and full of hope. "Annabel, my dearest, my heart—I've got a match for you!"

She had ushered Annabel's younger siblings outside to play, ignoring the trepidation on her eldest daughter's face, and continued, "Now, don't give me that look. It's been weeks since the scandal. Mend that heart, and let's move on."

"Actually," Annabel smiled weakly. "Perhaps instead of looking to marry right away, I might look at bookbinding as a trade?"

"No, darling," Arva dismissed. "I don't mean to mince words, but you'll die in poverty."

"Mummy!" Affronted, her daughter added, "I've been doing it at the church for two years, and more importantly, I'm good at it. I may have left my heart there, but I got to keep my kit." She smiled proudly. "The priest said I was excellent. He's never seen anyone fix a hymnal faster."

"That's lovely, sweetheart. Is that the same priest who told you not to return to the church until your public penance is over?" Arva asked dryly.

"How I loathe public penance," Annabel whispered. "It makes me want to sink into a hole and never come out. And the gossip...just because I fell in love with Paul. As though I don't already harbor enough guilt."

"He was our vicar," her mother scolded, throwing a look at her daughter as barbed as her tone. "They don't marry outside of the gentry. I could have told you that myself if you hadn't seen him behind my back for two years."

"I'm sorry, Mummy," whispered Annabel, covering her eyes. "I truly am. I feel terrible for lying to you, and it was honestly the biggest mistake of my life."

In a softer tone, Arva said, "I know you're sick of the penance. Not to mention...this situation is not making it any easier to marry off your sisters, who actually want to find husbands."

"Thank you." A scowl hovered on Annabel's face. "Did you not hear me speak of the guilt I harbor? Why must you add salt to my wounds?"

"I'm only saying, sweetheart..." Her mother placed a hand on her daughter's shoulder and gently rubbed her back. "It's time to get you out of our house and into your own. Preferably somewhere far from here where you can make a fresh start. Wouldn't that be nice?"

"Far from here?" Annabel swallowed hard. "Are you looking to send me away?"

"Of course not." Arva waved her hands. "I'm looking out for your health and happiness. You'll fare better away from the gossip. And bookbinding is a lovely trade, dear. I'm not saying it isn't, but no one in this town will hire you after hearing of the scandal—so please put your dreams of being a self-made spinster at trade to bed. It takes a village, sweetheart, and that village starts with a man."

"I know I'm not self-made. I didn't say I was." Annabel tried again. "Perhaps I could work on Bettina's boat. They're the third-best fishers in the region, you know, and our friendship would get me a good deal on my own fishing boat."

"Not a bad plan." Arva cocked her head. "But know that if you become an old fisherwoman maid after all you put us through at church with your only attempt at love—you might just break my heart as well as your father's, who's already got what amounts to a broken back. Are you prepared to live with that?"

Annabel swallowed hard and looked down at her hands. "No. I'm not trying to be selfish."

"I would never say you were." Arva patted her daughter's shoulder, pushing on, "Now, Paul was never right for you–really, an older man dallying with a farm girl. He should have known better, even if you didn't."

"God's head, Mummy." Annabel buried her head in her hands and groaned. "Please stop speaking of this. I'm beyond mortified. It's the end of my world."

"If you believe that, you really are a fool." Her mother waved her hand.

"This new opportunity lies far enough away from prying eyes. Leave it behind, and those who love you will visit."

"You've already married me off, it sounds like," Annabel muttered. "Where should I sign?"

"My love." Her mother smiled. "Let this new suitor call. If you don't fancy him, that's the end of it. You can stay home forever if that's your wish, and I promise never to mention it again. But won't you give me one more chance at grandchildren before I'm old?" Arva smiled at her daughter, affection and worry wearing on her face.

"I'll do my best but promise nothing." Annabel crossed her arms, smiling despite herself. "And who is this, pray tell? The last man you tried to set me up with had a lack of teeth and humor."

"Ah, but my darling, he was the only man I met who dared to taste your soup," Arva cheerfully replied, brushing off her daughter's tone. "Richard Granger is the farmer's name. Castle Rowley is his home, or the grounds, anyway."

"A castle?" Annabel replied, surprised.

"Yes. To be clear, you'd be in a farmhouse on castle grounds." Her mother continued, "He has a tenancy under Baron Rowley, and they grow barley as we do! So, you've already got a foot in the door, practically speaking. And think of the security of a castle." Her voice grew animated. "Isn't that lovely to imagine? Of course, it's not as it once was, as they've stripped away the embellishments. I've been to see it from the outside, and it's no fairy tale; the moat's quite murky—but it looks safe, which is a mercy with the war being in our minds, mind you; what's safer than a castle with high walls and plenty of food?"

"I've heard stories of Castle Rowley." Annabel had frowned and begun setting the table for dinner. "Ghost stories, mind you." She shuddered. "There's a story of a ghost in the Rowley River bend who pulls at the feet of women who swim there."

"What story are you talking about?" Arva asked suspiciously. "I've never heard it."

"Legend has it…" Annabel rubbed her hands together. "Long ago, a maiden with hair as dark as the midnight sky met a tragic fate in the waters of the Rowley River bend. On a moonlit summer's eve, she ventured to the river for a clandestine swim, but as she frolicked beneath the silvered moon, an unseen force seized her ankles, pulling her down into the river's murky depths." She paused, then slipped a foot to touch her mother's ankle under the table, making Arva jump and shake her head at her daughter.

Standing and crossing the kitchen to pull out the bread and slice it, Arva chuckled. "Oh, my little storyteller. May the cruel world never quash your spirit."

Annabel grinned and walked to the cabinet to pull out a pile of napkins.

"How many extra tonight? Three?"

"Four." Arva handed her a stack of plates. "I'm not finished with this subject, by the way. Never mind about ridiculous river ghost stories. Richard is a good prospect, a respectable farmer like us—so you'd better be finished putting on airs, dallying with a literate man. I love you, sweetheart, you know I do, but no farmwife needs an educated husband."

"Noted," Annabel sighed. "Remind me, how far away is Castle Rowley from here?"

"It's at least a quarter-day's ride away," Arva said.

"That's a bit far." Annabel frowned. "Why would he seek a wife from such a distance?"

Her mother shrugged. "Well, he's a widower. He wants to find a woman who doesn't know his wife to start fresh. That's what he said, anyway."

"Well, that's something," Annabel sighed.

Arva suddenly chuckled. "Oh, goodness, that reminds me. A little bird told him you could read, and he said he didn't mind. In fact, under his roof, you can read whenever you like." She winked at the startled smile pulling at her daughter's mouth. "Goodness. Perhaps I should have mentioned that earlier?"

A light came into Annabel's face. "Yes, Mummy." She laughed. "I'd say you should have led with that." Looking down at her hands, she whispered, "You win; I'll meet him."

"You mean you win, my darling." Arva beamed. "Richard is from a respectable family; he has Baron Rowley's favor, three brothers, and two field hands allotted for the property. He's not searching for a young bride; he says he wants someone strong and appreciates a smart, courageous woman with a level head—perfect for you," she had added affectionately.

Annabel flushed at the praise. "Thanks, Mummy. He does indeed sound like a good match. You know me well."

"Marvelous," Arva had said with a satisfied sigh. "It could be such a lovely, fresh start. He'll call on you tomorrow afternoon."

When he arrived to call on her next day, Richard Granger's charm was evident in the sparkle of his blue eyes and the tilt of his head as he handed Annabel a small carved wooden box.

"Why Richard, thank you!" Intrigued, she eagerly opened it to find gingerbread and parchment scrawled with endearing words. After reading it, she looked at him with amused astonishment and asked, "Is this a poem? Can you write?"

Richard sheepishly confessed, "No, but I heard you can. I paid someone to write it for me." His grin widened, and he added, "I wagered you'd be worth it."

Annabel couldn't help but smile at his honeyed words, a flush creeping over her cheeks as she carefully tucked the poem into her skirt pocket and sampled the gingerbread, her mouth filling with the taste of autumn and rosewater, and she smiled despite her nerves. "This is delicious. You must be quite confident," she added shyly. "Not minding a potential partner who reads while you do not."

"I appreciate clever women—and you clearly are one," Richard replied, his voice lowering with an air of intimacy. "I know my way around a column of numbers, but I'm more skilled in manual labor, to tell you the truth. I welcome your advice."

Annabel gestured gracefully to the kitchen table. "Shall we sit, then? Ale or tea?"

Richard nodded appreciatively, and the way his gaze followed her was a balm on her recently wounded pride. "Ale would be most welcome."

As Annabel poured the ale and they settled at the table, she broached the topic that was in the forefront of her mind. "I wish to be transparent with you, so I may as well ask. Are you aware of the scandal?" She smiled wryly. "By that, I speak of what happened between me and the vicar."

"I am aware," Richard replied with a nonchalant shrug. "We all make mistakes, do we not? What truly matters to me is getting to know you."

Her heart leaped at his words, and as he kissed her at the door, she felt a warmth she hadn't experienced in weeks. The sadness and guilt that had lingered since her heartbreak began to fade, replaced by the promise of a new connection.

And now, just two months later, with her nerves tingling and her heart soaring as she fought to quiet any lingering doubts, Annabel stood ready to exchange her vows.

"Annabel!" Richard's voice echoed through the grand hall as he entered.

His confident smile reached her, instantly calming her nerves. "Today is the happiest day of my life. And Arva, it warms my heart to see you again. I trust the pair of you had a pleasant journey?"

Annabel followed him through the dimly lit corridors of the ancient castle, captivated by its haunting atmosphere. But as she meandered through the majestic halls, an eerie, mournful scream suddenly pierced the air, and her step faltered.

Swallowing her nerves, Annabel wondered if she had imagined it, but then it came again, and her ears strained to discern its origin. Her mother glanced back, surprised, but swiftly shook her head, perhaps to herself, urging them to continue.

Curiosity piqued, Annabel leaned closer to her fiancé and asked softly, "What was that?"

Richard's voice held a hint of amusement as he loudly whispered, "Ghosts," and her daughter was surprised to see Arva tremble with fear.

"A funny jest," Annabel retorted, attempting to mask the tremor in her voice. She began to scratch at her suddenly itchy, anxious palms. "Though it does sound like a tormented soul, does it not?"

"Sorry, dearest." Richard chuckled. "Yes, it's only a joke. It's merely the cry of a fox caught in the ongoing hunt that has just commenced outside the castle walls—the Baron holds them often."

"A fox hunt!" Arva exclaimed, her voice filled with awe. "Have you ever witnessed one? Tell me all about it; I'm curious about how one catches a fox."

"Of course." Richard extended his arm, offering it to Arva. They continued down the corridor, their heads close together as they spoke in hushed tones.

Annabel momentarily lingered, her gaze fixed on a painting adorning the wall before hastening her pace. A cheerful wave from a tall, freckled brunette folding laundry in front of a closet captured her attention, and her step slowed again. In her opinion, something relaxed and playful in the other woman's face made Annabel feel like she would be a good storytelling audience—always the mark of a good person. Encouraged, Annabel waved back before continuing on.

She felt a tap on her shoulder as she walked and turned around. A lovely woman stood there, wearing thick gloves, black hair severely pulled back behind her linen cap, and clothes streaked with soot. "I'm sorry," she whispered. "You dropped this." She gingerly handed over a tiny notebook with the ends of her fingertips, and Annabel's eyes widened.

"I don't know how to thank you," she whispered. "This has all my favorite ideas written down in it." Annabel gave a little laugh. "Not that I'm going to do anything with them. But it's nice to dream. I need to stop carrying it with me. But if I get an idea out of the blue..." Shaking her head, she grinned. "I'm Annabel Barlow, and I'm just on my way to get married. What's your name?"

"Hattie...it's nice to meet you." The girl smiled tightly. "I've got to get back to the fire." As Hattie disappeared down the hallway in the opposite direction, Annabel quickened her pace again.

Finally, they reached the chapel, where Richard went to the altar to wait, and Arva hugged her daughter tenderly. "Now, I know you prefer to get changed alone with your thoughts, so go slip into your wedding dress, sweetheart, and comb your hair. Let me know if you need anything."

As Annabel slipped into the vestry and opened her suitcase, contemplating the removal of her tunic, she paused, ears pricking at a noise

that sounded oddly like paper being moved. "Who's there?" As the rustling grew louder, Annabel wondered if she preferred the unseen disturbance to be a ghost or a rat. Carefully, she took off her shoe and held it aloft. "Come out, or I'll have to think the worst."

"Which is?" A delicate redhead, who looked to be no more than eighteen, unfolded herself from one of the cubbyholes where many rows of stiff vestments were hanging. She regarded Annabel nervously. "Are you going to hit me with that shoe?"

"No," Annabel smiled, putting the slipper back on her foot. "I thought you were a rat."

"Not today." The girl reached back into the cubbyhole, her torso disappearing from view.

"What were you doing in there?" Annabel asked curiously.

"Never you mind," muttered the girl, her voice muffled. "What are you doing in the vestry?"

"I'm changing." Annabel gestured to the dress over her arm. "I'm marrying Richard in about ten minutes."

"Richard Granger?" the girl moaned. "What a fool you are. God's bones, is this stuck?"

"Sorry?" Annabel asked, affronted.

"You certainly will be," the girl called back sharply. "Oooh!" Suddenly, whatever she had been pulling on came loose, and she fell on the floor amid fluttering pages. Her cheeks reddening, she began to scoop them back up, muttering under her breath.

"Stop that," Annabel put her hand on the girl's shoulder. "You'll curl the pages."

The girl looked at her as if she was mad. "What are you talking about?"

"I used to fix books at our church back home. Your journal came loose?" Annabel held her hand out expectantly. "It's drawings." The girl gathered the pages into a neat stack, face down.

"The binding I've mended a thousand times with cloth caught on a hook back there and tore it all apart." Cecelia shook her head reproachfully, but her chin wobbled as her eyes looked anxiously upon her pages.

"I've got a spare leather cover you can have. This is my kit here." Annabel set down her wedding dress and rummaged in her suitcase for a large leather pouch. She pulled out a small pair of scissors. "May I?"

"Aren't you getting married?" Cecelia frowned. "Not in a hurry, are you?"

"There's always time for a quick read or a fast stitch," Annabel winked. "Last chance."

"Fine. Don't look at the pages." The girl hesitated before handing it to her. "I'm Cecelia. Cecelia Rousseau. My mother Bridgette's the housekeeper, and my father James is the Baron Rowley's steward."

"I'm Annabel Barlow. You must have at least five signatures here, and what lovely paper." She put a strong clip on the sheaf of pages, then

carefully stripped off the old binding. Aware of Cecelia's curious eyes watching her every move, she opened a tiny pot of glue and applied linen strips to both sides of the torn binding.

Setting it aside, she withdrew a curved needle and strong linen thread, then began expertly sewing up the papers. Then she applied glue to the spine and slipped a new leather cover onto the stack, carefully aligning the pages with the cover. Smiling, she poked holes in the middle of the cover with an awl, threading a larger needle with a leather cord and stitching up the spine. Gingerly, she handed it back to Cecelia. "You should press it under something heavy for a day. When it dries, I wouldn't mind doing a nice embellishment stitch along the s pine."

"Thanks." Inspecting the cover suspiciously, Cecelia remarked, "Why would you do this for me?"

"I like fixing books." Annabel shrugged, beginning to shrug out of her shift and into her wedding dress. "And I love artists! I envy you—I can write but can't draw anything resembling anything. What do you like to sketch?"

"People. Squirrels. Rats. Annabel, don't move here," Cecelia said suddenly. "I mean it. You will regret such a decision, mark my words."

A rapping came at the door, and Arva poked her head into the room.

"What is taking you forever and a day, my darling?"

"Nothing, Mummy," her daughter said reassuringly, but her throat was suddenly dry, and she rubbed it. "Give me another moment." As Arva sighed and closed the door again, Cecelia tried to slip away, and Annabel gently caught her arm. "Cecelia. Where do you think you're going after saying something like that?"

"Never mind." The young woman shook her head. "Go and attend to your family. Forget all about it."

"That's going to be quite impossible." Annabel crossed her arms. "I'm going to need a bit more, I'm afraid."

"There are ghosts here, ghosts who haunt the halls and the fields and beyond, anywhere a Rowley has been," whispered Cecelia. She smiled nervously. "Have you heard of the ones in the river?"

"Yes," Annabel said evenly, watching Cecelia's face. "My mummy said it was rubbish. A silly story. I won't be swimming in the water anyway."

"There's loads more than that." Cecelia shuddered. "The ghost of the later Baroness Philippa Rowley haunts the stables, and her late aunt Amelia haunts the castle." She swallowed hard. "Legend says

Amelia Rowley was locked in an old trunk on her wedding day, and her husband locked her in it and died to get her money."

"I see." Annabel gave her a tired look. "Might you have any warnings that have naught to do with ghosts, child?"

"I'm not a child. I'm eighteen," Cecelia said reproachfully. "And I was just trying to prepare you. I daresay you won't last a minute here—I'd place bets on it, in fact." Scowling, she suddenly slipped behind Annabel and out the door, where Arva's face soon appeared again.

"Are you ready, sweetheart?" Her mother's smile was tired but hopeful. "Who was that?"

"One of the young castle residents trying to scare me with stories. Am I ready?" Hesitating, Annabel's smile froze on her face. She cleared her throat, looking more confident than she felt and her mind turning over whether Cecelia's warning was worth heeding or merely a game at her expense. She blurted before she lost her nerve, "Yes, I believe I am ."

Half an hour later, Annabel found herself reciting her marriage vows, standing before the second love of her life in the chapel of the crumbling castle.

Annabel noticed Richard's trembling hands beside her as they prepared to embrace. Her thoughts wandered to their wedding night, and as he held her close and their lips met, a mixture of excitement and apprehension rippled through her. Her heart overflowed with gratitude for this opportunity and the chance to leave her past mistakes behind.

Richard seemed on edge suddenly, his anticipation palpable. When they broke apart, her mother quickly scribbled on the parchment as a witness and slid it before Annabel, her face beaming with pride. "Congratulations, sweetheart."

"Once more unto the breach," whispered Annabel under her breath. "*Henry the Fifth*." With a flourish, she took a deep breath and signed her name on the wedding contract. She had accepted a new path and was as ready as she'd ever been.

CHAPTER TWO

THE PIG AND THE PIRATE

Richard held Annabel's hand firmly, pulling her aside as Arva spoke with the butler and prepared to leave. His voice, filled with tenderness, resonated softly. "My wife, my darling wife...it is so sweet to repeat those words. I consider myself the luckiest man in all of England." Slipping a large hand to her neck, he lifted her face to his and kissed her soundly, stroking her freckled cheek tenderly with his thumb.

Annabel blushed, her heart fluttering at his words while her mind brimmed with hopeful dreams for their future. Clearing her throat, she suggested, "Shall you show me our house? I can't believe I haven't seen it yet. The castle feels so far from home." She paused, correcting herself. "Not home. Castle Rowley is home now. You understand what I mean." She rubbed her hands together, looking up at him eagerly. "What crop do you plan to plant after harvest season? I was thinking on rye."

"None," he said quickly. "We'll have a fallow field."

"Didn't you have one last winter?" Annabel asked in surprise. "You said you grew only barley last year."

"Yes. I know barley," Richard laughed. "I don't care to learn another crop. We're paying our rent and taxes. Baron Rowley is happy with our lot... that's the important thing. Don't worry about it."

"Richard..." Annabel smiled. "It's extra money, and the rye is a good hardy winter crop—it grows deep roots to make for good soil. When you put in the barley again, you know that planting rye leads to fewer weeds, don't you?" She tilted her head in memory. "And if you plant it at night, even better. I used to garden by the moon with my neighbors in between plantings so the seeds could enjoy the moon's cool light before the harsh night of the day." She winked. "All this to say, I'm no stranger to farming, and you might let I have a hand in our crops if I'm going to live here. My mother always helped my father, a nd..."

"Oh darling, I love the way your pretty little head works. You're right, I'm sure—look at you, already being so helpful. I can't wait to see what you do with the place." Richard chuckled warmly, but as Annabel reached for him, his expression grew solemn, and he tenderly brushed his fingers against her cheek. "Unfortunately," he murmured regretfully, "a family matter has arisen."

"We're each other's family now." Annabel reminded him. "How can I help?"

He sighed, his voice sorrowful. "My mother's health has taken a grave turn. She needs my immediate attention, so I left her side only to come here today." Smiling wanly, he added, "Of course, I wasn't about to miss our wedding."

"Oh!" Annabel exclaimed sympathetically. "I'm so sorry, Richard. I can only imagine how much this must weigh on you."

Richard nodded, his gaze filled with pain. "She has been pure, un-wavering support throughout all my hardships. In fact, I must leave you now to tend to her needs. If I depart at once, I should be back to sleep with you in our marriage bed before nightfall." He leaned in, kissing Annabel passionately and leaving her breathless before turning to go.

"Oh…" Richard's new wife's eyes widened, her heart sinking at the realization that he intended to leave so soon after their wedding. "Wait," she exclaimed. "I'll accompany you. I can assist you in caring for your mother. I can make a good honey onion syrup for cough, and I have mullein tea; I can prepare herbs for a cleansing steam…"

Richard shook his head sadly. "I wish you could, my love. You must trust me—my mother is a proud woman who would not want you to witness her in such a weakened state. I must go alone, but perhaps she may feel differently after we have been married a bit longer. You understand, don't you?" He smiled wistfully. "I know this is less than ideal for both of us. I

feel like a poor husband to you already."

Annabel bit her lip, struggling to hide her disappointment. "It is indeed less than ideal. Could I not accompany you and wait in another room if she will not see me? I can cook and clean, and I never have to see her. If she has

been sick, surely she will welcome any help."

"Aren't you the most generous wife?" said Richard. "I'm afraid the answer is no. I truly wish it were possible—know that I hear your words and will convey your disappointment to my mother."

"No…" Deflated, she shook her head. "There is no need. Convey my best wishes."

Richard patted her arm. "I'm glad to hear it. I know you are eager to meet Mother in due time." Lowering his voice, he added, "I cannot wait to meet you again tonight."

Annabel smiled nervously. "Neither can I."

Taking her hand to kiss it, Richard gestured toward the tenant farmhouses she had passed on their way in. "As you know, the loss of Agatha hit me deeply." She nodded. "Of course, may she rest in peace."

"A man should not have to endure the loss of a wife at my age," he sighed. "Especially due to a simple skin abscess. I am immensely relieved that you possess knowledge of managing household ailments. Not to speak ill of the deceased, but my late wife was not well-versed in such matters."

Richard shuddered at the thought. "I have been unable to face any of it on my own—since Agatha's death, I have been sleeping at my mother's house."

"You haven't even been back to your own home since she passed?" Annabel asked in surprise.

He shook his head slowly, a rueful smile on his handsome face. "It may seem silly, but a man needs a woman, Annabel; there's no denying it. I couldn't even bring myself to enter the house alone, the very place where she...where she passed away. I didn't know what to do—having you here has changed everything. You bring me great solace." He kissed her temple. "All I need from you while I'm gone is to tidy things up in our home for when I return. Can you manage that?"

She nodded weakly, and a wave of loneliness passed through her as they exited the chapel. Feeling a bit foolish, she embraced Richard tightly, then turned to hug her mother. "Thank you for everything, Mummy," she whispered.

Arva nodded, her eyes welling up with tears as a tired yet radiant smile adorned her face. "I am overjoyed for both of you, my darlings."

Leif opened the castle doors, signaling their departure, and Annabel steeled herself for the moment.

Suddenly, the air was pierced by a high-pitched scream, and to their astonishment, a tiny piglet darted through the great hall toward them in a flurry of pink tails and hooves.

"Don't let him out!" cried a small child, racing after the piglet at breakneck speed, only to stumble in her pursuit, knocking the wind out of her. "Oh no!" she gasped, gulping as the piglet slipped through the door.

"Please, stop him!" Tears streamed down her face. "That's Gavin, my dearest friend in the world!"

Hearing the urgency in the little girl's voice, Annabel dropped her suitcase and lifted her skirt without a second thought. Sprinting after the nimble piglet, the young woman paid no heed to the calls from her husband and mother, her determination fueled by the little girl's plea. Fear gripped her heart as she realized the piglet was heading for the murky, swampy moat that encircled the castle. Annabel suddenly had a mad image of herself wading into the sewage after the poor pig even as it sank, and her desperation increased.

Breathless and frantic, Annabel spotted a group of farmhands closer to the moat than she was, and, cupping her hands around her lips, she shouted, "Please! Catch that pig!"

The men erupted into uproarious guffaws, their laughter filling the air, except for one kind soul who broke away from the group with startling speed. Moving swiftly, he scooped up the tiny creature, rescuing it from an imminent plunge into the moat.

Approaching Annabel, the man exuded a friendly, affable demeanor. His face, defined by a wolfish jawline and a brown patch secured over his right eye lent an air of mystery—but his expression, which seemed to demand nothing, put her at ease, and she smiled back. His freckled forearms shifted as the piglet wriggled in his arms.

As they walked back to the castle together, their breaths still ragged from the chase, Annabel mustered a tentative grin and introduced herself. "I'm Annabel Granger, nee Barlow—thank you so much."

"Pleasure." He nodded politely, a hint of a smile playing on his lips. "Charlie Wright. I work for you and your husband now, among others. Depending on the day, I'm one of the farmhands—or a stableman. What are you doing, risking yourself for a wee animal? I saw you take off running first before I snatched him."

"I suppose I could ask you the same question?" Annabel chuckled. "It's hard to turn down a request from a child—that little girl back there; I thought from such cries that her heart would surely break without this little thing. I thought I could grab him, but I overestimated my speed and underestimated the pig's agility."

"I'm more accustomed to catching chickens, myself," he remarked lightheartedly. "They tend to move slowly if you do."

The image of the friendly man moving deliberately to catch a wandering chicken brought laughter to Annabel's lips. "In our household, we've always assumed it should take at least an hour, so we'd send the children after our errant small animals to tire them out."

Chuckling, Charlie added, "Meanwhile, Cassidy Rowley has practically turned this pig into a master of escape. I suspect it's her way of evading her lessons."

Their laughter subsided as they reached her mother and husband, only to find anger on their faces. "What's wrong?" she asked in confusion.

Arva looked at Richard and then at Annabel, shaking her head in exasperation. She took a deep breath and brought her daughter in for a quick embrace, whispering in her ear, "Even the most patient husband won't tolerate you chasing after every little distraction. Compose yourself, dear. And my goodness, you're a married woman now—step away from that filthy pirate." Kissing her cheek, her mother released her. "You've got a husband, now."

"I—" Annabel's brows knit together, and her throat went dry as she looked from her mother to her husband. She shook her head, the color rising to her cheeks. "I'm sorry."

Wearing a forced smile, her mother turned toward her new son-in-law. "Richard, it was a pleasure." She patted his back before heading toward the waiting carriage.

Richard's voice was low as he replied, "Indeed, it was. Annabel, what possessed you to run off like that? You could have been injured."

As her mother departed, confusion clouded Annabel's expression, and she rasped, "But...did you not see the pig or hear the child's plea?"

"Of course, I saw them," he snapped, fixing her with a stern gaze. "Everyone in the vicinity saw them."

Taken aback, she cleared her throat and stammered, "It only seemed right to catch it before it reached the moat. The pig belonged to the little girl!" Annabel turned to Charlie. "Yes?"

"She's right, Richard," Charlie interjected, his words tentative. "There's no harm done—"

"Charlie," Richard's clipped voice interrupted, cutting him off. "You work for the farmers, not the other way around. Hand the pig over to Cassidy, and return to your duties. And Annabel—my darling, I never want to witness such behavior from you again." He offered her a patient smile, and before she could respond, he dropped her suitcase, clasping his hands together. "Ah, there's Bridgette." A tangible sense of relief cascaded across his features, and Annabel shifted her gaze to witness an older woman drawing near, her visage marked by weariness.

Strands of red curls tumbled from beneath her bonnet, framing a face etched with the fatigue of many years.

"Hello," Annabel greeted her. "You must be Cecelia's mother? I'm Annabel Granger."

"What is it, then?" Bridgette sighed.

Richard took Bridgette's arm. "Bridgette, please see my dear wife to her new home, would you? I must be off." He kissed Annabel's forehead, leaving her momentarily stunned, before striding off, and she watched him hop into the next carriage and close the door.

"I'm the castle housekeeper, mind you, not yours." Bridgette coughed loudly into her sleeve. "Come with me." Annabel followed her towards a small, dilapidated farmhouse.

Once they reached the porch, Bridgette began counting Annabel's tasks off on her fingers. "Once you're done in here, you'll need to tend to the privy, that's it, the little shed there. There used to be chickens around back, so the old coop needs cleaning—seeing as they've gone back to graze with the main flock in Richard's absence, Baron Rowley will require a fee to take them back. Extra cleaning supplies can be found in the closet on your way to the kitchen." Casting a grim look towards the house, she nodded stiffly and held out the key. "Good luck to you, Mrs. Granger, and good morrow."

Annabel took the key and stood on the porch for a moment. With only a few hours left in the day, she hesitated, surveying the sprawling property before her. Vast grass fields stretched as far as the eye could see, grazing cows dotting the landscape. Sturdy red barns housed chickens coming and going. Barley and wheat fields extended into the distance. And in the distance, she caught sight of the magnificent, lavishly adorned stables rivaling the king. Calmed by the scene, she took a deep breath, forced a smile, and, biting back the disappointment at no husband to sweep her over the threshold, opened the door to her new home.

Her initial horror was overwhelming, and Annabel instinctively brought her hands to her face to shield herself from the repulsive stench that filled her nostrils.

As she glanced around, her eyes widened further. Discarded, greasy bones lay on the table, swarmed by flies. Mud caked the wooden floor in

patches. The walls exhibited signs of an alarming black muck that she hoped wasn't mold. Rusty tools hung haphazardly from a workbench beside a fireplace clogged with soot, the hearth covered in thick, congealed wax.

Quickly retreating outside, Annabel leaned against the porch, her head spinning. She closed her eyes and took another deep breath.

"There is nothing either good or bad," she finally whispered to herself. "But thinking makes it so. *Hamlet.*" She marched back inside, set her suitcase down changed her clothes, and fetched two pails of water from the well, along with a thick bar of yellow soap from the trough at the side of the house.

Slipping back inside and locking the door, Annabel thoroughly scrubbed down the wash basin, the kitchen table, all four corners of the house, and a bench, then turned to the bed. Shuddering at the apparent bugs in the mattress, she hauled it outside to change out the straw. Upon returning inside, Annabel threw the blankets in a heap in the laundry basket. She spread her grandmother's quilt from her suitcase on the long wooden bench.

Annabel glanced out the window, guessing it had been an hour. Smiling, she whispered to herself, "Come on then. You deserve a treat, and then you can return to it."

Rinsing her hands in the basin, her heart dancing with excitement, she opened her suitcase again and drew out her greatest treasure: a small stack of books. A few were gifts from the church, copies of books they had a great deal of and had passed on to her. Some had each been bought for a handful of carefully saved shillings and a bottle of Barlow family beer—the latter to compel the peddler to allow a woman to buy from him—and she smiled in memory, lighting a candle.

As she settled onto a worn wooden bench, she carefully arranged the booklets on her lap, each a treasure trove of knowledge and imagination. The covers were made of thick, textured paper, bearing intricate designs that spoke of craftsmanship and attention to detail. Annabel marveled as she did each time at the delicate ink drawings and fine script adorning her sparse collection:

The English Gardener by Leonard Meager

The English Housewife by Gervase Markham

Pamphilia to Amphilanthus by Lady Mary Wroth

Orbis Pictus by John Amos Comenius

The Practice of Piety by Lewis Bayly

The Duchess of Malfi by John Webster

Poems and Fancies by Margaret Cavendish

The New Atlantis by Francis Bacon

As Annabel swept her gaze over them all, she slowly caressed the edges of the pages made from rough and unpolished paper, enjoying the luxurious texture beneath her fingers, thinking on the skill of the artisans who labored meticulously to create such delicate works. She let out a sigh, reminiscing about the hours spent in the church, her hands pristine as she lovingly tended to the exquisite books.

The New Atlantis boasted a slightly thicker cover than the rest. As she tilted it, the metallic sheen of the ink used for the title caught the sunlight, adding a touch of luxury that sent a happy thrill down her arms. Wishing she had the time to devote to it, Annabel gently set it down.

Her eyes sparkled as she opened *Orbis Pictus,* reveling in the wealth of illustrations. As her eyes swept over the rag paper, she smiled at the intoxicating interplay of words and pictures on each page. Suddenly, the tattered textbook brought to mind the children she hoped to have, but as she slowly looked round the filthy room, a startling sense of dread filled Annabel as the image of her child toddling across the dirty floor swam before her eyes. Shaking her head, she set the second book down.

With a sense of anticipation, she finally selected *Poems and Fancies.* As she gently opened the slim volume, the soft crackling sound of the paper filled her ears, and as she relaxed her shoulders and smiled involuntarily at the familiar prose, she finally began to feel more like herself.

Annabel was enveloped by a lovely sense of escape from her current sorrows. The words on the pages danced before her eyes, igniting her imagination and filling her heart with wonder. She'd always felt that books were a precious window to the world, broadening her horizons beyond the fields she knew so well and filling her soul with dreams of adventure and knowledge that would stay with her for a lifetime.

After a good half-hour of secret reading in the darkened farmhouse, during which she filled herself back up with renewed determination, Annabel put her treasures away. She resolved to finish cleaning the wretched mess that lay before her. She promised herself she would earn the reward of curling up with a story again once the arduous task was complete.

A hopeful smile tugged at the corners of her mouth, and a surge of strength coursed through her veins.

Throwing open the drapes and lighting the hearth and an oil lamp as the daylight began to fade, Annabel moved from room to room, taking inventory and noting needed repairs in her notebook.

She uncovered a child's bed frame with no mattress, accompanied by a threadbare rug and two chipped cedar trunks at the foot of the bed. A dresser and an uneven bench beside half a broken wardrobe provided the scant furniture. Annabel shook her head in dismay, jotting down another task in her small notebook.

Her stomach growling, Annabel searched for signs of a root cellar. Eventually, she stumbled upon it, but there seemed to be little there than massive salt barrels. Digging through the shelves, she found sacks of barley in various sizes. There were a few pots of jam. Continuing her search, she found a small larder containing a pile of rancid bacon wrapped in parchment. Shuddering, she discarded the spoiled meat and scrubbed the spot the maggots had been with vinegar and clove oil she had brought with her.

During one of her trips outside to fetch tools from a shed, Annabel spotted two small children following their nursemaid down the path and smiled warmly at them, a pang coming to her heart as she realized how much she missed her brothers and sisters.

The boy regarded her with fear while the young girl pointed and beamed.

"You're the one who saved my piglet, Gavin! He's safe in bed now, thanks to you."

"It was mostly Charlie," Annabel modestly protested. "The farmhand, Charlie Wright. He's the one who rescued Gavin."

"We know Charlie. But he wouldn't have seen Gavin if it wasn't for you," the little girl reminded her. "You've got a good set of pipes."

Annabel laughed. "Aren't you funny?"

The girl sighed dramatically. "You're supposed to say you're welcome."

Chuckling, Annabel nodded. "You're quite welcome. I'm Annabel Granger."

"I'm Cassidy," the girl whispered. "And this is my brother, Talon." She proudly displayed her carved wooden horse. "And this is my horse. He may not be alive like Gavin, but he feels real. Look at his legs!"

Talon rolled his eyes. "A wooden horse can't feel real. Don't be such a girl."

Annabel accepted the intricately crafted wooden horse, examining it with genuine interest. It was a beautiful piece, its delicate hooves in perpetual motion.

In awe, she remarked, "What kind of playthings you have in a castle is remarkable. Back home, a toy like this wouldn't last a day among our rough-and-tumble bunch before being broken. Does your horse have a name, then?"

"Panza." Cassidy nodded solemnly. "His name is Panza. He's scared of the dark but trying to be brave. It's not easy when you can break so easily, you know."

"That's not why." Snorting, her brother mocked, "It's because *you're* afraid of the dark."

"I have bad dreams!" Cassidy hissed at her brother. "It isn't my fault."

"It is," laughed Talon. "Your very presence lets in the evil. Second twin, twice the sin."

"You're the one who tells me ghost stories, and then I can't sleep," grumbled Cassidy.

"Did you hear the one," Talon asked Annabel while Cassidy put her hands over her ears. "About the two orphaned children left in the woods by their wicked uncle? He meant to steal their inheritance, but instead, the children expired in the dead of night and had their deaths avenged by their own ghosts."

"Stop!" Cassidy moaned. "Don't say a word. Don't give him the satisfaction."

"Panza is so fortunate he has you to keep him safe," Annabel whispered with a smile, eliciting a radiant grin from Cassidy as she carefully took back her toy. Talon rolled his eyes. With a tired smile, the nursemaid led the children away, leaving Annabel with a newfound warmth.

At one point, Bridgette made an appearance. Standing in the doorway, she raised an eyebrow at seeing the transformed house, and upon entering the clean room, a wry smile tugged at the older woman's lips. "Still have quite a way to go, but you've done a decent job on the fireplace," she remarked, hesitant approval in her tone.

"Thank you," Annabel replied automatically, a sense of pride welling up within her. "Bridgette— how long ago did Richard's first wife pass away? The state of the house suggests it has been longer than I expected."

"Aren't you a dipper of honey?" Bridgette's eyes twinkled with amusement as she chuckled. "Oh, it's only been two months, give it take. Richard isn't one for cleanliness. I've never seen him lift a finger to clean anything that wasn't crop-related. He expects his women to take care of his home."

"The feast smells wonderful—I've enjoyed the aroma each time I walk by the castle," Annabel said softly. "Richard doesn't seem to have much food. Are there ever any leftovers, by any chance?"

"Only for those who complete their work before the day is over. And at this rate, I wouldn't count on it." Shrugging, Bridgette swept her eyes over the farmhouse, threw an amused look at Richard's new wife, and left.

Anger simmered within her as Annabel stood in the center of the room. Taking a deep breath, she poured her feelings into cleaning for the next several hours. As the hours flew by, she scrubbed, folded, mended, and scoured every nook and cranny of the house. When the moon indicated it was at least past three in the morning, the house was almost clean, and a basket of neatly mended clothes sat at the foot of the bed. Exhaustion and hunger washed over her.

Annabel turned her gaze out of the small window facing the castle, her heart sinking as she realized the entire place lay in darkness. The feast had concluded, and everyone seemed to have retired for the night. All hopes for leftover food, however scant, evaporated before her, and incredibly, she had seen nothing to eat since the rancid bacon, except for a meager bowl of unseasoned boiled barley.

It hadn't escaped her notice that Richard still hadn't returned, and the weight of disappointment settled upon her shoulders, threatening to break her spirit. Shaking her shoulders as if to dislodge the dread settling there, Annabel fetched a fresh bucket of water from the well and mixed in lemon juice and vinegar, just as she had done for the floors. Scrubbing herself down until she could no longer smell the house on her skin, she dried off, slipped into clean clothes, and stepped outside.

Smiling, Annabel let the sweet, cool night air wash over her. The gentle breeze whispered against her skin, coaxing a small smile to her face. As her tense muscles relaxed, she allowed herself a moment of respite, finding solace in the soothing sounds of nature. Her gaze swept across the darkened fields, illuminated only by the soft glow of the half-full moon.

And then, a flicker of light in the distance caught her attention. Her stomach growled. The idea of food cooked over an open fire stirred her senses enough to set off purposefully in the dark, ignoring the voice within her that warned against such folly.

After a brief walk, Annabel reached a short stone wall. Peeking around it, she discovered a roaring fire in a pit encircled by large stones.

Approaching cautiously, she observed a figure sitting before the flames, its features obscured by a hooded cloak, and intrigued, Annabel inched closer, her curiosity getting the better of her.

Annabel watched with fascination as the person's hand delved into a sack, producing a carved wooden horse—one strikingly like the one Cassidy had shown her. To her astonishment, the person nonchalantly tossed the wooden horse into the fire.

Annabel gasped in shock, and the figure stood, his face charged with fear. It was Charlie, the farmhand who had saved the piglet.

"What are *you* doing here?"

CHAPTER THREE

FIRELIT FRIENDSHIPS

"What am I doing? What are you doing?" Annabel replied irritably. She sighed when she heard her own angry voice out loud. "I apologize—I'm so bloody tired. I must be seeing things. Do you mind me asking if you are truly burning children's toys?"

"I do mind, actually." He sat down again, regarding her suspiciously, clearly rattled by her sudden presence.

"That little girl you rescued the pig for, Cassidy, she has a horse just like it inside." Annabel frowned. "Why would you burn it? "

"This one's not hers," Charlie hedged, his voice laced with a hint of caution. "It's dangerous for you to be out here this late, even with the castle guards nearby."

"I'm not afraid," she retorted, her tone sharper than intended, while she tightened her coat around her. She glared over her shoulder into the darkness and added, "I can take care of myself. I've got a knife in the pocket of my skirt, and I'm ready to use it."

"That doesn't mean you shouldn't be afraid," he replied, and his remaining eye flashed in the warm glow of the fire, catching her off guard. "There are all sorts of unsavory characters lurking about. Much worse than *filthy pirates*." His voice turned flat, his expression guarded, and shame washed over her.

"That was my mother's comment, not mine," Annabel murmured, her voice remorseful. She swallowed hard and added, "I should have told her off. I'm sorry."

"No need. But go home," Charlie repeated with a note of urgency. "Don't shorten your already brief life."

"Well, I'm just passing through nature on my way to eternity," she remarked with a hint of defiance and turned to leave.

Unexpectedly, Charlie burst into laughter—a hearty, genuine laugh that rang into the night and seemed to shed years off his countenance. Annabel couldn't help but smile at the transformation as she looked back at him.

"*Hamlet*?" he asked, leaning forward slightly, the sack at his side revealing another wooden figure.

"Yes," she agreed in surprise. "How did you know? Can you read?"

"I'm afraid so." He nodded hesitantly. "Why do you ask?"

"It's only that I can, too." A rush of elation washed over her. "I used to fix books for the church. I'd read as I fixed them, for hours sometimes...Shakespeare when I was lucky." She sighed. "I miss it so much. I miss access to a great deal of books. I've got the smallest collection you've ever seen, none of them Shakespeare, but it's my greatest treasure."

"Better than nothing, by far," he agreed. "I've also got some good ones, mostly plays, that I don't mind sharing. Come by the stables sometime."

Hope rose in her. "Do you mean it?"

Charlie grinned, the fire dancing in his remaining eye, and at that moment, a connection sparked between them—a fleeting bond she tried to suppress. "If I tell you a lie, spit in my face and call me a horse," he quipped.

Laughing, Annabel remarked thoughtfully, "That sounds like Shakespeare, but I'm not familiar..."

"*Henry the Fourth*," he revealed.

A rustling in the nearby bushes made Annabel catch her breath while Charlie returned to stoking the fire. Just then, the tall, friendly brunette who had waved at her while folding laundry emerged with a wide smile. "Well, look at you. Good morrow!"

"If it's better than yesterday, it will be, anyway," muttered Annabel, immediately feeling guilt at her tone. "I'm sorry. I'm a bit out of sorts..."

To her surprise, the woman just giggled. "I hear you. I went to pick chives to liven up our meal and, hopefully, the rest of our day. Want a baked potato? We've got an extra," she said, her eyes twinkling as Charlie shot her an incredulous look. "Oh, come now, husband. You know food tastes better with company."

"I'm all for company," Charlie dryly replied, "But this is Richard Granger's new wife. If he finds out, you know he won't be happy."

"Oh, pish posh," dismissed Lise.

"I don't mean to cause trouble." Annabel bit her lip and took a step back towards the path. "I can leave."

Tutting her tongue against the roof of her mouth, Lise reassured her,

"Pay him no mind. No one cares what Richard does except his own mum and the Baron. Charlie doesn't like to get involved, but I have no qualms. Now, do you want a baked potato or not?"

"That sounds wonderful. Yes, please," Annabel answered before she could stop herself. "If you're sure I'm not intruding..."

"Of course not. Have a seat," Lise urged, nodding approvingly as Annabel settled onto a log opposite them. "Little warmth within makes everything better. New friends don't hurt either, and I think I like you already."

"Aren't you nice? Thank you so much," Annabel smiled at her thankfully. "I was having a horrid night, to tell you the truth."

"I can't help but notice you're out rather late," said Lise. "I'm here to keep Charlie company after the Baron's chamberlain made him fire keeper for the night. But what about you—are you a ghost? A wildling? A sleepwalker?"

"I wish." Annabel laughed. "I've been cleaning my nightmare of a farmhouse all day and nearly finished. I still haven't completed that mountain of laundry. I just needed some fresh air and saw the fire, then my feet decided for me."

"Ah, now that's how I met Charlie too—by the fire," Lise exclaimed, a mischievous grin on her lips. "I snuck up here at night, risking the archers catching me. You could've knocked him over with a feather."

"Scared me half to death," muttered Charlie as he deftly retrieved three blackened potatoes from the fiery coals using a pair of battered tongs.

"Oh, I did the same thing," Annabel groaned. "I'm terribly sorry if I startled you with my shouting."

"It's alright," he assured her, slicing open the giant spuds with a knife, releasing tendrils of steam that mingled with the smoke. "Salted butter and chives?" he asked, and Lise beamed when Annabel nodded eagerly. With practiced hands, he added a pat of butter from a small crock to each potato before taking out a small, flat wooden board and swiftly chopping the chives, then sprinkled them evenly over the plates.

As they savored the warm meal in silence, Annabel couldn't help but feel a sense of comfort emanating from the crackling fire and the newfound camaraderie among them. She took a bite of the potato, relishing its rich flavors with the crunch of the chives, and closed her eyes in bliss.

When she opened them again, she found both Lise and Charlie watching her curiously. Embarrassed, the three of them averted their gazes and pretended to focus on their plates.

Seeking to dispel the awkwardness, Annabel broke the silence. "So, Lise, what were you doing in the middle of the night when you first arrived and approached Charlie by the fire? It sounds like a story."

"I was on the run," Lise winked, earning another sharp look from Charlie.

"What? We can trust her. She's one of the good ones," Lise assured Charlie, her eyes dancing mischievously. "I can tell. Woman's intuition."

He raised his hands in mock surrender, a reluctant smile on his lips. "How could you possibly know that?"

"She smiled at me inside when I waved to her. She's no snob," offered Lise, as if Annabel was not in front of them. "I think she wants a friend more than a bargaining chip."

"Please forgive me, dear wife, but your optimism is quite ridiculous." Charlie laughed. "I never tire of your candor, though it may be the death of us all."

"You think about death too much," Lise sighed, making a face at her husband and smiling at Annabel. "I'm right, aren't I?"

Awash in the glow of new friendship and her curiosity piqued, Annabel nodded eagerly. "I would never dream of betraying your trust."

"See?" Lise beamed at her husband, gently prodding him in the side, and he gave her a wry smile. Her stage whisper turned more serious, and Annabel leaned in to hear the secret. "I used to sell wonderful tea in a town far from here. I had a good hand with it. But then I was falsely accused of witchcraft by a competitor—a lot of rubbish. I decided to leave before it escalated to a court case. Unmarried witches don't stand a chance. So, I changed my name, my trade, even my hair...and Charlie, being such a helpful man, helped me learn all the lies I needed to gain employment here. We were married within the month."

"God's head," Annabel said enviously, a mixture of admiration and jest in her voice. "I'm impressed by your fortitude—I hope some of it rubs off on me. And I promise again that I won't breathe a word of this to anyone."

"I believe you." Lise smiled. "And I'm glad to hear it.

They finished their potatoes around the crackling fire, basking in its warmth for a few peaceful minutes. Annabel closed her eyes and dreamily pretended that tomorrow she would wake up in her own bed at home, not in the dirty pit she'd spent the last half a day cleaning and sighed.

The tranquility was interrupted by Charlie's sigh, and his voice rose as he confessed, "I really wasn't burning the children's toys, you know."

Annabel's eyes fluttered open, and she looked at him groggily. "What?"

"It's not a completed toy. I'm a woodcarver." Charlie's hands shifted, still holding his fork and bowl, catching Annabel's attention. She looked curiously at his long, bandaged fingers, and he quickly put his bowl down, tucking his hands out of sight. "That was one of my castoffs." Charlie gestured towards the still-burning wooden horse figure. "I make them to sell at market for extra money and don't have the room to keep a graveyard of failed attempts." Looking at the fire, he muttered, "I just didn't want you to think I was some sort of terrible monster."

"He's really not. He's the best of the monsters," Lise teased, patting Charlie's back. "But he's not supposed to make them, so please, don't tell anyone."

"Sorry..." Annabel sat up straight. "You made them? Those carvings?"

"Yes," Charlie nodded. "My father taught me years ago, before he disappeared like so many around here."

"Disappeared..." Intrigued, Annabel's curiosity continued to bubble. "But why aren't you supposed to make them?"

Lise let out an irritated sigh. "The Baron has forbidden Charlie from it."

"But why?" Annabel frowned.

She shrugged. "Baron Rowley makes a cruel proclamation from time to time that makes little sense. You wouldn't think the likes of him would care, but Charlie's been warned it'll be twenty lashes straight away if he's caught carving. It's happened a few times already. His back looked like raw meat after."

"Lise," Charlie said disapprovingly. "Don't give the girl nightmares."

"She might ask well know the truth of this place," his wife argued.

"Why don't you leave?" Annabel asked in horror. "That's no way to live. If you're getting your work done, there's no harm done in enjoying something you love. How can he be so cruel?"

"I'm behind on my taxes, and some time ago, I tried to move away, unsuccessfully. The Baron doesn't like deserters," said Charlie. "I wager I'm still being punished. He'd send a falcon or a hunter after us if we tried to leave without him granting it. And I still owe loads of taxes and fees, which are always being added to. It's easier to stay out of his way and do what he wants."

Annabel shook her head, appalled by the unjust treatment.

Lise's voice dripped with sarcasm. "Welcome to Castle Rowley, where the madness knows no bounds. Just try to stay out of his way if you can."

"How kind of you to give Cassidy such a treasure when her father is such a brute," Annabel said softly. "She had named him and everything."

"I did not give it to her," Charlie protested, shaking his head. "I stashed a few things in the wall of the stables, and she got into it. I gave her the horse to stop her from saying anything about the rest of it."

"Little blackmailer," muttered Lise. "He could have gotten a full pound at the market for it. You're too soft, my darling—I likely would have blackmailed her right back."

Annabel couldn't help but voice another question. "May I ask you something else?"

Charlie frowned and suddenly cast his gaze upon Annabel directly, catching her off guard. "Sure, as long as it's not about my eye."

Her stomach turned, and she felt a surge of embarrassment flood over her. "Never mind," she muttered.

Laughing, Charlie reassured her, "It's alright. It's just that everyone asks the first chance they get, so I can't resist." Winking, he added, "If you must know, an eel ate it right out of my face—don't go swimming after eating meat."

"I can't swim, not even a little," Annabel said, aghast. "Truly, an eel?"

Lise snorted, unable to contain her laughter. "He's joking, of course."

"Sorry." Charlie laughed. "I only joke because the reality is so depressing."

"Never mind, then." The atmosphere shifted, and the warmth enveloped them seemed to wane momentarily. Sensing the change, Annabel tried to change the subject in hopes of answers. "Here's a better question I might be more entitled to ask. Do either of you know where my husband really is tonight? Richard Granger?"

Hmmm..." Lise looked wary, exchanging a glance with Charlie before responding. "Where did he say he was going?"

"He said he was visiting his ill mother, but I expected him back before nightfall," Annabel whispered, a knot forming in her stomach. The pity in Lise's expression was hard to bear. "Oh, please don't look at me like that."

Lise sighed, her voice tinged with sadness. "I'm fairly certain Farmer Granger is with his girlfriend tonight. There's a woman who sells herself—a local girl who grew up in this region and works at a brothel down by the harbor."

Charlie stoked the fire. "Her name is Gwyneth Jones."

"Gwyneth Jones, that's right," confirmed Lise, nodding. "As far as I know, she's been seeing Richard consistently, one way or another, since they were teenagers. I've seen her here more recently, easily less than a month ago."

Annabel's cheeks grew hot with embarrassment. "Richard has been courting me for *two* months."

"Well..." Lise's voice carried a hint of remorse. "Two months ago is when Agatha went missing. Farmer Granger bragged afterward that he would be locking down another girl from out of town to keep his tenancy clean." She scowled, her disapproval evident. "No woman here would have him after what happened to Agatha. And Nancy before her."

Annabel's heart sank, her world crumbling before her. "Agatha... what do you mean, she went missing? I thought she died from a skin abscess. That's what Richard said. And Nancy?"

"A skin abscess? That bloody man!" spat Lise. "No, she absolutely did not."

"Careful," muttered Charlie.

"Why, it's not even a good lie," she exclaimed. "What is that addled farmer playing at?"

"He's foolish." Charlie shrugged. "That much is obvious."

Lise's voice was charged with emotion as she turned back to Annabel. "Agatha is not dead. Mark my words—something happened to her, but she's alive. I just know it. I know that it might be hard to hear that his late wife is still alive if you're in love with him—"

"Well, I thought I was." Annabel swallowed hard. "If he was with a prostitute on our wedding night, I'm honestly not sure how I feel about him."

"Either way, his last wife isn't dead," Lise asserted resolutely, exhaling hard through her nose as she looked down, rubbing her hands together.

"We don't have any solid proof she vanished, "Charlie sighed. "But it does seem strange, how she was perfectly healthy one day, gone the next, with nothing but Richard's word that she had died naturally and been sent to the bodyhouse to be burned."

Intrigued by Lise's conviction, Annabel leaned forward, her eyes filled with curiosity. "Where do you think she is?"

"Oh, I don't know," her new friend admitted, voice uncertain. "I'm unsure if Richard sold her or if her family came to snatch her back," Lise said in a rush, then shuddered with her whole body as if trying to shake off the intensity of the memory. "But...I think it's one of those."

The weight of this revelation settled heavily upon Annabel's shoulders, and as the fire crackled, its flickering flames casting dancing shadows upon their faces, they sat in contemplative silence.

Charlie reached into his sack and pulled out three small apples, offering one to each of them. Annabel's heart swelled as she accepted the gift, feeling the warmth of their newfound friendship. She made a mental note to bake them both her mother's famous barley cakes.

"Change of subject. Have you heard of the story of the Rowley Riddles?" Lise asked, eyes dancing.

"No," whispered Annabel curiously.

"Not for nothing, but..." Lise grinned. "No one can tell it like Charlie."

"No one's going to," he quipped in a mock affronted voice, and both women laughed. Charlie's voice took on a storyteller's cadence again as he leaned closer, his green eye sparkling. "It all began eighteen years ago, in 1677, with the ill-fated love between Baron Henry Rowley and Baroness Phillippa Wick."

Annabel pulled her cloak tighter around herself, her eyes fixed on Charlie, eager to hear the tale. It had been so long since she'd heard someone tell a story, and she smiled as she felt her shoulders relax, and her curiosity grow.

Charlie began, "Henry, an older man of noble stature, and Philippa, a lady of eighteen, Baron and Baroness, embarked upon a union fueled by passion and dreams. It was a love match—they shared many common interests and openly expressed their desire for an heir to carry on their legacy."

"Too openly," Lise interrupted. "Oh, they made it quite public. Some even say they engaged in intimate rendezvous in the stables, claiming it captured the 'energy' of the horses." She shuddered.

Charlie snorted at Lise's comment before continuing, "Yet, as time passed, their fervent hope turned to anguish. Despite their efforts, Philippa did not conceive after eighteen long months. A child's absence soured Henry's heart and he began to suspect Phillippa of conspiring against him."

The fire crackled, its flames reflecting the tumultuous emotions in the tale. Charlie's voice grew softer as he continued, "To alleviate his sorrow, the Baron sought solace in the arms of other women. But fate seemed unyielding, and his endeavors bore no fruit. Whispers circulated, casting doubt upon the Baron's fertility, for no woman could conceive beneath his touch."

Lise shook her head. "But don't ever mention it to him if you know what's good for you."

"Indeed." Charlie continued. "In 1679, after two years of trying, Philippa's womb swelled with life. But, alas, rumors emerged suggesting that another man was Frederick's true father."

Annabel's eyebrows shot up in surprise, her mind racing to comprehend the twists and turns of the story. "Does anyone know who it is?"

"No one," whispered Lise. "Some say it's Henry's brother, Geoffrey. There was a bit of a scandal about them being found cavorting in the chapel, but he wasn't in the country when Frederick would have been conceived."

Charlie nodded. "The rumors have persisted, even though Philippa gave birth to twins in 1691, six years ago."

"Cassidy and Talon, the little Rowley troublemakers." Lise shook her head. "But the next part is the worst."

Charlie nodded. "The Baron's doubts and anger drove him to banish her from her books, her property she came to the marriage with, and her lengthy charitable activities. He locked her in her chambers."

Annabel frowned. "What a monster."

"He likes to control people and seems to feed on their torment," Charlie said thoughtfully. "I'd call him a sadist."

"Circling back," Lise interjected, "Philippa acquired and commissioned several pieces from remarkable artists in residence during her time."

Charlie's voice carried sadness as he continued, "But then, in 1692, when the twins were just one year old, after a year of the Baron's harsh rules—Phillippa vanished, and with her, the treasures she had gathered throughout their marriage. No one knows where they are or where she is. Henry destroyed many more artifacts in his rage, looking for them." He shook his head. "Her maids said she spent all her time writing before she died, burning the drafts, then everything else vanished when she did."

Annabel's eyes widened with curiosity, her voice barely above a whisper, "Vanished? Just like Agatha?"

Both Charlie and Lise nodded solemnly, their expressions mirroring the weight of the mystery. "Yes, sadly," Charlie confirmed. "She disappeared without a trace, leaving only whispers, unanswered questions, and the rumor that she had buried the lost treasures—and several clues to find them —deep within the castle. Her closest maid said she bragged of creating riddles leading to her sudden treasures as one last trick on Henry. It's thought by many that she fled England and is staying with Frederick's father, whoever that may be."

As the crackling flames cast dancing shadows upon their faces, Annabel felt herself drawn deeper into the story, her voice barely audible, "God's bones. What a story."

Charlie leaned closer, a glimmer of intrigue sparkling in his eye. "But there is more. Once, the Baron's daughter Cassidy stumbled upon a peculiar fragment of parchment in the library, stuck in the side of a wooden storage cabinet built into the wall. It was tattered and yellowed with age, and it bore a cryptic riddle, a small ink drawing of a treasure chest, and Philippa's signature."

Lise added, "We don't know if it's the first riddle or how many others there are, but thanks to children not being able to keep a secret around the castle, at least not around servants; we know the entirety of this one." Her grin widened as she recited the riddle alongside Charlie, their voices intertwining seamlessly:

Ascend your knees and look for birds,

Seek sweethearts entwined to find the words.

"Hmmm..." Annabel tilted her head. "If I imagine ascending my knees, I'm marching. Birds are in the sky..."

"There's a shack where soldiers used to store supplies during wartime," Lise sighed. "We thought the same thing about marching. We couldn't find it there."

Wrinkling her brow, Annabel said, "Sweethearts entwined...sweet entwined...like taffy, perhaps? Do they make candy here?"

"Sometimes." Charlie nodded. "We've scoured the kitchen, too. Nothing."

There was silence for a moment, and then Annabel clasped her hands. "When I walked by the staircase, past the chapel, there were what looked like little people embracing, carved into the baluster. You'd be ascending your knees if you went up the staircase!"

"There are birds carved into it, too," Charlie added. "At the banister at the top. You can see them from the bottom."

"That's bloody it." Lise was grinning, leaning forward in excitement. "Aren't you clever? What were you doing before this?"

"Thanks." Annabel's eyes sparkled. "Farming now, with a touch of bookbinding at the church."

"You're bookish like Charlie – that's why you're brilliant."

Lise clasped her hands together. "The staircase will be so easy to check. I'll find a way to check every piece tomorrow while laundering."

"This we have to celebrate." Digging into the bag beside him, Charlie pulled out a small wooden box and offered them the contents.

"Gingerbread?"

Lise eagerly took a piece. "It's been too long." Smiling as she swallowed half of it in one bite, she gestured to Annabel. "You've got to try some. It's Charlie's late mother Mara's recipe, and Maggie only makes it occasionally. If you can believe it, the last batch was stolen from him while he slept."

"I wouldn't say late." Charlie scowled. "If you can say Agatha vanished, Mara is just as likely to have done the same."

Annabel took a piece, closing her eyes in wonderment as the welcome flavor exploded on her tongue. She nodded silently as she savored it.

Charlie beamed with pride. "My mother was a wonderful baker. She invented four recipes still used in the kitchen here—you might taste rosewater and almonds."

"Rosewater, yes," Annabel echoed. She paused, the wheels in her head turning. "Funny...When we met, Richard gave me gingerbread that tasted like this."

Lise frowned. "Also in a wooden box?"

Annabel nodded weakly. "Yes, much like this one, with the stripe across the bottom and the inlaid circles on the sides. I assumed it was from a local vendor."

"Very local," laughed Lise. "I've never seen one with these embellishments that Charlie didn't carve. Those circles are his trademark."

"There was also...a poem inside." Blushing, she recited it. "Please tell me that wasn't yours as well, Charlie?"

His expression darkened into a scowl. "Then I won't tell you," he muttered. "That thieving git."

"Truly?" Annabel sighed. "There goes the last of my affection for that man."

"Don't let your love be lost on my account. Do you still have it?" Charlie asked. "The wooden box, I mean."

"Yes, though the gingerbread is long gone," she said, taking another piece.

Charlie explained, "If you push both circles on the sides in simultaneously, there's a false bottom that slides out."

"Actually, I figured that out." She grinned. "There's a little bird carved under the extra wood."

"It's a W," he muttered.

"Oh, for Wright. Your last name. Right, of course." Annabel's cheeks colored. "Do you want it back?"

"No." Charlie grinned. "It sounds like it was delivered into good hands. I don't have room to store too many, anyway, and my boxes are still not good enough to be sold at market."

"It looked perfect to me," she replied.

There was a pause as they all nibbled on gingerbread and stared into the comforting blaze before them.

"Listen..." Lise placed a comforting hand on Annabel's shoulder. "You're not alone in this. Despite our limited power within the castle, we're here for you. If you ever need anything, don't hesitate to find us."

Annabel nodded quickly and offered a shy smile, overcome by such unexpected kindness. "Thank you so much...both of you."

When Annabel finally returned to her house, her eyelids heavy, the moonlight cast an ethereal glow over the landscape. At the same time, a sense of determination swelled within her, fueled by the kindred spirits she had encountered on this peculiar night.

Chapter Four

Illusions of Love

Annabel splashed tepid water from the basin on her tired face the following day, smiling weakly as she swept her hair back and mused over last night's fireside conversations.

A gentle knock came at her door, and when she answered it, Lise stood there, arms laden with a neatly stacked basket of clothes.

"You mentioned not finishing your laundry," Lise explained, handing over the fresh garments in a manner that suggested accepting them was not a point of discussion. "If my eye is right, and it always is, these should fit you perfectly. I know you're supposed to do your own washing, but we're friends now, and you can consider me your official backup for cleaning henceforth. Besides, you've worked yourself nearly to death on your first day. Consider these clothes a welcoming gift."

"I accept. You're wondrous!" Annabel eagerly squeezed the soft bundle, inhaling the fresh, clean scent. "Honestly, if you weren't already, you're now my new favorite person. Come in, won't you? Can I ask you something?"

"Of course," Lise responded, closing the door. "It's a bit chilly in here...are you trying to freeze out the roaches?" She rubbed her hands together.

"I let the fire die out by accident," Annabel confessed, quickly stripping and changing into clean garments. "I slept as though I was dead."

"Oh, I'll get it back up for you," offered Lise, pulling a tinderbox out of her laundry bag and kneeling in front of the old wood stove. "One good thing about living here is cheap firewood, so take advantage of it."

"Thank you," Annabel said appreciatively. "Lise...you told me of Agatha's disappearance, but you also mentioned Nancy? That was Richard's first wife?"

"Yes." Lise hesitated. "Nancy's mother coerced her into marrying Richard, hoping to gain favor from the castle. Richard has the Baron's ear. Then Nancy contracted pneumonia, likely due to being imprisoned in the damp, frigid dungeon as punishment for disobedience for something she'd apparently done to Richard. They created quite a scandal, even dragging Charlie into it, and he certainly wasn't eager to be involved. Ultimately, she met her end down there." Lise's expression turned sorrowful.

"Right." Annabel absorbed this information, nodding thoughtfully. "Change of subject—what of yourself? What do you enjoy doing?" Lise pondered. "I suppose I'm partial to games like cards, backgammon, and dice. I have a fondness for attending plays. I often get word on when the cheaper shows are on, courtesy of a friend in a troupe."

"A play! Like Shakespeare's works?" Annabel's enthusiasm was palpable.

"Yes, they perform his plays in the region quite often," Lise -affirmed. "Unfortunately, the stuffy old Baron won't permit theater here at Castle Rowley, but other nearby nobles have arrangements with actors' groups or their own performers. Why don't we attend the next play I hear about together?" Having brought the ashes back to life, Lise shut the stove door, brushed off her hands, and sat gingerly in one of the unbroken chairs.

Annabel's eyes sparkled with anticipation as she joined Lise at the table. "I would love that. I've only witnessed one play before, but I've been fortunate enough to read a few donated to the church."

Lise sighed dreamily. "I often imagine myself on stage alongside the actors, a part of their world. And there are usually delectable treats on offer afterward."

"You've talked me into it." Annabel grinned. "Not that I needed convincing."

Just then, a rustling sound came from the door, and Lise jumped to her feet, a surprisingly guilty look washing over her face.

Richard strode in, looking well-rested and with his hair combed, casting a suspicious look at the laundress. "Good morning, gentle-women."

"Good morrow, Farmer and Mrs. Granger," Lise murmured, bowing slightly as she concealed trembling hands behind her back. Standing behind her, Annabel was taken aback by Lise's sudden, noticeable unease.

"Good morrow, and thank you—" Annabel's words hung in the air as Lise swiftly exited. Taking a deep breath, Annabel turned to her husband, who had entered the room with a distracted look on his face. "How was your mother?"

Richard stared at her blankly. "My—oh, yes. She's been feeling quite tired."

"Sick, I thought it was?" Annabel asked mildly. "So sick that you missed our wedding night."

"Right." He coughed. "It meant a lot to her to have her second eldest son visit. Thank you for your patience while I sorted things out with her, my love." Richard looked at her expectantly. "You *do* understand, don't you?"

"Yes." Annabel could feel the lies in his words as much as she could see on his face, but she mustered a smile, her hands fidgeting nervously. "I'm glad to have you back home," she offered. "Perhaps you'll stay awhile, this time?"

"I shall indeed." Richard smiled approvingly as he surveyed their surroundings with new eyes and set his hat on the table. "You've done well here."

"Thank you," she replied. "It was quite an undertaking." Annabel pressed her lips together, willing her expression to remain calm. She relaxed her face and smiled stiffly. "What are your plans for today, dearest?"

"I'll tell you." He sat down on the bed, patting the space beside him. "Won't you join me?"

She hesitated before taking a seat, curiosity mingling with caution.

Richard breathed deeply, and as he slid his hand up to the hair at the nape of his neck, he looked as though the world's weight were on his shoulders. "Annabel," he began softly. "I'd like to be honest with you."

"Please do," she encouraged.

Richard looked down. "Now that you're a married woman, it's important for you to understand that a man has responsibilities to himself, certain needs that can sometimes conflict with matters of the heart." He looked up at her intimately, then shook his head with a chuckle. "You are so innocent that you know not the ways of men in the world, but—"

"Oh, my. Are you going to tell me about your mistress?" Annabel interjected in surprise. "I had assumed you would continue hiding it from me." Her voice broke, and she took a deep breath, waiting for him to deny it. "So, you are dallying with another woman."

"Annabel!" Richard's eyebrows rose, and he sucked in his breath. "For pity's sake. How on earth did you find out?"

"You've just told me." Her eyes flashed with hurt. "How could you? You knew it was hard for me to trust people after Paul, and you violated our marriage vows in the space of a day."

"Again," he murmured testily. "Who told you? I was careful enough that someone must have let it slip."

"That matters not." Annabel averted her gaze, feigning modesty as she suddenly realized why Lise might've been so nervous. "Were you planning to bid her farewell along with your confession to me today, or do you intend to continue your affair?"

"Annabel, slow down." Richard smiled patiently, bringing his voice to a low, dangerous timbre. "No need for such theatrics. In fact, I'm glad you know now, sweetheart. It was the right decision to tell you, no matter what my mother said." Annabel sucked in her breath. "What have I done, marrying you? You are having an affair, and we've just married yesterday."

Richard frowned. "As I mentioned, I was devastated when Agatha died and with Nancy before her. My relationship with Gwyneth is far more complex than an affair. She's always been there for me, but my mother won't allow us to marry."

"I—I feel as though I'm supposed to feel sorry for the pair of you?" Annabel made a face. "You do remember making me your wife, Richard?"

"It was a marriage of necessity." Sighing, he added, "I am prepared to be your partner in this house, but I cannot, will not simply sever my ties with Gwyneth. I'd sooner sever my own throat."

"So you are planning to continue it. Why did you even marry me, then? You should have gathered your strength and defied your mother if you wanted to keep seeing her." Annabel's voice dripped with desperation. "Your actions are rife with cowardice."

"I'm afraid she cannot have children," Richard sighed. "I need a wife to leave a mark on this world, though I've had bad luck with that, I'll admit."

"One needs human decency, Richard," lamented Annabel. "Why could you have not told me of your plight? Why could you not be honest? This has upended me and everything I thought of you and what I'd hoped we could build."

"I was tired of looking for a wife." Richard shrugged. "What I had before wasn't sustainable. And since my mother forbade me from marrying Gwyneth, I had to choose someone else. Someone more suitable." His voice softened, taking on a more entreating tone, and he took her hand. "I am so fortunate that it was you, my dearest."

Annabel withdrew her hand. "You married me to be your cook and maid then and bear your children while you dally with the woman you love as often as you can?"

"Don't make it sound so dreadful." Richard scowled defensively. "You'll live on castle grounds and always have a place to sleep. Do you know, even if you couldn't sleep here one night, you could always curl up by the fire inside? You'll never starve or go hungry with the resources here." He straightened proudly. "I've done you a great service."

"You really believe that, don't you?" Annabel looked at him, her world eroding. "What do you mean if I couldn't sleep here one night?"

A frown appeared on his face, and something unpleasant flashed behind his eyes. "It was your mother who sought me out, you know. She was desperate to find you a husband. And let's not forget that you were equally eager once you met me. It was simply a matter of a poem and a few empty promises to win you over."

"A stolen poem," Annabel muttered angrily.

His eyes flashed. "It was Charlie who told you, then. I bloody thought so."

For a moment, her heart seemed to stop. "No. No, it wasn't. I guessed because you were out all night when you'd promised a return by nightfall."

"That one-eyed donkey is always wagging his bloody tongue," her husband growled. "I ought to have Baron Rowley cut it off. I've got his ear, you know."

"You..." Her heart seemed to freeze in her chest, and while a sense of steely resolve filled her, she swore to herself that she would protect her new friends. Swallowing hard, she sputtered, "You are a heartless man. I do not even know you."

He winked at her, his blue eyes filled with the mischief that used to make her heart dance but now repelled her. "Come now, dearest. After being so patient already, you won't make things difficult, will you?" Richard's gaze turned shrewd. "And in return, you won't lack for anything—I'll give you plenty of sons, keep a roof over your head and barley in your stomach. "He smiled confidently.

"Oh?" Annabel challenged. "And what guarantee do I have that you'll keep your word? What must I endure while you have your way? What's to stop me from being tossed out in favor of Gwyneth?" She crossed her arms. "Perhaps I shall tell the Baron of your misdeeds. You may have his ear, but I doubt he would approve of your misdeeds."

"He cares not." Richard chuckled at her daring. "My family has a longstanding history of tenancy on Rowley land, even outside of the castle, and it would take me no time to have this marriage annulled and take another wife. Everyone knows that I didn't spend the wedding night here. You have nothing to bargain with, I'm afraid."

"You banked on that," Annabel realized, incredulity seeping into her words. "From the beginning, you orchestrated this marriage to serve your cruel desires. And use me as a pawn in your game of hedonism."

"That's a cruel way to put it," Richard scoffed. "You're not even trying to understand my side.

"Richard," Annabel sighed. "This is not how marriages should be. Did you really grow up thinking that when you were a man, you'd actively step out on your wife, the future mother of your children, with a harlot?"

"How did you know she was a harlot?" Richard snarled indignantly.

"Oh, for..." Annabel leaned forward and put her head in her hands. "God help me." Taking a deep breath, she sat back up and looked at him. As his blue eyes rose to meet hers, they darted to the window and back almost too quickly to notice.

Annabel frowned and went to the window. Staring through the small pane, she noticed a carriage waiting at the front of the castle and squinted. A blonde woman sat inside, arms crossed over her chest, a bored look adorning her lovely face.

"My dearest." Richard's hand found her waist and pulled her to him, away from the window.

"That very word is a lie," she whispered. "As I am clearly not your dearest. I'd wager the hierarchy is rather: your mistress, your mummy, then me."

"No," he said quickly. "My mother will always come first. I wouldn't be here if it wasn't for her."

"I can say the same thing about mine, so I'm not feeling particularly fond of her at the moment," Annabel muttered.

Sighing, Richard muttered, "Perhaps it was a mistake to tell you. You've been so sweet this far; I imagined you'd be more understanding. Let's set this aside for now."

"Set it aside?" She shook her head. "You've just told me you love another woman and don't intend to leave her. I am your wife." She cleared her throat, the tears gathering behind her eyes and threatening to fall.

"But nor do I intend to leave you," Richard assured her. "I will honor our vows to the best of my ability. I have more than enough love and time to go around."

"By missing our wedding night, you have proven that is untrue," Annabel retorted, raising her eyebrows. "And I do not seek a third wheel on our cart of marriage."

"Well, I apologize for that." Richard frowned, beginning to look impatient. "Let's move forward, dearest. It's getting late in the day, and I need a few things from the market. I've prepared a list of supplies and arranged for you to use the Rowley carriage. I'll even give you extra money to buy something for yourself." Richard pressed a pouch into her hand.

"How generous of you," Annabel sighed. "Richard, she is already here. Will you send me off and bring her inside now that I've cleaned your house?"

Richard chuckled appreciatively, a glint of amusement in his eyes. "You certainly are smarter than you look, my dearest. Yes, but she doesn't know you're here, and I would appreciate it if you remained so while you make your way to the marketplace. Let's help each other, remember?" His voice seemed kind, but a muscle in his jaw seemed to twitch as he waited for her next move.

Annabel crossed her arms. "I still need to finish the laundry from yesterday. Most of the furniture needs fixing before people sit on it. I haven't had breakfast. Did you bring any food home? You can't simply arrive here and expect me to run to the market at a moment's notice."

Taking a deep breath, she tried to remain calm. "Please send away your mistress, sit down for a meal with me, and let us speak more of shared ideas on our future together."

"Speak *more*?" Richard groaned. "I tire of this subject and caution you to obey me."

Annabel pressed her lips together and sat down at the table in a wobbly chair. She set the pouch back down on the table.

Richard's tone was thick with irritation. "Very well. Don't go to market. But I need the house, and I won't be ignored." He grunted as he stood up, then, catching her by surprise, he leaned forward and effortlessly lifted Annabel over his shoulder.

Amid her shocked protests, he held her firmly in place with one hand, opened the door with the other, and walked outside. Annabel felt mortified as Richard carried her firmly out of their house and walked to the stables. All eyes seemed to be on her as farmhands paused to witness the spectacle. Ignoring their shocked faces, Richard walked into the open stables, tossed her onto a large pile of hay, and forcefully shut the door behind her before walking away.

Frozen in humiliation, she first dared not move, eyes flicking about, ears pricked as she attempted to discern if anyone else was present. Silence filled the air, and Annabel remembered seeing the horses grazing outside. Once she was reasonably confident the coast was clear, she cautiously climbed out of the hay and went to the window. Squinting, she watched in disbelief as Richard escorted the lovely woman at the carriage to the farmhouse she had just been expelled from. Neither of them looked in her direction.

Annabel sank back into the mound of hay, tears streaming silently down her face as she felt an overwhelming sense of loneliness and helplessness engulf her. With a heavy sigh, she finally wiped away her tears and surveyed her surroundings. "Brrrrr," she whispered, rubbing her arms together for warmth.

Suddenly, the unmistakable sound of hay shifting came from one of the stalls, startling Annabel. She scrambled to her feet, fear creeping into her voice. "Who's there?"

A figure emerged from the shadows, and she sighed with relief when she saw it was Charlie. "Sorry. I was just back here messing about. I didn't hear what happened, only that you were—" He avoided eye contact as he offered a handkerchief. "Well, it's clean, and you're welcome to it."

"Thank you." Touched by his gesture, Annabel used the handkerchief to wipe her eyes before returning it to him.

After tucking it back away, Charlie frowned. "Are you hurt? It sounded like you came down hard."

"No." Breathing deeply as she tried to compose herself, clearing her throat as the memory of her being tossed into the hay rose again and again, Annabel stammered, "I'm—I'm fine. Just embarrassed."

Setting down the horse brush, Charlie reached into his tunic and produced a small bag. "Roasted chestnut?"

Gratefully, Annabel nodded, and he used a horseshoe to crack open four chestnuts. She munched gratefully and sighed. "Are you the only kind person at the castle besides Lise?"

Charlie laughed. "No, and she's much kinder. I tend to keep to myself, but we're all friends now, thanks to her."

"How lovely to have friends in a new place," she sighed, nibbling another chestnut. "They're almost as important as food."

"Agreed." He grinned. "Speaking of Lise, she mentioned that if anything went wrong with Richard this morning, she would offer you her extra cot. In her room."

"What a gem she is," Annabel remarked. "But don't you sleep there, too?"

"No. Lise sleeps alone in the cellar, sometimes with another servant for company, though most would rather stay closer to the fireplace. The cellar is cold – she has a lot of blankets." He shrugged. "I sleep in the stable loft if the horses are sick; otherwise, I stay in the outbuilding with the other stable hands and field workers. It's the usual arrangement for someone in my position at the castle. They don't want those who work in the fields and stables to be mixing with the aristocrats inside." Charlie laughed. "We're far too dirty."

Annabel finished off the nuts. "Perhaps I'm to work in the stables now, as I'm no longer welcome in my home."

"God's bones, I hope that's not the new hiring process." Charlie smiled when he saw her mouth twitch. "What happened, anyway?"

She hung her head after recounting her conversation with Richard before he banished her to the stables. "I'm so sorry I let it slip about the stolen poem." Annabel swallowed hard. "He threatened to cut out your tongue. I've never felt worse in my life."

"Don't fret about that." Charlie waved his hand. "Richard is always making idle threats; they're his bread and butter. He'll have mislaid the memory by tomorrow."

"It did not sound idle," she worried.

He shrugged. "I guess we'll see. What else can I do but keep working?"

"Right. I'm sure you need to get back to it," Annabel sighed, suddenly self-conscious. "Thank you for listening." She sat down again resignedly on a bale of hay. "I'll just wait here."

"You know…" Charlie tilted his head towards the ladder in front of them. "There's lots of freshly laundered horse blankets up there, and the hay was just replaced. No one would mind if you snuck up there for a spell."

"Don't say that unless you mean it." She laughed. "I may have had the worst sleep of my life last night."

"It's comfortable." He paused. "And if you loosen the board on the wall behind the third shelf on the right, there's more food and something to read."

"Really?" Annabel asked in surprise. "You're serious. Just have a nap?"

Charlie nodded. "I find there are few situations in life that sleep won't improve."

"You may have a point." Annabel nodded, taking a deep breath, feeling guilty but so tired she was swaying on her feet. "Right. Perhaps I'm mad, but I'm going to dare. You don't think anyone else will disturb me?"

"On my word," he assured her. "I'll see from the fields if anyone enters, but they shouldn't, and it's not the worst place to hang your hat briefly. These horses are treated better than the serfs here, so it never smells too bad."

Annabel nodded, looking around. "This does certainly smell much better than our barn did." She grinned. "Third shelf on the right, you said?"

Once Charlie left, Annabel climbed up the ladder to the hayloft. Behind the loose board, she discovered a thick cloth pouch containing dried meat and apples. When Annabel put it back, she discovered another large pouch, this one made of leather. When she peeked in, she saw two thick books, and after selecting one, she found a cozy spot under the shelves, wrapping herself in two blankets. She couldn't help but feel a sense of relief as she nestled into the warmth. Carefully, she stashed the tin behind the loose board again.

In the solitude of the hayloft, Annabel lost herself in the words of The Canterbury Tales. The stories provided an escape from the harsh reality of her situation, allowing her mind to wander, and as she read, her worries momentarily faded away.

Hours later, after dozing off, Annabel heard a scuffling outside the stables. She snapped to attention, quickly stashing the book into its hiding spot.

As Charlie entered, he wiped his brow and offered her a basket. "I have some boiled eggs from Maggie. She's been the castle cook for decades and the sweetest woman over fifty you'll ever meet. She sleeps in a room next to the kitchen, and if you're nice to her, she'll save you things. Richard was right about you not going hungry here, but it's not because of him, mind you."

"My gratitude." She smiled and carefully cracked an egg, removing the shell to take a grateful bite, and then another. "You know, I do actually feel better. Could you use some help in the fields?"

"Absolutely. I'd welcome it," said Charlie. "I'm short-handed to-day."

"Now that I'm rested, I need to do something productive, or I'll go peculiar." She smiled. "Well. Moreso."

He smiled. "You'll get paid for working today, so that should be a comfort at least." As she finished a third egg and Charlie opened the stable door, he asked, "You harvested barley on your family's farm at home, so I assume you already know the ropes?"

"Yes," Annabel said confidently, retying her bonnet. "I'm ready."

CHAPTER FIVE

SHADOWS OF DECEPTION

When the sun had begun to drop low in the sky, Charlie looked at the horizon. "It grows late in the day—I'd best check in with your husband. He's been in the farmhouse all day, bit unusual for him."

Annabel nodded warily, dusting barley off her dress, smoothing her brow, and mentally preparing. "Right."

Charlie disappeared around the side of the house, and she heard him rap on the front door before opening it. After a few minutes, he returned with a grim expression. "Asleep."

"You can't be serious," said Annabel incredulously. "It's not even sunset. What do you mean, he's asleep? I'll go in and wake him up."

"There was a bottle by the bed." Charlie coughed. "If you catch my meaning."

She sighed. "So, you're saying that the man is passed out in a drunken stupor?"

"Well—Richard injured his back some months ago," he said. "It was hard for him to work, and a doctor prescribed opium dissolved in alcohol."

"I know what laudanum is. My father takes it." Shoulders slumping, Annabel shook her head. "God's heart."

"It will certainly be more trouble than it's worth to rouse him." Charlie shrugged. "Go on and bunk with Lise. We'll get some food from the kitchen on the way."

"You really don't think she'd mind? I hate to be a bother...I really shouldn't." Even as she protested, Annabel's heart swelled with relief.

"You aren't," he assured her. "She offered. I prefer someone being in there with her, to tell you the truth. It's good for her to have a companion nearby... I really don't think the castle is haunted, but something is odd; I just can't quite put my finger on it."

"What do you mean?" Annabel asked curiously. "Have you always felt this way, or just recently?"

"Always. The Rowley family is full of secrets," he murmured. "Some of us think there's something odd going on below the castle."

"What, in the dungeons?" Annabel whispered. "If not ghosts, then..."

Charlie nodded. "I may be paranoid, but something tells me there's a secret." He laughed, his cheeks coloring. "You think I'm mad?"

"I guess I'll have to wait and see." She smiled, and he laughed again.

"Fair enough." Shrugging, he gestured towards the castle. "Ready?"

"Yes." Feeling conspicuous, Annabel followed him to the mighty door, where they walked nonchalantly by Leif.

Charlie spoke to Maggie, the ancient cook, in a low voice that caused a broad smile to crease her face like a walnut, and as he took a small parcel from her floury hands, she leaned forward to fondly kiss his cheek. When they reached the cellar, he knocked softly.

There was a slight scuffling as Lise unlatched the wooden door from the inside, then opened it bearing an enormous smile. "Welcome! How fine to have a bit of company this night."

Annabel stepped in nervously. "It's lovely of you to let me bunk with you. I don't know how much you know…"

"Oh, everything," Lise shrugged. "They're horrible chin-waggers in and around the castle. And as much as he tries not to be involved, Charlie's no exception."

"I am so," Charlie grumbled. "Don't misrepresent me. I don't let things slip."

"I did," whispered Annabel. "Lise, I'm so sorry. I let it slip that I knew the poem was stolen, and he assumed it was Charlie."

"Oh, that's not good." Eyes wide, Lise gave Charlie a worried look. "Watch yourself."

"Don't worry." He grinned. "I'll sleep with one eye open tonight."

"Funny," muttered Lise, kissing the side of his head and whispering into his ear as he scowled in a good-natured way. He whispered back, and Annabel smiled to see the two so in love after two years of marriage. Could it be like that with her and another man? She closed her eyes and dwelled upon what a crushing disappointment Richard had turned out to be.

Once Charlie had departed, she swept her eyes around the room. Like the rest of the castle, the walls and floor were stone, and the only door was the one they had come through. The ceiling was low. Along each wall was a clothesline; one hung entirely with stockings, and the third appeared to have a schedule marked up heavily with slate pencil. A vast iron cauldron hunched in a corner beside a wooden trough.

It was gloomy, no doubt about it, but she smiled at the touches Lise had clearly added—colorful tapestries, garlands of dried purple flowers, a sturdy cedar trunk with vines carved into the lid and embroidered cushions on the narrow bed. On a small end table burned a fat beeswax candle. None of the furniture was broken.

Lise pulled out the trundle bed and a deck of hand-painted cards as she looked around. The two women stayed up talking and enjoying the food parcel for the next few hours until both finally drifted off.

Just before dawn, a distant yet piercing cry awoke them both. Annabel and Lise both sat up in bed and stared at each other. "Did you hear that?"

Another anguished scream. Lise shoved her feet into boots and pulled on her coat, and Annabel did the same with some hesitation. "Are you sure we shouldn't just stay here where it's safe?"

"Oh, honey, I'm not missing whatever that is," laughed Lise as she unlatched the door. "And don't be ridiculous—nowhere is safe."

Troubled, Annabel followed her out of the cellar and to the castle door, where they met a small group of servants whispering. "What's going on?" Lise demanded. "It's the middle of the bloody night."

A man bearing a scornful expression shook his head. "Someone's bloody screaming in the Granger house."

Annabel's eyes widened, and she looked at Lise nervously. Suddenly, the door opened, and a bald guard towered over them, an irritated look on his face. He glanced at Annabel. "You're Farmer Granger's new wife, aren't you? Pray tell what all that fuss is about? It's coming from your bloody house."

"I don't know," she admitted, looking down at her feet.

"Why not?" the guard snapped angrily. "Don't you know your own husband? What kind of a woman are you?"

"I slept in the cellar this night." She cleared her throat and faced him bitterly. "My husband was dallying with a harlot in our home and did not want me there. I apologize for the inconvenience."

"God's head. This is all I need." The guard sighed, exhaustion lining his face. "Let's go then. Show me to your house, and we'll see what's afoot."

When Annabel hesitated momentarily, the guard stepped forward menacingly, and Lise took Annabel's arm. "Come on, I'll go too. And Gregory here won't let him hurt you, will you?" She jovially patted the enormous guard on the arm.

Gregory frowned. "Of course, I won't."

When they reached the door, the screams had dampened into anguished pleas. Gregory looked at Annabel, who shook her head. He sighed and knocked sharply at the door, then tried the handle, to no avail. From inside came the sorrowful call, "Please do come in! Please, help me..."

Gregory immediately kicked down the door with the help of the thick staff at his side, hurried in, and gasped at what he saw. Lise and Annabel were close behind.

The woman in bed with Richard, who Annabel recognized as the woman she'd seen him walk into the house, was wailing. "He's not waking up," she moaned, fear streaking her face.

Sure enough, Richard's jaw was slack, and his face was pale and unresponsive. "Is he...breathing?" Annabel whispered.

"Yes!" Gwyneth nodded. "Slowly. He was so tired, and he'd been in pain, as he said. But I've never seen him look this bad. He's never been this far gone. I had to call for help before he expired in my arms."

"He's treating that pain with a bit of extra laudanum, I take it?" Gregory sneered. "It's no secret. You ought to throw this one back, Gwyneth. If you don't know by now that he's a lost cause..."

"Thank you for your concern." Her eyes flashed. "It's not my fault he's got a problem. The doctor gave it to him. Mind you, I certainly haven't taken any myself. He's usually fine." She looked down at him with a wretched expression and shook him fiercely. "Will you bloody wake up!"

Richard's eyes suddenly flew open. When he beheld the group of not only Gwyneth in his arms but Gregory, Lise, and Annabel around the bed, he looked angry. "What are you lot all doing here?"

"Your mistress's screams bade us come running to save her from you," retorted Lise. "How is the laudanum, you old wastrel?" She shook her head in disgust. "You've never been able to manage yourself."

"Shut it! You don't know what you're talking about," growled Richard. "I'm in pain. The doctors told me I can take it."

"Sure, and how about your wife?" Lise snapped. "Having to bunk with me in the cold cellar while she's got a fine farmhouse, or at least it used to be, that you've thrown her out of." Her eyes flashing, she hissed, "Isn't that just like you?"

Annabel swallowed hard, studying Richard's angry face as she worked up the nerve to say something without breaking down at the ludicrous situation unfolding before her.

"You threw her out of your house?" Gwyneth asked reproachfully. "You told me she was out of town visiting your mother."

"You use your mother as an excuse for everything," Lise scoffed, casting a contemptuous look at Richard. "What a sodding useless liar you are."

"If you don't go back to your cellar, little laundry mouse...you won't like what I'll do," Richard threatened, sitting up in bed and rubbing his red eyes. "This concerns you not. My life, my livelihood, my wives concern you not. Leave me be."

"You big bully." Lise shook her head. "You ought to be ashamed of yourself, tricking this nice girl into marrying you when you're still chasing after a harlot like a bloody fool."

With a snarl, Richard cast Gwyneth aside as he threw his covers back and lunged for Lise. Yelping, she bolted away from him, and seeing Gregory still in the way of the front door, she seemed to pivot and ran for the closet, pulling it open and thrusting the door out to shield herself from Richard's attack. The soldier seized Richard on his way to Lise before he reached her, and they both gasped as the closet swung open. She carefully peeked out from behind the door and did the same.

A small chest filled with coins lay open in the back of the closet, and four finely adorned dresses were hung. Lise went to stand by Annabel again, who looked skeptically at Richard. "Are those *yours*?"

"The chest bears the Rowley crest, and those frocks belonged to the late Baroness," said Gregory, his voice aghast. "Are you bloody mad, Granger?"

"Th—that closet was locked," stammered Richard. "I'd have staked my life on it." He started for the closet, but Gregory stopped him.

"Well, that's not going to hold up in the court of the law, never mind with the Baron," the old guard sighed. "Let's go, then."

"I locked it last night!" Richard protested and looked over at Gwyneth in alarm. "*Didn't* I?"

She looked at him angrily. "I don't bloody know—don't rope me in with your nonsense." Pulling her clothes back on, she muttered. "I'm never coming back here again." She stood. "Gregory is bloody right—I should have been done with you long ago."

"Gwyneth," said Richard, sounding hurt. "How can you possibly talk that way?"

"That's cold comfort to me. It's going to be a long day ahead, that's for sure," Gregory moaned. "After I throw you in the dungeon, I'll have to sit with the Baron all day to review what happened."

Richard stammered, "You can't be serious. Come along, Gregory, we're old friends. The Baron will never miss this; it's from the attic, for God's sake. Let me share with you and your family, and..."

Annabel couldn't help but let out a giggle, which was really more of a snort than anything else, and they all turned to look at her in surprise—as if they had forgotten she was in the room. She took a deep breath.

"Richard," Annabel said in disbelief. "Both of your past wives have died in mysterious circumstances. You kicked me out of the house the day after our wedding, spent the first two nights with another woman, you're abusing laudanum, it's just been found out you're a thief stealing from your employer as well, and you would like to add a count of bribery to the heap?" She laughed again and shook her head. "Put down the shovel, won't you? Your grave is far too deep already."

Lise sputtered in laughter. "Hear, hear."

"She's got a point," Gregory chuckled. "Now, if you come quietly, I won't mention the bribery." He picked up the chest of coins, tossed the dresses over his arm, and smiled patiently. "Let's go, then."

Richard scowled. "My kin is old friends of the Rowley family, going back many generations. Does that not count for anything?"

"Yes, we all know you've got the Baron's ear," Gregory sighed. "You've still committed a crime he won't appreciate."

"The Baron won't let me be put away." Richard had begun to sound desperate. "You will look worse for having taken me in."

"Let's find out," said Gregory, and as Richard sighed, he reluctantly let the guard escort him out of the house.

Now, it was just the three women. Gwyneth rose to her feet and addressed Annabel with more alacrity than she had expected, accompanying her greeting with a slight curtsy. "Hello, I'm Gwyneth Jones."

"Yes," said Annabel wearily. "I know who you are, all to well."

"My apologies." Gwyneth coughed. "Richard has been a regular customer for years, and he told me the two of you had an understanding, as he did with Agatha." When Annabel's eyes widened, she added, "I take it that is not the case in your marriage."

"An understanding," Annabel said uneasily. "Meaning—they both saw other people? Is that true?"

"It was more complicated than that," muttered Lise. "He's never been completely transparent with anyone about his situation, from what I've been able to surmise."

"That's probably true." Gwyneth swept her lovely eyes from Lise back to Annabel. "As soon as Agatha began seeing someone else, I understood Richard grew weary of the agreement. In fact, he stopped seeing me for a short time in hopes of making his marriage work." She sighed. "And as you, I had no idea he was a thief. What a fool. I thought the laudanum was the worst of it."

"So you thought his wife had agreed to let him cavort with you in the house?" Annabel asked skeptically. "Did you not see him throw me out?"

"That was you?" Gwyneth exclaimed. "For goodness sake. I saw him toss a girl in the stables, but I assumed it was that little ninny Cecelia."

Annabel frowned. "Why on earth would Cecelia be in our farmhouse?"

"She does hide everywhere," admitted Lise. "Little teenager's like a small roach. She can fit into any nook or cranny and likes to listen. Don't befriend the girl because you can't get rid of her if you do."

"Regardless of the misunderstanding," Gwyneth lifted her chin. "I would not be here if I had not been invited under what I thought were conditions agreeable for all parties. After today's events, I won't be back, I assure you. He's given me grief for years, and this is the last straw. I have enough customers who aren't deadbeats with a complicated history."

"I believe you," said Annabel, sitting back down at the table, suddenly tired. "Honestly, I'm too tired to be upset with you about this right now, and it's Richard's fault, anyway. How much does he owe y ou?"

"Oh!" Gwyneth looked surprised. "Two pounds."

"Two pounds!" Annabel exclaimed, aghast. "I made three shillings yesterday in the fields."

Gwyneth nodded, retorting with not a little bitterness, "Not that it does me any good. Who knows how long he'll be locked up—I'll never be paid."

"I don't suppose you know much money he takes in?" Annabel asked curiously. "I looked over his books. He does keep records. But they're disorganized to the point of being almost incomprehensible."

"That's by design, mind you." Gwyneth gave her a knowing look. "He gets a third of the harvest, and the rest goes to the Baron. This farm is twenty acres, so the annual harvest should be about two hundred bushels. At market price, two shillings a bushel, he'd get a little over six pounds for the harvest in a year, give it take. Besides any hustles he may have going. Booze, betting, bribes."

"So he owes you a third of his yearly salary," Annabel confirmed in an incredulous voice.

Gwyneth nodded shamefacedly. "He's not allowed at the DiMilo anymore. But he's always shared whenever he's come into the money before, from gambling and the like." She shook her head in exasperation. "It's been worth it in the past to keep seeing him, but he's never been this behind. Really, I'm only here today because he promised to fully repay me at the end of it." She crossed her arms. "I shouldn't have trusted him again."

"The DiMilo is the bawdy house at the harbor," added Lise to Annabel. "They have comics and players too." To both of them, she admitted, "I must say, I didn't think this encounter between the pair of you was going to be quite a bit more dramatic. Should we have a drink?"

"I'll pour some ale." Annabel laughed, walking to the stove and taking a bottle from the cabinet that Maggie had given her the day before. "I have no gripe with you, Gwyneth. Richard has proven to be far different than he represented himself, and that isn't your fault." She sighed and set out three mugs. "What's to be done? We might as well help each other."

"Well said," Lise agreed, sitting on the bed while Gwyneth sat on a stool with an uncertain look. All three of them took a drink.

"So, you said he bets—now it makes sense as to why he is in debt with you and living beyond his means," said Annabel thoughtfully. "What exactly, is he gambling on?"

"Underground fighting in the dungeon," said Gwyneth immediately. "That's his favorite." She laughed. "To be honest, it's everyone's favorite. Sometimes, they bring pirates here to imprison them before hanging, they fight, and people bet on the odds. It's great fun. Sometimes Baron Rowley pays for the accompanying pleasure of my friends and I, down there in the crowd." She looked at Lise pointedly, who scowled.

Annabel was surprised to see the laundress redden. "Have you been down to the underground fighting, Lise?"

"Sometimes," her friend admitted.

"Do you have...friends who are pirates?" Annabel asked in confusion as Gwyneth sniggered behind her mug.

"It's not only pirates," explained Lise. "Others participate, too. Friends of mine. I wouldn't say they're proud of it," she said to

Annabel's aghast look and Gwyneth's suddenly blank face. "But it's one way to make extra money that's not regulated or taxed. And the Baron won't allow a theater to be built here nor hire any real players; he says he can't find a troupe who only puts on the plays he likes."

"Well, it wouldn't be my first choice," said Annabel as she poured another cup for each of them. "Bloody fighting. As if we don't have a short enough life already? But to each their own." She shook her head. "I can give you one pound today, Gwyneth, from my savings." She dug out a carefully hidden pound from her luggage and gave it to the other woman. "So, truly, you have no plans to keep seeing him?"

"Well!" Gwyneth laughed surprisedly, inspected the pound, and tucked it into a skirt pocket. "Thank you. Not after all that, I assure you. Life is short, and he's a time-wasting fool. I should have been done with him long ago. This was a good kick in the skirts."

Annabel bit her lip. "Will the DiMilo come after Richard's estate for the owed payment?"

"Lucky for you, he owes me directly since they kicked him out, which I had to pay back myself," sighed Gwyneth. "I'll be tightening my belt for a bit. All you might have to worry about is me."

Shooting Lise a look, Annabel asked, "And should I—worry, that is?"

"No." Gwyneth shrugged. "I'll trust you. You seem like a good egg. And Lise clearly knows you." She threw the laundress a shrewd smile. "I'd never want to get on her bad side."

Annabel gave her a grateful look. "I promise I truly will keep on the payments."

"Bully for you," Gwyneth said calmly, finishing her tea. "You're quite different than Richard's last two wives, I'll give you that. Perhaps you'll survive."

Lise looked out the window, sipping her drink, looking suddenly weary.

Annabel said, "I never met them. But I heard the first one died in the dungeon, and the second vanished under mysterious circumstances—though Richard told me, she died of a skin abscess."

Gwyneth raised her eyebrows. "Yes, well…"

There was a slight commotion outside, and Annabel stood. "Excuse me—I had better see what that's about. Please do finish your ale if you like." When she walked outside, she noticed a frenzy of nervous activity, as everyone seemed to be especially hard at work. As she carefully looked around, she saw a prominent, hulking figure about the size of a bear headed briskly down the path, complete with beady eyes and drooping jowls. It was Baron Rowley.

Annabel gulped nervously. She continued sweeping the landscape as she awaited the Baron. She saw Charlie in the fields, gathering barley, and watched him spot them. His face jerked in shock, and his eye met Annabel's in alarm.

"Are you Mrs. Granger?" Baron Rowley growled. "Yes, I am." She faced the Baron and curtsied, trying not to wobble. "Good morrow, my lord."

"Not as much," murmured the Baron, turning beady eyes above thick jowls to her. "Are you aware your husband is in my dungeon and what he's accused of?" His voice was low and slightly accusing. "One can't help but wonder why his new *wife* hasn't been keeping out of trouble."

Annabel studied the large man. She wondered if he was baiting her and after some consideration, realized he probably was. If she admitted that Richard had been with Gwyneth, especially on their wedding night; she might have no claim to the house in his absence. "I understand he has been disregarding the law, God forbid," she agreed carefully. "I must apologize on his behalf—but please know that I was completely in the dark on his thievery and am ready to continue working through his absence, however long that may be."

The Baron chuckled dismissively, as did the two companions by his side. "No man steals from me and gets away with it, but I will not kill a Granger and invite the wrath of their family. He'll be in the dungeon for a few months."

"How unfortunate," Annabel said, her heart lifting as she resisted an urge to cry out in relief, even as her stomach filled with dread at such a punishment.

The Baron coughed. "Why don't you return home to your mother, my dear, and wait for the next step. There is no male heir, and this marriage is fresher than paint. I will give the house and crops to Richard's brother Frank to manage."

"What?" Her eyes widened.

"I'm sure you understand." He waved a hand. "Frank is already married. I can't have a woman living in that house alone, seeing to the crops, and I don't want to pay another chapel fee for you if Richard dies during his punishment."

"Would he—die, that is, for stealing your property?" Annabel asked curiously. "Is theft a death penalty?"

"No," the Baron admitted. "But the dungeons are a cesspool, and my temper is short for theft. People often die there." He smiled. "I prefer to plan ahead for the likeliest outcome."

"I beg your pardon, my lord," Annabel swallowed hard, summoning her confidence. "I can't help but realize that with no heir, as his wife, I am, in fact, next in line to inherit Richard's assets. You need not worry about keeping up the crops. I have plenty of farming experience to manage our crop share, and I've already worked in your fields."

"You what," laughed the steward who stood to Henry's right. "You don't have the time to run the inside and out of a farmhouse."

"With two field hands working every other day, which is the same as before, I think I can manage." Taking a deep breath, Annabel gathered her courage and pressed on. "I want to stay. I have the knowledge and experience to work the cropland just as Richard did. And based on what he shared of his plans, I believe I can even deliver a higher yield than he would have."

The Baron's face softened, but he couldn't hide his skepticism. "Are you a witch, then?" he asked, a faint smile on his lips. "Do you have any familiars I can meet? Black cats or birds we can bake into a pie?"

Annabel shook her head firmly. "No, my lord. I'm not a witch. I'm dedicated and hardworking with a strong farming background, exceptional organizational skills, and a few good ideas."

"Such as?" He sounded amused.

She waved her hand towards the fields. "Crop rotation. I'm told Richard grows barley each year here, and he should turn over the land to carrots or beets in between plantings. They break up the soil and make it thicker, and there's always an especially higher barley yield afterward. I've also got recipes for improving the soil and getting rid of bugs..."

The Baron dismissed her proposal with a wave of his hand. "I'd rather not invest in such an experiment, my dear. It would be simpler to pass the responsibility to Frank." He turned to leave, leaving Annabel desperate to prove herself.

"Please, give me just six months to show you what I can do here," she pleaded, her voice desperate. "You won't regret it, my lord."

Charlie's voice cut through the air, respectful but assertive, as the Baron continued walking away. "Baron Rowley, she can read."

The Baron halted in his tracks. He didn't look at Charlie, but with a curious glimmer of interest in his eyes, he turned to his steward. "Cole, is this true?"

The steward shrugged nonchalantly. "I'm not sure, my lord. Her mother never mentioned it in the interview."

The Baron then turned to the man with hooded eyes standing beside him. "James, fetch me the book on my desk blotter," he commanded. Without delay, James hurried off to retrieve the requested tome. During this time, the Baron observed and scrutinized Annabel while she smiled at him politely and breathed deeply through her nose.

When James returned with the book, the Baron instructed him to open it to a page marked with a ribbon and hand it to Annabel, whose heart raced as the Baron's suspicious gaze fixed upon her. "Go ahead," he said dryly. "If you truly can read."

Annabel glanced at the title page, which read Ovid, Metamorphoses, Book 9. Nodding, she looked at the page before her, taking a moment to compose herself. Then, she began to recite the passage with conviction. "If her name has ever come to your notice, Deianira was once the most beautiful girl and the jealous hope of many suitors. When, with them, I entered Oeneus's house, her father, and the man I sought as my father-in-law, I said: 'Accept me as your son-in-law, son of Parthaon.' Hercules, scion of Alceus, said the same. The others gave way before the two of us. Hercules declared that he could offer Jove as his bride's father-in-law, spoke of his famous labours, and of how he had survived what his stepmother, Juno, had prescribed for him. On my side I said: 'It would be shameful for a god to concede to a mortal' – He was not yet a god – 'In me you see the lord of the waters, that flow in winding rivers, through your kingdom. As your son-in-law I would not be a stranger sent from a foreign shore, but a native, and wedded to your own interests. Only don't let it harm my case that Queen

Juno does not hate me, and all the punishment of the labours, she demanded, passed me by!'" Annabel's voice had a storyteller's cadence, and James was beginning to look slightly impressed, though Cole still retained a look of mild indifference.

The Baron raised his hand to signal her to stop. "That's enough. Have you read this before?" he inquired, his interest evident.

Annabel nodded. "Yes, my lord. A copy was donated to my church as part of a collection that needed repairing—that's where I learned to read, at church."

The Baron leaned back slightly, considering her response. "And what do you make of it?"

Annabel considered this. "Two men are competing for the love of a woman and for her father's attention. Hercules thinks he should marry her because he's immortal, and..."

She was startled when the Baron burst into laughter. "And you're a farmer?" he chuckled, shaking his head.

Annabel nodded firmly. "Yes, and a good one, my lord, I can assure you."

The Baron's expression turned pensive, and he shook his head again. "Very well. We shall give it a try. Mind you, do not lose my money with your experiments."

Overwhelmed with relief, Annabel smiled, swallowing back her enthusiasm. "Yes, Baron Rowley. Thank you so much."

As the Baron retreated into the castle, Annabel took a moment to collect herself, her head throbbing from the stress and anxiety. Turning to Charlie, she raised her eyebrows. "What was that all about, with the reading?"

"Philippa always told Henry to welcome any woman who could read to the castle, as they bring good luck," he admitted. "She hired Maggie, years ago, who can read. The same goes for our gardener.

Philippa instilled in Henry, that women who can read are special, and I thought maybe he'd let you stay if he..." Charlie stopped. "Never m ind."

She smiled. "What?"

He looked her right in the eye and whispered, "Annabel, I've got to confess something."

Alarmed at his tone, she took a deep breath. "Yes?" Her voice came out higher than intended.

"Richard did steal from the Baron, but I caught him stealing weeks ago and knew he locked it in his closet. That's where he hides everything he steals, as I well knew. After you told me of his threat, Lise had enough. She snuck inside while he was sleeping last night, added valerian root to his laudanum bottle, and unlocked the closet door so she could pull it open today, exposing Richard for the thief he is."

Annabel gasped. "You and Lise are the reason he was apprehended, then."

"That's why I told you not to worry." Charlie sighed heavily. "Call it self-preservation—besides, he treated you so terribly, Lise and I couldn't bear it, especially after what happened with Nancy and Agatha. "She cooked up the plan yesterday while you were sleeping."

"Goodness." Annabel laughed in disbelief. "I'm a lucky woman to have friends like the pair of you."

"I'm glad you feel that way," Charlie confessed. "And our intention was never to truly harm him—just to make him sleep overlong, giving you a brief respite from your troubles."

Annabel admitted, "Well, your plan certainly achieved its purpose, but you could have told me."

"If you had been in on it..." Charlie shuddered. "If the Baron thought you'd tried to set up your husband in the dungeon and have the house for yourself, he'd probably have thrown you in the dungeon yourself."

Annabel's heart skipped a beat. "You're not afraid of Richard," she stated, her voice concerned. "But you are afraid of the Baron, aren't you?"

Charlie scowled, his gaze fixed on the ground as he picked up his sickle to harvest another sheaf of barley. "If you're as clever as you seem, you will be too."

CHAPTER SIX

A GHOSTLY TALE

After a long week of managing crops, Annabel was baking a rather disappointing loaf of bread when a knock came at the door. Alarm and nostalgia rose in her to see that standing stiffly on her porch was Paul, her Paul. Paul, the vicar of her church back home and the last man who had broken her heart. For one brief, ridiculous moment, she imagined him taking her into his arms and whisking her away from this mad place.

He bowed briefly as he came inside, speaking with the same soft, unassuming voice she'd known so well, smiling at her knowingly. "Annabel Barlow, look at you. Well done."

Annabel responded cautiously, "I must admit, Paul..." She swallowed hard as she realized it still hurt to say his name. "I am surprised to see you. I thought you wanted nothing to do with me."

"I know." He sat down at the table. "And I'm sorry for that. I was ashamed of my feelings and admit I handled it all poorly." Paul sighed deeply, his expression laden with remorse. "After much reflection and counsel from my wife, Eleanor, I have come here to offer my sincerest apologies."

Annabel's surprise deepened. "Oh?"

He nodded again, acknowledging his wrongdoing. "It was profoundly wrong of me to lead you on when my intentions were never truly to marry you."

The words landed heavily on Annabel's heart, stirring up old wounds. She felt a surge of sickness wash over her as the memories resurfaced, and pressed her lips together as she remembered how anxious each day used to be as she'd sought to contain the secret of their tryst.

"You were such an invaluable asset to the church, Annabel." Paul's expression shifted, his tone becoming more earnest. "Your rare literacy and skill in restoring our dilapidated books seemed like magic to everyone, including myself. I believed I loved you, to be sure, but it all grew to be too much for me."

Annabel absorbed his words. "So, you came here today to confess your wrongdoing?"

"No," he objected, his eyes wide with concern. "I have come bearing a gift for you." Paul tossed her a small coin pouch with a casual flick of his hand.

Annabel cautiously opened it, gasping as her eyes met the substantial sum of six pounds. She gazed at Paul incredulously. "Why?"

Paul's initial shock transformed into a resolute expression. "An acolyte mentioned you before my wife, and she learned everything. She discovered that you had worked here for two years without pay and how I had proposed in a foolish bout of passion; you'd gotten your hopes up only for me to break it off," he confessed, his voice laden with remorse.

Leaning back in her chair, Annabel's fingers curled around the pouch, her mind swirling with conflicting emotions. "So, you offer me money as recompense?" she murmured.

Paul recoiled at the suggestion. "No," he protested. "You never asked for money, and I never gave you any. This gift is from Eleanor."

Confusion marred Annabel's expression as she attempted to comprehend the situation. "Eleanor," she repeated, her voice filled with uncertainty. "Your *wife*."

"Yes." Paul's demeanor softened as he explained, "This is payment for all the bookbinding you performed. Eleanor believed it unfair that you were volunteering while anticipating the upcoming financial security of a marriage."

Annabel's fingers tightened around the pouch, her mind grappling with the weight of the unexpected windfall. "This is a substantial sum," she murmured, a mix of awe and trepidation coloring her voice.

Paul offered a nonchalant shrug. "For Eleanor, and now I, it is insignificant. She bade me come here to make things right. The question remains: do you want it or not?"

At that moment, Annabel let herself dwell on the power the six pounds held within her grasp—the ability to shape her destiny. With a resolute gaze, she nodded and clutched the pouch firmly, her mind filled with determination. When Annabel said goodbye to Paul, she did so with conviction and grace. There was satisfaction when she closed the door, as though she were closing the door on that part of her life, but on far more agreeable terms than before.

The next day was All Hallow's Eve, and the weariness that clung to her from the day's toil threatened to claim her. Lost in the grip of fatigue, Annabel succumbed to a peaceful early evening slumber, her dreams weaving a tapestry of restful bliss.

A pounding on her door roused Annabel from sleep, and she opened it to find Lise standing before her.

Her new friend exclaimed with contagious excitement and a mischievous wink, "Why are you in bed? It's All Hallow's Eve—come celebrate! There's a small gathering in the barn. Charlie's already there."

Despite her lingering weariness, Annabel's grin surfaced. "Alright. Let me shake off the drowsiness," she responded. Making her way to the speckled mirror over the basin, Annabel refreshed her appearance, pinching her cheeks to bring color to her complexion and applying a beeswax balm to her lips.

Lise's happiness was evident as she sighed, "I'm eager to let loose. It has been a peculiar week for more than just one of us. A celebration is just what we need."

"A celebration?" Annabel asked in delight. "I didn't realize it would be a proper party—with refreshments and libations?"

Lise's grin widened. "Absolutely! Apple bobbing, hard cider, crowdie cake, music, and ghost stories—we look forward to it all year. Everyone behaves themselves, lest they find themselves in the dungeon just like Richard. Let's join in the merriment!"

Annabel followed Lise down the dirt path to the barn as faint strains of merry music slowly reached their ears. Inside, a modest band played a popular tune, filling the barn with a lively rhythm. A few dozen people swayed and twirled in time with the music while others found respite on hay bales, engrossed in animated conversations, laughter, and merriment. Charlie was clinking a mug with other farmhands she'd seen working in the fields.

Taking Annabel's arm, Lise led her toward a group of women who had gathered nearby. With a friendly wave, Lise introduced Annabel to Helga and Ethel as the dedicated garden keepers and Myrtle and Viola, who diligently cared for the cows, goats, and chickens. The women greeted Annabel warmly, their eyes sparkling with camaraderie and excitement.

Ethel brandished a bottle and beamed. "Care for a drink, my dear?"

Annabel nodded gratefully, accepting a stream of hard cider into the mug Lise put in her hand. As she took a tentative sip, a delightful tang danced upon her tongue, causing her to wince and smile simultaneously. "God's bones, that's tart," she remarked, her voice brimming with a newfound appreciation. "Delicious, though. It'll surely put a spring in my step."

Myrtle chuckled, her tunic still damp from recent apple-bobbing adventures. "We've all just finished bobbing apples," she shared, pointing to her water-drenched attire with a good-natured laugh. "Starting with a drink helps set the tone and adds to the festive silliness. Pick an apple, toss it in one barrel, then bob for someone else's in a separate one."

Annabel's gaze shifted to a table adorned with vibrant apples. Her stomach growled in anticipation, prompting her to inquire, "May I partake of the apples as well as bob them?"

Lise, laughing alongside the others, took a long swig from the bottle. "That comes later," she teased.

Annabel selected a bright green apple and tossed it into the designated barrel. "I need to wet my whistle a bit more before embarking on apple bobbing," she admitted with a playful smile.

Lise grinned. "I know the feeling. Care to join me for another round?" she proposed, reaching for the potent cider.

Accepting the offering, Annabel clinked her mug against Lise's and took another sip, the effervescent flavors invigorating her senses. "Delicious, indeed," she commented, feeling the warmth of the cider spreading within her. "But it may have a direct line to my head."

"Will you watch my drink?" Lise asked her. "I'll be back after a quick run to the privy and back."

With a reassuring nod, Annabel affirmed, "Of course. Take your time." Savoring another hearty gulp of the cider, her gaze wandered toward the motley band, and her body began swaying instinctively to the fading echoes of the music. At that moment, her tiredness faded, replaced by a contagious joy that permeated the air.

Just as Annabel immersed herself in the revelry, the music stopped, and Lise returned. Charlie approached, a relaxed grin on his face. "Happy All Hallow's Eve," he greeted.

Returning his smile, Annabel and Lise exchanged greetings in unison. Lise handed Charlie a pewter mug and filled it. Together, they raised their drinks, toasting to the night ahead.

Charlie leaned in and whispered, "Before I forget, I ran into Gwyneth yesterday at the harbor."

Curiosity rose in Annabel. "Oh?"

"She mentioned that Richard's mother had recently visited the DiMilo. Although Gwyneth never held her in high regard, especially after their teenage years, it seems she's now trying to suggest your marriage be annulled in hopes of persuading Gwyneth to give up her profession and marry Richard at long last." His tone reflected his distaste for this idea. "If you can believe it."

"No!" Lise laughed. "You're kidding."

A shiver ran down Annabel's arm as his words sank in. "And what was Gwyneth's response?" she asked.

"Gwyneth laughed in her face, telling her to kick rocks," Charlie revealed with evident satisfaction. "She also mentioned that you had already settled some of Richard's debt to her?"

Annabel nodded. "Yes."

"A bit silly, if you ask me," Lise sighed. "You'll never see that money again, mark my words."

Charlie shook his head. "No, it was a smart move. Gwyneth is on your side, not Prudence Granger's. It's best to avoid being on the bad side of the brothel—you've managed to do the opposite." He grinned. "Well done."

"I welcome all the friends I can get," Annabel remarked. "You make it sound as though they hold influence in town."

"Well," he began carefully. "They happen to be the sole brothel in the region for a reason."

Lise added, "The tax collector takes a generous cut, the local judge believes it maintains social order, and bribes flow freely." Rubbing her hands together gleefully, she continued, "As the witching hour approaches, does anyone know a good ghost story?"

"Yes," Annabel replied without hesitation.

"Perfect," Lise exclaimed, taking her arm and leading them to a nearby table with more people. Charlie made to join them, but suddenly, the baron's man, James, approached Charlie and whispered something in his ear; then he and James departed quickly out the barn d oor.

As the rest of the small crowd settled into their seats, Annabel and Lise found themselves in the company of Helga, Ethel, Bridgette, and Cecelia at the table. Lise announced, "The new girl has a ghost story to share." Turning to Annabel, she whispered, "We're all ears."

Annabel's nerves fluttered within her, momentarily regretting her impulsive offer to tell a story. She smiled nervously at the anticipation from her companions, gathered her courage and began, "Once upon a time, there was a very wealthy old man and a very cunning young woman." The table leaned in, a collective curiosity shining in their eyes. Annabel's smile widened, and she felt her spirit rekindling with each word, hungry for storytelling.

Continuing her tale, Annabel revealed, "The wealthy old man entered into a contract with the young woman, binding her to work with him for six years. Unfortunately..." She paused, drawing out the suspense. "She never read the contract." Ethel shuddered, and Bridgette began fidgeting with her hair. Lise nodded encouragingly.

"Had she read the contract," Annabel continued, her voice hushed, "She would have realized that at the end of each year, the old man would claim and forever own another part of her body for himself."

Cecelia gasped, her eyes widening with a mix of horror and fascination.

"After the first year," Annabel whispered, "The old man came to collect his due from the young woman. He claimed her right hand and declared they would be married that day. And so, her right hand became his."

"God's ears," breathed Bridgette, unable to contain her discomfort.

"In the second year," Annabel continued, her voice laden with sorrow, "He returned to claim her left hand. She pleaded with him not to take it, begging him to leave her at least one hand to call her own. Moved by his growing affection for her, the rich man altered the terms of their contract, allowing her to keep her left hand in exchange for her right leg."

There was a moment of silence, and a creaking in the walls made Cecelia jump.

"This pattern continued," Annabel revealed, her voice ominous, "With the old man taking possession of her left leg in the third year, her head in the fourth year, and her neck in the fifth year. Finally, the sixth year arrived. By this time, they had children, and her life was revocably intertwined with his. Once again, he demanded her left hand. After all, he practically owned her in every other way."

Helga snorted at this, unable to suppress her amusement, while Annabel concealed a grin. "But the young woman, consumed by fury, had dedicated the past six years to him. Did he truly need every piece of her?" Annabel's voice took on a defiant tone.

"No," scowled Cecelia, her indignation mirrored in her expression.

Annabel's smile returned. "On the other hand," she continued, "The old man resented that he had given her so much of his time and wealth, yet she still held back a part of herself. In a fit of anger, he forcefully removed the glove from her left hand, intent on claiming it for himself. However..." Pausing for effect, Annabel's gaze swept across the table. "There was nothing there."

Cecelia emitted a small scream, her reaction catching Annabel off guard. "I'm sorry, I'm sorry," the younger girl mumbled apologetically. "Please, go on."

With a sense of satisfaction, Annabel resumed in a low, conspiratorial voice, "The old man recoiled in horror, unable to tear his gaze away from her handless arm. 'What have you done?' he cried."

Every eye at the table remained fixed on Annabel, the air thick with anticipation. With a slight nod, Annabel revealed the woman's triumphant response, "You will never find it. I have sold it to a demon who now possesses it. If I cannot fully possess my body, neither will you!" Sorrow clouded Annabel's expression as she continued, "The old man crumbled before her, tears streaming down his face. She left the room, and when she returned, he lay lifeless on the floor."

"How did he die?" Cecelia blurted out.

"Hush," whispered Bridgette.

Annabel's voice lowered further. "He died by strangulation," she declared. "On his neck bore the imprint of a large, gaudy old ring—the very ring the young woman had always worn on that hand, a cherished heirloom passed down from her great-grandmother."

She lingered on the words, relishing the attentive silence that enveloped the table. "The woman lived a long and fulfilled life, always striving to bring more goodness into the world than she had received. Having reclaimed the rest of her body, she hardly missed her left hand." Dropping her voice to a whisper, Annabel leaned in, holding the table's gaze. "But in the dead of night, the hand roams. It seeks out those who have been selfish beyond measure, demanding possession of others' bodies for their own relief. It feeds on betrayal, and when it finds such a person..."

Suddenly, a large, dirty hand materialized behind Annabel, gripping her throat, causing her to yelp in terror, gasping for breath amid the shrieks of the table.

"It's the ring! On the hand!" Helga screamed, pointing at the shiny bauble adorning the finger of the hand that had startled Annabel. "It's bloody *got* her!"

Relaxing into a grin, Annabel playfully held up her dirtied left hand, the ring gleaming under the dim light. "Got you," she laughed, her voice filled with mischief.

The table erupted in cries of laughter, some of the women around her pale but smiling. Taking a deep breath to steady herself, Annabel addressed the table, her tone lighter. "My apologies for the scare, everyone. A fine All Hallows Eve to you all."

Ethel, still catching her breath, spoke up amidst the laughter. "Oh, Annabel...that was terrifying and perfect."

Helga shook her head in amazement. "Well done, my dear. You certainly know how to spin a tale."

Lise, grinning from ear to ear, raised her mug in a toast. "Three cheers to the new storyteller at Castle Rowley! The action, the drama—I won't be sleeping peacefully tonight. I know I can't read, but you should write that down, honey—it's a keeper."

Annabel's cheeks flushed with pride as applause and laughter filled the barn.

Chapter Seven

FRUSTRATING SETBACKS

The following evening yielded another welcome visit from Lise. "Good day to you! Might I come in?" She grinned, adding, "I have news on the staircase for you to puzzle out."

"Excellent!" Annabel held the door open for Lise and locked it behind her. "Did you actually find the clue?"

"Yes!" She exclaimed. "I couldn't believe it. The carved wooden couple under the baluster comes out if you press into the heart between them. There was a piece of parchment right behind." Her new friend dug in her skirts for a small leather pouch and withdrew the parchment. "Careful. It's quite old."

Her voice high with excitement, Annabel read aloud,

In shadows, we gather, awaiting the next
Small missives echo through day and night
While strong, our lofty shoes are vexed
But often also bathed in light.

Snickering, Lise whispered, "Spooky, isn't it? I showed Charlie. I looked in all the fine old boots and shoes, trying to see if a slip of paper was tucked away in lofty shoes. Even got to the old ones in the highest attic tower—nothing."

Annabel shook her head sympathetically. "That must have been smelly work. Maybe the nursery, just in case the small missives are small voices?" Shaking her head, Annabel went to the counter and poured the tea she had just made into two cups, setting one down in front of Lise.

"Let's ponder," pondered Lise. "Lofty shoes..." Annabel's brow furrowed, and suddenly she smiled. "Shoes—lofty ones? Maybe it's souls, like the kind in church, bathed in light, like the heavenly ones?" His voice grew more excited. "If I'm writing a small missive, I'm writing a note. Notes echo. Could it be the chapel, perhaps?"

"Of course, the chapel!" Lise clasped her hands together. "Gathering in shadows before each service. Why didn't we think of that? Again, you're bloody brilliant!" Unable to contain her enthusiasm, she stood. "Do you have time to help us search in an hour once we've devised a plan? We should take advantage of the Baron being out for the day."

Annabel's mind buzzed with excitement and trepidation. Eager to uncover the next riddle, she nodded. "Of course."

Within the hour, Lise was back at her door. "Charlie has bribed the sacristan to accidentally spill some wine at the altar on the massive floor cushions, which they hate to move, so I have a reason to be in there—but he doesn't know why we want the room, and he's washed his hands of it. James just called for me to get the stain out, and I've told him I need to grab a breath of fresh air and my laundry cart in the cellar."

"I'm a breath of fresh air? Why, thank you," Annabel curtsied playfully.

"More than you know." Lise laughed.

"Can Charlie join us to search?" Annabel asked. "Three heads ae better than two, right?"

Lise nodded. "He's just washing up to get the stench of the horses off, then meeting us in the cellar. You should fit in the laundry cart just fine—I've modified it."

"Two heads are better than one," Annabel agreed. "Especially if we have limited time to search. And the chapel is quite large. The clue doesn't really allude to where within the chapel it is, does it?"

Once both women finished their tea, they walked from the farmhouse towards the castle. Lise continued. "You'll both get into my modified laundry cart... it's reinforced at the bottom so a person can easily fit inside. I'll take it to the chapel. Once inside, I'll draw the curtains and lock the door, and while I clean the wine stains, you and Charlie can search for clues." She rubbed her hands together. "We should have about forty-five minutes before James is done meeting with Cole and comes to investigate my progress, I'd wager."

"Do we really have to be so covert?" Annabel shrugged. "I thought the Baron was away."

Lise's voice turned serious. "His men are still present, unfortunately, that rude little Cole and Cecelia's father, James, the biggest chin-wagger at the castle, and they can't be bribed. It may be less dangerous without old Henry skulking around, and God knows his children don't care, but it's still risky with his spies about. Are you still in?"

"Yes, of course." Annabel nodded resolutely. "I'm ready."

Ten minutes later, after considerable sweating inside the carts, they were within the chapel, and Lise secured the door behind them. With purpose in her steps, she approached the altar, briefly acknowledging the cross before aggressively tending to the wine stain, furiously blotting and squirting the stain with vinegar.

"Where should we start?" Annabel whispered, her eyes sweeping over the large, quiet room filled with tall candles and gilded art.

"Hmmm..." Charlie pointed to the long row of hanging tapestries behind the altar. "Do you mind checking behind those and the candlesticks, and I'll search under the pews?"

Annabel agreed and meticulously examined each one while Charlie scoured beneath the pews, trying not to break his lantern. Despite their thorough efforts, thirty minutes passed without any findings. Then, a knock on the door shattered the silence, sending all three of them into a panic.

Wide-eyed, they exchanged alarmed glances and Lise whispered urgently, "*Hide!*"

With no time to spare, Annabel and Charlie frantically searched for a concealed spot that would elude immediate discovery. Spotting the altar as their best option, Annabel swiftly gestured for Charlie to join her, and they huddled together beneath the hanging fabric, their bodies motionless and hearts pounding.

Lise opened the door, her tone exuding annoyance. "Can't a woman have a moment to clean in peace?"

James's voice sounded desperate. "I've damaged the Baron's best rug! The lavender one in his chambers...I spilled ink on it. Please, you have to come right away."

Lise's fury mixed with concern. "Ink? You bloody fool. Could you have picked anything worse to spill?"

James stuck his head into the room, his eyes landing on the clean, damp cushions. "Well, you're clearly done here, so come along before it sets," James impatiently insisted.

"I still have some work to finish..." Lise's voice trailed off, but her protests were ignored as James dragged her away.

Annabel and Charlie exchanged relieved glances in the sanctuary of their hiding place. Yet, as they prepared to emerge and she lifted the altar fabric, Charlie's eyes widened with excitement. He pointed upward, drawing Annabel's attention to the carved words underneath the altar.

Grinning, she read softly aloud, "Downwind..." She furrowed her brow.

"Go on..." Charlie said patiently.

"Nothing else." She squinted again but shook her head sorrowfully. "The rest of it is scratched out."

Charlie's excitement dimmed. "Only the first word is legible?" He sighed. "Just our luck. Why?"

"Why, indeed." Annabel nodded, sharing in his frustration. "How disappointing."

He sighed. "We can't wait for Lise's return indefinitely, and we can't risk getting caught coming out of that door."

Annabel tapped her foot against the floor beneath the altar, a sudden realization dawning. "Altars often have storage compartments underneath. Some of the old ones even have tunnels."

"Really?" Charlie's face lit up with anticipation.

Driven by a shared determination, they removed layers of rugs, canvas, and rushes to finally reveal, to their delight, a large hole with a ladder at the top of it. Casting a cautious glance toward the chapel's entrance, they decided. Annabel gestured for Charlie to descend first, and she followed suit, carefully closing the door behind them.

Plunged into darkness, Annabel blinked rapidly, yearning for light, her heart racing.

Charlie's whispered voice broke through the abyss. "Hang on, I have a tinderbox." She heard the faint sound of rustling and tearing fabric before a flicker of fire illuminated the space. Charlie held up a small torch and whispered, "Listen, I've been down here before through another entrance, and I think I can guide us back to Lise's room. The cellar has another opening. But we must be swift—who knows who else is down here."

"Who knew there was an underground tunnel system beneath the castle," Annabel muttered. With a mix of fear and anticipation, they moved swiftly through the dimly lit hallways, their steps light and cautious. At moments when impending footsteps hinted at approaching danger, they froze in unison.

Eventually, they reached another ladder built into the wall, prompting a relieved sigh from Charlie. "This is it."

Scaling the ladder first, Annabel emerged into Lise's room within the cellar, extending a hand to guide Charlie out. Sitting on the floor, both slightly breathless, they savored the momentary respite. Charlie confirmed the locked door, ensuring their safety, while Annabel settled onto a nearby chair.

Once she'd caught her breath, Annabel looked thoughtfully down at the hidden floor panel.

"What are you thinking?" Charlie asked.

"I was thinking about how the cellar has a door to the tunnels, and so does the chapel." She grinned. "I wonder where else they are?"

"I only knew of the cellar entrance, and there's one to the Baron's chambers as well." Charlie nodded. "It would be good information to learn more."

"Perhaps they keep the castle floorplans in the library?" she suggested. "If we find the other openings..."

"That sounds dangerous," Charlie warned. "Sneaking into the library. The Baron would have our heads."

Annabel nodded thoughtfully. She stood and walked to the basin set in the wall, scrubbed her hands, and dried them. "Is there a vice in the library?" she asked suddenly.

"For holding books together? Of course," he nodded. "There's also a printing press."

"What?" Annabel was so excited she rose and came over to him. "Are you serious? There's a printing press in the library in this very castle?"

"Yes." Charlie scratched his head. "To my recollection, the baroness used it for her correspondence. She was trying to start some kind of newspaper about writers and artists around it before she died."

"Interesting," Annabel mused, rubbing her hands together.

"We should go." Stretching, Charlie asked, "And what is your plan for the clerks?"

Annabel considered this. "Where are the Rowley twins? Talon and Cassidy?"

He shrugged. "Probably in the playroom with Elizabeth, their nurse."

"Let's go," she said confidently. Charlie shook his head but walked with her to the door.

Annabel followed him through the great hall and to the bottom of a grand staircase, where she paused. "Upstairs?" she asked doubtfully.

"Sure, the nursemaid and the children's rooms are all in the west turret." He gestured, then smiled. "Don't tell me you're fearless in the face of ghost stories on All Hallow's Eve, but a little height scares you."

"It's the stability of the castle that scares me," she insisted, looking fearfully upwards. "It's so old. It's no one-story farmhouse."

"If the western turret were likely to fall, it would have done so when Talon first began launching catapults at the wall a year ago," Charlie offered. "Does that make you feel any better?"

"Not really," she muttered, ascending the stairs. As they walked in silence, she remembered. "You weren't *there* for my ghost story on All Hallow's Eve. You stepped out."

Charlie laughed as he reached the top of the stairs. "I don't want to alarm you, but everyone at the castle knows The Haunted Hand practically by heart now."

"Oh..." A foolish grin escaped Annabel's face, and she found it impossible to remove. "Truly?"

Charlie smiled. "Truly."

"Charlie!" Cassidy came racing down the hall. "How good to see you. Do you have any presents for us?"

He laughed, searching his pockets, and withdrew a carved wooden top. "Will this do?"

Scrutinizing it, she nodded. Curiously, she looked up at Annabel. "Welcome to the upstairs."

"Where is Elizabeth?" Charlie asked.

"Asleep on the chaise." Cassidy pointed down the hall. To Annabel, she asked, "I hope you've come to tell us a story? I'm dreadfully bored."

"Actually," Annabel knelt at the little girl's level. "I've come to ask you a favor."

"A favor!" Talon laughed, and they all looked up to see in in the hallway, tossing a small hatchet from hand to hand. "Neither of us is giving you any money, farmwife."

"No one is after your stupid money, Talon," Cassidy moaned. "And I will be very cross if you drive away our only visitors. Do you want us to be alone forever?"

"Sorry." Talon's tone was rude, but Annabel thought his eyes were sad as she watched the young boy absently playing with the small weapon.

Cassidy rolled her eyes in the direction of her brother. "Never mind him. I'll do the favor." She paused. "So long as it really isn't money. Father says I won't get any until I'm married."

Charlie scowled at this, and Annabel cleared her throat, speaking softly to Cassidy. "I have been here for over a month and have had no chance to fix books, one of my favorite pastimes." She patted her skirt pocket. "I've got my kit here, and I was wondering if you have any old books that are coming apart, which I could practice on. It would make my heart sing to fix a book again."

"You can fix books?" asked Cassidy in surprise. "Like Roland?"

"Roland comes from the city once a year to fix books in the library," Charlie told Annabel. "There's quite a stack waiting for him, to my memory. I don't think that he's due back again until Summer."

"Only once a year?" Annabel cocked her head. "Does he finish them all?"

"No," Cassidy shook her head. "And he never has time to fix our books." A grin broke out across her face. "But if you could repair my Aesop's Fables..." She bit her lip. "It's my favorite, but it's been in bad shape for

ages." She smiled shyly. "I'd love you forever if you fixed it."

"Don't say that, Cassidy," moaned Talon. "They're bloody peasants. You're being ridiculous."

She whirled on him. "Are you going to fix it? Or ask Father to have it fixed?"

"No," he replied petulantly, walking away from her. "Of course not."

"Then hold your tongue," she hissed loudly. To Annabel, she whispered, "Wait right here. I'll get it." In moments, the girl returned with a dilapidated old gray book, gingerly holding the pages together. "It's quite bad," she whispered. "Are you sure you can fix it?"

As Annabel began to inspect the damage, she ran a finger along the frayed edges and carefully flipped through the tome. "Have some of these pages been...torn out?" she asked in surprise.

Cassidy blushed. "Yes. Mummy gave me the book years ago—sometimes talking about her makes Father angry. And he doesn't like all the stories." Sniffling, she added, "Ooh! Mummy signed the third page; it's still a bit ripped. Can you save it?"

Exchanging a look with Charlie, Annabel fixed a smile on her face. "Yes, I can."

"Where should we go?" Cassidy asked. "Since Elizabeth is asleep in the nursery?"

"Well, I've got everything I need to fix it with me here, and I can indeed do so," Annabel confided, winking at the girl. "All I will need is a vice to press it together at the end to help set the glue. Where can we find one of those?"

"Oh!" Cassidy clasped her hands together. "The library! I'll show you."

Charlie gave Annabel an impressed nod as Cassidy started back down the hall and turned to the boy hovering in the doorway of his playroom. "Talon, I take it you're staying here."

"Yes. The library is so quiet and boring." Talon sighed. "Will you play knucklebones with me, Charlie?"

"Of course, lad," he agreed, their voices trailing off as Annabel followed Cassidy down the hallway.

When they had arrived in front of a grand wooden door, Cassidy stopped. She opened the door a crack and peeked in, then pulled it open the rest of the way. "Sometimes Frederick is in here...his chambers are nearby, and he gets annoyed when I enter the library. He says we're babies, and the library is for grown-ups."

"Frederick, is your older brother?" Annabel asked softly, taking a cloth out of her pockets and laying it on a table, then gently setting down the book.

Cassidy nodded. "He likes books better than people, though. So maybe he'll like me when I'm older, and I've read more books."

Annabel's heart broke a little for Cassidy, though she tried not to show it. "I know what it's like to have an unappreciative brother. He'll grow out of it."

"I hope so," scowled Cassidy.

With great precision, Annabel set to work. She removed the dust and grime with a small brush, then carefully disassembled the book, removing the old threads and glue. Cassidy watched with curiosity and admiration as she worked, her small face illuminated by a sunbeam streaming through the window.

As she slipped linen thread through a large needle and began to sew the pages together, Annabel whispered, "What's your favorite story from this book?"

"The Horse and the Lion," replied Cassidy confidently.

"Can you tell me about it?" She carefully laid out the rest of her tools.

"Once upon a time..." Cassidy began happily. "In a distant forest, there lived a horse and a lion who were the best of friends. They spent their days together, roaming the fields and hunting for food." She whispered, "Charlie will carve me a lion to play with for this story. He promised me he would."

Annabel smiled. "A wooden lion - think of the carved hairs in the mane!"

"Yes! Cassidy's eyes lit, and she continued, "But one day, the lion fell ill. He was too weak to hunt and feared that he might not survive. The horse approached the lion with a heavy heart and said, 'My dear friend, I know you are hungry and weak. I offer myself as your meal. Eat me, and let my flesh nourish you back to health.'"

"Oh, my goodness," whispered Annabel.

Cassidy nodded. "The horse's selfless offer touched the lion, but he couldn't bear to devour his loyal friend. He said, 'I appreciate your sacrifice, dear horse, but I cannot accept it. I would rather starve than lose a friend like you.'" She gave a satisfied little smile, and Annabel nodded encouragingly.

"Days turned into weeks, and the lion's illness gradually receded. With time and rest, he regained his strength, and they were the best of friends again!" She clapped her hands together in delight. "Isn't that lovely?"

"That is quite a story," Annabel shook her head. "I hadn't heard anything like it. I'm sure you know the lesson, but what do you make of it, yourself?"

"Who knows," shrugged Cassidy. She paused. "The lion should have eaten the horse. No one would have blamed him. It's nature's course. But he chose differently, and he got to keep his friend." Sighing, she added, "I like the idea of making a different choice than expected because you want to for yourself."

"I do, too." Annabel unrolled a piece of thick leather from her kit and carefully applied adhesive, gluing the pieces of the old cover to the new one. "Ready for the vice?"

"Yes!" Cassidy squealed, then clapped a hand over her mouth, her eyes darting around. "It's over here." She brought Annabel to a bookshelf across the library, where a mighty vice stood. Nodding appreciatively, she walked around it, looking over the device from all angles.

Intricate patterns of vines and scrolls adorned its frame. The center, massive, threaded screw of aged brass, extended skyward, its surface bearing the gentle wear of countless turns. She admired the wooden jaws, carefully lined with soft, worn leather, and the ornately carved and polished crank handle.

"You like books as much as I do," Cassidy remarked happily. "I can see it in your face. I thought you were a farmer? Peasants usually can't read, but my mummy said anyone can learn if they try."

"A wise woman, your mummy," Annabel smiled. "I learned at church. Now listen, the glue I've used is strong, but it means the book needs to stay in the vice for a night and a day to properly set. Can you manage that?"

Cassidy considered this. "You may be unable to assist me later in getting it back out."

Annabel nodded. "Yes, but I don't want you to hurt yourself opening it. Is there anyone else who can help you?"

"I'll ask Frederick," the little girl decided. "He won't mind if it's about books."

"You promise?" Annabel raised her eyebrows. "You won't withdraw the book without Frederick or an adult?"

"Yes, yes," Cassidy clamored impatiently. "Please, let's get on with it!"

Annabel dusted off the massive handle with another cloth from her skirts, wrinkling her nose when she folded it with the dirt inside and stuffed it into a different pocket. Carefully, she turned the crank to open the vice, dusted off the rest, and then slipped the book into the device's jaws. She squinted to confirm it was centered, then carefully turned the crank clockwise, slowly, as she ensured the pressure was even.

When the vice was in place, Annabel turned to Cassidy and let out a breath, beaming. "Thank you so much. That was absolutely wonderful." She rubbed her hands together. "I feel so lucky to be here. Thank you, Cassidy, you're a gem, you know that?"

Cassidy beamed back. "I wish I could pay you, but Father only gives Talon money. He says girls can't be trusted to manage their own finances."

She scowled. "Even though all Talon spends his pocket money on is candy and weapons."

"Actually," Annabel tilted her head as if the thought was occurring to her for the first time. "I don't suppose they keep the blueprints of the castle in the library, do they? There should be more to the root cellar under my house, and I'd love to see for myself without having to dig." She smiled, wondering if she sounded as innocuous as she intended.

Cassidy looked surprised. "Oh! The blueprints aren't in the library."

"They're not?" Annabel was crestfallen.

But the girl smiled. "They're in the archives. I can show you."

Annabel followed Cassidy carefully through the library and to a dark, adjoining room. The girl lit an oil lamp and gasped as she looked up, seeing large wooden shelves with numerous manuscripts and scrolls labeled in a spidery, fading writing. Carefully holding the oil lamp aloft, Cassidy led her to an enormous set of drawers and pointed. "They're heavy, but they're in there."

Her heart in her throat, eyes constantly flicking her eyes to the door and back, ears pricked nervously, Annabel looked through the indexed manuscripts.

She found one from about fifty years prior and carefully pulled it out, spreading it on the nearest table. Cassidy held the oil lamp high again as Annabel's vision swept over it, soaking in everything she saw. Her eyes widened when she found where her farmhouse was built, and her fingers itched for the journal in her pocket to write down notes, but suddenly, they heard a rustling coming from the library.

Annabel smiled, her throat suddenly dry, and she stood and slipped the blueprint back into the drawer. "Thank you so much."

"Did you find the extra root cellar?" whispered Cassidy curiously. "Was it there?"

"Yes," she whispered back. "I found just what I was looking for."

HIDDEN PASSAGES

After much deliberation, Annabel requested to visit Richard in the dungeon, feeling entirely too guilty at her regret when it was granted. Still deeply troubled by his behavior but determined to comfort her husband as a wife should, she carefully chose her attire and tried to remember the good parts she'd known of Richard, that he was the reason she was here at all, and how lonely he must be in the dungeon. Placing freshly baked barley bread and a couple of apples in a basket, she took a deep breath, steeling herself for the encounter.

It was James who reluctantly agreed to accompany her. Annabel cleared her throat as they walked down the dimly lit corridor, breaking the tense silence. "How often do you come down here?"

"More often than I'd like," James replied curtly. "You need not know more than that."

"I imagine you're a busy man." Annabel clucked sympathetically. "You're Cecelia's father, aren't you?"

"Yes, unfortunately, I'm the father of that lazy little sneak," muttered James. "It's just up here on the right. You have ten minutes."

Approaching the small window of Richard's cell, Annabel called out tentatively, "Richard?"

His weary figure emerged from the shadows, relief flooding his face as he recognized her. "Annabel? Oh, my dearest heart, I'm so glad you're here!"

Fresh guilt washed over her. "Of course. Are you all right?" In a soft voice, she offered bread and apples. "Please eat—I've brought these for you."

"My thanks." Richard's face reflected gratitude and desperation through the bars as he stuffed a piece of bread into his mouth, chewed and swallowed, and then spoke through his next bite of apple. "I won't survive much longer in this place, I wager."

Her heart twisted, and she searched her mind for ways to alleviate his suffering, coming up empty. "I'm so sorry, Richard. What else can I do?"

"*Are* you sorry?" His voice lowered to a whisper. "Are you truly?"

"Why, of course..." Annabel began uneasily. "It's not my fault you're in here; it's definitely yours, mind, but I'm still sorry for you."

"Offer to trade places with me." Richard's blue eyes were desperate. "Please, Annabel?"

"What?" She almost dropped the basket.

Smiling weakly, he explained, "If you tell James right now you want to take my place, he'll inform the Baron, and they may release me from this wretched place."

Annabel recoiled in shock. "Are you out of your head? I won't take your place; I didn't commit your crime. Would you have me suffer for your mistakes?"

"You're my wife—it's your bloody duty." Richard's plea grew more desperate. "And if you claim you stole the jewels, clearing my name—I promise to repay you threefold." His voice was strained. "I shouldn't *be* here, Annabel. I've done my duty..."

"Then why did you steal from the castle?" Annabel narrowed her eyes as her feelings of guilt began to wane.

"It's complicated. If only that shrewish little laundress hadn't..." He sighed. "Why did you come here if you weren't going to help me get out?"

"Who says you're getting out?" Anger surged within her, and Annabel turned away, ignoring his cries. Taking the basket of food with her, she exited the dungeon, ignoring the curious stare of James on her way out, determined to regain her composure.

Once outside, she placed the extra loaves on the porch table. Fulke, one of the field hands, glanced up curiously. "Is that more bread?"

Annabel nodded listlessly. "Help yourself."

Later that night, after a long day in the fields, Annabel locked her door and took out her notebook. She carefully removed four pages, assembled them to form a large rectangle, and attached metal fasteners where the pages met. She sketched a rough map, opening and closing her eyes as she tried to remember the placement she had seen in the blueprints. She sketched out as much as she could recall, then fell asleep at the table.

In what must have been hours later, Annabel awoke in the dark. Scowling, she stood and felt around for her map, then lit the candle on the table. She paused as she unclasped the fasteners and slipped the pages into her notebook.

There was a low rumble coming from directly below her. Tilting her head curious, she sat in the quiet darkness and listened. The rumbling stopped...then as she strained to hear, there seemed to be the faint sound of almost...could that be cheering? She frowned.

Feeling silly yet curious, Annabel slipped below the table and put her ear to the floor. After another couple of minutes, there seemed to be a rumble that almost shook the ground, and she sat up again, flummoxed. She stood carefully and put her journal away, lost in thought. Then she took out her journal again, put the pages together, and looked at it.

A delighted grin spread across Annabel's face as she put the journal away for the second time and slipped on a cloak, heading for the root cellar.

After a few minutes of inspection and consulting her map, Annabel put all her effort into moving a large salt barrel and found what she had seen in the blueprints...a panel on the floor. "You might be a fool," Annabel whispered to herself. "But there is no easy way from the Earth to the stars."

She cleared her throat, trying to shake off her nerves. "Seneca...*The Madness of Hercules*." She pried it open with cautious anticipation, revealing a ladder leading down into a dark passageway. It appeared to be a secret entrance to the castle's dungeon. Taking a deep breath, Annabel descended the ladder, her heart pounding with trepidation even as it danced a little at the sudden, unlikely adventure.

Navigating the dimly lit hallway by a lone flickering candle set in the wall, she followed the distant noise until it grew distinct enough to pinpoint its source. Standing before a door from which the murmurs emanated, Annabel hesitated, contemplating running back the way she'd come.

Her deliberation proved brief as the door suddenly swung open, revealing James. The sight of Annabel made him to jump. "*You,* again. *What* are you doing down here?"

"I'm here to…" Before the door could close, she caught a glimpse of a room filled with men shouting and cheering.

"Place your bets!"

"Hold!"

"You're bluffing!"

Card games! Clearing her throat, she assumed an authoritative tone to gain the upper hand, addressing James with a commanding expression.

"I've—come for the game." Trying to read his face and failing, she tried fishing. "To see Lise?"

He scowled, looking her up and down. "Then why are you just standing here? Are you here to play or spectate?"

Annabel faltered, suddenly confused. "To… spectate? I seemed to have gotten turned around."

Shaking his head with a sigh, James opened the door again. Intrigued, she slipped through to the room, startled when he slammed the door shut behind her, with him on the other side.

Nonplussed, upon entering the room, Annabel was greeted by a cacophony of rowdy shouts and cheers. A massive underground chamber lay before her, a grand stage at its center. In the stands, surrounded by a throng of boisterous men, sat the Baron himself, who, upon noticing her, called out with a bark. "You there! Aren't you that literate farmer?" Baron

Rowley's voice carried across the room, and Annabel's throat tightened. "Yes, my lord," she replied, her mind racing. She spotted a few women scattered among the crowd, including Gwyneth. With more bravado than she felt, she added, "I've come to watch the show, if you'll allow it."

The Baron frowned while Gwyneth smiled and cajoled, "Oh, Henry, can she please join us? Annabel's company has been quite enjoyable—she's my favorite wife Richard has *ever* had." She winked at Annabel, who smiled weakly.

As he tossed back his drink, the Baron slurred, "I don't care. Just take a seat before it begins."

A surge of apprehension gripped her. Annabel quickly settled in the space Gwyneth made, feeling the other woman's curious gaze upon her. "I didn't think this was your kind of entertainment," Gwyneth whispered. "Have you come to get your pound of flesh?"

As Annabel parted her lips to respond, a dramatic fiddling filled the air, setting the stage and cutting off their conversation. Two guards emerged, dragging forth a disheveled and weary man with a prominent gash across his face. He cursed in a thick Scottish accent, tugging at his unkempt beard and wailing. One of the guards forcefully pushed him to the ground and announced, "Baron Rowley, allow me to present the captured pirate Kit Blackheart."

Gwyneth leaned in and whispered in Annabel's ear, "I would never say this to his face, mind you, but he's quite handsome, isn't he?"

Annabel peered at the pirate, whose muscular physique was evident beneath tattered garments. The sweat on his well-defined forearms stirred an unexpected flutter within her. Squinting to glimpse his partially obscured face, she sensed a fiery intensity and simmering anger emanating from him and found she couldn't quite tear her gaze away. Silently acknowledging Gwyneth's comment, Annabel gave her an appreciative nod without breaking her gaze from the man, and the other woman chuckled.

The room erupted in applause as the pirate spat in the Baron's direction, only to be met with the guard's swift kick to his stomach, causing him to howl in pain. Annabel's eyes widened. Undeterred, the guard continued, "Blackheart awaits execution for his crimes of murder, torture, and thievery. But why not have some amusement with him while he awaits sentencing?"

Suddenly, a piercing scream sliced through the air, capturing Annabel's attention. She gasped as she recognized the figure of Lise, bound and writhing in agony, and she could feel Gwyneth's curious gaze on her again.

Overwhelmed with uncertainty, she sank lower in her seat, unsure how to respond to the disturbing spectacle unfolding before her and wondering if she dared risk her life speaking out against it. Amidst the tumultuous crowd, the swarthy pirate stepped forward, his black beard cascading down his muscular chest as he bared his teeth menacingly. The guards forcefully dumped Lise in the center of the room, where she frantically struggled against her restraints, her eyes filled with desperation. The pirate advanced toward her, a predatory hunger evident on his dirty face. At that moment, a bell rang out.

The two combatants circled each other warily. Lise lunged forward, swinging a rope she had managed to free, but Blackheart deftly evaded her attack and retaliated with a swift kick to her midsection. Though momentarily staggered, Lise quickly regained her footing and launched at him again, wielding two ropes.

The pirate proved a skilled fighter, but Lise was quick. They clashed with ferocious intensity, their movements a blur of limbs as they vied for dominance. Blackheart struck Lise, causing her to stumble backward, yet she retaliated by tying a knot in one of the ropes and swinging it, narrowly missing his head.

The room buzzed with anticipation as the battle raged on. While Blackheart seemed to hold the upper hand, Lise displayed unwavering resilience. In a surprising turn of events, she launched a surprise attack, swiftly wrapping a rope around Blackheart's neck, causing him to lose his balance. He stumbled and fell to the ground, gasping for air.

Lise grinned triumphantly, bowing dramatically to the roaring crowd as if she had emerged victorious, but unfortunately, Blackheart was not so easily defeated. Summoning a surge of strength, he broke free from the rope's grip and sprang to his feet. He lunged at Lise with lightning speed, seizing her by the shoulders and slamming her forcefully into the ground with a resounding thud.

Blackheart quickly regained his footing, reveling in his victory. Despite the pain, Lise mustered her strength and swiftly mounted the pirate's back, trying to choke him with her legs.

In a startling display, the pirate proved he had one more trick up his sleeve—he produced a concealed dagger from his boot and ruthlessly plunged it into Lise's calf. A spray of blood followed, and she dropped to the ground, writhing in pain. Seizing the opportunity, Blackheart pounced on Lise with a final, devastating blow, driving her to the floor as she emitted a piercing shriek of agony. The crowd erupted in wild cheers as Blackheart emerged as the undeniable victor.

Lise lay on the ground, gasping for breath, moaning, and clutching her bleeding leg, and quickly, two men came with a stretcher to carry her away.

Annabel's stomach churned with a mix of horror and concern. She whispered to Gwyneth, trembling, "I have to go." Without waiting for a response, she hastily headed back down the path she'd come, spotting the stretcher bloodied, leaning against the wall...then as she went to turn back, she recognized a clump of bloody cloth from Lise's dress, light blue with tiny purple flowers...now stained with blood.

Hesitating briefly, she took a torch from the wall and headed down the second dark tunnel, her eyes wide as she looked out for her friend. Finally, Annabel spotted a soft light ahead, and picking up her pace, she reached the end, where a ladder was built into the wall leading up to the cellar tunnel entrance.

Shivering, she lifted her eyes skyward and was relieved to see the beautiful tapestry she recognized from Lise's ceiling.

When Annabel climbed the ladder and emerged into the cellar, she was doubly relieved to find Lise sitting with her back against the door, calmly tending to her injured leg.

Sliding the wooden panel back over the entrance and rushing over to her friend, Annabel trembled, her mind returning to the shock of the spectacle she had just witnessed. Gathering her wherewithal, she stammered, "Lise! Are you alright?"

Lise looked up at Annabel, her expression puzzled. "Oh, honey, I'm fine," she reassured her, her voice filled with concern and amusement. "It looks worse than it is. Were you down there?"

Annabel nodded, her eyes filled with a mixture of emotions. "Yes, I saw everything," she confessed, her voice laced with a shudder. "I thought something strange was happening there, but I never imagined they would force you to fight. How monstrous."

"Well." Lise sighed at Annabel's revelation. "That's not exactly what—"

Suddenly, the panel on the floor opened again, and Annabel shrieked when she saw it was the pirate who'd fought Lise. She was surprised when Lise clapped a hand over her mouth, and with a gasp, Annabel staggered backward away from them both, pulled a knife out of her skirts, and brandished it threateningly at the pirate. "Stay back," she warned.

"*Annabel*," hissed Lise in her ear. "Keep your bloody voice down, or you'll wake the castle. It's only *Charlie*."

"It's…" The blood seemed to drain from Annabel's face, and as her eyes met the pirate's, he winked, and she sat hard on the bed behind her.

The swarthy, muscular, villainous Kit Blackheart sat on the floor, pulled a wet rag from a bucket next to Lise, and held it to his face. "Sorry to startle you."

Annabel stared hard at the pirate, who looked back at her warily. "That's *Charlie*."

Lise nodded. "Yes."

"But...he *stabbed* you." Annabel looks at Lise's now wrapped leg.

Picking up her discarded boot, Lise drew a quivering red mass out of it. "It's a bag of blood. A pig bladder."

Annabel looked first at Charlie and then at Lise before burying her head in her hands, her shoulders shaking. Her friends exchanged a worried look.

"Annabel, don't *cry*," said Lise.

"I'm not," whispered Annabel, as the laughter began to follow her shock of the moment. "The *pair* of you."

Lise made a relieved sound, and Charlie grinned. "I had you going, then?"

"You really did," she admitted, peering at him. "What marvelous actors the both of you are. Is that...horsehair?"

"It is," he confirmed. "And Lise is the one who does marvelous makeup. She's even touched up a few courtiers who visited here."

"Oh, it's nothing," Lise said, coloring.

"It's not nothing. You're bloody good," insisted Charlie. "The Baron has never once guessed that I'm one of the pirates."

"That's hardly a vote of confidence in my favor," remarked Lise dryly. "The Baron is always stupefied to drunk at these things. He never remembers much the next day... we've tested that theory."

"How does this all work?" Annabel asked curiously.

"It started with the baron's underground rooster fights," said Lise. "Then the surge this past couple of years with more pirates getting caught came, and you know how the king hates pirates. He doesn't want them at the palace dungeon so close to his family. The Baron offered to host the pirates awaiting sentencing in his dungeons and decided to make some money off them first."

"But the pirates kept injuring guards," said Charlie. "Four men died, one became crippled, then two pirates escaped and had to be hunted down. It became a problem."

Lise nodded. "So Charlie hatched this plan, where we act out fighting so we can throw the fights when we like and play to the crowd, then everyone's entertained, and no one is meant to get seriously hurt," explained Lise. "Pirates participate so long as they understand the rules."

"You were both in on this from the beginning," Annabel sighed. "Why didn't either of you tell me?"

Charlie pulled a large chunk of horse hair off his face and shrugged uncomfortably. "You're my employer, or one of them. I simply thought you wouldn't like it."

"I like it better than either of you fighting to the death for real," Annabel admitted. "It looked brutal out there. So you're both actors?"

Her friends laughed ruefully at this, and Lise sighed. "God's bones. I bloody wish. Neither of us has got any chance of that. You've got to have training to be an actor and have connections in the industry to even get started."

"Not to mention, I could only play one kind of character," added Charlie. "But I have to admit, it's loads of fun."

"It's a rare bit of jest," added Lise. "I don't expect it to last forever, but please don't turn us in for now. Don't tell the Baron we're two of the fighters."

"Why would I turn you in?" Annabel asked, rankled at her assumption.

Lise shrugged. "Technically, you're above us. You've got more to lose. I know we're all mates, but..."

"*Above* you." Annabel rolled her eyes. "I've been driven out of my home by pranksters, my husband's imprisoned for theft, and before he left, he chose another woman over me. He just asked me to trade places with him in prison. And who knows how long the Baron will let me stay without Richard here." She laughed. "I'd wager I'm the lowest I've ever been. Though I was never at the top, neither of you are at the bottom."

Lise made a sympathetic noise, and Charlie continued removing his disguise. "Well, wherever we are, we're in good company."

Annabel looked down. "I'm not going to pretend I understand your troubles, and I won't blow your cover. But be careful, will you?"

"Always," smiled Lise. "Wait a moment. How did you find the stage, anyway? How did you find the *tunnels*?"

Charlie laughed. "She tricked Cassidy into bringing her to the library so she could see the blueprints."

"You clever girl," laughed Lise.

"Luckily, I found my way from the tunnel under the root cellar to the stage, and then I was able to find my way back to the cellar. Thank goodness for all the torches in the walls and seeing some of Lise's clothes on the floor, or I would've been lost for sure. Your eye," Annabel said suddenly to Charlie. "Was that from this?"

"No," he muttered, and Lise looked away.

"It wasn't really an eel either, though?" Annabel asked, and Charlie gave her a pained look. "No, don't tell me."

Lise coughed. "Are you still okay after what you saw? I'm sorry that we scared you. I should've told you about it; I just couldn't think of how to bring it up in conversation and explain it so that you wouldn't worry."

"I'm just a worrier. There's no stopping that," shrugged Annabel. "More to the point, are you okay? You're both fine beating each other up for the Baron's amusement?"

"It's not just us," insisted Lise. "There are loads of volunteers. They agree to terms and place bets, and I make folks up to make regulars look like different characters. Everyone gets paid from bets placed. We recruit volunteers, establish rules, and stage the fights ourselves. It's mostly gruesome entertainment, but at least nobody gets as badly hurt as they would otherwise. And it puts the Baron into a good mood."

Annabel smiled. "You both have incredible talent," she said sincerely. "I wish there was a way for you to pursue your passion on a grander stage, but I won't stand in your way."

Lise's cheeks pinkened at the compliment. Then she whispered, "Want to sneak out and go to a real play tomorrow night? Just us girls. Charlie's got to work."

Annabel's eyes sparkled with enthusiasm. "Yes, that sounds wonderful. How do we get there?"

Lise leaned in, her voice barely above a whisper. "A caravan will be just outside the gate tomorrow, selling knick-knacks. We'll slip away at night and catch a ride in the caravan to the theater. A friend of mine, Colley, works as a player at Baron Rowley's brother Geoffrey's manor, and they're allowed to use the carriages to go audit other plays. He brings a message to the Baron and then goes to the play. We have a ride there and back."

"Perfect! Thank you so much for including me." Annabel's excitement intensified, and she nodded eagerly. "I can't wait."

CHAPTER NINE

THE PLAY AND THE SCOUNDREL

As the next day's sun cast a warm, amber glow across the sprawling fields, Annabel found herself winding down her tasks. The day's labor had been productive, and she could feel weariness in her muscles and a pleasant ache in her bones. After changing and refreshing her face and hands with water from the basin, Annabel went to the cellar to meet Lise.

On her way, she bumped into Hattie, who looked rattled. "Are you going to see Lise?" the younger woman whispered, her eyes darting around the great hall.

"Yes," Annabel smiled. "Do you want to come along?"

"No," Hattie mumbled. "I've got to go. But can you give her this for me? I know the pair of you are friends." She pressed a shilling into Annabel's hand.

"Of course," said Annabel. "But are you sure you're alright?"

"I'm fine," whispered Hattie, but she swallowed hard and quickly walked away, turning a corner before Annabel could say anything else.

As she and Lise left the castle, her friend revealed a jug of wine in her shoulder bag. "Shall we seek refuge in the barn and drink before venturing out?"

"Absolutely," Annabel replied, excitement for the evening ahead coursing through her.

They slipped into the barn with a sense of secrecy, their laughter dancing in the air as they entered. Inside, they found Charlie engrossed in cleaning a caramel-colored mare's hooves.

Approaching her husband, Lise inquired in a playfully conspiratorial tone, "Might we find sanctuary here, indulging in a touch of mild intoxication before we embark on our evening?"

He laughed. "By all means."

Lise suddenly sucked in her breath, and Annabel followed her eyes to an almanac clipped open to the day's date on the stool beside Charlie.

"Sorry..." He set down the pick and dusted off his hands. "I meant to put it away. I was planning..."

"I can't believe it." Lise sighed. "It's been three months today since Agatha's disappearance."

"Yes." Charlie's voice was soft.

Her voice smaller than Annabel had ever heard it, Lise whispered, "It feels like so much longer."

Annabel stood there, her heart aching for the sadness that shadowed their eyes. She wished she could conjure words of comfort, but they eluded her as she wondered, not for the first time, if she would go missing next.

"Try not to dwell on it tonight," Charlie advised. "You both look lovely, and I'd join you if the work here weren't so demanding. Tomorrow is a busy day—inspection and grooming so the horses can be ready ahead of the Baron's birthday."

Lise sniffed and struck a playful pose, shaking off her sadness and Annabel smiled. "Have you attended one of the plays at Scion Tower?" she asked Charlie.

He nodded enthusiastically. "They are quite the spectacle. You'll have a marvelous time, I'm sure. What for the programs, they oft bear handsome woodcuts."

"I will!" Annabel exclaimed. "Thank you."

"We best be off," Lise suggested, taking another sip from the jug and stretching her arms. "We shall meet my dear friend Colley's carriage at the foot of the hill. We won't be gone too late."

"Say hello to him for me," called Charlie absently, returning to his work. The play that evening exceeded all of Annabel's expectations. Determined not to miss a captivating moment, she resisted the urge to blink, her heart and mind fully engaged as she allowed herself to be swept away by the enchanting story, the intricately designed sets, and the magnetic performances of the actors.

An announcement reverberated throughout intermission, promising a competition for thrilling, innovative play ideas. Emboldened by a few sips of wine, Annabel seized the opportunity. Hastily scribbling down the tale she spun at All Hallow's Eve in her hidden leather notebook, she submitted it under an alias, holding onto her resolve firmly before self-doubt could take root.

Lise caught up in Annabel's fervor and treated them to celebratory drinks after the performance. As the curtains fell, an exceptionally handsome actor joined their company.

"Allow me to introduce Colley Jameson," Lise addressed the newcomer affectionately. "Colley, meet Annabel, a recent addition to Castle Rowley."

"You poor, poor soul, ensnared by that place as well," Colley chuckled. "It's a marvel that castle still stands. And how do they manage to pay anyone? Do you know how many souls languish in the dungeon?"

"Enough," Lise playfully brushed off the topic. "May I remind you that we live there, dear friend?"

"Mind, it's better than my own stack of bricks. I'm only jealous." Colley nodded amiably before directing his attention to Annabel. "Are you employed within the castle, or have its walls claimed you through marriage?"

"It's the latter," Annabel confided. "I am the wife of Richard Granger, who had the dubious honor of three wives: one deceased, one vanished, and myself. Now he lies below the castle in the dungeon for thievery."

"How terrifying," Colley commented, his interest piqued. "I'm duly fascinated. Here's hoping you remain alive and return for many more plays."

"Maybe now that he's locked away, I won't have to look over my shoulder so vigilantly," Annabel mused. "Perhaps he can change, but I fear not. Then again, who can predict the future?"

Her friend's dark laughter rippled through the air, and Annabel joined in, the tension of the day momentarily forgotten. "We all watch our backs, day in and day out," Lise declared, raising her glass in a toast. "Here's to good people, and I count you both among them."

Colley nodded in agreement. "Here, here."

Laughter rippled through them, the world's worries held at bay for those fleeting moments. "Am I truly good company, though?" Annabel wondered aloud, a hint of self-doubt seeping through her words. "Richard didn't have many kind things to say after our marriage—he much preferred to cavort with a harlot, however nice she is. I now doubt every sweet word he spoke, and as it was, I was still healing from my first heartbreak." She sighed. "I feel old and worn and battered of spirit."

"You're anything but that," Lise assured her. "You're lovely; any man would be lucky to have you. Just look at your teeth."

"My teeth?" Annabel's hands went to her mouth anxiously. "What of them?"

"Well, you've got them all." Lise shrugged.

"Yes, they're very nice." Colley asked suddenly, "Wasn't Richard the one who took an unexpected dip in the harbor after imbibing a bit too much while arguing with Gwyneth?"

"Oh, yes, but stop." Lise waved off the topic with a chuckle. "He starts out incredibly charming, and she had no inkling of what awaited her. You are positively radiant," she assured Annabel. "But anyway, who cares? With a household to manage and crops to tend, relish this time without another man causing havoc."

Annabel laughed. "That's good advice."

"Well put," Colley agreed. "I've certainly had my share of older men meddling in my life. That's why my first love is acting. By the way, Lise says you're marvelous at telling stories." He grinned. "Might we hear one tonight?"

"Oh, I didn't prepare anything." She blushed. "I could improvise, but it might be terrible. Give me a moment."

"Take your time." Colley grinned and crossed his arms, and Lise sipped her drink. Annabel stared off distantly for a couple of minutes, then grinned.

"I know that look," crowed Lise. "I saw it when you told the tale on All Hallow's Eve. Let's have it."

"In the heart of London," Annabel began. "The new Globe Theatre was all the rage. And in one such theatrical wonderland, two actors stood out: Percival Thatcher and Bartholomew Hawthorne. Both were gifted actors, but each considered himself the show's star. And oh, did they have a rivalry!"

"Sounds like you and Nathaniel Fairbank," snickered Lise good-naturedly to Colley.

Colley made a face. "It does *not.*"

Annabel continued, "One day, the theatre director announced that they were to put on a new play, a comedy that would require the lead actor to don the newly imported wig from France—a marvelous, voluminous creation that was whispered to have once graced the head of none other than King Louis XIV himself! Naturally, both men wanted the part.'"

"Naturally," Colley breathed. "I'd give my eyeteeth to wear a wig like that."

Annabel smiled.

'Clearly, the role is meant for me!' proclaimed Bartholomew. 'I've been told my cheekbones are the envy of the town. A wig like that would frame them perfectly!'

Lise laughed, and Colley began to smile.

She continued, "Percival Thatcher scoffed, twirling his mustache dramatically. 'Nonsense, Hawthorne! That wig requires someone with a forehead as broad and magnificent as mine!' The bickering continued until the director, in a bid to maintain his sanity, decided that the best way to settle this was with an acting challenge: each would be given a mundane, everyday object, and they would have to deliver a spontaneous, heartfelt monologue about it.

"Bartholomew went first. He was handed a spoon—a plain, wooden eating spoon. Clearing his throat, he embarked on an impassioned soliloquy, drawing connections between the spoon's humble nature and the human experience, the depth of its scoop akin to the depth of human emotions. Tears welled in his eyes as he concluded, 'For in this spoon, I see life, love, and the unending cycle of soup to mouth!' The audience erupted in applause."

"Hear, hear!" Colley nodded.

Annabel grinned. "Percival was up next. He was given a potato."

Lise giggled, slapping the table in her mirth. "My favorite! No butter?"

"No butter." Annabel gave her friend a sad look. "With a smirk, he held the potato up high and launched into his monologue, detailing the potato's journey from the New World, how it had braved oceans and pirates, only to end up in a 17th-century English pot of stew. 'This potato,' he declared, 'embodies the spirit of adventure, the risks of the unknown, and the undeniable fact that it would taste marvelous with a touch of butter!' The crowd went wild."

"Well, who won?" clamored Colley.

At this point, two other men had gathered to listen. In her nerves, Annabel pretended not to notice. "In the end, neither Bartholomew nor Percival got to wear the coveted wig."

"What!" shouted the two men behind them. "That's bollocks, it is."

She smiled. "The director, inspired by their ridiculous monologues gave the lead role to the prop master, who, in the final act, delivered a heart-wrenching monologue about... the wig."

The group chuckled, leaning in. Softly, Annabel concluded, "And so, in the bustling heart of London amidst the noise, drama, and newly imported potatoes, two rivals learned that sometimes, it's not about the wig—it's about the story you weave around it."

"Ha!" It was Colley's turn to slap the table. "My dear friend, that was perfect. You ought to write these down."

"Right!" Lise crowed as the men behind them wandered off, smiling at Annabel as they left. "It's only a matter of time, surely? Now you've got time on your own and a bit more money for paper and things."

"I think a woman writer still makes men too nervous," admitted Annabel. "I love stories, reading, and writing, but I also want to stay alive without being called a witch or a troublemaker. I've run into many people who think I might be a witch simply because I'm a woman who can read. It's ridiculous. I'd rather live than be a martyr for my cause. Is that terrible?" She laughed.

"That's easily solved." Collets shrugged. "Pen name. Like a stage name. No one needs to know who you are."

Lise rubbed her hands together. "Tell us, what would it be? Your pen name, your alternate identity?"

"I know this one." Annabel immediately giggled. "Daegal Godwin. Nice ring to it, yes?"

"Oh, so you've thought about this already!" Lise laughed, throwing her head back merrily.

Colley was suddenly rooting through his satchel, frowning. "I'll be right back—I left something backstage." As he departed, Annabel and Lise ventured to the privy, and after tending to their needs, Lise drifted to a caravan stall a few yards from the door, where vibrant fabrics were displayed.

Meanwhile, the melody of the music playing indoors caught Annabel's attention, drawing her gaze back to the stage where the play had unfolded earlier. "Live music even after the play?" Annabel marveled.

Lise's voice carried over to her from the stall. "Indeed. The musicians might not be the finest, but this is at least an opportunity to practice."

Savoring the music inside the door, swaying as she felt the warmth of the wine, Annabel felt a hand touch her shoulder. When she turned, she beheld a tall, lean man whose gaze gleamed with playful intent. "Would you honor me with a dance?" he inquired.

"I'm flattered," Annabel smiled politely, willing her expression to convey friendliness rather than romantic interest. "I am also married."

He chuckled, undeterred by her response. "Certainly, but you ventured here alone, so why not seize the moment?"

"No, thank you," she declined gently. "I'm with friends this night." She tried to walk around him back outside to Lise, but he swiftly blocked the entrance.

"Didolis Crowell, at your service," he introduced himself, unfazed by her rejection. "Are you a witch?"

"What?" Annabel rasped, the mere mention of the term sending a shiver down her spine. "Of course not." She smiled weakly, in what she hoped was a polite manner, and asked softly, "Come now, sir. Why would you say such a thing to a married woman who has done nothing to you?"

Didolis shrugged nonchalantly. "Oh, you look quite like a witch I saw hanging a month ago. You might even be her ghost?" He grinned, enjoying the game.

Annabel felt the warmth within her dissipate, replaced with nauseated unease as she stared at him. "Please let me pass, good sir."

"Oh, fear not," he said with a mischievous wink. "I'll gladly vouch for your innocence."

"Thank you," Annabel replied stiffly.

"Could I call on you?" Didolis purred suggestively. "Perhaps later?"

"I'm afraid not," Annabel admitted, her voice carrying discomfort. "I came here to relax and enjoy the gaiety of a play, and with all respect, I'm not interested."

Didolis's demeanor shifted suddenly, his words carrying a hint of rudeness. "Ah, so you're here just to tease the men? I saw you *drinking.*"

"For pity's sake, sir." Annabel shook her head. "I didn't intend to cause offense. Can you not please leave me to go about your night?"

"Come now..." In a swift movement, Didolis stepped closer, causing Annabel to instinctively move backward inside the building. Her heart was pounding as she considered screaming for her friends, but her throat felt dry. "Just give me a chance," he urged, his grip on her hand tightening as his other hand reached her waist. "You may enjoy it..."

With a mixture of panic and resolve, Annabel's other hand darted into one of her pockets, fingers closing around a small packet as she felt his hot, moist breath on her cheek. In one swift motion, she ripped it open and tossed the contents directly into his face.

Happily, he immediately released her, his hands clawing at his eyes as he emitted a piercing shriek of pain. She quickly stepped around him and slipped back outside.

"What is this?" he shrieked to her retreating form. "What in the name of all that is holy..."

"It's pepper," Annabel retorted, her voice laced with anger. "Perhaps you should wash your eyes in the fountain to cleanse yourself of arrogance." "You mad witch!" Didolis cried in fury.

"I am not a witch," Annabel hissed as she departed. Lise and Colley rushed to Annabel's side, their faces perplexed by the unfolding scene. "What on earth was that?" Colley asked, his tone edged with concern.

"Unwelcome advances from this cad," Annabel murmured. "Resulting in unwelcome peppered eyes."

Lise's fury blazed in her eyes. "Didolis Crowell, how dare you. Your company is as welcome as rain at harvest."

"Your tongue wags like a dog's tail," added Colley. "And to similar effect."

Looking wounded, Didolis glared back at them. "It was all in good fun...I was just about to leave."

"If only your departure was as swift as your advances," spat Lise.

Didolis stormed off, muttering curses, his eyes still watering and bloodshot.

Annabel swallowed hard, drawing deep breaths to steady herself and regain her composure.

As he disappeared from view, after a few shocked moments of silence, Lise whispered, "Pepper!" and then began to chuckle. "Really, that's bloody brilliant. I hope you don't mind if I steal that. I've thrown sand before or removed my shoe to defend myself against an untoward man..."

"I carry a cane for that reason," replied Colley. "People think you're lame, but you're always carrying a weapon."

"Large hairpins work for a similar reason," mused Lise. "But pepper. Now, that's creative." She giggled again. Her amusement was infectious, and Annabel couldn't help but join in.

Finally, Colley gestured with a grin. "Come alone, Lise and Daegal. Let's get to the carriage and bring you home."

Chapter Ten

DUTY AND HONOR

L ise leaned close to Annabel on the porch the next afternoon, her voice barely a whisper. "Hattie has disappeared."

"Oh! The scullery maid?" Annabel's brow furrowed.

Lise nodded. "Did you know her?"

"Not well," Annabel admitted. "When I first got here, I dropped my journal, and she returned it."

"Yes, she's nice like that." Her friend nodded. "Vanished without a trace. Her belongings have evaporated, too, like morning mist. The Baron isn't saying anything about it, but Charlie thought he looked like he was trying to hide his anger."

"Actually, I saw her yesterday," Annabel murmured, her heart quickening. "I wasn't the *last* to have seen her, was I? We spoke right before you and I left for the play."

"Not exactly." Lise's expression darkened. "James claims he saw her leaving this morning with a packed bag. But he won't share more than that, and no one else saw her."

"Hmmm," Annabel frowned. "That's a bit suspect."

"Right, it's strange, isn't it?" Lise's brow wrinkled in worry. "And what surprises me more is that if she did leave on her own accord, she didn't pay her debts before legging it...that's not in her nature. She owes me a shilling."

"Oh no...I completely forgot," Annabel suddenly realized, shaken, and dug in her pocket for the shilling. "She gave this to me for you just yesterday."

The two women looked at each other with concern, then suddenly, Lise's gaze shifted, and she gasped as if she had seen a ghost. "Oh..."

Curious, Annabel followed Lise's gaze and was shocked to see her husband standing in the doorway. "Richard! You're out."

"Yes," he sighed, his face hidden beneath a thick, mossy beard. "The Baron has forgiven my transgressions and released me from the dungeon."

"After a month?" Annabel exclaimed, surprised. "He must have a forgiving heart. Thank goodness." This last, she added with a nervous smile, wondering how much resentment he harbored from their previous encounter.

Lise lingered near the doorway as Richard walked in, her eyes worried. He sat on a sturdy wooden chair that Annabel had since repaired, his gaze wandering around the room as if appraising it anew. "Annabel, the place looks tremendous," he said appreciatively. Suddenly, he hung his head. "I feel bad about what I said to you in the dungeon. I was out of my mind, and please know that I bear you no malice."

"I'm glad to hear it." Annabel, relieved, nodded slightly to the unspoken question in Lise's eyes and sat down across from her husband, her eyes meeting his as her friend slipped out. In the resulting hush, she softly asked, "What path lays before us to your thinking, Richard?"

"An easy one, I hope." Her husband chuckled. "I haven't seen daylight in weeks but must have groveled enough to earn a second chance. The Baron's grace freed me, and I'm prepared to forge a path towards redemption, starting today." He smiled tenderly.

"How grand," Annabel responded warily, studying his face. "And what of Gwyneth?"

"I have joyful news." He clasped his hands around one of her own, and she fought the urge to remove it. "In his kindness, the Baron has agreed to pay my past debts to Gwyneth as long as I commit to being your husband. And I am ready to do that." He smiled and stood, an intimate look in his eyes.

Annabel's mind raced, weighing her words carefully. "How terribly kind of the Baron."

"And of you," Richard added, his voice soft. "I see you've fixed the furniture. And I heard that you paid off some of my debts yourself. Where did you get the money to do such a favor, my clever wife?"

"It's here," Annabel pulled a pouch from its hiding place in the case by her bed. "There's money I brought with me, money I've made while I've been here, and—money for debts settled," she added, thinking of Paul.

"Clever indeed..." Richard's eyes lit as he poured out the pouch and counted the money, biting one of the coins to test it and nodding approvingly. His gratitude was palpable. "My love, your presence grants me more solace than I anticipated," he declared, rising to his feet. "You've made good efforts here, and I was truly a fool to spurn you for the advances of another."

A surge of discomfort rippled through Annabel as his long arms enveloped her. The moment of shared intimacy was utterly empty of the deep connection she yearned for. This was her husband, the man she should offer her unwavering, loyal affection to. But instead, irritation simmered beneath all her memories of their marriage, and retreating from the embrace, Annabel mustered her resolve. "Richard, there is something I must say."

"Speak your heart," Richard's eyes gleamed with the spark of expectation, lowering his gaze to just below her neck.

"I yearn to trust in your transformation," Annabel began, choosing her words carefully. "However, the abruptness of this change, coupled with your past willingness to entertain wild falsehoods...I cannot brush aside my reservations about our future. What if you were to revert to past habits and cast me aside once more?" She sighed. "I cannot quell such thoughts."

Richard's demeanor soured, a shadow cast upon his features. "Do you doubt my intentions? I severed ties with Gwyneth and returned to your side immediately upon my release. Yet, your faith in my commitment wavers?"

"How can I be sure you won't discard me once your desires are met?" Annabel asked, hating herself for wincing as he leaned closer to her. "The Baron's favoritism toward you is clear, and I am wary of a life lived in trepidation." As he slipped the coins back into the pouch and tucked them into his tunic, she asked pointedly, "And what do you plan to do with the money?"

She stepped back as she stepped forward, and he frowned. "Are you fearful of me?" Richard's chest puffed with bravado while Annabel steeled herself. "Remember, your earnings are mine as well—we are bound by matrimony."

"Indeed, I am," Annabel acquiesced, her voice steady. "To be in the company of a man as formidable and resolute as yourself can be overwhelming. It's akin to a stoat in the presence of a fox." As she smiled demurely, an idea took root in her mind.

"I understand," Richard murmured, sounding magnanimous. "It may be overwhelming for you. I've been away, and you've managed the home alone. My absence while confined surely bore heavily upon you."

"That it did," Annabel affirmed, her demeanor demure. "May I ask you another question?"

Richard chuckled. "By all means."

"I am curious," Annabel ventured, "did you apprise Gwyneth of the shift in our circumstances?"

A trace of unease flickered across Richard's cold, handsome face. "Indeed, I did."

"So, you consulted her before approaching me," Annabel observed, her tone contemplative. "This confession is inconsistent with your initial account."

"Why quibble?" Richard's gaze averted, his demeanor veering toward indifference. "I am here now, devoted to you."

Annabel's thoughts raced. "Until when?" she questioned, aiming for realism rather than confrontation. "Until misfortune befalls you, until opium once more claims your will, restoring you to the beginning of our marriage? I am committed to doing right by each other, Richard, but I struggle to envision a future in which I am not shrouded in unpredictability."

"I tire of this argument, my darling." Richard exhaled audibly. "We go around in circles. What remedy do you wish for? How may I assuage your doubts?" His voice lowered. "Tell me, and I will do it, then put many sons in your belly."

Annabel's mind raced as her stomach turned, and she stuck out her chin more confidently than she felt. "Commit it to paper. I yearn for an affirmation from you, a document delineating that I shall inherit this tenancy, unencumbered by the stipulation of heirs, which includes a portion of the crop's yield. And we will decide together what to do with our money." She drew closer as though she might embrace him, but instead, deftly lifted the purse out of his tunic, kissing his cheek as she squeezed his arm. "Surely the man who appreciates a literate wife doesn't mind her helping to grow his coffers."

Desire swept his face as he smiled, looking oddly relieved by her request, and she wondered what he had expected her to ask for. "You continue to surprise me. It may not be entirely appropriate for a woman to have such control over our finances, but we can discuss investments. And all right, I'll go to the courthouse and change the inheritance from my mother to you. I do want you to be taken care of, you know." He smiled. "Of course, once we have a son, it will all go to him."

"That's fair." Annabel smiled. "I truly appreciate your understanding. Richard."

He inched closer, a conspiratorial whisper coloring his words. "Show me." His lips met hers with insistence, his muddy aroma lingering as she suppressed a shudder, and guilt filled her heart. Her husband held her, the man she was meant to love and cherish forever. Yet, all she felt each time he drew near was the encroaching weight of remorse. Annabel sighed heavily, and her heart wrenched as the realization overwhelmed her that if, in fact, she had ever truly loved him, she no longer did.

Her mother's words echoed in her mind, the promise that moving forward would bring true happiness. But she couldn't deny the recent moments that had brought her more joy than ever imagined—the quiet reading all to herself each night, storytelling on All Hallow's Eve, that play with Lise accompanied by a vast boost in her confidence as she finally stood up to someone, managing the increasingly bountiful crops, eating and talking with the Wrights. Living with a clear head on her own terms had sparked something exciting within her, and she longed for Richard to leave.

She forced a grateful smile. "There's another thing."

"What is it, my darling?" Richard took a bottle of barley beer out of the cabinet and took a swig. "Drink?"

"I'm aware of our overdue taxes, Richard." Annabel opened a drawer in the dresser. Before she turned back to her husband, she slipped one of the two identical little notebooks inside her skirt pocket. Both were filled with the same information, everything she had discovered about their taxes, each instance of missed payments, and holes where he had not filed the paperwork nor paid fees. She held the other aloft as she turned back to him.

"What are you talking about?" he muttered crossly, tipping his drink back. "Darling, don't concern yourself with taxes. You can help me do far better things with this money."

She approached him with the notebook, smiling patiently. "We should use some of the money I've earned to take care of this. I've spoken to Mr. Lansbury downtown and assured him I'll speak with you about it when you return."

"You didn't." His face contorted in anger.

"I had no reason not to," she replied calmly. "Mr. Lansbury's already been by with a small team, who noticed the barley wine crates, prompting an excise officer to visit. They demand back taxes for the wine sold to the Baron and for unreported land."

"You foolish little..." Richard trailed off, breathing more deeply than before. "This will cost me a fortune."

Annabel continued, "I'm willing to help pay off the tax debts with the money I earned. We can make a partial payment, at least."

"No." Richard looked at her sharply.

Annabel took a deep breath. "You have expenses and responsibilities, true, but we must address our financial obligations, or there will be trouble for us both."

Richard took another swig of barley wine, swishing it around his mouth before swallowing. "I'll put this money to good use. I have plans for it that are none of your concern."

Anger flared within Annabel, but she maintained her composure. "You had no knowledge of this money until minutes ago, Richard. We must prioritize our responsibilities and work together to secure our future."

Her husband's irritation was palpable. "I agree to the inheritance and crop share, but investments will be handled according to my discretion. And absolutely not, on this tax nonsense. I've never had any trouble ducking them in the past; you clearly don't understand how things work here." He took the book of careful notes and ripped the offending pages out, casting them into the fire.

"Richard..." Annabel forced herself to remain composed. "If you are not here one day, they may arrest me on your behalf."

Richard only shrugged, his lack of concern evident as he drew closer to kiss her. "Let's cross that bridge when we come to it."

"Richard," she whispered, then cleared her throat. "I would prefer to wait for our coupling until we return from the courthouse."

He scowled. "You want to work that all out now?"

"I will feel more comfortable continuing our life together if that life feels safe," she entreated.

"I'll make you feel safe," he rumbled, slipping a hand to her face. "Give me a chance, my dearest."

"At the moment and for the foreseeable future," she murmured. "I am still reticent."

Nuzzling her neck, he murmured, "Hush..."

"Richard," Annabel cleared her throat, trying not to panic. "Did you know—it's said that when a woman is afraid during lovemaking, there is a larger chance of a daughter?"

He drew away, looking at her sharply. "Are you sure?"

"I have read it," she lied smoothly. "But if you'd rather take the chance..." She slowly reached out her hand.

"No, that's fine." Richard shook his head. "Let us go to the courthouse now. I've never had to work so hard for a woman." He cast an irritated look at her. "You will share my bed without complaint once this is done?"

She smiled demurely. "Upon our return."

"Then we shall see to your demands now so you may meet my own afterward." Richard smiled and leaned in, attempting to embrace her again. Before their interaction escalated, thankfully, there was a knock on the door. Annabel hurriedly composed herself and went to answer it, suppressing the distaste she felt from her husband's kiss.

"Good morrow!" It was Charlie, his demeanor nervous and uneasy, and something tugged in her to see her friend standing in the doorway. "Oh," His voice faltered as he registered Richard's presence. "Welcome back, Farmer Granger."

Richard's tone turned careless. "Thank you, Charlie. What do you need?"

Charlie's gaze swept to Annabel, and she gave a slight, confident smile to communicate she was not in immediate danger. He cleared his throat and offered, "Apologies. I thought I heard a loud sound from within and came to offer my assistance."

"As if you bloody could," scoffed Richard. "No need. We're going to the magistrate to take care of a legal matter. Annabel, change into suitable attire, and let's get on with it," he instructed loudly, coming forward to shut the door. She dressed swiftly, and soon, they were on their way to the courthouse in the Rowley carriage.

As they approached the village courthouse, its stone walls radiated a sense of authority that commanded respect. The sturdy oak doors stood slightly ajar. The courtyard before it was abuzz with villagers going about their morning tasks, and Annabel swallowed her apprehension as they moved closer.

Upon arrival, Richard proceeded to the counter as they entered the building, engaging in boisterous laughter and conversation with the tax clerk. Once he finally explained what he wanted to do and they had both signed the paperwork, Richard and the clerk continued talking, ignoring Annabel, who slipped away from his side and approached the next clerk at two counters over.

"Good morrow." She smiled warmly at the second tax clerk, withdrew the second copy of tax notes from her skirt, and placed it before him. "My name is Annabel Granger. Recently, a tax collector informed me of our considerable overdue taxes. I'm afraid my husband disagrees with the urgency of payment."

The tax clerk cast a skeptical gaze in her direction, thumbing through the stack. "Did you compile these documents?"

"Oh goodness, me?" Annabel demurred, saying a small prayer to herself as she told her second lie of the day. "All I can do is assure you they're all correct. Our castle steward keeps meticulous records. My purpose here is to rectify the situation—I was advised that immediate payment is imperative. I am ready to make a partial payment. Unfortunately, my husband remains disinclined. He insisted on spending our money elsewhere."

"Really," The clerk raised his eyebrows as he thumbed through the meticulous journal. "This is quite bad, my dear. I haven't seen anyone this deeply in debt for as long as I've been at this post."

"Oh dear." Annabel wrung her hands, shaking her head. "That can't be good."

"Hmm," the tax clerk murmured, finishing his perusing of the papers with a furrowed brow. "Kindly wait here. I shall summon the magistrate."

The magistrate, an elderly figure with a penetrating countenance, listened attentively to the tax clerk's briefing. Clasping the papers firmly, he bellowed, "Richard Granger!"

Richard was caught off guard. "Yes?"

The magistrate quickly questioned an irritated Richard about the contents of the papers. Once their authenticity was confirmed, as he was clearly too caught off guard to lie, the magistrate motioned to the bailiff. "Take him in. The amount he owes is outrageous." Facing Annabel, the magistrate scrutinized her. "You are his wife, I take it?"

"Yes, I am," Annabel confirmed. "May I extend a partial payment toward my husband's debt?" She offered the pouch she had retrieved from Richard, augmenting it with two additional coins. "This amounts to six pounds. The tax collector can contact me for further remittance, or I can personally convey it."

"Six pounds!" Richard shouted in disbelief. "You gave me only four."

"I had to, dear husband," Annabel said, her voice steady. "I was afraid you would spend it on something else, as you had hinted. Our commitment to civic duty and compliance with tax obligations demands precedence."

The bailiff interjected with approval. "Well said, madam. We need more taxpayers like you. Now run along home, and word will be sent once a decision about your husband's sentence has been made. It should be at least a few weeks." As the words left his lips, Richard was taken away.

A sense of relief and satisfaction washed over Annabel, and with her head held high, she exited the courthouse, her heart a little lighter. Outside, the countryside stretched before her, bathed in the soft hues of the morning sun. Her steps were resolute as she walked back toward the carriage.

Once home, she headed straight to the kitchen, skimming the cream off the morning's milk and slipping it into the butter churn, whistling a merry tune. Propping open *The New Atlantis*, she began churning vigorously. Doubts and concerns were overcome as the adventures she read swirled in her mind, a small, worried smile slowly coming to her lips as she worked.

Once her arms were sore and the butter was packed and stored in the larder, Annabel ventured out to the fields with a firm smile. She worked diligently, pausing only for a thick tomato and butter sandwich with some dried fish until the sun descended below the horizon. When she was finally back inside and about to prepare for bed, she splashed water on her face, jumping when a loud pounding suddenly came at the door. Mystified, she went to open it.

James was there, looking haggard. "You must come with me."

"Why?" She frowned. "It's so late. What's the trouble?"

"You're the trouble," he sighed. "Put on a coat and come."

Sighing, trying to belie her fear with bravado, she put on a coat and buttoned it, slipping her stocking feet into boots and tying them up quickly. As she closed the door with shaking hands and followed James, she asked, "Do you know what this is about?"

"Please don't ask questions," he sighed.

Once they reached the castle door, he led her to the fireplace in the great hall, where Baron Rowley was sitting in an oversized, thick, dark wood chair sipping on a pewter tankard. When he smiled at her, his teeth were red with wine.

"Won't you come in," the Baron intoned menacingly. "Do you know why you're here, Annabel? Can you guess?"

This felt like a trap to her, but Annabel only smiled prettily and curtsied, her legs shaking as she tried not to look directly at him. "I know not, my lord."

When he held up a book, her heart sank. It was Cassidy's copy of Aesop's Fables she had so painstakingly mended. "Do you recognize this?"

"Yes," she began carefully. "Is something wrong?"

Henry's tone was low and dangerous. "Were you in my library?"

"Only briefly, my lord," she said, eyes wide. "The book needed fixing, and your bookbinder won't be back here again until summer, so I thought—"

"I do not tolerate farmers in my library," growled the Baron. "Is that clear?"

"Of course. It won't happen again," Annabel said quickly. "My apologies."

"Far worse, I am told you entered our castle archives," the Baron continued, fury in his voice. "Do you realize what you could have damaged? There are documents in there *worth more than your life.*"

Annabel swallowed hard. "I deeply apologize, my lord. If there is anything at all I can do to atone..."

Baron Rowley took a drink. "The penalty for entering the castle archives is a fine of four pounds. Typically, I would couple this with a day in the stocks."

Her eyes widened, and her throat went dry. "Please..."

"But I'm a resourceful man," he continued, ignoring her. "I believe the punishment should fit the crime. And since this book has been contaminated by the hands of a farmer..." He shrugged and tossed the book into the fireplace.

There was a scream, and when the Baron and James both jumped in surprise, Annabel realized it had been her. Blood seemed to roar in her ears as the book burned. Unable to stop herself, she suddenly ran towards it, ready to rescue the book from the fire, only to be snatched back from the flames by James. He grunted as he held her arms fast, firmly stopping her from going towards the fire again. "This woman is bloody mad, my lord."

"Search her," Henry sighed, taking another drink.

Annabel rapidly blinked back tears, swallowing the lump in her throat as James carefully went through all her pockets until everything was laid out: her bookbinding kit, dried fish and fruit, extra needles, handkerchiefs sewn by her grandmother, different candles, three small notebooks, blotting paper, and a few pencils.

"What kind of witch are you?" James asked scornfully. "You grow barley for a living."

"I am a farmer," she whispered. "And a bookbinder."

"No more," thundered the Baron. "If you are to farm here, it will be all you do. Keep to your work. Burn it all," he said to James.

"No," she gasped, her eyes filling with tears. "Please do not. Take it away from me, but do give it to someone else. The kit's expensive—it was a gift."

"Burn it now," repeated the Baron, glaring at James. "I prefer not to repeat myself."

"Yes, my lord," said James quickly, gathering everything together and bringing it to the fireplace. He slowly fed everything to the fire while Annabel watched, speechless.

"You may return to your empty house and figure out how you'll repay me." Baron Rowley took another drink. "And mind you, stay away from my books unless invited."

Annabel nodded stiffly, chin quivering, and fled the castle, her heart pounding in her ears, hatred for Baron Rowley growing with every step.

Chapter Eleven

FIRESIDE ALLIANCE

Annabel's restless slumber that night gave way to a fitful awakening, her heart pounding with the remnants of nightmares. She quickly rose from the bed, stirring the dying embers in the wood stove with a new log. Stripping off her nightclothes, she splashed her face with water and swiftly dressed, pulling on long underwear, a tunic and dress, warm woolen socks, and sturdy boots.

Stepping out onto the porch with a sigh, Annabel surveyed the darkened sky, seeing that dawn was still a couple of hours away. Closing her eyes, she took a deep breath, then another, and another, until she was calm.

Her gaze wandered across the horizon until she spotted the flickering glow of a distant bonfire, bringing the first smile to her face that night.

As she approached the source of the smoke, Annabel circled around the short stone wall to find Lise and Charlie again. "Good evening," she greeted them.

Lise offered a tight smile. "And to you."

Concern creased Annabel's brow as she sat down next to her friend. "Are you alright?"

"It's nothing," Lise whispered, but her pallid complexion revealed her lack of sleep.

"Not hardly." Charlie sighed. "She slipped on the stairs inside and sprained her ankle."

"Oh, Lise!" Annabel exclaimed. "That's horrible. What can I do to ease your pain? Say the word and I'll do it." She patted a reassuring hand on the taller woman's back. "Anything."

"I'm going to lose my job; I just know it," Lise lamented, rare tears welling in her eyes. "I can't keep up with all my tasks with a sprain. Charlie made me a crutch and a brace, but being on my feet is unbearable. I'm afraid the Baron or his men will notice my struggle and find someone else to replace me, and if they bring in someone new, they might be better, and I'd get turned out. Sprains don't always heal perfectly, and I might end up limping for the rest of my life if I push myself."

"You will *not* be pushing yourself," Annabel reassured her firmly. "I can help you. Tell me what needs to be done, and I'll do it."

"See," murmured Charlie to Lise with a grin. "There, now you told me it was good to have friends and this proves it."

"It won't work," Lise sighed. "If the Baron sees you doing my work, or one of his men does, he will punish me and perhaps cast me out."

"Both of us have hidden tunnels that eventually connect under our rooms," Annabel reminded her. "I can go back and forth. If you can help me with some of my inside chores with your leg up, I'll have time to work on yours in the cellar."

"Truly?" Lise's eyebrows rose in hope. "But what about Richard? He wouldn't like that at all."

"Back in the dungeon for the foreseeable future—the king's dungeon, this time." Annabel smiled weakly. "I've heard it's harder to get out of." Quickly, she told them the details of what had happened.

"I can't believe it." Lise exchanged a glance with Charlie on her other side. "I told her you would offer," he admitted. "And I'm here to help as well, you know. Don't forget that."

"I shouldn't let you," Lise sighed. "It's too much. You already have so much on your plate—both of you."

Annabel insisted, "I have allotted farmhands. Please, don't even *think* about saying no. You would do the same for me and we all know it. You began my second day with fresh laundry, and I may as well repay the favor."

"You're such a good friend," Lise murmured, burying her head in her hands. "Thank you."

"Here's to friendship." On her other side, Charlie rubbed his wife's back softly, saying, "We all hate relying too much on others, but sometimes we must overcome that."

Annabel smiled warmly. "Exactly."

Lise whistled. "I can't believe you got rid of Richard, even temporarily. My hat is truly off to you."

"Be cautious of the Baron, though," Charlie warned. "He might not take kindly to you taking matters into your own hands."

"I've already recently learned of the breadth of his unkindness," Annabel sighed, looking down at the fire. "Last night, he burned the book I fixed for Cassidy, as well as the kit I used to fix it with, right in front of me." She blinked rapidly.

There was a stunned silence, and Lise broke the silence. "Annabel, I'm so sorry. That's awful."

"It's very cruel, but it still surprises me," Charlie scowled. "It's peculiar for him to have that reaction since, historically, he's shown great respect for books. Bit out of character for him...I wonder what the old man's up to." He looked uneasy.

"I suppose it can't be helped," Annabel sighed, trying to keep the bitterness from her voice. "I'm trying to think of it in a positive light since I was a result, I came to know about the tunnels."

"Good thought." Lise nudged Charlie's arm playfully. "Go on, distract her with our rare good news."

"*Good* news?" Curiosity piqued, Annabel asked, "What is it?"

"Er... do you know Cecelia, the redheaded teenager? James and Bridgette's daughter?" Charlie asked.

"The tiny one with the drawing pad?" Annabel struggled to recall hearing anyone mention or refer to Cecelia except as the castle brat. "Yes. And?"

"Before we tell you..." Lise interrupted, "It should be known, Cecelia has a dreadful crush on Charlie. She snuck into one of the underground matches years ago and saw him dressed as a pirate. Ever since she's carried a torch for him. Can you believe that?"

"Yes." Annabel nodded absentmindedly, her mind wandering back to when she first glimpsed Charlie as a pirate. Suddenly realizing her damning silence, she cleared her throat and added, "Hot-blooded teenagers."

"Oh, she's just dramatic." scoffed Charlie. "I'm no bloody prize, for pity's sake."

"Now, we know that's not true," winked Lise. "The ladies in the crowds certainly say otherwise."

"Anyway, I don't fully trust Cecelia," Charlie admitted, shaking his head. "But I had an odd conversation with her yesterday morning—it's why I came to your door."

Lise grinned. "Tell her."

"She said she knows we're looking for the clues, and she says she has one," explained Charlie. "She's willing to share it if she can join our search."

"That's wonderful! *I* certainly don't mind." Annabel smiled. "Closer to the treasure is certainly better than no treasure at all, and after what the Baron did, now I want to find it more than ever."

Nodding, Lise suggested, "Shall we meet here again tomorrow night with Cecelia?"

Annabel and Charlie nodded resolutely.

After the morning's fieldwork, Annabel returned home only to find the young Rowley twins, Cassidy and Talon, waiting on her porch.

"What are you doing here?" she asked. Talon shrugged. "She wanted to apologize for Father."

"I'm sorry," Cassidy said in a wobbly voice. "Father never comes to the nursery, but he came and saw me reading the book, and I couldn't think of a good lie in time. I'm so sorry you got in trouble, and Father burned your things."

"I'm sorry he burned your book," Annabel said, taking a deep breath.

Cassidy sighed. "Me too. Can we come in?"

She nodded. "Of course." She unlocked and opened the door, and both children ran inside eagerly. She hesitantly pulled out a game of backgammon from under her bed.

Talon wiped his brow. "It's scorching in here. Can we play it on the porch?"

"If you take care not to lose the pieces." Setting them up on the porch with the game, Annabel pulled out an extra chair to watch them play and rest her feet, having been up and running since before dawn's first light.

"I overheard that you told a wonderful ghost story that scared Cecelia," said Cassidy. "If you don't know her, that's impressive...she scares me all the time and she's no slouch. Do you know children's stories, too?" The little girl had her carved wooden horse with her still, and now she set it on the porch railing next to the table.

Annabel blushed. "I like children's stories as well. I don't know if I'm any good at them."

"I'm sure you're wonderful," Cassidy insisted. "Please?"

"She won't stop asking," sighed Talon, and Cassidy stuck her tongue out at her brother. "Since you're responsible for Father burning her book, you may as well tell us a story."

"I suppose I can try," Annabel smiled tightly at the little boy, then thought for a minute. "Right. Once upon a time, in a magical forest, there was a horse named Panza, unlike any ordinary horse you've seen."

The smile that spread across Cassidy's face and the reluctant interest in Talon's warmed her soul, and she continued.

"You see, Panza was very special. He had been carved by a master toymaker who possessed a touch of enchantment at his fingertips. Panza was a beautiful carving, and he also possessed emotions that would sparkle in the eyes of anyone who looked upon him."

"Aw, is there magic in this one?" Talon asked scornfully. "I don't *like* magic."

Annabel smiled as she continued. "Now, this magical toymaker's workshop was a place of wonder where dreams came to life in the form of delightful toys. Every child in the village longed to have one of his enchanted creations, but Panza held a secret that set him apart. He was born in the stillness of a moonlit night when the stars adorned the sky like twinkling jewels. And when Panza opened his eyes, he felt an inexplicable fear deep within him - a fear of the dark."

Cassidy's eyes were like saucers, and both children had abandoned the game.

"As evening descended upon the forest and the golden sun dipped below the horizon," Annabel whispered. "The shadows played their dance amongst the trees. Panza would tremble and creak with anxiety, for the darkness seemed to wrap around him like a heavy cloak of uncertainty. The woodland creatures, who adored Panza, tried to console him, whispering tender words of comfort and encouragement.

"Fear not, dear Panza," they would say, "for the dark is nothing to be afraid of. It's just the absence of light, and you, my friend, are filled with light and love."

But alas, the fear remained, and night after night, Panza sought refuge inside a hollow tree, hiding his eyes and ears from the mysterious sounds and sights that came with the darkness. His sleep was restless, and he longed to be as brave as the heroes in the stories the children told.

One day, Panza resolved to face his fear as the leaves painted the forest in a tapestry of red and gold. Summoning every ounce of courage, he declared that he would spend the entire night outside in the woods, with eyes wide open, determined to conquer his dread of the dark. As the sun began to set, bathing the forest in hues of pink and orange, Panza stretched his legs and took a deep breath. Shadows danced around him, and a shiver ran through his wooden frame. But he held his ground, reminding himself of his quest.

Suddenly, a sound pierced the silence like a lightning bolt, and Panza released a terrified scream, leaping to his feet. But it was not a creature of darkness that greeted him; it was a tiny piglet named Gavin, his rosy snout twitching with excitement and curiosity."

Cassidy clapped at this, and Talon laughed. "I'd forgotten that you know Gavin."

"We met on my first day at the castle." Annabel smiled. "Gavin, unlike the other pigs in the farm where he had been raised, possessed a spirit of adventure that could not be contained within the fences. He longed to explore the world beyond, seeking thrilling escapades and daring feats.

That very evening, Gavin decided to embark on his own grand adventure. With a spirited squeal, he bid farewell to his fellow pigs and ventured into the mysterious woods. As fate would have it, Gavin's path crossed with Panza's, and the encounter would change their lives forever.

"Who are you?" the curious piglet asked, coming to a halt before the apprehensive horse.

"I am Panza," whispered the horse, "and I'm afraid of the dark. I wish I could find the courage to face it and be brave like the heroes in the tales."

Gavin listened attentively and smiled, his eyes shining with determination. "Why don't you go on a quest with me to find the brightest star in the sky? That way, you'll always have a little light with you, even in the darkest of nights. If you can't see it, stay home or look for fireflies."

He made it sound so easy. Panza's eyes lit up with excitement at the thought of going on an adventure with a newfound friend. He nodded eagerly, and together, they set out on their quest to find the brightest star. Panza's fear of the dark slowly began to wane as they searched for the elusive sparkle in the night sky, for he now had Gavin's joyful companionship and the promise of a radiant beacon to guide him through the night.

With each passing day, their bond of friendship grew stronger, and tales of their bravery and camaraderie spread throughout the forest, capturing the hearts of all who heard them. Finally, Panza felt brave enough to go out on cloudy nights, but he still preferred the comfort of the stars.

Annabel smiled warmly at the children, surprised and touched that they had sat still listening to her silly story for so long. "And so, never forget that true courage lies not in the absence of fear, but in facing those fears-and it doesn't have to be alone. Just like the brightest star in the sky illuminates the darkness, the light of love and companionship shines brightly in our hearts, guiding us through the darkest times."

A clapping behind her, quickly joined in by the children, made Annabel jump, and she saw it was Barnaby, one of the regular farmhands, and Charlie. She colored. "God's thumbs. How long have the both of you been standing there?"

"Long enough to be inspired by a pig," laughed Charlie. "I had no idea the little runt I saved was such a hero."

Barnaby prodded Charlie in the arm. "How much for one of the wooden horses who're scared of the dark? It's my youngest's birthday in a month."

"You can't afford me," said Charlie as Bridgette approached the porch.

"Thanks for looking after them. Hope they weren't too much trouble." Bridgette's face was tired. She scowled down at the children as she shooed them off the chairs and back towards the castle. "Lucky for all of us, it's time for their lessons."

"They were no trouble at all," Annabel smiled. "Come back and visit any time."

The next night, when Annabel came to the fire, Cecelia was sitting there with a satchel on her lap, looking pleased as Lise scowled at her. The three looked up when she came around the stone wall. "Welcome," murmured Lise. "I hope you don't mind babysitting."

Cecelia stuck her tongue out at Lise.

Shaking his head, Charlie offered, "Cecelia, you say you have another clue?"

"I think so. I was in the chapel, you know." She shot a look at Charlie, then Annabel, and smiled. "I saw the pair of you hiding under the altar."

"How?" Annabel asked in surprise. "And what were you doing in there?"

"I was in the alcove." Cecelia shrugged. "I like to hide. It's better than working."

She laughed. "You have me there."

"I heard you say that you couldn't read the whole clue," Cecelia explained. "Why are you trying to find the treasure anyway?"

"Charlie, Annabel," warned Lise. "Maybe this isn't such a good idea. Cecelia can't be trusted."

"You chose to trust me immediately, although Charlie was on the fence," replied Annabel. "What's so different about Cecelia?"

"She's a brat," muttered Lise. "And she's been after Charlie for years. Not to mention, she's a *child*—she'll just tattle to her parents. The three of them are the biggest chin-waggers here."

"You're thinking of my father. I turn eighteen next week, and I never tell my parents anything," Cecelia shot back. "I've never laid a hand on Charlie."

"It's about respect, which you have none of," retorted Lise. "Clearly."

"Respect must be earned," sniffed Cecelia, looking away with a petulant expression.

"Then *earn* it." Lise crossed her arms defiantly.

"Alright," Cecelia asked, putting her hands on her hips. "I don't know if I was the first one who found the altar clue, but I was definitely the one who scratched out most of it so that no one else would find it."

"*You* scratched it out?" Lise cried. "You absolute nutcase. Now, we'll never find the treasure."

"What did it say?" Annabel pressed.

"She can't read any more than I can," muttered Lise. "This is a lost cause."

Cecelia shrugged. "Lise is right; I can't read." She smiled shyly. "But I drew a picture of it."

Annabel grinned. "As good as the pictures from your sketchbook?"

"Yes," Cecelia confirmed. "Although, you weren't supposed to look."

"Well, I hope you enjoyed the binding since it's the last one," sighed Annabel. "Baron Rowley burned my tools, and Cassidy's book I fixed with it."

"He didn't!" Cecelia's jaw dropped. "That bloody madman."

"Yes, the Baron is a monster. We all know," Lise said impatiently. "So, shall we see your drawing of the clue?"

"I'll show you if you share the treasure with me." Cecelia smiled.

"Oh, for—" After glancing at Charlie and Annabel, Lise sighed and said, "You really drew it all out?"

"See for yourself." Cecelia pulled a drawing pad from the satchel at her side and flipped it open.

Lise whistled at the perfect drawing of the underside of the altar, looking at Cecelia with new respect. "Alright. I don't know what it says, but I've got to hand it to you–that looks quite well done."

Cecelia shrugged. "Thanks."

Annabel read:

Down winding path where shadows creep,
Explore where all his secrets sleep.

Up and down and left and right
You'll find it locked—but not so tight.

Lise groaned. "That's the dungeon. The treasure can't be down there... surely Philippa would have put it somewhere safer. That probably just leads to another clue."

"It does sound like the dungeon," Cecelia agreed. "Can't the pair of you sneak around when you're about to fight?"

"I'm lame in the ankle, but don't you dare tell anyone," sighed Lise. "So I can't, at least for a while. Probably a few weeks."

"I may be able to help." Cecelia rubbed her hands together. "My parents have been asking me to help with a dungeon project for months. I've been skirting them, but I could accept." She shrugged. "I could look for the clue and draw it again while down there."

"How fascinating that you can write, but you don't know what you're writing," Annabel marveled. "Do you *want* to learn how to write?"

"Not if it's a lot of work," grumbled Cecelia. "And I suspect it is. I prefer to draw things."

"That's certainly true," Lise smirked, and suddenly, she snatched Cecelia's sketch pad, flipping rapidly through the pages.

"Give that here!" Cecelia exclaimed and dove for it.

Lise opened the sketchbook to a sketch of a half-naked man. Annabel pressed her lips together as she leaned forward to keep the mirth from escaping. It was unmistakably Charlie, wearing not a stitch, though the drawing cut off just where his breeches would have begun.

Cheeks flamed, Cecelia took back her sketch pad and stormed off.

Annabel called out. "Cecelia! Lise is sorry."

"Well..." Lise opened her mouth and, at a look from Annabel, closed it and sighed. "Yes! I *am* sorry, Cecelia. I'm bloody jealous of your drawings, all right? I can't read either. I would give my bloody eyeteeth for your talents!" She yelled the last part, cupping her hands around her mouth, and after a minute, Cecelia returned, scowling. "I should not have snatched your drawings. But pray do *not* draw my husband," Lise huffed, crossing her arms. "If you're going to join us, you must promise that your pining for him is truly through."

"I haven't drawn him in *ages*," snapped Cecelia, then looked down shamefacedly. "I'm no longer pining, I'm just bloody bored. Most of our family is back in France, and I have no money or skills beyond cleaning and drawing. I have nothing to inspire happiness but my fantasies. I have no companions here...nobody my age at the castle but Fredrick, and everyone thinks I'm just an odd nuisance who hides in walls. Charlie's hardly the only man I've drawn in there...he's just the one I've known the longest." She shook her head. "I made those drawings a long while ago and haven't made any lately." She drew a breath. "I'm sorry I ever did."

"Fair enough," Lise repeated as Charlie looked at the ground. "Friends?"

"Yes." Cecelia nodded. "Oh—Annabel, I have something for you." She dug in her sachet and held out something shiny to her.

Annabel squinted at the object, but when she took it, a smile spread across her face, and she looked gratefully at Cecelia, closing her hand around it. "It's my finger guard! To protect me from the awl when poking jokes in the books," she added. "It was in my kit that the Baron—" She swallowed hard. "It was in my kit that the Baron threw in the fire."

Cecelia nodded. "I was in the kitchen when he did it. I overheard a little, not much, then I saw you go running back. When the Baron returned to his chambers, I found out what happened to my father, and after he left, I took a pair of tongs to it. That was the only thing salvageable."

"Thank you. It was my grandmother's," Annabel turned it over in her hands, holding up to the fire. "It's so clean! Even these little pockets which have always been dirty."

"I would have brought it back yesterday, but I wanted to clean it," the girl admitted. "Horsehair brush and breadcrumbs to scrub, vinegar and salt to polish."

"Cecelia," Charlie said in surprise. "That was really decent of you."

"Whoever said I wasn't decent?" she snapped. "I'm a good person."

"Who knew you could bring a sooty ring back to life?" Lise said. "I don't think I've *ever* seen you clean."

"That doesn't mean I don't know how to," Cecelia muttered, and when they all laughed, not unkindly, a sad smile slipped across her face. "Look, I don't *want* to be a lazy maid or help watch the children in the castle while their nurse is drunk all my life. I can't read, but I listen, and I know there's a whole world out there better than what we've got now. I want so much better than this."

"I think we all do," whispered Annabel.

Cecelia gently threw a stick at her feet into the fire, and the flames danced. Suddenly, she grinned. "Therefore, I want part of that treasure."

"Hear, hear," Lise agreed.

"Then let's join forces." Annabel smiled. "And we'll figure this out together."

Three days later, they met again by the fireside.

"I still want the treasure, but I wish I'd never told my parents I'd take that job," Cecelia moaned. "It's horrid and boring. I haven't gotten to meet one prisoner. I'm gathering and pulling a wagon of supplies down there and leaving them in front of locked cells for someone to return later and give them. It's awful grunt work."

"Well, what are you gathering and leaving?" Annabel asked curiously.

"The *oddest* things." Cecelia laughed. "Good clothes, scones and jams, teas, games. There was a game of some kind in each one. Two had several tins of what smelt like fancy fish. One had three jars of pickled lemons. Silk scarves. Pink salt. It's really quite odd, all of it. I don't know why they would give such good things to the pirates."

"I'm sure some of them down there aren't pirates," Lise said. "They're just the only prisoner I've met. Who else is the Rowley family keeping in the dungeons?"

"Who knows?" Cecelia shrugged. "None of the cells are marked, and Father won't tell me, though I'm sure he knows." She took out her sketch pad. "If it helps, I've made a map of the tunnels to the different cells I have to drop things off in front of and the ones I don't yet." They all hunched forward to see the drawing.

"Ooh!" Lise cried gleefully, her eyes sparkling with excitement. "That wiggly one!"

"*Down winding path*?" Annabel grinned.

Cecelia nodded, and as she ran her finger down the path on the page, out loud, she said, "*Down winding path*...you can see it winds in and out three times...then it goes up in a straight line, then this circle is a tunnel to a lower level." She swallowed hard. "I went down like it says in the riddle, and it was so cold—then likewise I went left, then right, and there was an ordinary cell door. Just one, but the inside must be massive."

"Have they told you to bring anything to that cell?" Annabel asked.

"Not yet. Tomorrow." Cecelia cocked her head. "I've got to go to the market—Father said to buy pickled cockles and blood sausage."

Wrinkling her nose, she added, "I don't even know what that first one is."

"Small clams in brine," Annabel said. "My best friend Bettina back home is part of a fishing family. They tried pickled cockles, but not for long; apparently, they weren't very popular. I like pickles, but the *texture*..." She grimaced.

Lise made a gasping sound in her throat, and when Annabel looked at her, she looked as though she had seen a ghost. "Are you all right?"

"It's just that..." Lise trailed off. Shaking her head and suddenly grasping Charlie's arm, Lise said, "They *are* disgusting. Absolutely revolting. In fact, all my life I've only ever known *one* person who enjoyed pickled cockles and blood sausage."

"Who?" Charlie asked in surprise.

"Agatha!" Lise cried. "Don't you remember? We went to that fish fair last year..."

He frowned. "What are you saying? Agatha is who Cecelia's bringing pickled cockles to?"

She deflated. "I suppose that's silly. It's been three months. Why would she be in the dungeon? She's no criminal."

"I know why," Cecelia retorted.

They all turned to look at her.

"Before Agatha disappeared," the girl explained. "Richard came to see the Baron in the chapel."

"Where you just happened to be hiding?" Annabel asked with a grin.

"Unfortunately." Cecelia shuddered. "Richard told Henry he thought Agatha was stepping out on him, but he didn't know with whom. He was ranting and raving like a child throwing a tantrum." She rolled her eyes.

"The Baron said Agatha didn't appreciate him enough, and he knew just how Richard felt, and that the best way to train a woman was to take away what she loves—until the man is all she loves."

"God save us," Annabel said, shuddering.

"This was the day before she went missing?" Lise demanded. "Why on earth didn't you tell us sooner? You knew she was mates with us."

"Well, *I* wasn't mates with *you*." Cecelia scowled. "You said yourself you never liked me. I'm telling you now because Annabel was nice to me, and I want to help find the treasure, so I may as well be friendly with you now."

"Thanks a lot," Lise spat angrily. "A woman could be dead as a result of your withholding."

"Not yet." Cecelia hugged her sketchbook to her chest. "And trust me—not that you will—but if I shared every bit of information I overheard while I was hiding out, everyone here probably would have already killed each other." She cut her eyes at Lise. "You've certainly got some secrets you wouldn't like known. Not that I plan to share them."

"Fair enough." Lise flushed, looking away. "Fine. Sorry, then."

"If the Baron was trying to play some sort of mind game to get Agatha to be more appreciative when she came back to Richard, perhaps that means she wasn't killed," Annabel said thoughtfully.

"Well, she didn't come back," sighed Lise.

Cecelia chewed on her lip, raising her eyes skyward as she seemed to be trying to remember something. "I asked Father what the lugging around carts was for, and he wouldn't tell me... I've heard him talk about it quietly to Mother, but I didn't understand it. It sounds like a baby talking." She paused. "Something like 'see the library' but not. See the librara? Something like libations or a library..."

"Coena libera?" Annabel suddenly leaned forward with interest.

"That's it!" Cecelia exclaimed, rubbing her hands together. "What does it mean?"

"Oh no," Charlie moaned. "That's the gladiator meal, isn't it?"

"Why? What's that?" Lise asked.

"It's the last meal fed to gladiators before they went to the Colosseum," explained Annabel with a shudder.

"Lise…" Charlie looked worried. "James told me that two matches after mine tomorrow night, there's going to be a wench fed to the pit of vipers."

"What do you mean, the pit of *vipers*?" Annabel cried in alarm.

"Baron Rowley was inspired by a circus," Charlie muttered. "But the box doesn't really have vipers."

"What is it really?" she asked.

He explained, "They're said to be illegally imported European Adders, which are venomous, but they're really painted Smooth Snakes, which are not. The skies are held aloft, the victim screams, gets pushed in a box, and the snakes are tossed in after."

Annabel shuddered. "Fascinating."

Lise added grimly, "What really happens when someone is dropped into the box is that they go through the trapdoor while the snakes stay in the box, and someone in the room under the trapdoor quickly kills the victim. It's later reported as a snake bite death."

"We're going to need to bribe the person in the room," Charlie said thoughtfully. "I'll work on that."

"Hang on," Cecelia held up her hands. "Is this where we're at? Agatha may be in the same cell the riddle led us to in the dungeon, so we're going to go traipsing down there on a hunch?"

"Well, we've got to check," Lise said firmly. "I'll never sleep well again if we don't, if it is her. And if tomorrow is supposed to be her last night, we can't let that happen."

"And how would you suggest we do that?" Cecelia asked. "I can get us down there, but I don't have the key to the cell."

"The riddle said it's locked, but not so tight," Charlie mused. "Could there be another way to get in? Perhaps if we brought a wedge and cudgel."

"Right! Maybe the door has a weak point that makes it loose?" Annabel suggested. "Cecelia, is there anyone else down there when you go? Any guards?"

"Not by the cells," Cecelia said. "Just at the main entrance. In the basement. The guards rotate—tomorrow, it's Gregory and Kent."

Lise looked at Charlie. "Could you..."

He nodded. "I'm the first fight tomorrow. I can finish it and then split off to help you get into the cell."

Cecelia shook her head. "You're all mad."

"I can't go," moaned Lise, looking sorrowful. "My ankle is still tossed. I can't believe this bloody timing. I will never forgive myself..."

"You don't have to." Annabel put a hand on her shoulder. "I'll go."

"Mad, the lot of you." Cecelia sighed. "I suppose that I will, too."

Chapter Twelve

BACK TO THE TUNNELS

The next night, Charlie, Annabel, and Cecelia stood ready to embark on their daring mission while Lise lay on Annabel's farmhouse bed, her leg up in a brace and her face worried.

While Charlie went onstage, Cecelia approached the dungeon entrance, her wagon full of pickled cockles and secretly Annabel made up to look like Agatha, under a blanket with several tools. She smiled weakly to herself as the cart went past the guards.

When they had reached the cell, Cecelia unloaded the two jars of pickled cockles, and Annabel climbed out. Trying to be as quiet as possible, they each took a tool and attempted to wedge the mighty door open. Ten minutes later, both were red in the face when they heard someone coming. Alarmed, Annabel tried to climb back into the wagon, then they both heard a scuffle in the hallway and froze to listen.

"Who's there?" James hissed. "And what have you got to my bloody throat?"

"A scimitar," came the rumble of another man, and Annabel's eyes widened when she recognized Charlie's voice. At Cecelia's look, she nodded, and they both crept closer to the wall to listen. "Tell me what I want, and no one gets hurt," Charlie growled, low and hoarse.

"Anything," said James quickly. "Please..."

"I'm looking for Agatha Coombs," Charlie hissed. "Where is she?"

"She's in the cell around the corner," James said immediately. "I was coming to bring her to the fights after her last meal."

"Why is she going to the fights?" Charlie demanded. "Why?"

"Punishment," cried James. "She's to be killed. If you kill me when they expect her, you'll die too. I can help you save her if you let me live."

"Go ahead," growled Charlie.

"All you have to do is...oh!" There was a scuffling, and it seemed that James had slipped loose. Then there was a loud thump. The two women waited with bated breath, each grasping a tool from the cart as the footsteps crept closer.

When Charlie appeared around the corner dragging James, both women breathed a sigh of relief. "Any luck?" he whispered. "He tried to run for it, and I had to knock him out." Pulling a coil of rope from his belt, he began to tie up the unconscious man.

"No luck at all. Let's blindfold and gag him, then put him in the wagon," Cecelia hissed, ripping a large strip off her skirt. "Annabel, Agatha is supposed to be going in now; you've got to run!"

Her stomach bubbling with nerves, Annabel nodded. "I look enough like her, with the makeup, false nose, wig, and all?"

Cecelia and Charlie nodded, and she took off. Following the familiar raucous noise, she ran down the hall, and following the map in her mind, she remembered from Cecelia's drawing and Charlie's instructions from the previous day, she made her way to the room and climbed up on stage, shouting to be heard above the din. "I am here!"

"Is that Agatha? Finally!" The baron's familiar slurred voice cut through the noise as she squinted against the bright lights. "Throw her in!"

A tall, sinister man with a shaggy beard came toward her, and when she recognized him as one of the kitchen lads, Annabel let him pick her up and throw her over his shoulder as Charlie had told her.

The man yelled into the crowd and beat his chest, drawing their hunger for action. "This woman is to be punished for the sins of adultery and sodomy!"

"Hear, hear! Toss in the sodomite!" Baron Rowley shouted, starting a chant that spread throughout the room. Annabel shuddered, then tensed as the man holding her jumped sideways to badly dodge what felt like a giant, squishy old tomato.

Another man staggered towards them onstage, laughing, and as he giggled manically, he bent towards the large pit and withdrew a hissing snake. She shuddered as he brandished it towards her and screamed in what had to be done convincingly since, although she'd been warned about the snakes, she was still terrified.

"If you insist," the man yelled, shrugging, and threw her. Annabel fell unceremoniously into a flat panel of wood, which she smacked as instructed when she crashed into it, it gave way as she did.

A floor down, she fell straight into a pile of hay covered in blankets. She shook the false hair out of her face to see Cecelia talking to a guard whose back was to her. "I really can't thank you enough for your discretion," she purred, signaling Annabel to move along. Gathering her skirts and wits, Annabel sped down the winding path to Agatha's cell.

When she reached Charlie, he held a finger to his lips and pointed at James: bound, blindfolded, and gagged in the wagon. He gestured to one of the tools, broken on the floor and the cell door, then, stepping closer to Annabel, whispered softly in her ear. "He's pretending he's still out, but he's awake. I can't figure out how he planned to get her out—he has no keys. I've searched."

Annabel faced the door, crossing her arms as she studied it for a minute. Suddenly she knelt and examined a small, squat knob at the base of the cell, and her eyes followed a seam up the middle of it. "It couldn't be that easy," she whispered. Shaking her head, Annabel grasped the knob and pulled it up, creaking along the cobwebby track; then, as she brought it up to the top, she heard something click into p lace.

She held her breath as she brought it back down, then pulled it all the way to the left and then to the right. She pulled the knob out, and the door popped open. Charlie stepped forward, eyes wide, craning his neck to see what the cell contained.

The room was dimly lit by a solitary candle, its feeble glow illuminating the pale countenance of a bound and gagged young woman, her eyes brimming with torment.

Annabel was relieved as he nodded at her, heading for Agatha's side to whisper in her ear and pull down her blindfold.

Just as Cecelia arrived, she put a blanket over James, still bound in the wagon. Annabel put a finger to her lips, and the other girl nodded. Charlie came forward to grab one of the tools out of the wagon and popped Agatha's remaining restraints open, gesturing for her to rise. Unsteadily, she drew herself to her feet, immediately reaching to lean on him.

Cecelia pulled Annabel away from the wagon and drew her lips close to the other woman's ear. "I'm going to dump Father in the room he uses for paperwork. Mummy brings him a snack in an hour, and she'll untie him then. Help Charlie get Agatha back through the tunnels to your house. Be careful, yeah? I've grown fond of you, but don't repeat that to anyone."

Annabel nodded quickly, squeezing Cecelia's shoulder and giving her a reassuring smile. Cecelia bit her lip and followed them with her eyes as she led the wagon back down the hallway.

Charlie pointed, and Annabel held the torch high as they descended the path. Agatha seemed to be trying her best to walk but clung to Charlie, her arms weak and fragile but her grip firm. Breathing heavily beside her, Annabel felt herself simmering with excitement and something like sand dancing within, and she wondered if what she was feeling was hope.

Suddenly, Agatha stumbled, and Annabel caught her under the other arm. "Thank you," whispered Agatha. "I'm sorry. I exercise every day, but in that cell, my muscles..." As Annabel's torch lowered, the other woman smiled through the grime on her face. "Are you supposed to be me? Is that Lise's work?" She looked at Charlie. "Is Lise all right? When I didn't see her with you, I thought..."

"She's fine," said Charlie, and they turned again, peered around the corner and kept moving. "Just a hurt ankle. She's waiting in your old house."

"Is Richard dead?" Agatha gasped.

"He's not dead," sighed Charlie. "He's in the king's dungeon. Annabel put him there."

"He was cheating on his taxes, and I helped expose him," explained Annabel, and Agatha snorted. "I don't know how long he'll be there. They won't give me a date for the sentencing."

Finally, they emerged into the passageway leading to Annabel's house. Agatha's eyes shimmered in the torchlight as they drew nearer.

Annabel remained by her side as Charlie ascended first, ensuring the path was clear and the entrance unobstructed, before returning to assist them. Annabel guided Agatha, wincing in pain, toward the ladder while Charlie reached out an arm to carry her weight. Slowly, they ascended, step by step, until Agatha was safely seated on the old sofa as Annabel smiled, holding the torch, realizing she recognized every creak and step of the house above her now.

Alone in the tunnels, holding the torch, she shivered. Peering down the dark tunnel where they'd come, she couldn't believe they'd done it. She smiled, taking a deep breath and exhaling. Laughing to herself, she pulled off the false nose and the horsehair, slipping the pieces of her disguise into her skirt pockets. She stepped forward to grasp the ladder's bottom rung, waiting for the all-clear signal to climb back up.

Instead, a strong pair of legs appeared, and she realized Charlie was climbing back down. He reached the bottom quickly and, facing Annabel, took the torch from her and placed it into a sheath on the wall.

"Is it all right to come back up?" Annabel whispered, uncertain. "You didn't need to climb back down—I can manage it alone."

Charlie's gaze lingered down the dark hallway behind them before meeting her eyes in the flickering light. "I know you can," he said softly, inching closer. "I've never met anyone like you, Annabel."

"Oh," Annabel whispered, feeling a surge of emotions coursing through her, a guilty flutter in her heart. "Charlie..."

In two swift strides, Charlie closed the distance between them and kissed her.

Annabel's heart suddenly swelled as if flowers had bloomed within her, and she reflexively closed her eyes, savoring the tenderness of his lips on hers. It was suddenly as though her heart was dancing a jig, and she almost moaned with how good he felt against her. Seizing the day as she never had before, she returned his kiss, relishing his comforting, delicious taste and the familiar scent of wood oil on his skin. She felt utter happiness at that moment—vibrant, alive, and hopeful. Annabel's hands, unsure of what to do, found solace at his firm waist, where he suddenly intertwined her fingers with his, a gentle caress that felt almost like love—and it was this incredibly intimate gesture amidst the intoxication of the moment that jolted Annabel back to reality. She suddenly drew away from him, gasping. "We have done a great wrong," she whispered in horror.

"No..." Charlie shook his head, his face paling. "No, you don't understand—"

"There's nothing to understand. I would never hurt Lise like this." Annabel's voice was filled with anguish. "That should never have happened. Please..." She shook her head, her resolve firm as he tried to speak. "Don't. You must leave. I can't *believe* I was so careless..." Her mind raced as she violently pushed away the yearning rising in her heart and wondered what her new friend would think of Annabel kissing her husband. She groaned at the thought, feeling wretched.

With a stricken expression, Charlie retreated, immediately putting distance between them. "I'm so sorry," he murmured, his voice laden with remorse. Shaking his head, he swiftly took the torch, then turned and walked quickly down the seemingly endless corridor; then she saw him turn left, disappearing into the darkness.

Annabel swallowed hard, burdened by guilt, momentarily considering lighting another torch, for there was another unlit on the opposite wall, and pursuing him—however, the absence of a tinderbox rendered her unable.

Casting a final, nervous glance toward the closet entrance above, she slowly ascended the ladder, determined to face the consequences of their transgression.

Annabel was greeted by a sight that left her speechless as she emerged at the top of the stairs. Lise and Agatha were locked in a clearly passionate embrace, their hands intertwined, faces radiant with naked joy, tears of happiness streaming down their cheeks. Stricken, she watched them for a moment, kissing as though they feared the world would end, oblivious to all else.

"But..." Annabel stammered, her words trailing off as she faltered. The two women looked up, startled by her presence.

Lise beamed, her face aglow. "Annabel, I could never thank you enough. Not in a million lifetimes." Her expression turned to concern. "Isn't Charlie with you?"

"He...no," Annabel whispered, her voice filled with worry. "He ran off. He turned left, so he might be in the cellar."

"He ran *off*? What do you mean?" Lise exclaimed in alarm. "What happened to the plan?"

"He *kissed* me," Annabel confessed, her tone filled with regret. "I sent him away—I was terrified that our friendship would be shattered, yours and mine."

"It will be if you don't go after him!" Lise's voice rose in frustration, but her chin trembled. "We can't afford for him to disappear now. *Please*, Annabel?"

"Of course, but..." A surge of irritation coursed through Annabel's veins. "Couldn't you have told me all of this? If I had only known..."

"I couldn't risk it," Lise whispered, her tone filled with vulnerability. "What if you saw me as an abomination?"

"You truly think that of me?" Annabel scowled, snatching a candle and her flint and steel pouch, ready to venture back into the tunnel without waiting for an answer, her mind racing.

Chapter Thirteen

APOLOGIES

Thankfully, Annabel navigated her way to the cellar, holding her candle tightly. She discovered Charlie there, removing his disguise, a weary expression etched on his face.

As she silently entered the room and closed the hidden entrance, Charlie looked down, avoiding her gaze. "I'm sorry about that—it won't happen again. You didn't have to come here."

"I was worried about you. So was Lise." Annabel stepped closer to him, watching his face.

"I'm fine." Anxiety blossomed on his brow at her approach. "I'll leave and see to her while you rest here, or I can head to the stables. You've done more than enough to help us." His voice lowered. "Sincerely, my apologies. I don't know what came over me. I'm usually so careful."

Annabel spoke softly, her voice filled with compassion. "I wish I had been informed about the true nature of your relationship. I had no idea Lise was trying to save Agatha because they were *lovers*."

Charlie scowled. "It's not exactly like that. We were friends with Agatha first, and then something blossomed between them. She's still my friend as well."

"I see," Annabel said, gazing at him.

"But..." Meeting her eyes, he murmured, "When Lise sought refuge with me that first night by the fire, it wasn't just to escape a competitor."

Her eyes widened. "No?"

Charlie continued, his voice heavy with the weight of the past. "It was the husband of a woman she had been involved with. He killed his wife when he discovered her in the arms of another woman. Lise barely escaped with her own life."

"She came here to find solace," Annabel whispered. "She came here seeking death," Charlie admitted flatly. "She confided her story in me, hoping it would make me hate her. She had brought a knife and begged me to end her suffering, saying that she was an abomination."

He laughed wryly. "As if *I* could kill someone."

"Instead, you proposed to her," Annabel said in awe. Her heart twisted with admiration for what he had done, and she smiled. "You're a good man, Charlie."

"Well, I don't know about that. It seemed like a good idea at the time—-preferable to murder, anyway," he laughed. "Besides, *you* know Lise. When you meet her, you can't help but want to help her. She's not my true love, but she's a remarkable person."

Annabel's heart swelled with tenderness as she reached for him, curious to reprise their embrace from before...only to retract her hand when he flinched.

"You will not allow me to stand near you," she noted, crossing her arms. "We are no longer friends?"

"I'm not sure I deserve your friendship," Charlie's voice was pained. "I took advantage of you in the tunnels. It was untoward."

"You're being too hard on yourself," she insisted. "I kissed you back."

Shaking his head, Charlie disappeared behind Lise's canvas privacy screen to change clothes. "Well, to make matters worse...if I'm honest, I already had feelings for you I've been repressing. Then, when the realization struck that you're not truly married, my pining got the better of me." He sighed deeply. "A momentary lapse. You needn't worry about it happening again."

"I'm not..." Annabel's voice trailed off. "God's bones. This means Richard's still married to Agatha, and my marriage to him isn't valid. I can't believe that didn't occur to me. I need more sleep."

"Yes, you're an unmarried woman, strictly speaking." Charlie laughed. "I'm ashamed to say that I've thought of nothing but that fact since we made to rescue Agatha."

She couldn't stop the smile from spreading over her face. "But this is wonderful news. Neither of us is truly beholden to another." Annabel wickedly closed her eyes and slowed herself to imagine him before her, half-naked while changing, his broad torso and muscled thighs exposed, slowly tugging down his breeches. A delicious shiver ran through her.

"Not entirely," he remarked, and she opened her eyes. "I still have a responsibility to Lise, even if we aren't in love." He grunted as she heard him take off his boots. "And it may not change things for you in practice. Agatha will likely need time to heal before revealing the truth. She may only desire freedom, not retribution, so your lack of marriage may not matter quite yet."

"You mean we can't actually do anything to bring Agatha justice, after all the suffering she endured?" Annabel asked in disbelief. "That's rather disappointing." Making a nervous hum in her throat, she added, "I suppose patience is a virtue, but I dare say it's such a boring one." She was rewarded by a low chuckle that warmed her heart as Charlie stepped out from behind the screen, fully dressed, his false

beard and makeup gone, face clean and unassuming as his gaze met he
rs.

Annabel's heart skipped a beat as she noticed—as she allowed herself to see him in this new light—his sensual jawline and determined
expression, an errant lock of hair over his ear she itched to slip back
with her fingers. She'd never noticed that freckle that disappeared
when he frowned and danced when he laughed. The beauty of his
remaining eye, which was a beautiful pool of green with just a hint of
blue, brought to mind the color illustrations she'd seen of the sea. A
surge of longing coursed through her, so sharp it almost hurt, and she
had to look away.

Charlie shrugged casually, oblivious to the whirlwind going
through her mind. "Our goal was to rescue Agatha, not to enact
revenge. We succeeded. Now, we must ask her if she wants to pursue
justice—we only know that she wants to live, eat, and be with Lise,
and now she can."

"I think I may want *you*," Annabel whispered as she looked back at
him. She blushed to say the words, even as she yearned to feel his lips
against hers again.

"We can't," he said firmly. "You were right the first time. Can we
not return to before I kissed you in the tunnels?"

"Charlie," Annabel said firmly. "If Lise gives us her blessing, and
I'm sure she would, especially since she has Agatha now, why wouldn't
we..."

"It wouldn't matter. On paper, in the eyes of the community,
you're still married to someone else," Charlie reminded her, not meeting her eyes. "If we're discovered together, the consequences could be
disastrous for you. I can't bear that."

"Women aren't sentenced to death for adultery," she argued. "We're
not living in the medieval ages."

"The legal penalties for women who commit adultery are severe, especially in this region, particularly on the land of an aristocrat," he explained. "You could face substantial fines, imprisonment, or even public whipping if you couldn't pay the fines."

Annabel's eyes widened in shock. "And what about *you*? Would you face punishment?"

"Perhaps I'd be castrated," he nonchalantly shrugged, causing her to wince. "Or perhaps not. There's no way to know. In any case, the blame would fall on you, as unfair as that may be. The consequences would be primarily yours."

"If you're so apprehensive about it, why did you kiss me in the first place?" she asked, irritation lacing her tone.

"I'm sorry... I know people always say this, but I shouldn't have," Charlie sighed. "I'm not usually that impulsive. As you immediately and correctly pointed out, it was a great wrong."

"That's not fair," she protested. "The only reason it felt wrong was because I thought you were happily married to our dear friend Lise." Annabel crossed her arms defiantly. "In my eyes, that was your only mistake."

He laughed nervously. "It would still be wrong to kiss you without firm intentions. I am not entitled to offer you anything but myself, not now or in the future. I have no house, money, or family."

"Charlie." She swallowed hard. "Do you not *want* to kiss me?"

"Oh, Annabel..." Groaning as if a man in pain, he hung his head. "I am absolutely sick with how much I'd like to kiss you."

She smiled. "I hope not too sick."

"But..." He took a deep breath and protested, "But I'd best not. It would complicate everything—more for you than for me. The right thing to do is to let it go."

Annabel pressed her lips together, feeling uncharacteristically bold and not intending to allow this dizzying new feeling of elation to leave her. She whispered softly, "What if I said please? *Please* kiss me again, Charlie."

"Annabel..." At the word please, an almost devilish look lit his eye, along with that boyish grin she'd grown fond of, causing a flame of desire to lick deliciously up her front, and she breathed deeply. For a moment, he looked as though he might come to her—then he looked down again, shaking his head. "Don't say such things. You deserve someone better than me—a married, one-eyed laborer, fighting illegally every week, deeply in debt to the Baron of the castle. I'm not allowed to work my trade or ride in the carriage. I'm no bloody prize, Annabel, and I won't pretend I will ever be good enough for you." He laughed weakly.

"Don't disparage yourself," Annabel objected. "You may be those things, but you're also a clever, literate, patient woodcarver who is good with children and can act better than people I've seen in *plays*." Drawing a sense of satisfaction at his resulting proud smile, she added, "And I hate to remind you, but I'm an aging farm wife with two recently failed romances under her belt, who is afraid of heights, poor at cooking, and already getting into trouble here."

"You're doing fine," he whispered, and her heart lifted as his previously beleaguered expression seemed to shift to a more hopeful one. "Your crops are thriving. Lise said she's never enjoyed talking with someone so quickly. And you know that everyone feasts on your stories like the best venison."

She smiled at the compliment. "Perhaps we are both just humans with flaws and fancies?"

Charlie nodded. "Perhaps."

"Then hear this: your kiss made my heart come alive, Charlie." Annabel brought her hand up to her chest to thump it insistently. "It felt quite a bit like happiness, which, to be quite honest, I wasn't sure if I'd recognize after recent happenings. And I'd like another go at it—if you do too." She swallowed hard.

"Of course, I do." Charlie swallowed hard as he met her eyes, and she saw his eyes darken even as he whispered, "But when you plan your life with ideally the eventual subtraction of Richard, whenever that may be, you should look to set yourself up to be with someone with less problems and a better future. And know that I won't be offended if you do." He coughed, looking away as she watched him try to convince himself of the words he was saying.

With a flutter of her heart, Annabel found herself inexplicably drawn to him. Slowly, as if guided by an unseen force, she stepped closer, the distance between them diminishing until they stood face to face. His gaze held a hint of mischief and wisdom that stirred her, sparkling with intelligence and depth. Time seemed to stand still as their eyes met, an unspoken connection forged in that single electrifying moment.

"Charlie," Annabel said reasonably. "I like you very much, and if you're prepared, I'm going to kiss you."

"Fair enough." He laughed, a loose, joyous sound that pulled at her heartstrings, and his tensed shoulders finally seemed to relax. "What I mean is...yes, please do, Annabel. I'd like nothing more."

She stepped closer, her heart leaping as his breath drew in sharply, and when she stood inches from his lips and hesitated, savoring the feeling of closeness, his hot breath on her parted mouth, his knotted belt grazing her skirts. Annabel took a deep breath in and out again, hardly daring to believe it, tilted her face up, stood on her toes, and kissed him.

Charlie's skin was warm, and the kiss felt like sunshine gleaming through her, yet at the same time, she felt as though she was drinking water after years in the sun. As she strained to remain within range of his lips, he bent his muscular frame down to meet hers, kissing her back fervently. As his firm lips caressed hers, his hands slipped to her waist, then slowly past her breasts, barely grazing them, and he twined his long, nimble fingers in her tousled hair.

Pulling briefly away, he stopped to look at her, his gaze resorting to her eyes, cheeks, and the freckled span of her collarbone. "Oh, Annabel," he whispered. "You are bloody enchanting." He bent and kissed her neck, his lips igniting little fires of pleasure along her skin.

"Then move not," she whispered, wondering if he would recognize the play. "Thus from my lips, my sin is purged by yours."

"I hope I am not in such a tragedy as Romeo and Juliet, but I do like where you're going with this," he continued with a moan, kissing slowly across her collarbone and facing her again, his expression hungry. "Oh, teach me how I should forget to think."

"Sin from my lips?" Annabel continued. "Oh, trespass sweetly urged! Give me my sin again."

"Gladly..." Suddenly, he reached down and swept her into his arms, sitting down hard on the bed with her on his lap as she laughed, and they fell back onto the blankets together, her on top of him. Kissing him again and again, she curled her fingers in his dark hair, running her fingernails down his scalp, and he moaned again as her breasts pressed firmly against his hard chest.

Several minutes later, they came up for air, clothes rumpled and lips bruised with wanting. "I'm sorry to disappoint you, Charlie," said Annabel solemnly, sliding off his lap and onto the bed beside him. "But that was, in fact, good enough for me. You worried for nothing."

"Aren't you funny?" He chuckled, rolling his eyes. "You pretty rogue."

When she reached out her hand, he took it, and her heart danced a little livelier in her chest as she realized that even her fingertips were responding to Charlie's presence. "What are you thinking?"

"You first," he suggested, taking one of her hands in both hands and massaging her palm.

Annabel smiled. "I think we should probably head back to Lise and Agatha, but I'd like to do that again at some point, as well as get to know you better. And you?"

"I'm afraid I'm a bit of a cynic. I'm wondering if you'll regret this after our blood stops rushing." He began to gather supplies into a bag, his face flushed.

"I supposed only time will assure you of the contrary," she whispered, admiring his forearms as they worked.

"And you're right," he continued. "We should indeed return and check on them. I'm sure Lise has already tended to Agatha's wounds with the supplies we left, but we should bring more. Extra clothes, too."

"Fair enough," she nodded. "Let's head out." They gathered the necessary items, slipping back to Annabel's house. Charlie wasted no time getting a fire roaring inside the cast iron stove and a stew going over it, and a grateful Agatha was already in bed with clean bandages, playing cards with Lise, looking tired and happy.

Chapter Fourteen

THE BARON'S RIDDLE

The next day, Lise guided Annabel in the laundry tasks, including cleaning and drying while she and Agatha handled the mending and heavy scrubbing. Lise and Agatha had agreed to take care of the indoor chores to the best of their abilities, with the shades always drawn. Agatha was an excellent baker, taking her time kneading the dough, and had a large loaf of barley bread baking in a Dutch oven nestled in the coals before dawn. To their delight, the farmhands each received a weekly loaf.

As Charlie suspected, Agatha hesitated to reveal her new status of being alive. Instead, she focused on healing, keeping herself busy with chores, long talks with Lise, and restful, deep sleep.

Annabel couldn't help but steal constant glances at Charlie. When he stretched in the fields, a delicious thrill ran through her to see his forearms reach the heavens, the sinewy muscle twisting on his capable arms. Upon him bending over, she regretfully bit her lip instead of his firm thighs. And he helped change Agatha's bandages; he was tirelessly patient. Unlike most of the men she'd known, he seldom complained, and she realized how much she had come to depend on his presence.

After a great deal of thought, her only concern was his belief that he wasn't good enough for her. She couldn't bear the thought of loving a martyr and wondered if, if they did decide to try being together, he would give her up at the first sign of trouble or fight for their relationship. At the end of a long day of laundry, Annabel was ready to find Charlie and let him know her feelings remained unchanged, hoping for another dizzying, wonderful kiss. Wickedly, she grinned and wondered what else they could do together.

When the laundry was finished, she slipped back home, locking the door securely behind her and smiling gratefully at Lise and Agatha. "How are both of you doing? And is that a meat pie?"

"Venison. Help yourself," Lise grinned. "Great news: I can stand on my leg without wincing as long as I don't move it from side to side. Progress!"

"This is wonderful," Annabel sighed, standing over the pie with a slice in her hand. "I wish I could make something like this."

"You and me both," Lise agreed, helping herself to another serving.

"I'd be happy to teach you," Agatha beamed. "It feels so bloody *good* to be out of that dungeon and have access to a hearth and stove again."

"And you're truly feeling better?" Annabel asked worriedly. "How are your wounds, and are you *sure* you don't need a doctor?"

"Thank you, but I'm honestly feeling stronger than even I expected." Agatha shook her head. "Being out of the dungeon and having my life back, and Lise back too, feels like a dream. It's wonderful to feel useful again without being confined." She let out a merry laugh. "Well, I suppose it's still confined, but it feels much better. I wouldn't mind running through a field with my arms spread wide, but I can wait while I acclimate myself back to the world in small steps."

"Good for you." Annabel began preparing tea. "Please stay as long as you like. I don't know if you've thought about what you want to do next..."

"I have. "Agatha smiled. "Charlie knows a merchant family willing to take me in and provide room and board in exchange for work. Once I've healed, I might move in that direction to regain my footing and replenish my purse before heading to court." She grinned. "By the way, thank you for helping put Richard away for the time being."

"I hope it lasts and we have time to plan for his return. I was told by the magistrate that we have at least a few weeks until there's more news of his sentencing." Annabel paused, asking curiously, "Cecelia said you were thrown in the dungeon for punishment. Is that right?"

"Yes, that's right." Agatha shuddered. "Richard never caught Lise and me together, but we had a few close calls. Then he noticed that I was happier after seeing Lise, and he figured it out. He brought me before the Baron and I refused to confess anything, making him even more furious. They threw me in the dungeon for a week—every day, they asked if I wanted to confess, and I kept refusing."

Lise reached out to take her hand and rubbed it reassuringly. "I'll never forget what you did to protect me. I wish you hadn't had to."

"So do I." Agatha sighed. "Then, one day, I was so desperate to be out of there that I said I would confess. I was brought out and given a hot meal and a third-hand bath." Shuddering, she spat, "The Baron asked if I was fertile."

"What?" Annabel asked, horrified.

"He said if I stayed with him in the castle and willingly gave him a child, I wouldn't have to return to Richard." She shook her head angrily. "I'm sure he wasn't serious, but I don't know what bloody game he played. When his back was turned, I tried to escape. James caught me before I left the room and threw me back in there. I can't believe it's almost been three months."

"They're both so bloody horrid," hissed Lise savagely. "I hope they drown in a cesspool."

Agatha laughed, then turned the question on Annabel. "And what about you? Why did *you* marry Richard?"

Annabel sighed. "Honestly, I was desperate for a second chance." She swallowed hard and explained, "I fell in love with our vicar back home...he was the only man at the time who encouraged my reading." She sighed at the memory.

Lise nodded to Agatha. "This one read a page of the Baron's book in the field with muck on her boots. It was bloody wild. He was ready to send her away and move in Richard's brother, then he let her stay as soon as he found out she was literate. Gwyneth and I were right here where you're sitting."

"That's quite something." Agatha looked impressed. "How did you manage to build that skill?"

"Late nights and early mornings of practice. I never needed much sleep," mused Annabel. "I washed every day after my chores and did bookbinding for the church three days a week. If you want to know the truth—honestly, I felt a bit wicked for reading, and I thought maybe if I was with Paul, a man of the cloth, it would help to make up for it. Isn't that silly?"

"Oh, yes," Lise agreed. "You're probably the least wicked person I know."

"Well, I disobeyed my mother to see him and hid our relationship for two years," Annabel admitted. "He must've known all along that it was foolish, but one day, he impulsively asked me to marry him; then, just as suddenly, left me for another woman the next day: The lovely, kind, wonderful daughter of one of the church's biggest donors. I honestly haven't a single bad thing to say about her, and I fully understand his choice. He's already made up for it—I have no reason to b e sour."

"Ah, don't talk like that." Agatha shook her head. "Feel what you feel. He had no right to treat you that way."

Annabel sighed, looking down. "Well, I was humiliated at the time. I— coupled with him the day he proposed. He'd promised we'd wed the next day." She shuddered, not meeting their eyes. "I was so ashamed. I'm *so* lucky it didn't lead to a baby. When it all collapsed, I thought no one would ever want me again....and well, then I met Richard." Her face was red.

"I completely understand. Timing," muttered Agatha. "Isn't it the dearth of us all? Richard also made my future seem brighter, and then I learned how he truly is."

"Right!" Annabel nodded. "He swept me off my feet. He knew the gossip about the vicar but didn't mind...he made a new life together for the both of us sound so appealing."

Agatha shuddered. "My mum met Richard once and thought he was the best chance at turning my interest over to men." She rolled her eyes. "If she could see me now."

"I'm your family now," Lise whispered. "Don't ever forget it." Smiling gratefully, Agatha squeezed her hand.

"I'm starting to realize how easy it is to make those mistakes in judging character." Annabel sighed.

Lise's eyes sparkled with warmth. "Well, let me tell you, I couldn't be happier that you're here. Not only have you become one of my newfound favorite companions, but you're helping our quest to unearth the Rowley treasure." She sat back happily, a dreamy expression on her face. "Do you know how our lives could transform if we succeed?"

Annabel sighed. "Well, unfortunately, we hit a dead end there."

"For now." Lise waved her hand. "So, onto you and Charlie...."

Agatha grinned. "Right. Let's discuss how the two clearly fancy each other. All those stolen glances both ways when the other's back is turned."

"*Is* he looking at me when my back is turned?" Annabel asked hopefully.

"*Yes,*" Lise laughed incredulously, "You truly haven't noticed?"

"He really *kissed* you in the tunnels?" Agatha asked.

Pressing her lips together, cheeks reddening, Annabel nodded. "I kissed him back."

Lise shook her head. "Hand to heart, he's never made a single move on me in two years of marriage because I told him I wasn't interested in men. I know he kissed a few girls in his youth, but I wouldn't have thought he'd have the nerve. He's always been so cautious. Like an old man before his time, but don't tell him I said that."

"Well..." Annabel's heart stirred as the memory resurfaced. "After he helped Agatha up, he came back down, said some pretty words that warmed my spirit, and then came the kiss. After enjoying it, I was horrified, as I didn't know the situation—so I bade him leave, then once you sent me back after him, I found him in the cellar, he'd apologized about fifty times, then *I* kissed him." Annabel took a deep breath and let it out. "It was...well. It was bloody spectacular."

The affectionate expression that came over Annabel's face when she recalled the moment made Lise gasp. "Why, Annabel Barlow Granger, the *glow* on you. Pray tell, are you in *love* with my husband?"

"Goodness," Agatha remarked, snickering at her partner. "What is she, your child?"

"No!" Annabel protested. "Of course not. I hardly know him. And yes, please don't ever say my name like that again. You know I'm not really *married* to Richard now, not technically." She made a face.

Agatha laughed darkly and shuddered. "I do not thank you for the reminder—another reason not to make myself known just yet. If you don't mind."

"Take as long as you need," Annabel assured her. "Let's both enjoy the respite."

"Fine. But you want to kiss him again, don't you?" Lise smiled. "The mere mention of his name sends your temperature rising; it's undeniable."

"She's right," agreed Agatha.

"Fine. But if there's *any* chance it could mean the end of yours and my friendship, I'll wipe the thought from my mind," whispered Annabel. "I'd rather never see him again if that's what you prefer. It's no skin off my nose, so if it makes you feel oddly in the slightest, I swear I'll never give him another feverish thought."

Agatha grinned. "What an awful liar you are—we should all play dice sometime." She pulled a deck out from under the bed. "Or cards?"

Lise laughed and playfully pinched Agatha, eliciting a giggle. Then she turned to Annabel and said kindly, "You have my blessing, whatever you decide to do—wild stallions couldn't keep me from our friendship." With a reassuring smile, she added, "Charlie is a good man, and I will always love him dearly, if not in that way...and he deserves a second chance as much as the rest of us. Go talk to him now before you lose your nerve."

Annabel swallowed hard, daring to hope. "You're absolutely sure?"

"I am." Lise paused. "And I'm sorry I wasn't entirely truthful with you about my tale of woe. I should have been honest—if anyone understands how life can turn so quickly, it's you—but please know it was simply a matter of self-preservation."

"I understand now why you didn't," Annabel smiled. "And thank you. There's no judgment from me, and I'm happy for both of you."

Suddenly, a knock interrupted their conversation, causing them all to freeze. Following their practiced plan, her two friends silently moved to their hiding places just before Annabel opened the door.

It was Cole, the Baron's steward. He looked over his shoulder, clearly distracted. "The Baron has sent for you," he said impatiently.

"Why?" Annabel asked in surprise.

"I don't know, and I don't care," Cole sighed. "Come along now; I haven't got all day."

"Of course," Annabel said curiously, stepping onto the porch and locking the door behind her.

Annabel stood before the Baron's desk within minutes, trying not to glare at his pendulous face. "Good evening, my lord," she greeted him as she heard Cole scurry out of the room.

"Indeed," he sighed. Surprisingly, he rose slowly to close the door behind her, then sat back down and gestured toward a small sofa at the side of the desk. "Sit."

With a sense of unease settling in, Annabel sat gingerly on the elegant silk. As she thought of Charlie, Lise and Agatha, she resolved to maintain a composed demeanor in the face of the man who had laughed while he burned her property. She took a deep breath and imagined her spine was made of steel, her face of granite, and with this in mind she waited patiently, a calm smile at the ready while the Baron shifted in his chair, scowling as he strove to get comfortable.

Eventually, he pulled a quill out of his seat and tossed it on the desk angrily before fixing his gaze on her.

"Annabel, you may not know this, but my late wife Phillippa, the mother of my three children, passed away some time ago." Henry's voice carried a touch of sorrow.

Apparently, there was to be no mention of their last encounter. Perplexed by the direction of their conversation, Annabel folded her hands in her lap, offering a sympathetic look from across the table. "I'm sorry for your loss, Baron Rowley. From what I've heard, your wife was a remarkable woman."

The Baron nodded, his expression melancholic. "Phillippa was a woman of beauty, strength, and intelligence. She ran this household with an iron fist, loved and respected by our people. She was a lady, but she was no shrinking violet." He paused, a fond smile gracing his lips. "She was the love of my life. Even now, her absence weighs heavily on me." His gaze shifted to a cord at the side of a curtain, and with a tug, a large portrait of Phillippa Rowley was revealed.

"Oh!" Annabel's eyes widened as she took in the lifelike depiction of the late baroness surrounded by horses. "How very elegant and regal she looks in this painting."

"In her honor," Henry sighed, "I keep this magnificent likeness. But it's cold comfort, merely a reminder of what I've lost." He poured himself a glass of wine and gestured for Annabel to continue. "Today marks the anniversary of her death, you know."

Still uncertain of the purpose behind this conversation and feeling a bit foolish, Annabel nodded politely at the mad old man. "I wasn't aware, but I'm sorry for your loss, Baron Rowley. It must be a difficult day for you."

"You are a kind and understanding young woman, Annabel," the Baron said, sipping his wine. "I appreciate your grace during this meeting after what transpired this week. You accepted your punishment with aplomb."

"Clearly, I overstepped," she said evenly. "You will not find me in your library again. Again, I apologize for my behavior, and I thank you for allowing me to remain here at the castle."

"I was told by the nursemaid that my daughter ceased her nightmares after you fixed her book," admitted Henry. "Then, apparently, she resumed them after it was destroyed. It appears I may have made a misstep in my attempts to assert my will."

"Oh, I'm sorry to hear that," Annabel said mildly, her brows drawing together. "She is a very clever young girl."

"As are you," Henry demurred. "Compassionate, intelligent, efficient— much like Phillippa's younger days. And it is with this perception that I find the courage to appoint you to a special task."

Annabel tried to keep the fear from her voice. "Oh? And what is that?"

The Baron walked to the bookcase and patted the side of it absently. "My late wife and I had a particular ritual. She lay down in her nightdress on this bed and read to me until I fell asleep, providing me peace and comfort. It was a cherished tradition between us." His voice cracked and then purred as he added, "Lavender was my favorite color on her."

"How very nice," she said, beginning to see where he was heading with such a suggestive tone, and dreading his next words.

"You will spend the night in my room and read to me in her nightgown until I fall asleep," Henry said decisively. "This is not a request. It will bring me solace on this day of remembrance and help me move forward."

"I'm a farmer." Annabel was perplexed. "Surely there is an eligible lady at court whom you would prefer to perform this activity?"

"Oh, *now* you're only a farmer, are you?" Laughing as if she were the mad one, he explained, "Obviously, I can't ask a lady of nobility or a potential wife for such a vulnerable request. I will seem less of a man, an object of spectacle and ridicule, and my future wife must respect me. This will ready me for her, whoever she may be."

Annabel's mind raced. "How admirable it is that you loved your wife so deeply," she remarked, carefully choosing her words. "I would be honored to read to you to bring comfort and peace on this difficult day."

Henry nodded, smiling magnanimously down at her in the low chair from his great height. "Splendid. Go through that door behind you; a bath is drawn. I hope you don't mind removing the residue of the crops before handling my books."

"Of course." She stood and backed nervously toward the door, a stiff smile on her face. Inside, she was splitting her sides with nervous laughter, and she clamped her lips shut to avoid a wild giggle at this odd situation.

Entering his side chamber, her nerves were calmed by the brisk maid to the Baron, Constance, who introduced herself disapprovingly. The lukewarm water and grit in the bottom of the tub indicated it had been drawn sometime before and already used, but she tried not to dwell on it. After washing off the dirt and grime, Annabel dried herself with a towel. To her surprise, Constance had a starched, bright lavender nightdress waiting and was not prepared to take no for an answer.

"Could I not fetch one of my own?" Annabel asked timidly. "You need note trouble yourself."

"This is what you're wearing," Constance ordered. "Unless you'd like to go back without a stitch."

"When you put it that way..." Annabel sighed as she stepped into the garish nightgown. "It's just lovely."

When she had returned to the Baron's chambers, he was wearing a nightcap and had poured himself a tankard of wine. He motioned her to the sofa again, settling himself in the middle of the bed. "You may begin where it is marked," he said, indicating a hefty tome on the end table.

Annabel's eyes widened as she skimmed the lengthy, daunting page, fighting a grimace as she wondered if she could stay awake. The book was The Poetry of John Donne. Taking a deep breath, she began reciting the verses.

"Many these Poems have, for several impressions, wandered up and down trusting (as well they might) upon the Author's reputation; neither do they now complain of any injury, but what may proceed either from the kindness of the Printer, or the courtesy of the Reader; the one by adding something too much, lest any spark of this sacred fire might perish undiscerned, the other by putting such an estimation upon the wit & fancy they find here, that they are content to use it as their own: as if a man should dig out the stones of a royal Amphitheater to build a stage for a country show."

Shaking her head at the monotony as she paused to draw breath, she continued with a sigh. The words flowed from her throat, though her voice grew raspy. The candle finally burned out at one point, and when she lit it again, the Baron appeared asleep. Annabel crept quietly to retrieve a blanket from the shelf and settled back on the sofa, preparing to spend the night there.

As she got comfortable, the Baron stirred, murmuring in his sleep. "Forgive me," he mumbled, his voice laced with sorrow. "Please..."

Annabel's heart skipped a beat. She listened intently as he continued, his voice filled with longing. "Forgive me, Philippa. I'll do anything...I swear, I'll even let you go if you only love me again."

Frozen in place, Annabel's eyebrows rose.

"Of course," moaned the Baron. "But no more lies. Lie to me again, and I'll kill you—for real this time." He then groaned, turning on his side.

As the Baron's snoring filled the room, Annabel could not succumb to sleep. With a quiet resolve, she slipped off the couch, breathing deeply in anticipation at the collection of books. Quietly, she slipped one off the shelf, looked slowly through it, and put it back, then did the same thing with another and another.

The smell of parchment surrounded her, and her shoulders relaxed as she dreamily inhaled the scent. She took down a seventh book, and a slow grin spread across her face as she discovered a bookmark within the pages. She realized the handwriting on the bookmark bore a striking resemblance to the carving she had uncovered beneath the altar.

Squinting at the tiny script, she read the inscription, the words resonating with intrigue and adventure within her mind.

In a steel coffin where shadows dwell,
Seek the valiant and the swell.

It had to be one of the riddles, and Annabel's mind raced with possibilities. She pondered the significance of the words, imagining the mausoleum as a potential hiding place. The thought sent a shiver down her spine, mingling excitement with apprehension, and Annabel carefully returned the book to its place, her mind consumed by the mystery ahead.

Drifting off to sleep, her dreams were filled with cryptic phrases and hidden passages.

When she woke the following day still wrapped in the thick blanket, her throat sore, she found Henry stirring from his sleep. He greeted her with a contented smile, claiming it was the best night's sleep he had in ages. "I feel rejuvenated, Annabel," the Baron declared. "Perhaps now I can venture into the world and find a suitable wife. I believe I've finally properly mourned Phillippa."

Annabel offered a polite smile, though her mind remained clouded with questions. "I'm glad I could be of assistance, Baron Rowley. "

He nodded appreciatively, his gaze drifting towards the desk. "You may go. Return the nightgown after the laundress has seen to it."

She took a deep breath. "May I have back the clothes I came in?" "You may not," Henry frowned. "Please leave." Tilting his head, he gave her a small smile, and she realized he was wondering if she would make a scene.

With a gracious smile and a curt nod, Annabel turned towards the door, but as she stepped into the hallway, she found Cecelia standing there, her eyes widening at the sight of her nightgown. "Your mother is waiting for you in the great hall," she muttered.

Annabel's excitement of seeing her mother overshadowed the lingering perplexity from her encounter with the Baron. "Thank you, Cecelia. I'll go to her now."

Hurrying through the corridors, Annabel's steps quickened with anticipation. She entered the grand hall, scanning the room until her eyes met her mother's familiar face. Arva Guernsey stood nervously, tapping her foot as she watched her daughter approach.

"Mummy!" Annabel exclaimed, unable to contain her joy. "I'm so happy to see you. How have you been? Is everyone well at home?"

Arva gave her daughter a hug, her eyes filled with excitement. "We're all just fine, my darling. I've come with some wonderful news."

"News?" Annabel asked curiously.

"I spoke to a priest who said we might be able to get your marriage annulled." Arva glanced around, lowering her voice. "And I've found you a new husband."

Chapter Fifteen

DISCUSSION

Annabel recoiled in surprise, disentangling herself from her mother's embrace. "Who?" She sighed in exasperation. "Mummy—"

"Montgomery Hayworth, your old neighbor," her mother proclaimed proudly. "I do listen to you, you know. I received word that your husband will soon be sentenced to perhaps years for theft and tax evasion. We've got a good case for annulment." Her voice grew high. "Annabel, my heart, I am so sorry about this. I really thought Richard was a good man. But if I know you, I doubt you lose any sleep over a thieving husband. I promise I'll fight Parliament on your behalf if need be...this is more than enough reason to separate you from that man."

"Mummy," Annabel tried again. "You don't have to go to so much trouble—"

"Now, we all hate to think of these things, but we must find your next husband promptly and have someone lined up for the future so the house and opportunity aren't taken," her mother interrupted eagerly, a smile of expectation. "I'm only thinking of what's best for you. You know that, don't you, my darling?"

As Annabel opened her mouth to object a third time, her mother hurried on. "No, no, let me finish. Monty hasn't fathered any children and is just a few years older. He's stronger and younger than your previous match. He works on his father's farm, a decent family. They have many children, like us, so he should be fertile—"

"I remember him, and not pleasantly. He bullied me when I was a child," Annabel finally interjected. "Mummy, I mean no disrespect, but I didn't ask for your help finding a new husband."

"Annabel Guernsey. I still have your three younger sisters to marry off, who don't talk back as much as you," her mother snapped sharply.

"I know," Annabel replied softly.

"It's a miracle I found this match for you at all," Arva scolded. "He initially inquired about your younger sister Dorothy, but I have someone else in mind for her. Stop complaining."

"I'm not saying I don't appreciate you." Annabel's stomach churned uneasily. "Dorothy is only fourteen. Must she be betrothed so quickly?"

"Well, we've seen what happens when we wait," Arva muttered, shooting Annabel a pointed glance. "She turns fifteen in May, and her future husband has a fine stable of horses. She's always loved horses, that one."

"She does," Annabel acknowledged. "It feels like just yesterday she was learning to ride. Pity we had to sell Dapple and Barry."

"How time flies," her mother sighed. "I can't stay long. I need to sign her contract before nightfall. I've been working on your new match for weeks, but I couldn't inform you until it was certain."

"So it's certain, so long as Richard is sentenced according to your timeline?" Annabel muttered. "Won't you please give me the book you've written about my life so I can at least follow along?"

"I wouldn't do that even if I could." Arva rolled her eyes. "Don't give me that tone. Your father is still injured, probably for the foreseeable future—"

"Is that what the doctor said?" Annabel asked, stricken.

"Yes," her mother sighed. "His farming days may well be over. And you're my responsibility, along with your siblings. This is the best course of action for you, with the scandal still fresh in the minds of the town. Haven't you already proved you need help knowing what's best for yourself?" Her face softened. "There's nothing wrong with accepting a little help, dear one. You needn't do everything yourself."

"I'm not disagreeing with you there, but making decisions and learning from mistakes is part of growing up. I should be able to find a husband who meets my standards when I'm ready," Annabel expressed, surprised at her boldness as she worked to keep the tremor from her voice.

Arva scoffed, "Oh, please, don't start with that nonsense. For all your talk of independence, you're still just a young woman. You're doing fine now, but what if something happens to you? What do you know about managing land?"

"I'm handling it," Annabel insisted. "Better than expected, even. I've learned a lot from you. You know I've been helping manage our family's land for years. As you say, we reap the seeds of our heritage."

"You remember too much." Her mother sighed. "I worry about you just the same. First a lying vicar, then a thieving farmer?"

"Mummy!" Annabel frowned. "You chose the thieving farmer."

Arva pressed her lips together. "Monty was thrilled when the engagement was proposed and said he could visit Castle Rowley within the week. Richard won't be back by then, will he?"

"He better not," Annabel muttered. "Mummy, I won't marry Monty, whether Richard dies or is sentenced. I mean that."

"Listen, my love," Arva chided. "Keep your head down, work hard, and you'll have a strong husband and a wonderful life as a wife and mother, who will support your happiness just as we have."

"Mummy," Annabel sighed. "I appreciate your efforts to help. I'm just worried I'll never be the person you want me to be. And as hard as I try, I'll never make you as happy as I could make myself."

"Oh, my darling, you're probably right," Arva said, looking at Annabel affectionately. "But don't forget, happiness is cold comfort if you don't have a place to live, a warm bed, or a family around you."

Annabel was silent for a moment, then met her mother's gaze. "I'm willing to chance it. And if you love me, you must trust me."

Arva closed her eyes, took a deep breath, then opened them again. "I'm unsure if I can do that, my darling." She smiled sadly, then sighed, "But I'll delay this match for now and check back with you in a week. I'm afraid that's the best you'll get out of me now."

"Thank you, Mummy," Annabel smiled. "I love you."

"You never love anyone as you do your first child," Arva sighed, squeezing her daughter. "I do have to go onto my next errand. The Baron is allowing me use of one of his carriages! The perks of a castle, I tell you. Take care, my dearest...I love you very, very much."

"Safe travels," Annabel whispered, hugging her mother back fiercely.

Arva climbed back into the carriage and waved as it departed. Annabel watched it for a while, dreading the idea of Montgomery Hayworth, for he was truly awful. She would need to find a way to push him away and stand up to her mother, but she couldn't make a fuss that might result in her eviction.

Annabel longingly thought of her connection with Charlie, hoping their last kiss wasn't the final one. Peeking out the door to ensure no one spotted her, she quickly set out to find him.

When she approached Charlie behind the stables, it was with a growing sense of anticipation. As she neared, her heart fluttered, and she couldn't help but notice how confidently he stood, like an oak tree in the wind, his gaze fixed upon a large cauldron simmering over a small fire.

"Good morrow," she greeted him warmly.

Charlie nodded. "Indeed, it is," he replied, his face reflecting the water. "A perfect day to be outside."

"What are you making?" Annabel asked, her nose catching the refreshing scent.

"I'm preparing peppermint water and warm mash for the horses," Charlie explained. "It's to treat colic. The mint leaves have a soothing effect."

Annabel took in a deep breath, relishing the delightful aroma. "It smells refreshing," she remarked, her senses captivated.

"Indeed," he agreed, not quite looking at her, and anxiety rippled under her skin. Swallowing hard, she tried to remember her recently acquired backbone.

"I've been hoping to talk to you," she said gently. "A few strange things have happened, and I'd love your ear on them."

"What you do is not my concern," he replied calmly. "You need not keep me informed. Perhaps you should seek advice from Lise and Agatha."

Dread washed over her. "You heard where I spent the night, I assume then."

"I heard," Charlie murmured. "It matters not to me."

"Cecelia told you, didn't she?" Annabel scowled. "I know the lavender nightgown was ridiculous, but please don't be bothered. It was truly nothing."

"I'm not bothered," he insisted. "I have no right to be bothered. I told you to go off and do better than me, and I'm glad you did." Charlie shook his head. "Don't concern yourself with it—we need not have this conversation."

Annabel closed her eyes momentarily and counted to ten in her head. When she opened them, he was looking at her dubiously. "Why must you dismiss me as so many others do? It hurts more, somehow, coming from you."

"That's not fair." Frowning, he protested, "I'm not trying to dismiss you...only to be realistic and save myself the heartbreak."

"And you want to know, just a little bit, perhaps, if I dallied with the Baron," she retorted, noticing his suddenly furrowed brow. "Don't you?"

"No," he blustered without conviction. "It's none of my bloody business anyway. You don't need to tell me anything. Don't tell me anything."

"Fine," Annabel said graciously. "If you don't care, I'll be on my way. Good day to you."

Charlie scowled. "Did you?"

"Did I what?" she challenged.

"No," he murmured. "Forget it."

"Charlie Daly." Annabel crossed her arms. "Speak your mind."

"If you did dally with him, I think it would have been the sensible thing to do, and I wouldn't fault you for it," he said lightly. "The Baron has a history of rewarding those who share his bed."

"Of course," she said, her voice laden with irony. "I forgot myself! I'm irresistibly attracted to giant oafs who throw women in dungeons for the smallest acts of defiance. You saw from my tears how much I enjoyed Richard throwing me in the stables, so I must like it with the Baron. Do I have that correct?"

"I don't care if you do!" Charlie almost shouted, then made a face. His voice grew softer. "God's head. I'm not allowed to care, Annabel."

"Yes, you are," Annabel said softly, and she noticed the tension in the way he was standing, the tightness in his shoulder. "Something else troubles you, which this situation has only worsened."

"I can't believe you can tell that just from my face. I haven't a chance." Charlie glanced over his shoulder, then, satisfied that no one was nearby, he sighed. "Yes—I've just discovered that years before my father, Lucas, disappeared, he had an affair with the late Baroness Rowley, Philippa."

"Oh," Annabel gasped in shock. "Your father? With Baroness Philippa Rowley?"

Nodding grimly, he continued, "And as you might recall from the story, Lady Rowley could not conceive for two years after marrying Baron Rowley...until she met my father, as the timeline suggests," he added.

Her eyes widened. "Are you saying..."

"Yes," Charlie muttered. "The Baron's so-called son, Frederick, is my brother. And now he knows too."

"Good Lord," she sighed. "Do you think Baroness Rowley knew that Frederick was your father's child when she died?"

"She most certainly did," he replied. "Frederick found a letter addressed to Philippa from my father while rummaging through old attic boxes—I'm lucky the sour teenager showed me. He's never so much as spoken to me before."

She shook her head slowly. "What else did the letter say?"

"Oh, my father spoke of their affair as a mistake and that my mother had forgiven him. He expressed his desire to see me grow up and never have any contact with Philippa or her son, to raise their child as the

Baron's own and leave him be." Regret washed over his face, and she knew he was thinking about what could have been.

"He must have loved you very much," she said softly.

"But after that—both my parents, Lucas and Mara Wright, disappeared without a trace," Charlie sighed.

"Oh," Annabel whispered, horrified.

"Right," Charlie sighed. "They were almost certainly both killed by the Rowleys. It's far too convenient otherwise."

"I'm so sorry, Charlie," she whispered. There was a long pause when she searched for the right thing to say. "Shall I off Henry for you?"

Startled at her phrasing, he shook his head, but a smile touched his lips.

"Let's see..." She rubbed her hands together. "I could loosen the ropes in the dining hall and bring a chandelier crashing down upon his head."

"Many thanks, but no." Charlie laughed, tossing her a small smile that seemed to slip into her heart.

"Please let me know if anything changes." She smiled lightly as she tried to avoid looking directly at his face, afraid she might throw herself at him.

As her vision caught a tree, she suddenly imagined him sweeping her up in his strong arms as he'd done before in the cellar, only this time slamming her into a tree, his hot breath on her cheek and his hands on her hips...

She blinked away the fantasy, swallowing hard as she finally looked him in the eye. "What are you thinking?"

"I fear..." Charlie ran a hand through his hair, his voice heavy. "I fear that kissing you was dishonorable. Both times. My father was with a married woman when he was married, and so was I. How can I judge him?"

He shook his head bitterly.

"Well, we know I'm not married, and yours is in name only. The circumstances are quite different." Tilting her head, she asked, "Is honor truly what's bothering you?"

"No," he admitted. "Truthfully, in the forefront of my mind is you. And that's a problem, because I'm starting to want to be selfish."

Annabel couldn't help but smile. "Oh?"

"Are you some sort of witch who has cast a spell upon me?" Charlie whispered. "With your powers to bring forth truth and desire?"

She gave him a playful look, rubbing her hands together as she inched closer. "And if I were?"

"You have witchcraft on your lips," Charlie murmured, his eyes darkening as her breath quickened.

Annabel laughed. "That's Shakespeare, isn't it?"

"Yes." He grinned. "Henry the Fifth. I'd gladly assist you with your potions and help fix your broomstick if you have one. I don't care what you are," Charlie murmured, facing her so close she could feel his breath, and her pulse quickened. "I want you more than I can bear...I fear I might do anything for you, given the opportunity."

She tilted her face up as he slipped his hands to her waist and pulled her to him. As desire for him surged through her, tingling in her groin, lips, and belly, she met his gaze. "Are you doing anything tonight?"

"I'm yours if you're mine," he murmured. "Well, even if you aren't."

"What do you mean?" Annabel asked.

"Nothing," he muttered.

Annabel's eyes widened. "After all that, you still wonder if I dallied with the Baron?"

He shrugged. "As I said…"

"Oh, for heaven's sake, Charlie," Annabel shook her head. "Do you really think I would do so the day after kissing you? Do you think so little of me?"

"Plenty of smart women have slept with the Baron," Charlie replied. "He wants more children, and there are many reasons to be on his good side. I understand. As I said, I'm not upset about it." He coughed. "Cecelia informed me with no little satisfaction that you were seen leaving his chambers wearing a nightgown."

"You bloody chin-waggers." Crossing her arms, Annabel added sharply, "The Baron did not touch me, bed me, or even witness me undress. We did nothing in his room except eat, talk, and sleep. I changed in the adjacent servant's quarters—you can ask his maid. Constance? He insisted I wear his late wife's nightgown for reasons I'd rather not dwell upon while I read to him until my voice grew hoarse." She shuddered at the memory.

"Oh, is that all?" Charlie laughed. "What a bloody relief."

"I thought you didn't care." She crossed her arms, frowning. "So why on earth would it be a relief?"

"Why didn't you tell me immediately and spare me the anguish?" He grinned and cocked his head, cutting his eye at her. "You played a game with me."

"What anguish? Again, you said you didn't care," she repeated. "Instead, you listened to others and made up your mind before even talking to me about it."

"Alright, I bloody care, far more than I care to admit," he sighed, rubbing his neck. "But I didn't make up my mind about anything. And neither should you until you've explored all your options."

"Charlie, get off the cross," Annabel said sharply, startling him. "We need the wood."

"A joke." Charlie laughed. "You're so bloody funny. I love that about you."

"Thanks." She smiled despite herself. "What I mean is, I've had enough of your slagging off on yourself. I could easily live the rest of my days without your martyrdom." Saucily, she added, "Frankly, I'd rather be kissing you than hearing you talk about how horrible you think you are."

His laughter resonated throughout the clearing. "Your direct way of speaking is truly refreshing," he confessed with a genuine smile. "It's a quality I find myself deeply drawn to."

"How lovely," she replied. "It has always been my most disparaged trait." Her voice softened as she took his hand, offering reassurance. "Charlie—you're allowed to care. And to feel. I don't share these feelings with anyone; I want to know you better. That's all."

"It's good to hear that," he said, a trace of concern lingering in his eyes. "You weren't harmed by the Baron at all last night?"

"No," she shook her head, vividly recalling the unusual evening. "It was an unexpected turn of events. It turned out to be the anniversary of his late wife's death. We dined in his chambers, and I read to him from The Poetry of John Donne for hours, wearing that silly nightgown as if an apparition of his wife."

"What a bore," Charlie laughed.

"It really was," she agreed, shuddering. "The Baron said he used to do that with Philippa before bed—she would read to him until he fell asleep. He said those were the best nights of his life."

"Understandable, I suppose," Charlie said. She recounted Henry's mumbled words about Philippa in his sleep, and he appeared troubled. "I wonder what he's feeling guilty about. What did he do to her?"

"I am beginning to wonder if he threw her in the dungeon to punish her, like Agatha," she whispered.

"I wouldn't put it past him," Charlie remarked. "Then she never did what he wanted, so she died there? Who knows, perhaps her ghost still haunts this place."

"There was also a bookmark!" Annabel remembered, and closing her eyes, she recited the riddle she had discovered.

When she opened her eyes, Charlie looked at her with unease. "I really don't want to go to the mausoleum."

"That's what I was afraid of," she sighed. "If I got in trouble for going to the library, I would certainly get in trouble for going to the mausoleum."

"Unless we snuck down there at night," he suggested. "Perhaps when the Baron is out of town again. Next week?"

"Yes. Oh, Charlie, I've missed you—your sharp mind, your calming presence, even if only for a day," Annabel sighed. "Do you mind me saying so?"

"I do not mind at all." He looked at her with longing in his gaze.

"How I wish it had been you I was reading to last night," she said softly. "And only you."

"Annabel, I wish I could give you the world," he murmured.

"I don't want it," she whispered. "I only want to read and perhaps to kiss you."

"Fair enough." After a momentary pause, he smiled and asked, "Would–you like to meet me by the stables later this evening?"

"Yes," she said, her voice filled with anticipation. "Very much."

"After dinner?" asked Charlie.

Annabel grinned. "It's a date."

Chapter Sixteen

Getting to Know You

That night, the two lovers met outside. A waxing moon peeked out from behind the clouds, casting its silver glow upon Annabel's face, and Charlie whistled as she drew near. "You are beautiful. I'd attempt to carve your likeness in wood, but fear I could never do you justice."

"Everyone is beautiful in the moonlight." A smile tugged at Annabel's lips. "You flatter me."

"Never," Charlie shook his head, a playful glint in his eyes. "It's not flattery if it's the truth. I'd love to illustrate your fire, your excitement—what your thoughtful expressions do to the curve of your brow. It's captivating."

Their tender moment was interrupted as the moon disappeared behind a cloud, plunging them into darkness. Annabel's gaze shifted towards her farmhouse containing Lise and Agatha, realizing she hadn't been alone with a man in such an intimate setting since her uncomfortable encounter with Richard.

She turned to Charlie, her voice laced with anticipation. "Should we head to the stables? You honestly keep it so clean; I don't mind spending time there if it means we can talk in peace."

"We could do that," Charlie grinned mischievously. "But I had another idea. After roaming around after a match the other night, I discovered a tunnel leading to a long-abandoned room under the library, which bypasses the dungeon completely and connects to the stables. I asked around the servant's quarters why it was not on the list to be cleaned regularly. Apparently, Philippa used it as a study… she'd go straight from the room to the stables, avoiding anyone who might disrupt her from one of those activities. Sometimes, she'd leave food refuse down there, lemon peels, fish scales, and such, and a maid would have to retrieve it. It's thought to be haunted now, so it stands unused." He lowered his voice conspiratorially. "I can take us there no w."

"You're not kidding, are you?" Annabel gasped, her eyes widening with excitement. "Yes, please do!"

She helped him pull back several hay bales, a large canvas sheet, and a heavy piece of wood to reveal the hidden entrance. They replaced the pieces and stealthily entered the tunnel.

Charlie took Annabel's hand and guided her through a maze of passages until they reached a small, dusty door. He unlocked it, removed a board knotted over the handle, peered inside briefly, and then opened the door, gesturing for her to enter.

As Annabel stepped into the room, the flickering light from the torch unveiled a scene frozen in time. The space, nestled deep beneath the castle, was veiled in a thick layer of dust that had settled upon every surface. Weathered shelves sagged under the weight of neglected tomes, their leather covers cracked and faded. Rows upon rows of books stood in solemn silence, bearing witness to the untold stories and lost wisdom in their pages. Delicate cobwebs clung to the corners, remnants of a time when this room was cherished and tended to.

"God's hands," Annabel whispered reverently as Charlie set the torch into a sheath on the wall. The air in the room carried the scent of aged parchment and forgotten knowledge, creating an atmosphere of mystery. Her eyes darted from shelf to shelf, drinking in the beauty before her. The room held the promise of endless hours of knowledge, patiently waiting to be unraveled—but as she skimmed the titles, she shivered as she realized they all had to do with the supernatural or the occult.

Charlie guided her to a small, dusty bookcase. "Just a moment..."

"This place is incredible," she whispered. "Bit dusty, but..."

"Oh, yes," he agreed, feeling around under the bookshelves and pulling a small lever underneath each one. "Leave the dust. Ideally, it should look as though no one was here in this first part of the room, if one was to pop their head in briefly."

"That's going to limit us as far as our activities this evening." She raised her eyebrows playfully. "Unless you had only planned on a conversation?"

"We can do whatever you like." Blushing, Charlie pulled a lever on the bottom shelf and stood, running his hands along the side of the bookshelf. "Conversational or otherwise."

"Tell me more about otherwise," she teased. "What things between men and women do you know of? If you don't mind me asking."

"Let's see..." He considered this, running his hands through his hair. "I had a childhood sweetheart, a relationship which ended with my losing an eye, so that's not a terribly good memory. Shortly before Lise, I dallied with Maggie, then Lise and I went to an orgy a month after our marriage—her idea. I did not couple with any of them, just everything but, mind you. I wouldn't risk leaving someone with a child I couldn't yet support. Lise and I discussed it, but ultimately, she preferred not to, and I wouldn't be able to perform if I didn't think she was equally eager."

"Maggie?" Annabel asked in surprise. "The old cook?"

"That, I have no regrets about." He grinned. "She's a handsome woman who is now remarried to the butcher but happily still fond enough of me to pass on extra food to my wife, friends, and myself. What about you?"

"Well, you know of Richard. We have done nothing but kiss and caress...happily." She sighed. "There was also a man named Paul, the vicar at our church. After two years of hiding our love, he proposed, and we made plans to elope—but he broke it off the next day in favor of another."

"Oh." Charlie looked shaken. "What a cad—how dreadful of him. I'm so sorry you had to endure that."

"Unfortunately, we did—couple, that night he proposed. I was so foolish," she whispered shamefully, stumbling over her words and looking away as she blinked back the anxious, unwelcome tears that had suddenly appeared and took out a handkerchief. "Oh, for the love of God, I am so sorry. I don't know why I'm suddenly so emotional—if you want to take me back to the farmhouse..."

"Of course not. No need for apologies," Charlie said quickly. "If you want me to take you back, I will. But I still want your company if you'd like to provide it."

"Thanks," she hiccupped, looking down. "I was so afraid of what you might think of me. It was not my proudest moment. I worry a bit that I'm ruined."

"You aren't. You can't think it's your fault that a man took advantage of your good nature. He misled you into marriage—that is nothing but his loss." Charlie's voice was filled with affection as he slipped his hand to the side of her face and stroked a tear away with his thumb. "Even if he had not misled you, I wouldn't mind. Know that you are still endlessly compelling and wonderful to me."

She beamed through her tears.

Then Charlie leaned forward and pulled the knob sticking out of the bookcase, and Annabel jumped as the massive piece of furniture suddenly receded, small wooden barriers popping up in front of each line of books.

The entire thing slid into the wall as he put his shoulder into it. He grinned as he jerked his head in the position of the open doorway as she stared in astonishment. "I know, I'm impressed I figured it out, too. This is where I was thinking we could enjoy the evening."

Annabel followed him through where the bookcase had been, examining it in fascination on the way, and stopped suddenly to marvel at the cleanliness of the second room instead of the first. The floor was swept, and the air smelled faintly of lemons. The faded upholstery of a plush mauve sofa matched the quiet, cozy theme of the room and was draped with a patchwork quilt. There was a fading, beautifully painted mural of wild horses against rolling green hills covering one of the walls, and the others were painted softer green. An enormous map of the world was hung.

On the opposite wall, an ornate wooden desk stood adorned with quill pens and ink pots, and an open wooden box was thickly stuffed with parchment. A firmly, sturdy-back chair had flowers and feathers carved into it. Charlie walked to the desk and ran his hands over the surface. "It was filthy from lack of use but with good bones," he remarked. "Now you'd never know—it cleaned up well. I can bring you down here and guard the door anytime you want to read or write in peace outside of the old farmhouse."

"Write?" Annabel asked in surprise. "I'm not a writer. I was a bookbinder, but the Baron destroyed my kit. I'm sticking to farming now, as ordered."

"That's silly. Don't let the Baron ruin your fun," Charlie gestured at the desk. "No one comes down here because they think it's haunted. I figured it's logically your next step. You must write down the one about the possessed hand, Gavin's friendship with the horse Panza, and any others you have tucked away. Lise told me of a tale you spun to her and Colley about a wig?" He laughed.

"Oh, those are just silly stories," she muttered. "Silly stories made to entertain friends in the moment. Not something that should be written down for posterity."

"When repeated throughout a community with this much appreciation, they're more than that. The twins always ask their nurse for yours; she knows them, mind you, but she can't spin the yarns as well as you can. You could do great things with your stories if you wrote them down." He shrugged. "You don't have to. But you could."

"Charlie," Annabel whispered, her voice filled with wonder as she finished looking around the cozy space. "Did you clean out this second room for our meeting and my writing?"

"Well, I only discovered it today," he protested. "I didn't have enough time to clean the entire space. But I thought you might like it."

"You were right." She grinned, settling on the sofa and pulling the neatly folded quilt over it onto her lap. "Join me?"

Charlie sat down beside her. "How have you been feeling? I know it's been an extra burden for you—taking care of the laundry, tending to the fields, managing the house."

"It helps that I'm doing it for good people," Annabel replied. She felt a sudden chill and rubbed her hands together for warmth, but her feelings for him burned brighter than ever. Changing the subject, she asked, "Can we come back again? Will anyone notice?"

"Yes. No one ever comes in here—I checked." Charlie shook his head. "The main reason people believe this room is haunted is because Philippa used it to store her books and simulacra of ghosts and spirits."

Annabel's eyes swept the room again in light of this new information, landing on the desk where a red book lay face down on the blotter. She smiled, feeling a surge of curiosity. "What ghost story is that?"

"Poetry," he replied, wiping his hands on a handkerchief within his tunic before picking up the book. "I brought it myself. Shall I read you some? I also have wine."

"Oh, yes, please, to all of it." she agreed.

Charlie retrieved a bottle of wine and two worn pewter tankards from the desk's bottom drawer. He handed her one, and they both took a sip, savoring the moment. After Charlie had set his glass back down and gingerly opened the book, squinting at the delicate text that adorned soft yellowed pages, he muttered under his breath, brows knitting together in frustration. With some hesitation, he walked over to the desk and gently pulled open the top drawer.

Casting a quick glance at Annabel, he whispered, "You must never tell anyone about this," before slipping on a pair of slim spectacles crafted from wood and glass.

Annabel couldn't help but playfully swoon, draping herself into the quilt as if overcome by his transformation. He scowled at her, a twinkle of amusement in his eyes. With his glasses firmly in place, he returned to the book, ready to delve into its verses. "Can you read without them?" she asked, her voice laced with curiosity.

Charlie nodded. "Yes, but it's a struggle, especially with small words. A worthwhile one, mind you, but it's definitely easier with them on," he admitted with a hint of vulnerability. "I don't need them over both eyes now, of course, but I find the balance of glasses more appealing than something like a monocle."

"I quite agree," she said, taking the excuse of admiring them to draw closer to him. "They're absolutely marvelous."

He smiled. "They're also always hidden—I don't want to invite teasing or risk them getting broken. Keep it under your hat that I have them, if you don't mind."

Annabel's heart swelled with warmth, realizing the significance of his willingness to wear the glasses in her presence. "Where on earth did you get such things?" she asked, her eyes tracing the unique contours of the frames. "They're exquisite."

Charlie smiled, pride glimmering in his eyes. "I'm fortunate to know a merchant in town who deals in such treasures. The Sutars," he explained. "I'd be happy to introduce you."

Picking up the book again, he flipped through the pages until he found a passage that captured his attention. "Drink to me only with thine eyes, And I will pledge with mine," he began, his gaze meeting hers with a tenderness that made her heart skip a beat. "Or leave a kiss but in the cup, and I'll not look for wine." Clearing his throat, he added, "Ben Jonson."

Charlie turned the page. "Had we but world enough and time, this coyness, lady, were no crime. We would sit down and think which way to walk and pass our long love's day. Andrew Marvell."

Annabel's gaze remained fixed on him, her heart fluttering with each word. The room seemed to fade away, leaving only the two of them.

"She weaves through words, the classics dear, with eloquence, her voice sincere. Her wisdom, like a hidden gem, should yet be writ, if not now, when?" He grinned at her, and she felt lightning dancing along her insides. "Charlie Wright."

Suspiciously, she looked at the page. "Did you really come up with that all on your own?"

"Hand to heart." He shrugged. "I don't always have carving tools, and I have to do something to keep my mind off this place."

"I actually forgot you could write poetry," she admitted. "But I remember the poem Richard stole from you. That was beautiful, Charlie... I've never had a poem written about me before."

"Not that you know of, anyway." He winked at her, and she blushed.

Smiling at him ruefully, she whispered, "I appreciate your shameless push for me to write. Maybe I'll take you up on it."

Charlie set the book down and reached for the quilt that had started to slip off her lap. Draping it over her shoulders, he rubbed her arms through the blanket, his touch comforting and electrifying. "Take care not to catch a cold," he murmured. Then, he removed his glasses, delicately placing them on the side table, and leaned closer.

At that moment, time seemed to stand still. Annabel could feel the heat of his breath against her skin, her entire being consumed by anticipation.

Charlie closed the distance between them, and their lips met in a kiss that ignited a fire within. It was a kiss filled with the yearning building between them for far too long. The intoxicating taste of desire lingered on their tongues as they surrendered to the depths of their shared longing...but his fervent kisses did not stop at her lips. They traveled a path of fiery sensations, exploring the soft curve of her neck with tender nibbles, sending shivers cascading down her spine.

Annabel's breath hitched in her throat, a gasp escaping her lips as his warm breath teased her earlobe, stirring a whirlwind of sensations within her. His hands caressed the contours of her back, leaving trails of fervent desire in their wake as they slipped downward, then pulled back briefly to look at her earnestly. "Is this all right?"

Overwhelmed by the intense connection that enveloped them, Annabel summoned the strength to express her yearning. "Oh, Charlie," she gasped, her voice a symphony of pleasure and longing as he momentarily pulled away. "Of course it is. Please don't stop now..."

Quickly, he moved the book of poetry from the quilt to the desk, and a deep, throaty moan escaped him, its resonance echoing through the room, his voice aching with desire. With the next kiss, she intertwined her hands through his thick locks, feeling the texture of his hair, which curled in short waves above his ears.

The faint scent of wood oil, sweet hay, and beeswax mingled with the intoxicating aroma of books, engulfing them both. Delicately, she traced her nails along his scalp, eliciting a guttural groan of pleasure.

She shivered with anticipation, and after she whispered yes to the question on his face, he slowly unlaced her bodice. Carefully, he traced the outline of her nipples, sliding his warm hands over them, slowly kissing down her stomach, back up to her torso, kissing her breasts, lips, and neck. Dipping his head, he brought one of her breasts into his mouth, and she moaned with pleasure as he sucked gently on her nipple until her jaw went slack.

Finally, when she would have done practically anything if he would only keep touching her with such intentional adoration, he whispered into the hollow of her collarbone, "Can I...slip under your skirts?"

"Oh!" This caught Annabel slightly off guard, and her eyes flew open. "I don't have the birth control tincture on me; it's in my dresser in the house." She spoke softly, faltering as he kissed slowly up her neck. "Besides..."

                    MATILDA LOCKWOOD

"No," His head came up. "I'm not trying to do something like that on our first evening together. I told you I wouldn't risk that without being able to care for you and a child…as much as I'd like to."

Annabel smiled. "Then what do you mean, under my skirts, you silly man? Massaging my feet?"

Charlie laughed. "No, although I'm happy to do that too." He kissed down to her breasts, then lifted her legs atop his lap. Running his hands slowly up her stockings, watching her curious eyes as he reached her garters, he paused his hands to look at her lasciviously. "If you're interested, this is when I'd part your legs and dive between them to spell the poetry silently with my tongue. Well…you don't have to be silent."

"Oh!" she exclaimed, blushing furiously. "Well. I've never done that. Are you sure you want to?" Her tone was skeptical. "You are talking about…."

"Yes. Would you like to?" Charlie asked, sliding his long, deft fingers down her sensitive legs to massage her calves. "I'll stop any time you like."

"There's a play I've read bits of, Venus and Adonis…" she recalled. "They…mentioned it there. Graze…" She swallowed. "Graze on my…"

He grinned. "Graze on my lips, and if those hills are dry, stray lower, where the pleasant fountains lie?"

A thrill ran through Annabel, and she wondered if it was from the quote, which seemed to roll off his nimble tongue, or the anticipation. "But you like to do that?" she asked nervously. "To a farmer?"

"Very much, Annabel," he whispered. "Be you farmer, bookbinder, or writer."

"Even though I'm not a virgin?" she stammered, hating herself for a moment, but he only shrugged.

"What a fool that man was," said Charlie. "No, I don't care if you're a virgin. It doesn't matter to me or change how I feel about you. Your past is your business. I hope it was consensual at the time—aside from how he misled you?"

"Yes," she said. "It made sense since I thought we'd soon be married. I just wanted to mention it in case you didn't want to."

He smiled happily, his hand sliding to hers. "I still want to. Do you?"

"Yes..." she admitted weakly, flopping back on the blanket, her cheeks flaming. "Yes, please." She suddenly felt slightly out of her depth, but not enough to stop him. His strong hands were still massaging her calves in no hurry; his touch felt blissfully indulgent, and then he gently kissed along her inner thigh, making her shiver. His thumbs stroked the soft skin where her thighs became her hips, and her feelings became increasingly animalistic as he continued.

Charlie's roving mouth worked up her legs, through parts of her body she knew little of, then just as she buried her hands in the cushions beneath them, he glided his tongue into her. She moaned, pulling her hand up over her mouth to stifle herself. He flattened his tongue then and held it against the most sensitive part of her, letting it soften and flex again and again as his hot breath exhaled against her nakedness, and she let out a long, shuddering breath.

She was surprised to realize that she was suddenly shy no longer, at least past her stomach...in fact, she was practically bucking her hips against his mouth, and he was cupping her buttocks as he buried his face in her with wild abandon.

Then suddenly, after several minutes of bliss, the pressure within her, which bubbled in her like a cauldron all day long—finally, at long last exploded, and she came in a wave of pleasure, grabbing his shoulders, running her fingers down to grasp his scalp, satisfied and gasping.

As their heartbeats gradually slowed, he shifted to lie beside her, their bodies still basking in the afterglow of their passionate union. A moment of serene tranquility enveloped them, their shared intimacy creating an unspoken bond that words could never fully capture.

With a casual tone, he broke the silence. "That was alright?" he asked, sincerity shining through his gaze.

Her eyes met his, searching for any sign of jest, but found only tenderness. A soft smile graced her lips as she let out a breathless whisper,

"Yes, yes, it was." The intensity of their connection lingered in her voice, and she marveled at the deep satisfaction and contentment that washed over her.

Concern suddenly washed across her. "And what can I, er...do for you?"

"You already have," he assured her, his voice infused with warmth. "I have just...taken care of my ardor while enjoying yours. I'm afraid it's been too long for me to hold off." He delicately folded a handkerchief, which he slipped into another handkerchief within his breeches pocket.

Relief washed over her, mingling with a sense of exhilaration. "Oh, grand," she smiled, her heart feeling lighter. "I'm so glad to hear it. Perhaps I can do something for you next time? That was...exquisite, Charlie."

"Yes, it certainly was," he sighed. "I feel like I've seen God again between your legs."

"You are an irreverent imp," she laughed. "Please never stop."

"I'm becoming far too fond of you with each moment," he admitted. "I fear you are melting my reservations, and perhaps we should continue."

"I fear that not only are you correct, but it will be well worth it," she offered. "I'm willing to wait for our relationship to become public until the time is right and we are both publicly unattached, but I make no mistake, I want to do this again." She blushed. "Well, a meeting, I mean. I wouldn't mind the other thing, too."

"Agreed," he whispered. "I'm already dreaming of our next encounter. I want to know everything about you, Annabel Barlow."

Their bodies melted into one another, their embrace becoming a sanctuary from the outside world. With each brush of their lips, a current of desire surged through them, binding their souls together in a dance of shared longing and affection. It was a moment etched in their hearts, a stolen fragment of time where nothing else mattered except the connection they shared.

As they pulled away, their breaths mingling, Annabel's eyes met Charlie's, the intensity of their gazes speaking volumes. They lay there, wrapped in the warmth of the quilt and the blossoming love between them, their hearts entwined in a dance of hope and possibility.

Chapter Seventeen

THE MARKETPLACE

The air crackled with anticipation as the day of the baron's birthday celebration arrived at Castle Rowley. The grand event was set to be a lavish affair, complete with a magnificent feast, joyous dancing, and an influx of hundreds of guests. It was the largest gathering the castle had seen in years.

Annabel's spirits soared as she reveled in the continuously joyful atmosphere. Lise's injured leg had healed remarkably, and Agatha proved to be an excellent companion, lightening her workload and bringing warmth to their interactions. Amid it all, she and Charlie continued to share blissful nights in the secret room beneath the castle, gradually making it their haven with each visit. Often, he would read one of the many old books afterward, and she tried her hand with writing, always carefully hiding her pages afterward.

One day, as Annabel went to see Lise in the cellar, her friend had news that would leave her stunned. "Annabel, I was just about to come find you. You won't believe what I've heard," Lise exclaimed, her excitement evident as she closed the door behind them. "You've won!" she whispered excitedly, clapping her hands together in glee.

Annabel's expression showed her confusion. "What are you talking about?"

"Well, I visited the pub to see Colley yesterday. You remember him, my actor friend who got us into the play," Lise explained. "Do you recall entering that short story idea into the bowl for the contest?"

"Oh, *that*. "Annabel's memory stirred, and she replied, "A jest inspired by wine. I never expected it to be taken seriously. Besides, I didn't even use my real name."

Lise's eyes sparkled with excitement as she revealed, "Only because women weren't allowed to enter. But your submission, under 'Daegal Godwin,' which might I remind you, you told us both of at the table, won the contest. They've been looking for you. Colley remembered that funny name and told them he knew the man, and they instructed him to find you to collect your winnings."

"Winnings?" Annabel gasped. "How much?"

"Three pounds!" Lise squealed in delight. "And a dictionary!"

"Three pounds and a dictionary?" Annabel echoed, astonished. "That can't be right."

"It *is*, Annabel. And I believe it's only the beginning," Lise beamed. "You have some talent, my friend, and should run with it as far as possible."

Annabel smiled hesitantly, daring to hope. "Do you really think so?" Before Lise could respond, Annabel waved her hand dismissively. "Oh, but women aren't allowed to enter the contest. I would get into terrible trouble. Tell Colley to have them give it to someone else."

"Don't you dare even think about forfeiting," Lise asserted, her voice firm. "All we need to do is find a man to pose as Daegal Godwin, collect the winnings, and then return it to us. We might have to offer him a small portion as compensation."

"Oh, that's all?" Annabel chuckled. "How many men do you know who would dare to break the law, impersonate another person, and retrieve the money without keeping it all for himself?"

"Killjoy." Lise rolled her eyes. "Some actors assume different names when they perform. It's not unheard of for writers to do the same, penning their works under a pseudonym to protect their true identity."

"Do such people who would help in this *particular* situation exist?" Annabel questioned skeptically.

The laundress shrugged. "Why don't you ask Charlie? He has a family in the marketplace who used to work with his family before he was cut off from the industry, and they have the most opportune connections. Sometimes, he meets people at the river when the baron is away—I believe he does woodcarving jobs for them, and they give him money or things for bribes. Maybe there's something there."

"The Sutars." Annabel remarked curiously, "Perhaps I should ask him to come, too."

Lise sighed and replied, "Unfortunately, the baron forbids servants or unaccompanied women from summoning a carriage on the Rowley account. Charlie's forbidden outright. And they're exorbitantly expensive if you have to pay for them yourself." She wrinkled her nose. "So, if the person he thinks of is at the marketplace, you might want to ask him if he's got any ideas for that as well. Colley can borrow the carriage he has access to, in order to bring you to collect your winnings, though."

"Thanks." Annabel smiled. "I'll go talk to him now. I won't be able to get a thing done with this on my mind otherwise."

Finding Charlie mending the stable door, Annabel wasted no time relaying Lise's news—after first admiring his bent, muscular form. He smiled broadly, and her heart beat a little faster. "Congratulations, that's fantastic!"

"Especially if anything actually comes from it." She laughed. "Do you have a contact who could help me, perhaps in the player community? I'm not holding my breath, but unfortunately, I will probably need a man's assistance to collect the prize."

Charlie pondered momentarily before responding. "I'm sure my friend Kunal would be willing to help. He associates with the players and has a penchant for supporting playwrights and struggling artists."

"Really," she said in surprise. "That's handy. Kunal...what's he like?"

"Trustworthy," said Charlie. "Literate and with the physique of a veritable giant; you'll be safe in his company when collecting your winnings. He must be between six and seven feet tall, I think? He's strong, kind, good manners. You can find him at the Sutar stall—they're the woodcarvers I work with." He smiled wistfully. "I don't get to see them much anymore, but they're like a second family to me."

"They made the beautiful wooden glasses, I take it?" Annabel guessed.

"Yes," Charlie nodded. "Kunal's mother Sarala designed the glasses, and his father Manik carved them out of Sheesham—Indian rosewood. They also have a daughter, Rupa, who mostly manages their accounts, but she carves as well."

"An entire family of carvers," Annabel sighed. "How wonderful. I like their names—where are they from?"

"They came over from India," Charlie replied. "But if you'd like to hear the story..."

"I would." She grinned shyly. "Where is India?"

"It's to the east of Europe and separated from England by a vast expanse of land and sea." Charlie went to the basin on the side of the stables to scrub his hands with a bar of yellow soap, then gestured for her to follow him inside. "The Sutars come from the lands within Rajasthan, amidst the northwestern territories of India, a realm of princely states and a stronghold of Rajput pride. It's a place where the air is thick with tales and traditions." He closed the door behind them and brought the bolt down.

"What marvel," she sighed. "I've never been outside of England. Have you?"

"Only in stories, which might not be as good, but it's something." They shared a grin at this.

"Go on about the Sutars," she urged.

Charlie continued, "Captain Harrington of the East India Company chanced upon their stall and, bewitched by their products, namely a carved wooden panel of the Mahabharata..."

"The what?" Annabel asked curiously.

"The Mahabharata. It's one of their grand epics." He smiled in memory.

"Harrington offered them a life here as their benefactor; they discussed terms at length and agreed to brave the journey."

"Incredibly brave," she whispered. "I can't imagine traveling so far. They didn't have any trouble?"

He shrugged. "When they arrived, they were like a fish out of water. But Harrington is wealthy; he secured them a place in the market, and soon, their booth became a sensation. Kunal's father Manik's intricate works were like magnets, drawing people from all corners, while Kunal catered to the everyday Englishman with his smaller crafts, becoming one of my best mates. His sister Rupa also carves, but her main strength is doing their accounts. And his mother Sarala regales customers with stories of their homeland, making every piece seem like a portal to India."

"Storytelling through carpentry," Annabel breathed. "How marvelous. How did you come to meet them?" asked Annabel.

"The late Baroness Philippa Rowley connected to their benefactor. One of her many business relationships with artists and their investors that dried up upon her disappearance." Charlie sighed. "He's a confident man. Henry hates him."

"Why?" Annabel asked curiously.

"Oh, the Baron makes no secret that he despises immigrants," Charlie sighed. "It could be why he forbade my carving. My father was best friends with Manik, and they worked together mostly on musical instruments. I used to play with their children, Kunal and Rupa."

Ooh," Annabel clamored. "Can you play a musical instrument?"

"No," Charlie laughed. "And Manik mostly makes furniture now. His daughter Rupa makes the instruments."

She nodded. "What does Kunal make?"

"Games. Chess sets. Wooden boxes. I can mimic his box designs, but you can still see the difference side by side," Charlie sighed. "I'll write you a note. If you deliver it to Kunal at the market, he can help, and he has a horse and cart at his disposal. Come inside."

Slipping into the back of the stables, he loosened the hayloft board and drew out a wooden box with parchment and quill and ink, beginning to write a message.

"That solves one problem," Annabel said. "But do you know how I should get to the market? Lise mentioned it's costly and that you're not allowed to go. I don't have any reason I can think of to go to the market today."

Charlie paused in his writing. "Frederick needs to collect his coat from the tailor at the market today."

"Frederick—the Baron's son?" Annabel exclaimed in surprise. "Why on Earth would he help me?"

Charlie scowled. "Ever since he found the letter where his mother admitted that we share the same father, he's been eager to establish a connection with me, albeit not in front of his father, for both our sakes. He wants to be secret brothers or some such nonsense."

"That's actually rather endearing," Annabel remarked with a grin. "So, he might be willing to assist me on your behalf?"

"I can't say for certain," Charlie sighed. "But he recently delivered a heartfelt speech to me expressing his everlasting desire for an older brother. He offered to help me if I needed a favor or wanted to practice fencing together sometime." Chuckling softly, he added, "As if I've ever held a sword in my life."

"Now is your chance." A smile curved Annabel's lips. "Is there anything I can return from the market for you?"

Charlie nodded appreciatively. "If you speak to Kunal, he'll give you something on my behalf." He handed her a flat wooden box and inserted the note inside. "Would you also deliver this to him? But refrain from opening it," he teased, giving her a playful wink. "I'll go find Frederick."

Hastily changing her clothes and attending to her duties with the field hands, she retrieved a small shopping list from the friends in her house and money from Lise and secured her rucksack. Carefully wrapping a scarf around the wooden box to protect it, she stowed it deep within her bag.

As she made her way toward the castle path where the carriages awaited, she noticed Frederick emerging from the imposing doors of the keep, his face etched with a sullen expression. She had often seen him wandering the castle grounds, always wearing a frown. "You must be Annabel," he stated matter-of-factly.

She nodded, feeling a hint of apprehension in the air. Frederick didn't look entirely happy. "Are you...going to the market?"

"Yes, come on then," he sighed, walking toward the carriage and opening the door for her, then quickly climbing in through his own side, his impatience evident.

Perplexed but undeterred, Annabel climbed into the carriage, closing the door behind her. "You don't seem particularly thrilled about this," she observed.

"Did he tell you all?" Frederick inquired, his voice lowered as he covered his mouth slightly, gesturing toward the carriage driver. He leaned closer to her and whispered, "Short, nondescript answers that reveal nothing. The driver is listening."

Surprised, Annabel replied, "Yes, he did."

"Well, I'd rather spend time with him than with you. No offense meant," he added as an afterthought.

"That's not a great start," she admitted evenly. "From what I have surmised, he usually prefers the company of those who are more polite."

"Perhaps you're right," he muttered, glancing out the window. "What makes a married barley farmwife so special, anyway?"

Annabel faced the window and rolled her eyes. "Not much, I suppose. We appreciate things about each other."

"He mentioned you can read," Frederick mused, his gaze fixed on the passing scenery. "That's probably it. You're not as pretty as Nancy. Again, no offense meant."

A sudden chill ran through Annabel's veins. "What did you say about Nancy?"

Frederick turned to her, a flicker of fear momentarily crossing his features. "Nothing. Clearly, you're more his type since he's actually plunging forward. Forget I said anything."

Annabel narrowed her eyes. "I thought you and Charlie never spoke before recently."

"We didn't. I mean, everyone knows about what happened..." Frederick's discomfort was more evident than ever, his eyes darting nervously. "Let's not talk about it. Er...on my orders. Silence, please."

Biting her lip, Annabel's mind raced, and her stomach turned nervously as the carriage carried them the remaining way to market.

Upon reaching their destination, Frederick grumbled, "Meet back here in two hours," before swiftly departing without waiting for her response.

Annabel took a moment to observe her surroundings, appreciating her height from the carriage before she descended into the crowd. It had been some time since she had roamed a market alone, without children tagging along. Slowly, she maneuvered through the bustling crowds, inching closer to the various stalls. She had set aside some extra coins to indulge in something for herself, and her eyes scanned the seemingly endless array of goods, feeling overwhelmed by the choices.

With her fingers dipping into her rucksack to reassure herself of the box's safety, she began her market exploration at the Sutar booth. Hesitating briefly, her gaze sweeping over the vibrant landscape, she meandered until she reached the stall. Surveying the exquisite wooden wares on display, she inhaled the intoxicating scent of various types of wood.

Her eyes traced the myriad hand-carved spoons, bowls, inlaid boxes, puzzles, games, toys, frames, talismans, beads and jewelry, trays, walking sticks, and animal figurines adorned the stall. "God's fingers," she whispered in awe, a sense of reverence filling her. As Annabel lifted her gaze, she locked eyes with a man with tawny golden skin, whose presence felt as solid as a boulder. He seemed to peer through the crowd without singling out any individual. "Spoons on sale," he called. "It's four spoons for one shilling."

"Do...do you...is Kunal here?" she stammered nervously. "Your wares are magnificent."

"Thank you," The man nodded. "I'm Kunal. Who's asking?"

Summoning her courage, Annabel began, "I'm Annabel Barlow." She retrieved the box, with the letter resting atop it. "Charlie Wright, from Castle Rowley sent you this letter and box." She lowered her voice. "The most beautiful box I've ever seen, apart from your wares here."

A smile stretched across Kunal's face, and he reached out, his long-fingered hands accepting the letter and the box. "You're right. He's getting better." Upon carefully unfolding the letter, he raised an intrigued eyebrow at her. "Did you read this or open the box?" Kunal inquired.

"Of course not," she responded honestly. Though the temptation to read Charlie's words had crossed her mind during the carriage ride, she had been too preoccupied with her thoughts on what Frederick had said to peek.

Kunal read the letter as Annabel perused their selection and selected four spoons, two pencils, and a bookmark. "So, you're the writer then?" he mused, squinting at her with an impenetrable expression.

"Yes," she admitted nervously. "I write, or at least I try to. I haven't been published, of course. But I've been crafting stories in my mind since I was a child. And, well, something I wrote—a mere idea—won a contest, and..."

"Sure, it's all in the letter," he interrupted, his gaze fixed upon her. "I'll do it." A broad smile graced his face as he brushed off his imposing shoulders. "Daegal Godwin is a grand name, and I'd be proud to portray him so you can claim your prize. By the by, what was the story about? That's not in here."

Annabel proceeded to outline the tale, pausing to answer questions and provide clarifications when needed.

"I like it," Kunal exclaimed, rubbing his hands together in excitement. "Just let me know when and where. I don't mind lending a hand to a female playwright starting her journey."

"I don't know if I'm a female playwright," she said nervously.

"If the playhouse likes your idea and you've won a contest, they likely want you to make it into a full play for them." He shrugged. "Are you planning to reveal yourself as a woman once you succeed, or do you prefer to work behind the scenes, with me as your frontman?"

"I'm not entirely sure," she confessed. "I thought of it one night out of frustration."

Kunal nodded in understanding. "Our best writing often stems from our emotions," he remarked. "You'll figure it out. Take your time to consider. Shall we arrange to retrieve the winnings on Tuesday? I can bring my horse and cart to the castle."

"Yes, thank you," Annabel beamed. "Are you a writer as well, or an actor?"

Kunal shook his head. "Neither. I'm better with my hands than my words. However, I can bluff convincingly; I admire plays, and I have a love for reading."

"Will it put you in danger to assume an identity?" Annabel asked in a worried voice. "His, would it even work?"

He shrugged. "I'll tell our benefactor I'm interested in playwriting. He'll write a letter of recommendation for the stage name preferred. It's no trouble."

She was surprised. "It's as simple as that?"

"I shouldn't think there would be more to it than that." He smiled warmly. "Harrington will be thrilled that the family who has made him so much money wants to branch out further."

"Why would you help me?" Annabel asked. "You seem very friendly, but it all seems like a terrible inconvenience for you. Looking at all you do here, it's hard to imagine it would be worth your while." Kunal leaned forward and spoke in a low voice. "Everyone in my family is passionate about something. My sister has her numbers, and my dad has his furniture. I like the plays, people, playing chess and games with them. And my mother—my mother does a bit of everything." He glanced around discreetly. "Officially, she does most of the sales that really make people want to buy, but her real love is for storytelling. She holds workshops, you know, where she tells stories while carving them and invites others to do the same."

"Really..." Annabel raised her eyebrows, a grin spreading across her face. "I had no idea. That's truly wonderful." She bit her lip. "Your mother isn't here today, is she?"

"Of course she is," Kunal assented, pulling a nearby rope that emitted a faint gonging noise from the back of the tent. "So is my sister."

In no time, a pretty young woman emerged. She had long, plaited dark hair, dancing eyes, and a smile that fairly shone across her tawny face. Wood shavings adorned her apron, and she appeared impatient. "What's happening, Kunal?" she inquired, eyes on Annabel as she offered a small wave.

"Rupa, this is Annabel." He jerked his thumb in her direction. "Charlie's friend. Annabel, this is my sister, Rupa Sutar."

Annabel weakly waved back. "Hello."

"Annabel's got a box from Charlie, and it's intact," Kunal explained, a glimmer of excitement in his eyes. She's a writer."

"Well, I..." Annabel dithered. "I'm not published. I don't know if you can say I'm..."

"Really!" Rupa's eyes lit up. "Oh, please bring it back here. Kunal, can you lift the barrier? Thank you. Annabel, come back this way! Don't be shy. Any friend of Charlie's is a friend of ours." With that, she disappeared into the shadows, passing through a flap in the tent stall.

Chapter Eighteen

THE SUTAR FAMILY

As Annabel followed Rupa into the tent, she gasped, her eyes widening as she slowly took in the room before her.

It was a wooden wonderland, a realm of intricate beauty. The room was adorned with various exquisitely carved wooden objects, some painted with tiny scenes. There were chairs carved with a scene of the sun setting over the river. Annabel breathed deeply as she walked further in and inhaled the faint, pleasant scent: a combination of freshly carved wood and just a hint of aromatic spices.

She continued to take in the roomful of treasures, Rupa watching her in bemusement as she removed her apron. Annabel noticed walking sticks in a corner carved intricately from top to bottom, which looked solid and hardy. Beautifully carved jewelry boxes depicted a handsome couple in a forest. A table stood proudly in the center of the room with a beautiful tray carved elaborately with flowers, in the process of being inlaid with brass. Tearing her eyes away from this mesmerizing sight, Annabel retrieved the small box from her pocket and handed it to Rupa. "But it's locked," she cautioned.

Rupa carefully lifted the tray to another surface and placed Charlie's box on the table. She nodded, a mischievous wink in her eye. "Have you tried to open it?" Rupa asked.

"No!" Annabel protested. "Why would I?"

"It's just a joke." Rupa chuckled, shaking her head. "When he sent the box with someone else before, they attempted to pick the lock with a hairpin."

"On my grandmother's grave, I promise I would never do that," Annabel assured her.

"As a result, Charlie can be quite secretive. He doesn't trust easily, that one," Rupa said with affection in her tone. "We've been missing him."

"I completely understand if you'd rather not show me what it is," Annabel said. "It's your business, and I'm content enough without prying, though I'm certainly a devoted admirer."

"Do you have a fondness for woodcarvings, then?" Rupa inquired. "Kunal probably wouldn't have sent you back here if you didn't, but..." She shrugged.

"Of course I do," Annabel assured her, her eyes gliding over the surrounding masterpieces. "I can hardly fathom the artistry involved. It seems like pure magic, to tell you the truth."

"That's good enough for me." Rupa walked toward a large box in the room and unlocked it with a key hanging around her neck. Within that box, she found another key, which she used, wearing gloves, to open the smaller chest that Charlie had sent with Annabel.

Curious, Annabel peered over the box to glimpse its contents. Nestled within, carefully cushioned with straw, lay several crescent-shaped pieces of wood, all a few inches long, with intricate grooves across t hem.

Rupa leaned against a stool and crossed her arms across her chest. "I'll give you three guesses as to what they are."

Annabel laughed. "I fear I shall need more than three."

"Go on then." The other girl grinned.

"Perhaps these are ornamental carvings meant to adorn furniture or walls?" Annabel guessed. "I see the sun over the river on the back of the chairs, so maybe these are moons?"

"Good guess. The sun is setting over the Ganges." Rupa smiled again. "But no."

Annabel stepped up to the table to see the pieces closer. "Could they be a tool for working with wool or flax? Or maybe they're used in cooking or baking?"

"Maybe not," Rupa replied.

Flicking her eyes back to the tent flap where she had left Kunal, Annabel guessed, "Could they be pieces for a game, like draughts?"

Rupa laughed. "Have you ever played draughts?"

"No," admitted Annabel. "Are they religious in nature? Tokens or amulets of ward off evil spirits or bring good luck?"

"They're religious to my nature," Rupa said, a faraway look in her eyes. "But no."

"Some sort of tackle for fishing - a fancy lure?" Annabel frowned as Rupa shook her head. "Fasteners for clothing. Children's toys?"

"I'm afraid not." Rupa smiled. "I've enjoyed this, but I'd rather put you at ease." She went behind Annabel to a padded cart and carefully lifted out a beautifully carved and polished instrument with a round end and a long neck.

"Now I remember Charlie said you make instruments," Annabel breathed. "I feel like a fool. It's beautiful...what is it called?"

"It's a sitar," Rupa replied. "And this piece..." She took one of the carved pieces from Charlie's box. "Is the heart of the instrument. The bridge. It's called a jawari." She tilted it in the light to show off the grooves. "The sitar's unique sound comes from the strings vibrating over it." Rupa nodded to the stool she had been leaning against. "Have a seat, and we can see how he did."

"I'd love it," Annabel said, taking a seat. "The instrument, I mean. I've heard not much more than a fiddle and a flute."

Rupa carefully positioned the jawari on the sitar, then plucked a string, producing a twangy note that resonated throughout the large tent. "Oh, that's nice." She turned it, then played a haunting melody. "That's Raag Bhairavi...it's better when accompanied, mind you."

"I wouldn't know it," Annabel whispered. "But it's mesmerizing."

Rupa nodded. "Yes, he did well with this. I'll fit the others later." With a wink, she played Greensleeves while Annabel clasped her hands in delight.

"You are wonderful! It's marvelous how you pluck many strings while playing." Annabel shook her head. "You're very skilled and practiced."

"Why, thank you," Rupa grinned, then, after some hesitation, sang aloud while she played the next song. "It was a lover and his lass, with a —"

"With a hey!" Annabel joined in, and they sang together. "And a ho, and a hey nonino! That pretty country folks would lie. In springtime, the only pretty ring time, when birds do sing...hey ding ding; sweet lovers love the spring!"

They laughed, and Rupa set the instrument down carefully, a bemused look upon her face.

Annabel stood. "That was marvelous. You know As You Like It!"

"Thank my ma," Rupa rolled her eyes in mock annoyance, then smiled. "She taught me many of the bard's songs when teaching me English."

"Well, I've never heard anything like such playing," Annabel nodded appreciatively.

"I can tell. "Rupa smiled. "My family has been making wooden things for generations. I have the training but don't love forming each jawari. They're finicky, and Charlie's great at them. My father Manik taught Lucas, Charlie's father." She raised her eyebrows archly. "You must be a close friend of Charlie's if he trusts you to carry his wares?"

"Yes," Annabel replied, trying to keep the fondness in her voice. "I moved to Castle Rowley a few months ago, and Charlie has been one of the high points. Alongside Lise, of course. They've been terrific friends to me."

"He faced a great injustice at his trial before the Baron for his debts," Rupa remarked. "I remember it well. Our benefactor testified on his behalf when we asked him to, although it didn't yield enough to squash old Henry's connections at court." She sighed regarding the box. "He's a talented amateur carver, one of the best I've ever seen. Too bad no one will hire him except for us since the Baron seems to own far too many people in this town."

"Exactly," Annabel sighed. "He's a monster, the Baron, to all around him. I've first-hand knowledge."

Rupa put the sitar away. "Did Charlie tell you not to divulge his involvement in these woodcarvings? Not only is he not supposed to carve himself, but the Baron doesn't look kindly upon businesses like ours from those who aren't local."

"Yes, he did. May I?" Annabel gestured toward Charlie's creations. "It's a shame that the Baron is so narrow in his view."

"He thinks we're all dirty. Speaking of which…" Rupa handed her a cloth while mimicking scrubbing her fingers. "*All* people are dirty. Wipe your hands thoroughly with these first, please, and put on the gloves."

"Of course." Annabel went to work on her hands with the towel Rupa handed her.

Rupa tilted her head. "It's funny, but you clean your hands like Charlie does." Suddenly, the other girl gave her a knowing look. "You're not…involved with him, are you? Not for nothing, but you seem like his type, and you've got a particular *look* in your eye when you speak of him…"

"Well, he's married," Annabel replied cautiously, studying Rupa's expression before she went back to looking through the jawari pieces. "And so am I, actually. Though, it's a bit complicated."

"Well, I know Lise," Rupa shrugged. "And I know all of it. So, again—*are* you involved with him? I won't tell." She smiled. "I would be happy that he's happy, I promise you."

Annabel hesitated for a moment before answering. "Yes, but please do keep it a secret." Summoning her courage, she continued, before she lost her nerve, "You don't have to answer, but I must admit to some concern about living in Nancy's shadow. Charlie cared for her deeply, didn't he?"

"Oh, goodness," Rupa exclaimed. "Yes, he did. I'm surprised he mentioned it. He usually avoids discussing her at all costs. That whole horrid thing with his eye…" She shuddered.

"His eye…" Annabel's guilt and curiosity battled each other, and she considered coming clean. "Of course. I'm sorry to bring it up—I don't want to hurt him either."

Rupa's following words did little to assuage her unease. "Don't worry about Nancy. She's long gone now, and if Charlie is finally reaching a point where he can talk about it comfortably, that's a positive sign. It's a sign of healing." She nodded encouragingly.

"Thank you," Annabel sighed. "I appreciate your kind words."

"Of course, I won't say anything to anyone," Rupa assured her. She tilted her head and added, "And you're a writer? I hope you don't mind that I overheard your conversation with Kunal."

"I don't mind at all. I enjoy storytelling, although I hesitate to call myself a writer," Annabel admitted. "But I aspire to it, I suppose. And Kunal thinks I might have to write an entire play...which I'd love to do."

"My mother teaches writing," Rupa told her. "Well, she calls it storytelling. She can write, but she prefers to carve while she tells stories. Would you like to meet her?"

"Yes! Kunal mentioned that, but—" Annabel's face blanched. "Does she offer lessons to commoners?"

"To 'commoners'!" Rupa laughed in amusement. "What do you think *we* are?" She tugged twice on a rope hanging in the corner.

"Merchants, tradespeople," Annabel blanched. "I'm a farmer."

"Fine, then." Rupa smiled. "My mother teaches everyone who wants to learn. If she likes you, that is."

"Even farmers—if anything, they're hard workers, and I love to teach hard workers," a voice chimed in, causing Annabel to startle. An older woman with silver hair and a serene presence entered the room from a slit in the back of the tent, her smile warm as she addressed them. "Rupa, my dear, I am not a teacher; don't you lead this poor girl on. I lead storytelling workshops while I make products to sell, make no mistake." She smiled at Annabel.

"I'm not afraid to tell you," admitted Annabel. "I would die happy if I could make a product to sell from my stories."

Rupa introduced them. "Mummy, you probably heard this is Annabel Barlow from Castle Rowley. Annabel, this is Sarala... Kunal's, my mother, and the best saleswoman you'll ever meet." She winked.

"It's a pleasure to meet you, Sarala," Annabel greeted her.

Kunal tells me you're writing a play," Sarala agreed. "You're at Castle Rowley? Let's meet by the Rother River fork, and I can give you what amounts to a writing lesson and then tell you when the next workshop is. Shall we say two shillings? Do you have time on Sunday?"

"That's more than fair," Annabel replied. "Yes, I can come on Sunday."

"We'll come get you Sunday after lunch." Sarala smiled.

"Perfect," Annabel responded, a sense of joy bubbling within her. "I can't wait."

"And you're involved with young Charlie?" Sarala asked, her tone subtly teasing.

"Maa," Rupa laughed. "Don't press the girl. I already have."

Annabel shifted uneasily. "Yes... we're trying to keep it discreet due to the circumstances, but suffice it to say that we've gotten to know each other."

"Ah, yes, he's still married to Lise," Sarala recollected. "Lovely girl. But I've understood their relationship lends itself more to convenience than long-term happiness. Are you looking to enjoy that with Charlie?"

"I cannot say," Annabel admitted. "And technically, in the eyes of the public, I am still married to Richard Granger. Though—" She stopped.

"Oh!" Rupa exclaimed, realization dawning. "So *that's* why you asked about Nancy. What a coincidence."

"It wasn't planned," Annabel sighed. "But when we discovered..." She trailed off, her voice faltering.

"No!" Sarala suddenly grasped Annabel's and Rupa's arms at once, a sense of urgency in her touch. "Did they *find* Agatha? Thank the lord..."

Annabel nodded. "We found her, and she's good and well. She was wounded, but it's nearly healed now." She laughed nervously. "I hope this is all fine to discuss so openly."

"We're all friends here," Rupa assured her. "Our lips are sealed."

"Oh, that's marvelous." Sarala's relief was palpable. "I'm so relieved for them. Will you tell her we're here for her if she needs additional sanctuary?"

Annabel nodded. "Of course I will. I'm sure she'd love to be out of hiding in the closet of my farmhouse."

"Give me an update when we meet next week if you don't mind," Sarala said, a grin spreading across her face. "And please remind Charlie that we are here to provide refuge for anyone who needs it. We always have before."

"Maa expects results, make no mistake," Rupa laughed.

"And send him my warm regards," Sarala added softly. "His path has not been an easy one. The Baron Rowley has taken a toll on his spirit."

"More accurately, Baron Rowley has been slowly torturing Charlie for years, hoping to force him out or break him," Rupa interjected.

"What a place for a young man to grow up," Sarala murmured, shaking her head.

Rupa let out a sigh. "Be careful."

"I will," Annabel promised, her eyes lingering on a music box featuring a twirling kitten before abruptly starting. "Oh, bother; I must finish shopping before I meet the carriage. I should return to the market."

Sarala disappeared behind a standing wooden screen made of several intricately carved panels, their ears catching the sound of coins being handled. When she emerged, she held a small, knotted pouch. "For his efforts."

Annabel nodded. "I'll get it to him. It was an absolute pleasure to meet both of you." She discreetly stowed the pouch in her inside skirt pocket.

Rupa gave her the box, locked it again, and gave it to Annabel. "Tell him his receipt is inside," she said, winking.

"Good morrow, Annabel," Sarala chimed in. "Here's a homework assignment for you. Take a look at it once you return home." She slipped a small notebook into Annabel's rucksack. "See you on Sunday."

After Annabel had smiled gratefully and merged back into the bustling crowd, she purchased quills, ink, and chocolates. Gathering all the items on Agatha and Lise's shopping lists, she met the carriage promptly. Fredericks' silent demeanor accompanied the journey back to the castle.

Once they arrived, the Baron's son hurried indoors, and Annabel swiftly checked on the fields and the house. Then, she set off to find Charlie.

CHAPTER NINETEEN

NANCY

After ensuring no prying eyes were upon her, Annabel discreetly slipped into the stables to discover Charlie skillfully braiding ribbons into one of the horse's manes with his deft fingers. A warm grin spread across his face as he saw her, causing her heart to flutter despite her sudden reservations.

"How was your trip?" he inquired.

"It was quite enlightening," she replied, watching his face. "I didn't expect to discover you were involved with Richard's first wife."

Her question wiped the smile from his lips as he dropped the ribbons. Annabel sighed in frustration as they fluttered to the ground, and he quickly scooped them back up. "Why did you keep this from me? Is our own relationship merely a façade to seek revenge on Richard?" Her breath caught in her throat.

"No," Charlie thrust the ribbons into his pockets and rubbed his face wearily. "I apologize, Annabel. I intended to tell you sooner, but it's honestly the most painful part of my history—it's how I truly lost my eye, and I detest discussing it. Everyone here knows, of course. I've been teased about it for years." He swallowed hard, looking regretful. "I'm so sorry..."

"Fine," she replied, her voice frosty. "Keep your secrets. But I refuse to accept affection mixed with lies—I've grown weary of deceit, and I must admit, I expected better from you." She crossed her arms and looked away.

"No, I want to tell you. I genuinely do," he insisted earnestly. "But the experience tore me apart, and I didn't want you to pity me."

"You have my word that I would never pity you," she whispered. "I promise."

"Nancy was my childhood sweetheart," Charlie sighed. "I knew her before Richard did."

"Oh," Annabel responded, caught off guard by this revelation. She sat down on a firm hay bale. "You misled me a-purpose, Charlie."

"Yes, I did," he admitted. "And I understand if it's unforgivable."

"Go ahead and tell your story," Annabel muttered. "I want to hear it, if you will speak the truth to be at last."

"Nancy and I were in love from ages fifteen to eighteen," he continued. "Then her mother presented her with a list of eligible suitors. I wasn't included on the list, but Richard and his brother were. They hailed from a respected family."

He rubbed his temples. "We discussed running away, exploring our romantic options. However, she didn't want to be disowned and ultimately chose Richard."

Annabel leaned forward, resting her elbows on her knees, eager to hear the rest despite her irritation.

"I refrained from any involvement with Nancy for two years," Charlie insisted. "Then, one day, she approached me under the pretense of friendship. She informed me that Richard was undoubtedly infertile and asked if I would father her child. She planned to raise the child as a Granger." Disgust seeped into his voice. "Initially, I intended to leave, but she kissed me, and in my loneliness, I foolishly kissed her back."

"I suppose that I can understand that," Annabel whispered.

"Richard walked in on us amid that moment," Charlie revealed, his hands trembling as he recounted the memory. He took a seat on the opposite hay bale, facing Annabel. "He was furious. We endured his relentless screams for an hour in the house before he had both of us dragged before the Baron in his private chambers, who had already displayed his disdain for me. Henry summoned his son."

"Frederick?" Annabel asked. "Not Talon."

"Yes. Fred is the bookish type—he doesn't come out much when his father is around," Charlie explained. "It doesn't help that Henry shouts at him for every action he deems unsuitable. I've never witnessed a man so cruel to his son, driven by an unwavering determination to mold him into a particular image of masculinity."

"So, what happened next?" Annabel asked, dreading the answer.

Looking down, he continued. "The Baron asked Frederick how he should punish me. And Frederick scowled; he refused to take part. He hid behind his book. The Baron goaded him, not allowing him to leave the room, threatening his inheritance, until finally he put the book down." Annabel's eyes were huge. "And?"

Charlie covered his face with his hands. "I can still hear him so clearly like it was yesterday. All he said was 'I...' and then he clapped his mouth shut, shook his head, and turned back to his book, ignoring his father. The Baron laughed, said, 'Have it your way,' grabbed me by the hair, and gouged out my left eye while James held my arms."

"No!" Annabel gasped. "That's why he did it? Because his son said 'I,' Baron Rowley gauged out your eye, just to teach you a bloody lesson?"

"Yes. Henry said it was a good learning experience for everyone in the room." Charlie's voice shook. "Then he threw Nancy in the dungeon for adultery, where she died weeks later of pneumonia. Her mother glared daggers at a funeral at me, sobbing into Richard's coat. Of course, I still wasn't allowed to leave Castle Rowley. The Baron added more money owed to my balance afterward. Then I was ostracized by the entire castle, for the most part, save Maggie, until I married Lise."

"Oh, Charlie," she whispered, absorbing his words and the emotions behind them. "It must have been a harrowing experience for you," she commented softly, her voice filled with compassion.

"It truly is a coincidence regarding Lise and I, Richard and his wives," Charlie insisted. "And now you understand how I lost my eye, and I'm afraid you'll forever pity me as everyone else does." He sighed. "Thank you for not laughing."

"I didn't laugh because it's not funny. You can rest assured that I'm not going anywhere if only you tell me the truth going forward, and I don't pity you," Annabel assured him, her voice warm with sincerity. "Why would anyone find such a tragic story humorous?"

Charlie let out a bitter snort. "The Baron found it most amusing." "People often find humor in the most peculiar things," Annabel replied, nodding in agreement. "I can understand why you harbor animosity toward Frederick."

"Oh, I don't, not really. It wasn't his fault–I always thought he was spoiled because he never speaks to anyone. But I never really got to know him until recently." Charlie's gaze softened, his eyes filled with a tender longing as they met hers. "You truly have no intention of leaving me after hearing that story and after I shamelessly lied to you?"

"Well, I will decide for myself that torture trumps lying. But please don't do it again." Annabel's voice resonated with unwavering determination as she shook her head. "And if anything, I'm glad I understand your past better."

A current seemed to pass between them at that moment, drawing them together. Charlie leaned forward, his lips meeting hers, and Annabel kissed him back, nibbling his lower lip, kissing the freckle near it, giggling as he pulled her closer into his embrace.

When they briefly broke apart, their breaths mingling, Charlie's gaze held hers. He whispered, "No more lies, I swear it. I'm so grateful that our paths crossed."

"Likewise," Annabel murmured affectionately.

Sitting back, their eyes locked in a shared understanding. Charlie's voice was filled with remorse as he spoke, "What a weight off my shoulders. Once again, I apologize for not telling you sooner."

Annabel nodded. "I forgive you. But please trust me. I can handle the truth, can't I?"

"Yes." Charlie's expression grew pained. "I can actually think of another truth I should tell you right now."

"Oh!" Annabel tilted her head. "Go on."

"A while back I—paid Gwyneth for a night," he admitted, his face coloring.

"You *dallied* with her?" Annabel asked in surprise. "With Gwyneth Jones?"

"Not exactly," he sighed. "It was after Nancy and before Lise. I didn't touch her, but I paid Gwyneth to read a book while I—pleasured myself."

He made a face. "At the time, I just wanted a release, but I was still so into Nancy I didn't want to court anyone else. Gwyneth had always been nice to me."

"Apparently," Annabel whispered, chuckling. "Goodness, it never occurred to me to pay someone for reading."

"I truly didn't touch her, though," he promised. "I wasn't ready for that, in the state I was in. Just listened while she wore something revealing and read aloud. Then we switched and I read silently while she danced."

"It's in your past, and I have one, too, so I'm not worried." She kissed his neck. "As long as I don't have to worry about another woman reading to you behind my back." She winked. "What book was it?"

"*The Story of Venus*," he said. "Otherwise known as, *The Ladies Delight*. It was written fifty years ago in French and translated into English about thirty years ago. It's about two women having a very forthright discussion about sex, then it goes right into coupling with one of the women and her fiancé." He hung his head. "It's terribly weird, isn't it?"

"Yes," she agreed. "I still want to read it myself, mind you. Anything else?"

"Well, I do gamble quite a lot at the fights," he sighed. "I'll never pay off what I owe to the Baron, but I need to pay just enough not to get kicked off the land."

"Be careful." She shook her head. "Are you quite finished?"

Charlie smiled weakly and replied, "I may remember more later."

"I look forward to it." Annabel nudged him playfully. "Are you finished attending to the horses?"

Shaking his head, Charlie answered, "I still have four more. Most of these horses belonged to the late Baroness, and it seems the Baron believes her spirit resides within their souls. You know they're all named after Greek Gods? He sometimes speaks to them as if they were a lifeline to her, often staring into the stables for hours, a cloudy look on his face."

A shiver ran down Annabel's spine as she responded, "That's rather spooky. Will you be making a fire again?"

Chuckling softly, Charlie replied, "No, tonight the Baron wants me to stay in the stables and sleep there. He's concerned that an attendee might attempt to steal one of the horses."

"I'm volunteering tonight–in case a maid is sick, I'll be drafted in to clean for a few extra shillings." Annabel's smile turned mischievous as she suggested, "Would you mind if I paid you a visit in the stables after the party?"

Charlie's eyes lit, and he responded with a grin, "Please do. Everyone else will be occupied unless some drunkard embarks on a wild horse ride, which is thankfully a rare occurrence."

Annabel laughed, finding amusement in the thought. "What a spectacle that must be," she commented. "Oh, I met Rupa. I have your payment." Reaching into her pocket, she retrieved a pouch and handed it to Charlie. As he slipped it into his inside pocket, she stretched her legs onto a nearby hay bale, leaning against the wall. Charlie leaned forward, his hands beginning to massage her calves with deliberate ca re.

A pleasurable moan escaped Annabel's lips, and Charlie asked, "Did my letter convince Kunal? Will he be assisting you?"

Beaming with delight, Annabel replied, "Yes! He's agreed to accompany me to collect my prize this weekend. Although I'm feeling a bit overwhelmed."

Charlie offered, "You might be doing something you're not used to, but you can handle it." Leaning forward, he kissed her fondly, but then he suddenly withdrew his lips and dipped his hand back into his pocket. He weighed the bag of coins in his hand, a curious expression on his face.

"This is more than usual, and it's unlike Rupa not to be pay me to the exactly shilling." he noted. "Why is it over?"

Annabel shrugged, a hint of confusion on her face. "I don't know. She said your receipt is in there."

Charlie regarded her perplexedly before reaching into the pouch and retrieving a note. His smile widened as he read and put it away, and he chuckled softly. "It's not a receipt. The note says the product is excellent, and she liked you–something you said must have driven her to tip me."

Annabel's smile grew warmer. "I was completely spellbound when Rupa played one of those sitars fitted with your jawari. I had no idea such marvelous music existed. You should feel incredibly proud of creating the bridge that makes that music possible."

Charlie grinned. "Thank you. The jawari pieces are small, so they're relatively easy to hide here, and all I need to make them is the wood, a chisel, a file, and sandpaper." He smiled in satisfaction. "The Sutars, they're a good family...truly upstanding folk. I'm glad you got to meet them."

Annabel leaned in, her voice barely above a whisper. "They spoke highly of you, and Sarala wanted me to remind you that she can hide anyone you send her. She guessed about Agatha." She pressed a kiss against his neck, a thrill coursing through her from lips to legs at the sweet scent of his neck. "They agreed with me about you being a good man."

A heartfelt appreciation shone in Charlie's eyes. "You're lovely," he replied, his voice filled with affection.

"You're wonderful," she whispered, kissing his neck softly.

"I hope I can continue working with the Sutars," Charlie expressed, his gaze briefly shifting toward the castle. "But I wish we could get away from here, both of us. This place is cursed in many ways."

"Run away?" Concern etched across her face, Annabel asked, "Where?"

Charlie shook his head and gently rubbed her cold hands between his warm palms. "I don't know. If you could choose, where would you go?"

Annabel pondered for a moment before responding, her voice tinged with longing. "Somewhere I can indulge in reading, storytelling, perhaps writing, and you. Perhaps a garden with chickens near a well or a spring. We used to live near a spring, and I'd heat a kettleful of fresh spring water in the morning, let it cool to warm, and pour it over myself." She laughed.

"My kingdom for a hot bath, Charlie."

"I hear you. I've only gotten used to washing so I won't sully the books." Charlie grinned, his eyes dancing. "That sounds lovely. A place to be at peace with each other and live our lives."

Annabel's thoughts wandered as she admitted, "I haven't had much time for daydreaming lately. But I do enjoy it."

Charlie laughed, and the sound of it warmed Annabel's heart. Leaning in, she kissed him deeply, their connection intensifying as she sank into his embrace. He kissed her back with equal fervor, and her heart filled with joy as his hands glided along her back, drawing her closer.

When they parted, their lips still lingering, Charlie's eye met hers, and in that unspoken gaze, Annabel felt a profound sense of safety and vulnerability. She whispered, her voice overflowing with sincerity, "I'm so glad I met you. If I could play an instrument myself, I'd write you a song of how much I enjoy your company."

"I feel the same." Charlie whispered, "If music is the food of love, play on."

CHAPTER TWENTY

A BIRTHDAY FEAST

Annabel trudged through hours of grueling labor the next day, feeling the weight of exhaustion settle upon her. Seeking respite as the sun lowered in the sky, she returned to the house, splashing cold water on her face and patting it dry with a hand towel.

Inside, Agatha sat in a rocking chair hemming a sheet, her intent gaze lifting as Annabel entered. "Welcome home," she greeted.

"Thank you," Annabel replied, lying down on the bed. "What a day it has been—I regret volunteering to clean tonight. Lise is working hard back in the cellar now that she's nearly healed?"

"Yes." After a brief silence, Agatha cleared her throat. "I hope you don't mind, I'm sure you don't, but I've been considering moving in with the Sutars. They've offered, and living in constant fear of being discovered has become untenable, not to mention that I'm...not quite ready to go to the authorities. I hope you don't mind...I know it affects you. I hate to leave you holding the bag with Richard. I just *can't*."

"No, I understand." Annabel nodded. "You'd like some time to heal from being in the dungeon for three months. Would you think I'm crazy if I said I've been entertaining the thought of escaping from this place, perhaps with Charlie?"

Agatha's eyes lit up with hope, and responded, "No, not at all. Perhaps we could all find a new town, far from here, and start afresh—when the time comes."

Annabel's smile widened, but a knock on the door interrupted their shared moment of joy. Agatha quickly concealed herself, and Annabel opened the door to find James standing there, visibly annoyed, holding a bucket of soapy water and a dress draped over his arm. Uncertainty filled Annabel as she asked, "May I help you?"

He let out a weary sigh. "Yes. You can scrub down, put this dress on, and come to the castle without any backtalk."

Puzzled at the quality of the dress, Annabel furrowed her brow. "That's not a maid's uniform."

"No. It's a piece belonging to the late Baroness." The exasperation was thick in James's tone as he explained, "The Baron wants you to read aloud at the feast like a fool."

"Oh," exclaimed Annabel, delighted. "Well, that's a bit odd. But it is certainly better than cleaning. He must have enjoyed my reading before."

"If you say so, farmwife." James grunted. "Will you hurry? The longer you delay, the more poorly it reflects on both of us."

"Of course," Annabel replied calmly, gingerly taking the bucket and dress before closing the door in his face.

Turning to Agatha, she shook her head, and Agatha responded with a curious expression. Slipping behind a screen, Annabel stripped, scrubbed up and down, dried off, and tugged on the dress, grimacing as she realized it was not entirely her size.

Agatha made a face when she stepped out and gestured for her to come closer. Expertly, the other woman used tiny sewing scissors to let it out slightly, quickly tucking and sewing the fabric back into place. She set down her needle and pinned up Annabel's long waves, offering her a small pot of beetroot for her lips and a brush of talc for her face. Leaning in, Agatha whispered, "Be careful. The Baron enjoys embarrassing people."

"It's just a reading," Annabel whispered back, her nerves tingling. "How bad could it be?"

"He'll find a way to ruin it for you, mark my words," the other woman warned. Annabel impulsively embraced her, bringing a smile to the surprised woman's face, and Agatha patted her on the back in a comforting, motherly way. "Good luck."

"Thanks," Annabel replied, mustering her courage. Taking a deep breath, she straightened her posture and went outside. She approached James and whispered, "Do you know what I'll be reading or why the Baron wants me to do this?"

He shook his head grimly. "Some poem or another. Who knows? Maybe because he's drunk or mad, or maybe both." He cast a sharp look at her, his words slurring slightly. "You didn't hear that."

"Of course not," Annabel laughed.

Upon entering the crowded ballroom, filled with boisterous laughter and merry drinkers, Annabel noticed the predominance of men. The Baron's loud cheer startled her, drawing the room's attention. He handed his tankard to Cole and applauded enthusiastically as Annabel stepped forward. James quickly left her side to stand at the Baron's left.

"Gentlemen!" Baron Rowley boomed, his voice carrying across the room. "And the few ladies left among us." Laughter rippled through the crowd. "We have gathered here to witness a poetry reading!" He gestured towards Annabel, drawing everyone's gaze in her direction.

Feeling her nerves rise, Annabel offered a nervous smile, debating whether to curtsy or not. Taking his tankard back from Cole and sloshing half of its contents over his chest, the Baron staggered forward, his hand slipping onto Annabel's back as he guided her towards an overstuffed red chair surrounded by cushions. "Go on," he whispered in her ear, his breath heavy with the scent of whiskey.

Sitting in the chair, Annabel scanned the room, her eyes darting from one face to another. She couldn't shake the feeling that there was a hint of malice in their eyes, causing her stomach to churn. Baron Rowley handed his empty glass to James, wiped his hands on his brown cloak, and received a small book with a slim leather cover from Cole, who would not meet her eye.

Drawing close to Annabel again, she noticed a menacing glint in the Baron's eyes, though he maintained a smile. "Mrs. Granger," he rumbled.

"Yes, Baron Rowley?" Annabel's anticipation tingled beneath her skin. She felt somewhat foolish in the borrowed party dress, but at least she was clean and presentable.

"You are to read every word in the book loudly and for the entire room to hear," he said in a low voice, his mustache twitching as a sly smile curled upon his rubbery lips. "It's my birthday, you know."

"Of course." Puzzled, Annabel glanced at the small, untitled volume in her hands. "Many happy returns," she added, her tone tinged with uncertainty. She raised her gaze to meet his, searching for an explanation.

"And if you fail to do so," he continued, his voice laced with a threat, "You will be expelled from Castle Rowley and sent back to live with your mother in Lower Broach."

"That seems rather severe," Annabel murmured, taken aback by the harshness of the consequence.

Shaking his head, Baron Rowley insisted, "I will not tolerate disappointing my guests, young lady."

Realizing the extent of his madness, Annabel offered him an indulgent smile, her mind racing. She nodded and gave him a reassuring look while pondering how long she would have to endure this charade.

"Don't even think of running away," the Baron warned, his tone filled with sadistic glee. "My falcon, Percy, would be more than eager to chase down a pretty girl like you. He'd make a *mess* of your neck and shoulders."

Annabel was speechless, rubbing her neck. "What on *earth* are you talking about?" she asked in disbelief.

"You heard me, my dear," the Baron rumbled, thrusting the book into her hands before stepping away to accept a fresh tankard from a serving maid.

Running her fingers carefully over the thin book, Annabel cleared her throat, preparing to begin.

Just then, Frederick and another boy, carrying a fiddle, entered the grand hall. Pointing towards a cushion in front of Annabel, the Baron called out, "Amos, over here! Accompany the young farm girl while she reads. Let's

liven things up a bit," he added, snickering.

The fiddler jumped at the Baron's request, taking his position on the cushion before Annabel, arranging his hands on his instrument and looking up at her expectantly.

Annabel sat on the proffered cushion and opened the book as the murmurs in the room subsided. She took a deep breath.

"Stand!" the Baron suddenly bellowed, and Annabel obeyed, her nervous smile directed at the room. She turned to the title page.

"Ladies and gentlemen, I present to you Mrs. Richard Granger!" Baron Rowley announced, prompting mild applause.

Still bewildered, Annabel read aloud, "The Imperfect Enjoyment, by John Wilmot, Earl of Rochester."

There were titters, and she turned the page. Suddenly, her eyes widened, and her mouth fell open. She looked up at the Baron with fury. In return, he toasted her, his face contorted with lecherous intent.

Annabel stowed her anger, took a deep breath, and continued, eyes down. "Naked she lay, clasped in my longing arms, I filled with love, and she all over charms. Both are equally inspired with eager fire, melting through kindness, flaming in desire. With arms, legs, lips close clinging to embrace...she clips me to her breast and sucks me to her face."

After a stunned pause, the fiddler Amos at her knee whispered to her, "How—how about to the tune of Greensleeves?"

Closing her eyes briefly, imagining just briefly that she was back home again, Annabel took a deep breath, opened her eyes again, and nodded. The fiddler began to play the familiar melody while Annabel adapted her reading to match the tune.

"Her nimble tongue, love's lesser lightning, played within my mouth, and to my thoughts conveyed, Swift orders that I should prepare to throw—the all-dissolving thunderbolt below. My fluttering soul sprung with the pointed kiss, hanging over her balmy brinks of bliss. But while her busy hand would guide that part...." Annabel swallowed hard. "Which should convey my soul to her heart...in liquid raptures I dissolve all o'er...." She paused, cheeks flaming, her throat dry, and she coughed loudly.

The Baron burst into laughter, and several of his comrades guffawed. "Go on, little farmwife! Or have you had enough?" His voice was cruel.

She heard a throat clear below and looked down to see Frederick holding a goblet of ale up towards her, away from himself, without looking at her face, a bored expression on his face. Accepting gratefully, she sipped at it and continued, this time in a much bolder, more robust voice.

"Melt into sperm and spend at every pore. A touch from any part of her had done 't: Her hand, her foot, her very look's a cunt." At this last word, Annabel somewhat bit off the last word, as if it were a piece of carrot, and tossed a wink into the crowd, resulting in several laughs that seemed to be on her side. "Smiling, she chides in a kind murmuring noise, and from her body wipes the clammy joys...."

The reading went on like this for over an hour. There was talk of panting bosom, virgin blood, and even an 'oyster-cinder-beggar-common whore' before it ended. Annabel held her head high, gave the crowd a frozen smile, and curtsied.

The unexpected applause filled the room, catching Annabel by surprise, and the fiddler held out his hat for tips, which he graciously split with her.

Glancing at the Baron, she saw him scowling as he sipped his ale. "I can't believe we almost stayed home!" whispered a gleeful spectator to her friend, who enthusiastically agreed. Annabel attempted to slip away, but James hissed at her to remain seated in the chair.

Frederick, who seemed well acquainted with the fiddler, conversed with him in low tones before approaching Annabel. "Well," he said. "My father is quite twisted."

"Thank you for the drink, Lord Frederick," she replied quietly. "I truly appreciate it. I'm not sure I could have made it through otherwise."

"It doesn't matter," the teenager sighed. Glancing at a man approaching them, he added, "Brace yourself. My eccentric uncle Geoffrey is here—my father's brother."

If Baron Rowley resembled a bear in stature, his brother Geoffrey had a more buffalo-like presence. Robust and barrel-chested, he wore a cape beneath his long, curly hair, both of which he nervously picked at. He flashed a timid smile as he slowly made his way towards them. "Good evening, young Frederick. And you, young lady," he said, bowing slightly in their general direction.

"She's no lady," Frederick scowled. "She's a farmer's wife who somehow possesses the ability to read. Father thought it would be amusing."

"Well, I must say, humor was the furthest thing from my mind," murmured Geoffrey. "I found the reading quite impressive. In fact, would you be interested in doing a reading for me? My birthday is in two weeks, and I've just hired a new maid for the occasion but find myself without a jester. I'm Geoffrey Rowley, by the way."

"Lord Geoffrey..." Annabel chuckled nervously. "You can't be serious?"

"I have a manor house on High Green," Geoffrey continued. "I may not draw a crowd like this, but I assure you, I can compensate you handsomely."

"You're a mad old man," Frederick snickered. "She means she doesn't do readings. This was merely her playing the role assigned by my father."

"I never said that," Annabel interjected. "I'd be more than happy to do a reading. My name is Annabel Granger, née Barlow. Furthermore," she added with a stroke of inspiration, "I also compose original pieces. I'd gladly write a poem featuring yourself and recite it aloud." She nodded at the fiddler. "What about him?"

The fiddler eagerly nodded. "Amos Bell. I can perform in two weeks."

"Excellent!" Geoffrey clasped his hands together. "I'll be in touch and arrange for a carriage to pick you up on the morning of the event." His eyes swept across the room suddenly. "Freddy...Talon and Cassidy aren't still awake, are they?"

"I highly doubt it, given that it's past midnight," Frederick sighed. "The Great Hall is finally clearing out."

"Well read," Amos grinned at Annabel. "Thanks for the unexpected job. I'd have paid to get a job outside Castle Rowley."

As the ball drew to a close, the Baron staggered off to his bedroom without speaking to Annabel since her reading. Frederick and Amos disappeared down the hallway. Annabel made her way to the kitchen to return a few abandoned tankards. Startled, she nearly jumped out of her skin when she noticed movement in the back. "Who's there?" she whispered loudly, her hand instinctively gripping her knife.

There was a clinking sound, and Cecelia stumbled out from between piles of dish towels, clutching a jug of wine. Upon closer inspection,

Annabel recognized it as the Baron's private vintage. Relieved, she sighed and chided Cecelia, "Have you been hiding back here, getting drunk all night?" Taking the bottle from Cecelia, she realized it was nearly empty. "You are a handful," she muttered, surveying the room.

"I hate my bloody life," Cecelia moaned.

Annabel sighed, low on patience, as she tidied up the toppled towels, separating the dirty ones. "Why is that?"

"Well, I have no future," Cecelia slurred. "Not that I had before, but now that you're getting what you want and just got here, I'm more aware of it."

"Don't envy me; I've no idea what I'm doing," Annabel added softly, "Can I help?"

"No. I'm sorry." Cecelia pulled out a handkerchief and wiped her nose. "I've been making a fool of myself, and I'm finished." She sighed. "What was the last riddle you found?"

Annabel closed her eyes and recited it.

In a steel coffin where shadows dwell,

Seek the valiant and the swell.

She shuddered. "Charlie and I are trying to work up the courage to plan a trip down to the mausoleum."

"I don't know any coffins that are made of steel." Cecelia wrinkled her nose.

"Oh." Annabel considered this. "That's true. I supposed they're usually made of wood, aren't they?"

"Yes. But old Henry used to put on his armor and stroll around the castle saying he would go to war," Cecelia remembered. "Philippa used to look at him and say he looked like a swollen snake digesting an elephant in a steel coffin."

"Did she *really*?" Annabel clamored. "Do you *know* where the armor is? That particular set of Henry's armor?"

"Of course. I know where everything is." Cecelia yawned. "It's next to the fireplace in the great hall."

Five minutes later, Cecelia lay in wait by the kitchen, ready to distract someone at the front door if need be, while Annabel crept, candle in hand, to the dark corner where the suit of armor towered. Unfortunately, thirty sweaty minutes searching the pile of metal yielded many tiny cuts and no clue. Annabel was ready to give up when she happened to look underneath the visor–and gasped.

Crafted with exquisite detailing, engraved on the rim of the inner side of the visor, was a fine, delicate script that blended seamlessly with the existing embellishments on the armor, making it difficult to detect at first glance.

"Cecelia," she whispered in excitement. "I found it!"

She came running. "Is it paper?"

"No, it's tiny words on the underneath here." Annabel squinted in the firelight. "It's hard to read. Where could we get a glass?"

"Be right back," Cecelia whispered. When she returned, she was brandishing a magnifying glass and giggling. "Here."

Annabel threw her a suspicious glance. "What is it?"

Cecelia shook her head. "Sorry. I'm sworn to secrecy. What does it say?"

Holding the glass carefully, Annabel read:

Journey to where the truth lies,

Discover where secrets upon sheets rise.

She looked at Cecelia blankly. "Any ideas?"

After a pregnant pause, Cecelia laughed. "Are you having a go at me?"

"No," said Annabel. "Why? Sheets that rise?"

"I'm never letting you live this down, you odd old reader," Cecelia cried gleefully. "Where the truth lies? Secrets upon sheets? Sheets are pages that rise when you turn them. The truth lies in a book."

"God's teeth!" Annabel almost jumped for joy. "Cecelia, you're brilliant!" But then her face fell. "Oh—but that's where the clue to the chapel was found. In the library."

"So we are back to the dungeon?" Cecelia groaned. "Bloody perfect."

"Yes," Annabel sighed. "Can you draw out the map you had before, but near each cell on the map, draw what you've dropped off there and any messages you can find down there?" She took a deep breath. "If we find this..."

"It will change everything." The other girl nodded purposefully. "I will."

Chapter Twenty-One

A Game of Love

After Annabel stealthily made her way out of the castle and into the farmhouse, past a sleeping Agatha to change into a clean frock, she hung up the borrowed dress gathered her strength and ventured toward the stables.

Charlie's sweet, familiar face appeared at the door, looking weary. "Long night?" he asked, and she nodded, weariness evident in her expression.

"It was...not the best evening," she admitted, her lip trembling as the evening flooded back to her, and she tried to hold in hot, shameful tears. "But we did find another riddle that doesn't lead us anywhere, so that's something."

"I don't care about the riddle—what's wrong?" Concern etched across Charlie's face as he reached out to touch her shoulder. "What is it?"

Annabel gestured past him at the barn. "Can we...go inside?"

"Of course. No drunken party guests managed to find their way in tonight, thankfully," he said, holding the door wide open as she walked in and securely locking the bolt behind them.

"It's good to be with you," she whispered, not meeting his eyes.

"You must be utterly exhausted," Charlie remarked as they entered and climbed the stairs to the hayloft together. "Can I give you a massage? You can lie down and let me work on your back." The sweetness of his offer filled her heart with warmth, and Annabel nodded before climbing onto his makeshift bed and lying on her stomach.

Charlie began to rub her back in silence, his hands skillfully loosening her gown to reach her knotted muscles. He worked slowly and deliberately, his firm, muscular hands soothing her physically and mentally.

After a few minutes, he spoke softly, "Are you alright? You don't seem quite like yourself."

Annabel let out a sigh. "The Baron deliberately tried to humiliate me tonight. I don't know what his game is, but I fear that now I have unknowingly begun playing, he will not allow me to cease it."

Charlie's hands paused on her back. "What do you mean? What task did he have you perform?"

Struggling to find the right words, she stumbled over her explanation. "I was summoned to read at the party, so I immediately complied. I arrived wearing a ridiculous dress he had sent with James, assuming it would be another boring piece from his chambers like the other night."

Charlie puzzled, "And it wasn't?"

"It was a poem about *sex*. A man *experiences ejaculation*," she whispered, her eyes closing in embarrassment.

He sucked his breath in sharply. "The Imperfect Enjoyment?"

"You've read it?" she asked in disbelief, opening her eyes. "About the woman laying naked, and..."

Looking chagrined, he nodded. "If there's something dirty that someone's written down and published, I promise you I've enjoyed it more than once." Charlie shook his head. "They sell dirty books at Gwyneth's brothel, too. But really, what a horrid old man to make you do that."

"Just before I left the house, Agatha warned me," Annabel pondered. "She said that the Baron would find a way to ruin my reading."

"He didn't, did he?" Charlie asked curiously. "That doesn't sound like you."

"No, he most certainly failed. *No one* could do such a thing," she grinned. "But he certainly tried, and it was terrible." She proceeded to recount the Baron's threats if she defied him. "It was truly terrible, Charlie." Her shoulders trembled at the memory. "He said he would release his prized falcon, Percy, to chase after me if I tried to escape."

"I'll bloody kill him," Charlie said softly, an edge creeping into his voice though his fingers resumed the soothing massage on her back.

"Don't even joke about that," she sighed. "Charlie, you're *not* that kind of person, and I don't *want* you to be."

"I can become that kind of person for someone who threatens you," he insisted, scowling as he ran his hands through his hair.

"Maybe a dead one," she said. "I just need to find a way to avoid him."

"Good luck." Charlie grimaced in disgust. "He's such a bully. And when he has an audience, it fuels his cruelty. He revels in the spectacle at someone else's expense." His tone grew pensive. "Maybe I shall slip some arsenic into his coffee."

She chuckled. "No need for that."

He continued, pretending to be lost in thought. "Or perhaps I could spray him with atropine while he sleeps, and he would endure a slow, miserable death, as he deserves."

"No, but please, go on," Annabel encouraged him. It was comforting to listen to his soothing voice.

Charlie grinned, enjoying the game. "Another option is to gather leopard's bane, which grows in a lovely meadow nearby that I can show you, and mix it into his salad with pansies. It would gradually stop his heart while causing uncontrollable bowel movements and hair loss," he declared.

The vivid scene he described sparked laughter in her, and she nestled into him, lying on her side with her head in his lap as he caressed her hair. "Thank you for the jest; I needed that. How do you even know such things?" she asked softly.

"I have a book," he replied.

She looked up at him. "Here?"

"Oh no, I keep a few crates with Rupa's family where I pay them for storage," he explained. "The Book of Venoms, written by Magister Santes de Ardoynis. It belonged to my father. Full of information about poisonous plants and animals, their effects, and whether they can be helpful or harmful. I studied it to ensure I didn't harm myself while gathering wood for carving."

"That sounds fascinating," she said. "I would love to see it sometime. By the way, I have a writing lesson scheduled for Sunday, just the day after tomorrow, by the river! I'm so excited." Sighing, she added, "Or, I was until tonight. Now I feel like crawling into a hole and never coming out."

Charlie sighed dramatically. "If you truly won't let me take care of him, so to speak—"

"I won't let you put yourself in danger," she interrupted. "I'd never forgive myself."

"Then all you can do is try to be resilient around him," he advised. "The Baron thrives on reactions. It's what he lives for. It's best not to show how much he upsets you if you can manage it." He added, "Unless he's physically harming you—then wants to see the pain on your face. It's a delicate balance."

She sighed. "I honestly don't know if I can do such a thing, in the face of his cruelty."

"Just say the word, and I'll find a safer place for you than here," he offered. "I'll start researching, anyway."

"Couldn't you leave as well?" Annabel watched his face intently. "I want to be with you."

Charlie shrugged. "As long as everyone I leave behind is taken care of. I wouldn't want to leave anyone in the lurch, and it would require careful planning. I do worry about what would happen if I left without paying the debts Henry has piled on over the years."

"Yes?" Annabel prompted. "But you'd do it? You'd leave here with me?"

"I'd be forever looking over my shoulder, as would you," he warned. "The Baron doesn't like to let people leave. He considers it a liability. Loose lips sink ships and all that. It makes me nervous to think about what he might do."

Annabel frowned. "It seems like the next step is getting rid of the Baron."

"How?" Charlie chuckled. "He's far too careful. Don't get caught talking about that, either—he has ears everywhere. To be honest, either goal feels equally unattainable." Then he winked at her. "But you know, the best dreams often seem that way initially. Just like you."

That prompted her to kiss him, sitting up and melting into his embrace. He reciprocated deeply, holding her as though she were valuable, worth protecting, the way she had always yearned to be held by another person.

"Oh!" He suddenly broke away and went to the hidden panel in the wall. "I almost forgot. I have something for you."

"No, you don't," she said. "You don't have to give me gifts...you have so little already."

"You don't know everything I have," Charlie said lightly, handing her a parcel. "Here it is."

Despite her hesitation, she eagerly began to unwrap it, carefully folding the paper behind the gift. As she uncovered it, her eyes widened. "Mr. William Shakespeare's Comedies, Histories & Tragedies," she read. "Oh, my stars! Is this..."

"It's all thirty-six of his plays," Charlie grinned. "You mentioned you hadn't read them all. I couldn't bear to live in a world without having experienced all of Shakespeare's works. These plays have kept me sane these years." He laughed. "Well, more sane than otherwise."

"This is... all of them?" she whispered, her heart overflowing with excitement as she tightened her grip on the book. "All?"

He grinned intimately at her. "Yes, every single one. Please read it soon so we can discuss them together."

"Oh, *Charlie*, thank you so *much*!" she exclaimed, pulling him into a hug. He smelled so comforting, like trees and hope, as she rested in his strong arms. Charlie's chest was firm and warm beneath his patched tunic, and he remained steady as she practically crashed into hi m.

"You've given me a tremendous gift, even more than the sun of it," she whispered. "Instead of today being the day I had to endure the humiliation of speaking sexually to a room full of drunken fools at a party, it's now the day I received the greatest gift of my life." She opened the book slowly. "I can't wait to memorize my favorite passages after reading them countless times."

"I'm so glad you like it." They lay together for a while, him stroking her hair as she reverently turned the pages. "What are you doing tomorrow after work?" he suddenly asked. "Would you let me do something for you?"

"Yes," she agreed, yawning. "I'd like that. Honestly, I'd like to stay in your arms until dawn. But we probably shouldn't fall asleep here..."

"True." Charlie tilted his head to observe the moon's position from the window. "You know, Frederick came to see me before the feast. Did he tell you about Nancy?"

"Not directly," she admitted. "He mentioned something in passing that led me to suspect some connection between you and Nancy. Then I mentioned it to Rupa, and she confirmed my suspicions." She grimaced.

"Apologies for being sneaky about it."

"Oh, you only pulled the threads I left open with my intentional omissions," he sighed. "Fred came to apologize himself anyway and surprised me by sharing a whole laundry list of things to blackmail him with, as he says," Charlie chuckled. "And he claims he still owes me a favor. I might go riding with him this week."

"He brought me a drink during the reading when my throat was dry," she recalled. "It was a thoughtful gesture."

"Good lad. Then I'll definitely go riding with him this week." Looking at her, he added, "You know the play 'As You Like It'? It's my favorite."

"I've read it," she replied. "I like the character of Jacques the best."

"Me too. But one of the characters, Rosalind, disguises herself as a man named Ganymede, and a shepherdess named Phebe falls in love with Ganymede." He grinned. "Lise likes it. She feels represented."

"Of course," Annabel nodded.

"There's also a play, 'Troilus and Cressida,' about the Trojan War," he continued.

"Yes, the Greek myths!" She grinned.

"Right." He smiled. "Well, two Greek soldiers, Achilles and Patroclus, are fighting in one of the stories. They're very close—some, not me personally, but some say, closer than men should be. Not I, but some. The Baron, mostly."

"And?" Annabel was puzzled.

"And to make a long story short, Frederick fancies himself as Achilles and that musician Amos as Patroclus," Charlie explained. "It was one of his confessions to me; he said it was alright to tell you. His father suspects it, which fuels most of their arguments. Frederick—has never been with a woman that wasn't forced upon him by his father. And he doesn't wish to be."

"Oh!" she exclaimed. "I've heard that can happen in aristocratic families—fury if anything interferes with their lineage."

"Exactly. It sends him into a rage, the thought of not fulfilling his father's legacy and producing grandchildren," he explained, shaking his head. "It doesn't help that the Baron suspects him to be illegitimate. Fred constantly tries to hide his feelings and fears of being disinherited."

"What a way to live," Annabel sighed. "Listen," she added. "I'm serious about not wanting you to do anything reckless with the Baron, no matter how horrible he is. We must find a smart way to get rid of him without bloodshed. Let's think on it."

"I know," Charlie said. "And you're right. I couldn't just kill someone impulsively. I don't think I have the stomach for it."

"That's a good quality, not a bad one," she assured him. "It means you're not a murderer or a sadist like some people."

"Sure, I'd still like him dead, though," he sighed. "If he started choking in front of me, and we were alone, I might let him die."

"I think I have just seen the perfect response to that..." She opened the book and flipped through it, running her finger down a page and looking at him with a grin. "Men have died occasionally, and worms have eaten them, but not for love. As You Like It."

"That's a good one," Charlie said thoughtfully, continuing the game. "His unkindness may take my life, but it can never tarnish my love. Othello."

"Oh, I hope not." She flipped through the book again and paused. "So are you to my thoughts as food to life or sweet-seasoned showers to the ground...Sonnet 75."

"I'd love to kiss you under sweet-seasoned showers." Charlie winked, and she shivered with desire at the mental image. He added, "Speak low if you speak of love. Much Ado About Nothing."

After a moment of reflection, without looking at the book, she said, lifting her eyes to his, "A heart to love, and in that heart, courage to make love known. Macbeth." She bit her lip, feeling a surge of desire while love bloomed in her heart. "Charlie..."

Charlie took her hand and whispered, "Doubt thou the stars are fire..."

"That's one I know. Hamlet again." She grinned. "Doubt that the sun doth move." She swallowed hard. "Doubt truth to be a liar..."

They finished the stanza together. "But never doubt I love."

Annabel whispered, "I love you, Charlie."

"I am very much in love with you, Annabel," he whispered. "I love you yesterday, today, and more—with every dawn, my heart for you does soar."

"That's not Shakespeare, is it?" she asked.

"No," he whispered. "Just myself."

He took her in his arms and kissed her then, and they lay there with him for another hour on a horse blanket, nestled in each other's arms, discussing dreams and aspirations for the future.

CHAPTER TWENTY-TWO

IN HOT WATER

The next day proved to be an exasperating and arduous one for Annabel, as if every possible thing that could go wrong had conspired against her to do so. First, her plow broke, then her harvester. Strange weeds had been discovered in her fields, unlike other farmer's crops. Dealing with each issue swiftly, she had pushed herself to exhaustion.

During her brief lunch break, she hastily consumed her food while standing, and when she finally completed her chores, it was nearly dinnertime. Breathing deeply, her weariness overwhelmed her. With a sigh, she collapsed face-down onto her bed and almost wept to find solace in the fresh, soft blankets that had not been there when she'd left that morning.

"Who's about?" she mumbled.

Lise laughed from the larder, coming out and shutting it. "Agatha left yesterday—she doesn't like goodbyes. But she left three loaves of bread, and she'll be back. I'm just here getting the last of my own things." Her friend came to sit on the bed and observed her with mild concern. "Are you alright? There's a surprise for you at the castle arranged by Charlie, you know... I'm supposed to help escort you back to the cellar."

Annabel sighed heavily. "I'm too exhausted to do anything. Today has thoroughly defeated me."

"Too tired for a surprise?" Lise winked mischievously. "That's just silly. I think you'll find it worth your while."

Suspicion rising in her voice, Annabel asked from the bed, "What is it? Do I have to move?"

"Yes. It's in the basement. Charlie is waiting on the porch," Lise replied, her grin widening. "Oh! Frederick is in charge, with the Baron away for a week, and we've all got extra supplies all around as a result. Can you believe that? That boy isn't as useless as I thought. Do you know he's actually listening to Charlie?"

"I'm glad to hear it," grumbled Annabel. "But if I never have to step inside the castle again, it would be too soon. I can't stop thinking about who saw me read aloud at that bloody feast. "

"Pity," said Lise airily. "I can personally vouch that you'll find it worth the effort. But if you've decided now is the time to stop trusting me, I won't be hurt...much."

Reluctantly, Annabel sat up and slipped her feet into her shoes. "You are far too convincing."

Stepping out onto the porch, Annabel saw Charlie on the path. His face lit up when she caught his eye. "Good day."

"Can we cancel our outing?" she sighed. "It's been an incredibly challenging day. Week. Month, actually..."

"I'm not sure anything within these castle grounds could be considered a proper outing," he replied. "This is something just for you. It's not far."

"Can you promise it's not far?" she sighed, rubbing her temples. Charlie winked. "I do. I promise."

With a resigned sigh, she followed him down the path, Lise closing the door behind them. They entered the castle through the kitchen's side door and entered the cellar. Lise grinned and motioned down the hallway to the basement. "I'm heading to bed for a proper nap, myself. I'll see you all later."

Once Lise had departed, Annabel groaned as she gazed down the dimly lit corridor and sat on the steps. "Charlie, you promised it wouldn't be far," she lamented. "That hallway looks endless."

"I can carry you if you'd like. We won't encounter anyone else on the way." He grinned mischievously.

"No?" Curiosity sparked within Annabel. "You shouldn't, really. With my height and build, I'm called good farm stock for a reason." She laughed nervously.

"Come on," he urged, his grin widening. "I carry around sacks of feed heavier than you."

Rolling her eyes, she stepped forward, and Charlie leaned in, effortlessly sweeping her into his strong arms. Her heart skipped a beat as she rested her head on his shoulder, daydreaming of him carrying her away into the sunset, far from this place. He navigated the maze of hallways with agility, seemingly aware of every turn. "I must say, you're quite fetching when you're grumpy. I was beginning to think you never stopped smiling, so it's honestly a relief to remember you're human like the rest of us."

"Aren't you funny?" Annabel yawned. "I'll have you know that my smile is a proactive defense against being called a witch. How much farther?"

"Isn't that sobering...here it is!" Charlie exclaimed. He carefully unlocked and opened a thick wooden door.

As Annabel peered into the room, she gasped. The room was small, devoid of people, and spotless. Three beeswax candles were lit, and a bench held thick towels, pink-wrapped soap, and sponges. But the most captivating sight was an enormous washtub, foam across the top, steam still curling from its depths.

"Charlie. Is that…" Her voice rose before breaking as she slipped off Charlie's back. "I must be imagining things. Is this a hot bath you've brought me to? Or is it a mirage? I don't think I've ever even seen a bath that hadn't been used by another."

"It is indeed a hot bath," Charlie confirmed. "For you, and you alone. You said you liked to wash, that it relaxes you." His voice sent a deep thrill through her. "No one has used it. The tub was scrubbed down with vinegar before being filled." He kissed the back of her neck. "The water is so hot, your skin could peel off. You'll have to test it before slipping in."

"You silver-tongued devil," she whispered, her voice in disbelief. "I've never had a hot bath in my life. How on earth did you manage this?"

"This used to be Lady Phillipa Rowley's private lounge," Charlie explained. "Henry never comes down here since it reminds him of her, and he's out of town anyway. The rest of the castle inhabitants believe it to be haunted, much like the room under the library. It had been neglected for years until earlier today."

"God's legs. I knew I loved you, but this surpasses my dreams," she marveled.

"Oh, dream bigger." He grinned. "It wasn't much. Maggie approved to heat extra water, and Gregory and Leif carried it down here—in exchange for ale from Frederick. Lise contributed her rose-scented soap and towels."

"Goodness," Annabel breathed, her gratitude overwhelming her. "That was incredibly kind of them all. And so unexpected."

Charlie shrugged. "They're all right. The important thing is, do you like it?"

"It's the most wonderful sight I could see right now." Her eyes threatened to well up as she envisioned sinking into the inviting, steaming water. "You know me better than I realized."

"Ah, good. That was the goal. Enjoy," he added, his voice filled with warmth. "I'll be right outside, ensuring no one disturbs you."

Annabel stood before the bath, rendered speechless as Charlie departed. With deliberate steps and a radiant smile, she approached the inviting tub, a sigh of contentment escaping her lips. Slowly, she shed her sweaty, greasy clothes, letting them fall to the floor, and gracefully slipped into the steaming embrace of the pristine water. Unwrapping the rose-scented soap, she inhaled the sweet aroma and set the paper carefully back on the shelf as she lathered up the soap usually meant for aristocrats.

"Oh, yes," she whispered, submerging her head and cleansing her dust-streaked face and hands. Her attention then turned to her weary feet, giving them the attention they deserved. Finally, with just her face above the water, she floated, surrendering to the blissful serenity of the moment, allowing the weight of the past few arduous days to dissolve.

Once fully relaxed, she gingerly rose from the tub and lathered up again, enveloping herself in a velvety foam cocoon. Submerging herself in the water again, she rinsed away the suds, reveling in my sweet indulgence. It was a feeling of decadence she had never experienced. Gazing dreamily at the flickering glow of the candles, she felt like a princess, her imagination weaving tales of daring spies and clandestine adventures. As she luxuriated in the bath, time seemed to lose its hold, and her happiness multiplied exponentially. Feeling like she had transformed into a thousand iridescent bubbles, she couldn't resist the wicked thought that crossed her mind.

"Charlie!" she suddenly called out, her voice full of mischief.

The door creaked open, and Charlie's voice inquired, "Are you decent?"

"No," she replied innocently, crossing her arms over the tub's rim. "I washed up, but I'm still dirty. I desperately need someone in here to wash my back."

"Oh, you don't have to invite me in," The blush on his face made her feel giddy. "That was not my intent for all this. It's truly not a date. I just wanted to help you relax, I promise."

"I know you're an honorable man," she said, slipping away from the rim, bringing her hands up to pull her hair back, and lifting her breasts out of the water. "I love that about you." His jaw dropped, and he quickly stepped into the room to close the door behind him and lock it.

"Annabel..." Charlie said as he began to walk towards the tub, not taking his eyes off her. "I would never be one to impose on your will, physically or otherwise. I would never treat you as Baron Rowley has, or Richard, or that vicar Paul."

"I know," she whispered.

"You can say no to me at any time," he added. "If you change your mind, I'll leave."

Her heart fluttered, his words stirring a passionate desire within her. "You drive me mad with desire when you say such sweet things," she whispered. "You are the most wonderful man I've ever met."

As he finally reached the edge of the bath, hunger burning in his eyes, he bent down to her, holding onto the edge of the tub as he claimed her lips in a fervent, longing embrace. Then, slowly, he slid his hands down to her breasts, his thumbs sliding over her nipples and belly. She moaned and opened her eyes. "Won't you get in with me?"

Charlie's gaze simmered with lust, and he nodded. He pulled off his tunic, undershirt, pants, and undergarments. Entering the water beside her, he leaned back, devouring her with his gaze as she handed him the soap, and he began gathering. "All the times I undressed you with my eyes, I had no idea you were this beautiful, completely naked."

"I've never felt so good being naked before." She smiled when he set down the soap, reaching for him, and he took her in his arms, sliding his strong hands up onto her back.

For a few minutes, they felt electrified, embracing each other with mounting passion. "Annabel," he moaned. "I fear I cannot do this much longer without...."

"You'd bloody better," she whispered firmly. She leaned forward and slowly kissed Charlie's thigh, lifting him in the water to float on the surface. Slowly, she took his stiffness in her hands and stroked the whole shaft, slipping her palm over the base of it.

He groaned, "Oh, Annabel, that feels..." shuddering as she stroked him gently, harder, faster, until she finally bent down and licked at his tender thighs, feeling dizzy with lust when he curled his hands in her hair. Flicking her eyes at his face, seeing his eyes closed, she realized how much she loved how he looked. She wanted nothing more to straddle his hips, thrusting him inside her suddenly, but somehow managed to restrain herself.

Taking him into her mouth carefully, she sucked the head of his manhood with her soft lips then licked from the top to the base slowly, languidly. Suddenly, he pulled her to his face to kiss her, and it was as though a stroke of lightning jolted between them. She stroked him now vigorously with both hands as her thighs pressed against his legs, and he suddenly looked around feverishly and seized a hand towel, coming into it with a shudder she found incredibly sexy.

Charlie's breaths were steady and deep, his eyes opening to meet her gaze as he tossed the towel to the floor. "You're truly incredible," he murmured.

"You're not so bad yourself," she whispered, her voice warmed. "I still have those tinctures—not that I ever used them."

"Obviously, I'd love to help you test them out," he sighed but shook his head. "But though they're better than nothing, tinctures can fail. If by chance you conceive and something were to happen to me, my meager wealth would not pass to you. Our children would face a life of poverty, and I cannot bear the thought of such a possibility."

Before she lost her nerve, Annabel asked, "And how would you feel about a more...legitimate future together?"

"In a heartbeat," he responded without hesitation, his voice brimming with sincerity. "I would consider myself the luckiest man alive to have you by my side."

Her smile widened. "I feel the same." Picking up the soap, she playfully teased, "Shall I wash your back?" Her fingers grazed a bruise on his side, and she jokingly chided, "Is this from a fierce battle with a horse or perhaps a daring encounter with a pirate?"

He pridefully confessed, "I still find myself drawn to the fights. It's hard to explain, but it offers a certain release. Something I hadn't had until more recently," He winked at her over his shoulder, and she blushed. "And it's one more way to make extra money, I don't have to immediately turn over to the Baron."

She nodded understandingly. "Fair enough," she acquiesced. "Just promise me that you won't depart from this world prematurely. I'm not ready to bid you farewell."

"I wouldn't dare leave this world without savoring your lips again," Charlie whispered, his voice filled with devotion, as he leaned in to kiss her tenderly.

Running her hands gently down his back, a sigh of contentment escaped her. "This moment is pure bliss."

"Can I do something else memorable for you?" he asked, tracing her thighs softly with his fingers under the warm water, and her breath caught in her throat. "Yes, please..."

Chapter Twenty-Three

PERCY THE FALCON

Annabel had been harvesting barley for about ten minutes the next day when she heard her name being called. She walked up to the castle door, surprised to see the butler Leif throw her a contemptuous look. "There is a gentleman here to call on you, Mrs. Granger."

"What?" Annabel's mouth went dry. She thought she had more time. "My mother said..."

"Arva sends her regards," came a cheery voice, and Montgomery Hayworth stepped out with a winning smile. Monty saw Annabel looking rested, clean, happy, buoyed by love, and was immediately charmed. "I must say, you're fairer than your mother said."

She stared at him in distaste. "We knew each other as children. Once, you ripped apart my catechism and tore off my skirt. I mean this in the best possible way, but no, thank you."

"Sure, I remember you now!" He grinned at the realization. "You were a skinny little thing–you look far better now. I believe you'd make a fair wife."

Annabel's patience was wearing thin. "Montgomery, we are not engaged, and I am still married. This is highly inappropriate, and it matters not that you've spoken to my mother. Please leave."

"Oh, come on, now," entreated Monty. "Let's just spend a bit of time together, and perhaps you'll change your mind when the time comes." He smiled flirtatiously. "You like Shakespeare, don't you? I'm his great-grandson."

"You are a liar." Scowling, Annabel informed him, "Shakespeare doesn't have any descendants. His only granddaughter died twenty years ago."

"Ugh." Monty rolled his eyes. "My mistake." Drawing closer to her, he suddenly smiled. "I don't have to woo you, by the by. Your mother and my own have already agreed–you're mine as soon as your husband is executed or dies in prison."

"For..." Annabel stepped away from him and strode to the front door, with him on her heels, as she began to panic. Taking a deep breath, she said, "Look, Monty, I'm sorry if I've wasted your time, and I should have said something before today after my mother came by, but I've been terribly busy—not to mention still married. My mother did not get my consent nor blessing on another marriage." To his blank face, she confirmed, "To be clear, again, I will not be marrying you."

"Oh, yes, you bloody will be," he snapped, rankling her. "Our parents didn't spend hours hammering out an agreement so that some ungrateful little farmer's wife who doesn't know her place can turn me down."

"I'm sure you will make another girl very happy." Annabel remained calm. "But it will not be me."

"This isn't how things are done," groaned Monty. "I'm not giving up just like that. You'll be a sitting duck when your husband is gone, and like it or not, you'll need a man around here."

"Look, Monty, you don't want to marry me," Annabel said desperately, in what she hoped was a reasonable tone. "Surely you have better prospects. I'm old for marriage, and I'm sunworn. I'm not a good cook. I don't want a lot of children. I'm practically bad luck with my history—as you so kindly pointed out, my husband is a criminal, possibly about to make me a widow, and before that, I was left once already by our town vicar."

"I know," he winked. "I heard all about what happened with the vicar. What a saucy woman you are."

Her desperation increasing, Annabel stammered, "I'm–cantankerous. Three of my teeth are crooked. I like to stay inside reading, and I'm no better at sewing than cooking. I'm certainly not much fun for a man like you."

"Oh, the part I care about the most is putting a baby in you," Monty whispered, turning her stomach with his tone.

"I'm afraid I must insist that you leave," said Annabel in the firmest voice she could muster as she steered him away from the castle, walking him towards the carriage. "I have work to attend to. Please go home."

"No," Monty snapped. "Why don't you take me to the Baron, and I'll sort this out with him. We should have done that in the first place—you don't have to worry about a thing."

Annabel felt as though she was having a waking nightmare. She knitted her brows in frustration and looked past Monty to spot Frederick walking down the path, headed towards the stables. She suddenly remembered, with relief, that the Baron was still out of town.

"Lord Frederick!" she called, realizing how stilted and high her voice sounded, just as Charlie stepped out of the stables. Meeting

Frederick's eyes nervously, trying to silently signal for his assistance, she said, "Won't you please come and meet Montgomery Hayworth?"

Frederick looked wary but came slowly towards her as Charlie stopped in his tracks. Annabel gave them both a silent, grateful look. "Lord Frederick is the baron's son," explained Annabel to Monty, who appeared nonplussed. "He's in charge of the barony while his father is away, which he is, for several days."

"Oh, fantastic," sneered Monty. "Lord Frederick, won't you talk sense into her? This woman's got her mother's permission to marry me once Farmer Granger's passed on."

Wrinkling his face, Frederick looked crossly at Annabel. "What is this?"

"As I have told Montgomery," said Annabel. "I have rejected the proposed marriage contract with him."

Frederick looked surprised at that. "Have you? Alright." Shrugging at Monty, he said, "Guess you don't have any business here, then." He began fidgeting with a dagger at his side. "Is that all?"

"Are you *mad*?" Monty looked incredulous. "No, that's not all. Her mother as good as promised her to me. There's land involved, which is going to be mine. She has no rights."

"I think she does," said Frederick in a bored tone. "Now, I'm no expert, but we've got several prisoners of the kingdom here, mostly pirates, being held for murder."

Montgomery looked worriedly at him and stepped back. "You have murderers in your dungeon?"

Frederick continued with a sniff, "Of course we do. How versed are you in this region's penitential laws?"

"What?" Monty asked, clearly lost.

"It's true that when aristocratic women become betrothed, they have a little right of refusal due to the familial land involved," ventured

Frederick, trying not to look at Annabel. She glanced at Charlie's face to see him looking worried, albeit mildly impressed.

Frederick continued, "But Annabel was not an aristocrat when she came here and signed her marriage contract; she was, and is, a peasant. And peasants have the right of refusal for marriage when there is no land involved."

"There is bloody land involved," argued Monty angrily.

Frederick laughed. "Castle Rowley doesn't award land to peasants. It's a tenant farm, a rental. She gets money from selling the barley but still has to pay quarterly for the house and land from the estate. We like to make money here, after all. You wouldn't have any rights to Annabel or her land unless you were married."

"You what?" spat Monty. "Did you not hear me? Her mother arranged it."

"Her mother is free to arrange, but Annabel is free to refuse," repeated Frederick.

Annabel breathed a sigh of relief. "Now will you go?"

"That's ridiculous," said Monty, shaking his head. "I can just take her myself when the time comes; I've got her family's blessing, after all." He winked conspiratorially at Frederick. "It's a man's world, after all, right?"

Frederick's eyes flashed, and he cleared his throat. "I've always found it fascinating what Castle Rowley, our barony, is best known for in this kingdom. It's certainly not our exports." He looked beyond Monty and spoke loudly and sternly. "James! Won't you please enlighten this man here?"

James, who had come up behind them on the path, looked stricken. "What?" Frederick repeated the question, and James swallowed hard. "It's punishment."

"Is it *really*?" Monty began to look green.

"Oh, yes." Emboldened, James continued. "We may have the largest dungeon in the region and certainly the most occupied."

"Hmm," Monty said uneasily. "I didn't know that. But..."

"What's the punishment for rape and abduction, James?" Frederick asked in a bored voice, picking at his fingernails.

"For rape, either the Baron or the victim is to gouge out the rapist's eyes and cut off their balls," said James, grinning as he began to enjoy the game. "For abduction, it's torture. Baron Rowley likes to use either the Judas cradle or the iron chair."

"God's bones," said Monty in a shocked voice. "Back home, it's only a fine for rape and the stocks for murder."

"In this region, we are quite devoted to punishing every man convicted of a criminal act in a way that deters it," said Frederick darkly.

"Really, even for peasant women?" Monty asked skeptically. "I thought that was just for aristocrats."

"For pity's sake, get off your high horse, Monty," Annabel muttered.

"As long as she lives on the castle grounds, she will abide by our rules," proclaimed Frederick, crossing his arms and throwing Monty an irritated look. "Aren't you a peasant?"

"Yes," growled Monty.

"Well, I'm an aristocrat," Frederick sneered. "And it's time for my supper. So why don't you leave here before I lose my appetite."

Monty shot them each a look of death and stormed down the path, ignoring the carriage. James walked off in the opposite direction, muttering, and shaking his head.

Frederick gestured silently to Charlie and Annabel, then the castle, and the three quickly entered it. As soon as Leif had shut the door, Annabel and Frederick broke down in fits of laughter while Charlie looked at them incredulously. "I'm glad you both think that was funny. I'm shaking in my bloody boots here."

"Sorry," snickered Frederick, hanging his head. "But that angry look on his face...like a child with a ball taken away. It was almost too pitiful to be funny, and yet..."

"I assure you, it's nervous laughter," said Annabel. "I was starting to get a bit frantic there. I hoped Frederick could help me get rid of him, but I didn't realize how good he'd be at it."

"Oh, I made quick work of him," said Frederick, smiling and bowing to them both dramatically.

"You think he's gone?" asked Charlie reproachfully.

Frederick scowled. "Of course, he's gone. I told him to go, and he went."

"Did you hear him say he was leaving? I didn't," Charlie scoffed. "I bet you a day's pay he's standing right outside. He's waiting for her to leave, then he'll grab her and have his way with her in the middle of the cornfield, using it as leverage to marry her later on." He looked at Annabel's aghast face apologetically. "Sorry. But I've helped break up a few assaults in the cornfield."

"Bet." Striding to the window, Frederick slumped. "God's arms, you're right. Bloody git. How dare he?" He absently handed a surprised Charlie a a handful of coins from his purse and began pacing outside the kitchen as Maggie looked at them from the baker's block, kneading and shaking her head with some amusement.

Annabel sighed bitterly. "So, I've got to stay inside all day and miss the writing lesson I've arranged, due to this nonsense?" "Perhaps there's another way we could entreat him to leave," suggested Charlie mildly. "A way that would not endanger ourselves."

Frederick stopped clenching his hands and drew out the dagger. "I'll go out there and make him leave myself. I'm not afraid to bring a fight with weapons or fists."

"Is that the best idea?" Charlie asked mildly. "He's perhaps ten years older, and you don't know if he can fight or any of his handicaps. Without planning, there are also others outside you could injure by accident."

"So we'll send James out there to scare him off," sighed Frederick. "Or Leif."

"And get them in trouble when he returns later to officially complain to Henry, with Annabel's mother in tow?" asked Charlie.

"Do you think he will?" Annabel asked uncomfortably.

"I do think so," he said to her, winking. "If it was me, I would fight for you."

She smiled, her heart and cheeks warm.

"Then what?" asked Frederick crossly. "I can tell you have an idea, Charlie, so out with it already."

"Percy," Charlie sighed.

His eyes alight, Frederick crowed, "Of course! Bloody brilliant idea."

"Who is Percy?" asked Annabel warily. "Oh, dear. That's not..."

"Percy is Baron Rowley's prize falcon," said Charlie. "He's trained to chase after people."

"I recall that now, in far too much detail," Annabel sighed, shuddering.

"Right. Father threatened you with Percy on his birthday." Scowling, Frederick replied, "Bugger. It's best to have a piece of the twat's clothing."

"Of that man standing outside?" called Maggie from the kitchen. "He left his hat. Not that I'm listening in, mind you."

Charlie grinned. "Brilliant."

He took the hat from Maggie with thanks, and Annabel curiously followed them up the stairs to the east-facing turret. There was a small wooden hut, and Frederick dipped in and emerged with a bird in a hood on his gloved arm.

"God's bones, it's huge," remarked Annabel, marveling at the enormous animal.

"Oh yes, he's a beast," said Frederick. "He's worth his weight in gold. My father loves this bird. He's taken it to church. He loves it more than he loves me and far more than he ever loved my mother."

"Now, that's not true, Fred," sighed Charlie. "Did you bring the meat?"

"Oh shoot, I forgot," lamented Frederick. "Will you please get it?"

"Yes," said Charlie. "I'll be right back." He touched Annabel's back reassuringly, fleetingly, and left quickly down the stairs.

When they were alone, Frederick spoke softly to the bird. "We're going to keep our voices low to not scare this bird. He's ferocious, a mighty beast, but also very skittish when he first comes out, aren't you, Percy? Yes, you are," he said fondly.

Annabel took a slow, deep breath and carefully peeked out of the turret. Sure enough, Monty was pacing in front of the cornfield.

"You must fancy Charlie rotten, right?" asked Frederick softly. "To break your engagement like that."

"Truthfully, I knew Monty in childhood and hated him. I didn't want to marry him anyway. It was not an engagement for me," she said firmly. "But yes. I do quite fancy Charlie."

"He said he's in love with you, you know," said Frederick. "That must be grand to be in love. I've never been able to get close enough to anyone to fall in love." He sighed. "It's terribly lonely here."

"Really?" Annabel asked in a surprised voice. "Charlie told you he loved me?"

"Yes." Frederick grimaced, looking affronted. "Why, didn't he tell *you*?"

"Yes," she shrugged. "I didn't realize he'd shared such a thing with you. I suppose you got your wish to be closer to your brother."

"Hardly." Frederick sighed. "I hate my father, and my father hates Charlie. We'll never be able to be close like real brothers." His voice was bitter. "I'll be honest with you, Annabel. Castle Rowley is a terrible place. You and Charlie should both get out of here."

"Perhaps you're right." She rubbed her arms, suddenly feeling a chill. "But be careful. If my father thinks you're trying to help Charlie, you'll go missing," stated Frederick flatly, and Annabel looked at him in surprise.

"You sound pretty sure of that," she said nervously. "What do you know about people going missing?"

He shrugged. "It's what happens. Are you and Charlie going to run away together?"

"I don't know, truthfully," she said. "But he doesn't want to leave while people still need him here."

Frederick laughed. "That could last forever and a day. Just take what you can, bunk with some friends underground, and run far from here." He paused. "Do you hear something?"

Charlie was back with the meat. "Leif says Monty tried to bribe someone to let him sneak in. And running away would be a death sentence. The Baron doesn't tolerate deserters. This very bird would hunt us down."

"Hattie left," Annabel remembered. "She wasn't hunted down."

Shaking his head, Charlie said, "Who knows if she truly left on her own or not? She was here one day, gone the next."

Wrinkling her forehead, she remarked, "Are you sure? Lise said that James saw her leaving with a packed bag."

"James, the castle chin-wagger, and the Baron's steward?" Charlie laughed.

"He's bloody lying, no doubt about it. Maggie has just told me the castle door never opened that night nor that morning. And just like Agatha, she had no family, no friends outside the castle."

"That bloody figures." Frederick removed the falcon's hood but kept his leash on and threw a tiny piece of meat on the ground.

The bird dove for it. Then Frederick showed him the hat, and the falcon carefully inspected it. Frederick withdrew the leash, and the falcon flew into the air. The three of them clustered around the windows to watch, peeking from where they could not be seen from the ground. Charlie took Annabel's hand, and she squeezed it.

Percy began coasting, perusing the ground as he seemed to trek through the air. He quietly went flat once he had him in his sights. Suddenly, he swooped down over Monty's head, causing the young man to jump around erratically, looking for who could be there. The regal falcon was already twenty yards up in the air and swooping down again. Percy screeched and grabbed Monty's shoulder, scraping shoulders and ripping fabric, making the man scream.

"Get the bloody hell away from me!" he yelled, picking up speed and sprinting away from the barony. The bird continued to duck and chase Monty until he was entirely out of sight, upon which Frederick blew a whistle and unpacked a more significant portion of meat.

Percy was back within seconds and happily enjoyed the meal. "Good boy, Percy," said Frederick softly. "That's a bad man."

CHAPTER TWENTY-FOUR

DAEGAL GODWIN

Once they were sure Monty was gone, Annabel beamed at Charlie. "That was impressive. You and Frederick certainly have quick thinking on your side—for a while, I thought I would miss my lesson."

"She's meeting you by the river, yes? Let me saddle you a horse." They began walking back downstairs. "That's all right, Fred?"

"Yes, of course," Frederick grinned. "Good day to you both...in my father's absence, I've got a rare music lesson, if you take my meaning." He quickly departed.

They made their way to the stables, where Charlie saddled a horse, patting the animal's neck affectionately. "This is Athena."

"Why must I take a horse?" Annabel asked, slightly puzzled. "It's just a short walk by the river. I can easily go on foot."

"Just in case you and Sarala need to make a quick getaway and ride off for any reason," he explained. "Just as a precaution."

She frowned. "Do you think there's a real danger?"

"Yes, honestly," he replied. "Some people around here don't take kindly to women learning to read and write." "Oh, should we meet indoors instead?" she suggested.

He shook his head. "Believe it or not, that might be even worse. As if you're hiding something."

"Are you serious?" she asked, surprised. "I hadn't realized it was quite *that* bad. I thought it just made people uncomfortable."

"Too uncomfortable. Mind you, I don't make the rules—I just learn them so I can break them discreetly," he commented. While handing her the bridle, he suggested, "Once you're there, tie the horse up to graze. You can ride her back. Don't worry too much. Kunal is there for protection, but I feel safer knowing you have a horse nearby by the river."

"What kind of people are opposed to a girl learning to write better, for pity's sake?" she muttered.

"I agree. Literacy is always a good thing. Some people are just mad—or make odd choices in superstitions," he said, shaking his head and looking about to ensure no one was watching them before squeezing her hands as he handed her the bridle.

She grinned as he waved her off. When she reached the spot by the river where Sarala was waiting patiently, Annabel saw that they had set up a tent, propped open to let in the fresh air, with two stools outside.

Sarala stood, a broad smile on her face. "Annabel! I'm so glad you made it. And you remember Kunal."

He tipped his hat to her from his place atop the cart, a book in his hand.

Annabel nodded, hardly believing that this was really happening. "Thank you so much for doing this. What do we do first?"

"Have a seat here, dear." Sarala gestured for Annabel to sit on the low, carved wooden stool at the table outside the tent.

Sitting down, Annabel couldn't help but ramble. "I've wanted to learn to write better for years. It was always impossible when I was living at home, helping raise my twelve brothers and sisters. I can't believe I'm finally here. Is it even possible for someone my age to become a good writer?" Her voice dropped. "Most of the writing I've done is in my head."

"Yes, it really is. And you'll be hard-pressed to find a writer who hasn't done more writing in their heads than on paper." Sarala took out some paper and a red book with no words on the cover. "So you were living with your family before, and now you're at Castle Rowley? Are you safe here?"

Annabel nodded. "I'm finding some of it grand, some of it painful. Perhaps in the future, if I can save enough money, I might try to leave."

"Oh?" Sarala inquired. "Do you have any particular place in mind?"

"No...just dreaming right now." Shaking her head, Annabel looked down her head. "Is that naive, do you think?"

Sarala shrugged. "Naivety simply means you haven't learned enough yet. You'll figure it out as you go. We all do. Now, why do you want to become a better writer?"

Annabel pondered this. "Well, I recently won a prize for submitting an idea for a play. Telling it out loud sparked something in me, and I wanted to be ready if they did ask me to write the play. I want to learn how."

"Well done, you." Sarala's smile grew wider. "First of all, for all you don't see many women reading in public, you're certainly not alone. The number of men who can write is just under a third; for women, it's a little over a tenth—and growing, that's the important part. And I believe in you. All of us do."

"Why, thank you," Annabel said, feeling encouraged.

"Have you completed any writing projects before? Can you recall any challenges you faced in the past—internal, not societal?" Sarala asked gently.

"Lack of time was always the biggest challenge," Annabel shrugged. "Beyond that, no one thinks a peasant should read."

"Is there anything else you're currently trying to learn?" Sarala asked.

"Stoicism," she replied. "To face up to the Baron and his games. Oh, and playwriting, of course."

"Excellent," Sarala said. "I think we're going to get along marvelously. Let's begin." She opened the red book, and by the rushing river, Annabel embarked on her first writing lesson in earnest.

Hours later, the lesson ended with her mind buzzing with new-found knowledge on character development, hooks, and plotting, and her rucksack filled with a beautiful composition book meticulously notated by Sarala.

Kunal saddled up Sarala's horse, then turned to Annabel. "When do you want to go and pick up your prize? I've got the letter."

"Tomorrow afternoon?" Annabel asked hopefully. "Is that all right?"

"Of course." He grinned. "I'll bring along food for the ride."

Sarala smiled warmly. "Congratulations again on your win, dear. That's quite an achievement."

Annabel nodded. "I'm worried I might get caught, to tell you the truth. I'm not used to this kind of thing."

Sarala smiled. "Yes. I'd love to tell you to forge ahead and demand your winnings under your name, but that would likely only put your life in danger. The best option I've found is to surround yourself with like-minded individuals, become astute at reading people, and, whenever possible, get rid of those who perpetrate harm or move on."

Annabel nodded. "I appreciate your insight."

"I suggest you go down there, assess the situation, and if necessary, pretend that Kunal is your husband if anyone becomes brutish. Most men are afraid of him, and that will work to our advantage, as he would never harm you or me," Sarala advised. She smiled at Annabel. "You're a thinker, and I can see that. Just be cautious."

"Thank you," said Annabel softly. "Thank you so much for everything."

The next afternoon, in front of the theater, Kunal looked at Annabel.

"Ready?"

She nodded, excitement and nervousness churning in her stomach. Slowly, they walked through the tall hallway adorned with colorful scarves. Approaching the ticket counter, Kunal rang a small bell as Annabel stood nearby. After a moment, a short man with fiery hair appeared at the window. "Can I help you?"

"Daegal Godwin, here to collect contest winnings," Kunal announced in a deep rumble.

The man's eyes widened. "Are you Daegal Godwin?"

"In the flesh," Kunal lied smoothly.

"The piece you submitted was quite dark," the man whispered. "I've never read anything like it. Can you tell me if it's part of a series or if there will be a full-length play?"

Kunal shook his head. "I'm currently working on something else. Inspiration can lead me anywhere."

The man looked disappointed. "What a shame."

Giving the man a discerning look, Kunal murmured, "You're not so young that you've had enough disappointment. Embrace it; it builds character."

Rolling his eyes, the man disappeared back inside. Kunal appeared unsurprised, but Annabel whispered anxiously, "Where is he going?"

Kunal jerked his thumb back towards the spot where the man had been. "He doesn't have the money. He's going to fetch it or find someone who does."

"Why did he waste time talking about the play then? This whole situation makes me nervous," she whispered.

"He was just fishing for information," Kunal explained. "People are nosy. Sometimes, a diversion is enough."

"I suppose you're right," she mumbled as another man in a suit and an excited expression entered the room.

Kunal nodded at the man. "Are you here to present my winnings? If I've ever seen an outfit fit for a presentation, that's it."

The man chuckled. "Why, thank you. I am, indeed. Lionel Black."

Kunal pulled out a leather roll and handed over a letter recommending a Daegal Godwin matching Kunal's description. The man nodded and handed Kunal a bag of coins and a package. "This is the dictionary," he explained, "and the winning amount is all there. Please reconsider writing a full play. 'The Haunted Hand' was the most captivating ghost story, and although I've never read your work before, I'd love to produce a full version of it."

"You *would*?" Annabel asked, astonished. "Truly?"

Lionel glanced at her as if just noticing her presence. "Ah, and who might you be?"

"I'm..." The words caught in her throat momentarily, and Lionel regarded her with suspicion.

Placing a hand on her shoulder, Kunal interjected, "She's my dear friend, who has had a fright recently. You see, my story draws inspiration from true events." He winked at Annabel as Lionel turned his attention to her with curiosity.

She cleared her throat. "Yes, I have been plagued by...spirits lately. Please forgive me if I've given any other impression."

"Well," huffed Lionel. "What do you think, Mr. Godwin? Is working together on a production a possibility?"

Kunal shrugged, looking pointedly at Annabel. She pressed her lips together, and anxiety coiled in her stomach, threatening to overpower her. "Yes, I think you could do it, Daegal."

"Fantastic," Lionel exclaimed, clapping his hands together. "Do you have time next week to sit with me and show me more of your work?"

Kunal considered the request. "Make it two weeks," he said after Annabel discreetly raised two fingers behind Lionel's back.

"Of course, of course. Thank you so much, Mr. Godwin." Lionel shook both their hands with enthusiasm.

As they made their way out, Annabel confided in Kunal, "I'm feeling an extra spark of confidence now, and I wouldn't mind doing something with it. Could we stop by my mother's house to tell her to stop setting me up with men and let me live my life? I can pay you to be my escort."

He laughed. "Your money is no good here, Mr. Godwin. I'm happy to take you to your mother's and then back home."

Annabel smiled in gratitude, and when they arrived at the Barlow house, she squared her shoulders and marched right up to the house.

When her mother opened the door, she gaped in surprise at the sight of her eldest daughter. Without losing her nerve, Annabel declared, "Mummy, I won't marry Monty or anyone else you send my way. You have to stop this right now, or..." Annabel paused for a moment, searching for her words. "Or you'll wake up one day and have a grandchild you'll never meet. You won't see me again if you don't stop meddling." She held her head high.

"What?" Arva asked, confused.

"I need to make my own decisions," Annabel sighed, softening her tone. "You have to stop trying to live my life for me. No more matchmaking."

"My darling child," her mother whispered, taking Annabel's hand. "I only ever wanted you to be taken care of. I'm afraid you'll be left with nothing if I don't secure your future. I don't want you to be all alone." Her voice quivered as she fought back tears. "A girl needs a village, or at the very least, a man. I'm sorry, sweetheart, but it's how things are."

Suddenly, a little face peeked out from under Arva's arm. "Jack!" Annabel cried out with delight, ruffling his hair affectionately. "You little bean, I can't believe how much I've missed you." Glancing inside the house, Annabel noticed something was amiss. "Where's all the furniture?"

Her mother's face fell, and she appeared to struggle with her words. "It's been sold. We're moving," Jack announced.

"Moving?" Annabel repeated. "Where to?"

"We're going to live with the Ramseys," the little boy replied. "This is our last week here."

"Jackie, my love, go inside and finish your supper," Arva mumbled. Turning back to Annabel, she confirmed, "He's right. We can't afford to keep this farmhouse anymore. Everything's been sold to pay the creditors." She shook her head. "Your father can't handle all the chores in his condition, which isn't improving. My children are being worn down every day before my eyes." She blinked back tears. "Just as you were

."

"Is that why you were so quick to marry me off to Richard and Monty?" Annabel asked. "And Dorothy?"

Her mother nodded sadly. "The Ramseys offered us a place to live with the three little ones in exchange for helping with chores, but nothing more. I've been trying to secure homes for you and all your sisters since they only have room for a few of us."

"Why didn't you *tell* me?" Annabel cried.

"I have my pride," Arva lamented. "A mother must create a happy home for her children, and it's a father's responsibility to work and provide for that home. We've failed on both counts." Tears began to gather in her pale green eyes, and she wiped them away with the back of her hand.

Annabel stepped forward to embrace her mother. "You haven't," she reassured her softly. "No one could have predicted that Papa would be injured by that tree. You've done the best you could with what we have. And you've taken steps to ensure we won't end up on the streets." Annabel squeezed her mother's hand. "I'm proud of you, Mummy."

"Oh, don't start. I've run out of clean handkerchiefs—they're all on the line," Arva sobbed, and Annabel offered her one from her pocket, which her mother gratefully accepted. "I'm sorry things didn't work out with Monty. His mother gave me an earful yesterday about things that made not one lick of sense. He said you have demons at the castle. Flying ones." She shook her head, mystified. "Either that boy's seeing things, or you're in the thick of Hades at Castle Rowley."

"Goodness, wouldn't that be something," chuckled Annabel. "I'm afraid it's nothing quite so interesting. The Baron Rowley's son helped me chase him away with his father's falcon."

"Well!" her mother exclaimed. "How did this friendship come about? That's plenty interesting enough for me."

Annabel shook her head. "I've made friends at the castle, Mummy. I've found my village without Richard. I've formed connections and even earned extra money doing things I like." Suddenly, her hand dipped into her pocket. "Do you need any?"

"No," her mother replied quickly, shaking her head. "No, sweetheart. But thank you. No, when you move out and start your own life, whoever is in it, you must use that to build your future, not ours."

"If you ever need anything, I'll be there, Mummy," Annabel promised. Arva took a deep breath and smiled. "Now that we've almost sorted things out, I look forward to living with the Ramsey family. Sarah Ramsey is a fantastic cook, and her husband, John, is a strong and patient bear of a man. He doesn't mind helping your father get around. They've grown to be mates; they have." Arva's gaze shifted past Annabel to the carriage, where Kunal sat reading a book under the shade of his hat. "Well, and who is this new man of yours?"

"Actually, he's not," Annabel said, smiling. "But he's part of my village, so to speak. He brought me here, and he'll bring me back to the castle."

Smiling at her daughter, Arva's shoulders seemed to relax, and she nodded. "Good for you, then." She hugged Annabel tightly and whispered, "I'm proud of you too, sweetheart."

CHAPTER TWENTY-FIVE

BETTINA SOLEDAD

One day, Annabel received a summons to the castle, which left her with a sinking feeling. But to her great delight, as she entered the great hall, she found her childhood best friend waiting for her.

"Bettina!" Annabel exclaimed with joy. "It's been ages! How long was that fishing trip?" She laughed. "I'm so glad you're here."

"Annabel, how I've missed you!" Bettina threw her arms around her friend's neck. "I'm sorry I didn't come to visit sooner." She grinned. "Do you love living at a castle? Are you getting every meal at last? And is it really haunted, as they say?"

"I am indeed getting every meal, and there are parts of it that I love," Annabel whispered, glancing around to ensure no one was listening. "I don't think it's actually haunted, but it's still a bit of a mystery, to tell you the truth. Do you want to go for a walk?"

Just then, Lise approached with a pail and a large laundry basket, stress lining her face. "Annabel, I'm behind on my tasks. I know you have company, but please do me a quick favor? I'll repay you in trade."

Annabel nodded. "Of course, what do you need? Lise, this is my friend Bettina Soledad."

"Oh, God's thumbs, how rude of me. Good morrow, pleased to meet you," Lise said, her face flushed. "I'd shake your hand, but I'm a mess today."

"No worries." Bettina smiled. "Nice to meet you. Any friend of Annabel's is a friend of mine."

"What's the favor?" Annabel asked. "Preferably something outdoors—I hoped to take Bettina to tour the property a bit."

"It is," Lise replied. "I have a net bag of the Baron's worst socks that need to be tied at a spot in the river so they can finally get clean. The river is the only thing that can remove the grime from this fabric."

"Oh, that's all?" Annabel said. "No problem. How about a new set of stockings?"

"Deal," Lise agreed, handing her the pail.

As Annabel led Bettina out of the front door, her friend looked at her admirably. "Look at you, not doing everything for nothing. Maybe this place really is good for you."

Annabel smiled, and as they passed by the stables, she paused. "We should each take a horse so we can go riding later. Also," she whispered, "I should tell you—I'm secretly seeing a man. Don't mention it to anyone, but I had to tell you. Richard, the man my mum found for me, the reason I moved here—turned out to be the worst part of all of this, a drug-addled brute who slept with a harlot on our wedding night and doesn't pay his taxes, and with him put away, Charlie has been..." She smiled. "Perhaps the best part."

"Oh!" Bettina playfully nudged Annabel's arm. "Annabel Barlow, you've been holding out on me. Tell me everything, please." She paused and added kindly, "Might I say, dear friend, that your face is more alit now than I ever saw it speak of Paul."

"Paul is like a slim volume containing a few stories, while Charlie is like an anthology of literature." Annabel smiled. "I'm not cheating on Richard, mind. He was already married twice, and his second wife is still alive, though you didn't hear that."

Bettina's eyes widened. "For goodness sake. Your life sounds like one of those plays you like to read."

"Not for nothing." Annabel quickly filled her friend in on the background. Smiling, she added, "Charlie simply melts me—and he can read. We work together in the fields some days, then others he works in the stables—he's meant to be a woodcarver, but it's a bit complicated. "She grinned. "Betty, this man had a hot bath drawn just for me. There was steam curling off it."

"God's legs, I'm bloody sold," laughed Bettina. "Will we meet him if we take the horses, I hope?"

"I think so," Annabel whispered as she carefully opened the stable door. Charlie was brushing down one of the horses, accompanied by two stablehands.

One who she had come to know as Fulke scornfully told Charlie, "I don't see why you won't do it."

The man on the other side agreed. "It's just a bit extra money won gambling. You can tell us the outcome of at least one fight, surely. We can pay you."

"Are you going to pay the ferryman for my passage?" Charlie laughed.

Seeing Annabel and Bettina, he stopped and put down his brush. "Good day to both of you. Fulke, Nathaniel, why don't you both take a break."

"Good day to all of you," Annabel greeted, smiling at the others, and the two men nodded back at the two women before departing. "Charlie, this is my best friend since childhood, Bettina Soledad."

"It's a pleasure," Charlie said with a friendly grin. "Nice to meet the best friend of the best woman I know."

Bettina smiled as Annabel asked, "I hoped to borrow a couple of horses? We're going to the river to do a favor for Lise, then heading to market."

"Sure," Charlie said, and he saddled up the horses.

"Thanks," Annabel whispered, briefly squeezing his fingers.

After Charlie returned inside and they turned the corner of the stable, headed for the river, Bettina cleared her throat. "I didn't want to say anything, Anna–but I know I'll regret it if I don't. I've asked around and heard things about it here. There's a rumor that people have gone missing and never returned." She lowered her voice. "Nothing has happened to anyone you know here, has it?"

"Actually, yes," Annabel admitted. "We actually banded together to rescue a woman from the dungeon who was sent there unjustly." She shivered. "I still can't quite believe we weren't caught. To tell you the truth, I keep expecting to be hauled before the Baron, the truth forced out of me."

She took a deep breath. "I've had a few nightmares about it... he's a very cruel man."

"That's not a way to live, my friend," Bettina protested. "You shouldn't have to endure such fear. You don't have to. It's only a matter of time before you get punished for something trivial–I've heard stories about how they treat the lower class here."

"I can't give up now. I've come so far and am too close to achieving what I want to turn back now." Annabel sighed.

"Come live with my family and me," Bettina said. "You can read and write on the side; no one will stop you. Work at the Soledad Fishery and stay on one of our houseboats—Pa said he'd pay you thirty percent above the living wage to start. He's seen you cast and thinks you're a natural with a fishing net."

"Oh, Bettina," Annabel said, touched. "I'm so grateful. And if your offer stands, I might take you up on it soon if things change. But for now, I must stay. It's what I want."

"Alright," Bettina sighed, smiling at her friend. "I won't push you, but please be careful."

"I will," Annabel assured her. "How is your family? Is your dad still telling his endless stories while making fish pies? Tell me the latest one."

"It's funny you mention that," Bettina remarked. "He was asking about you. He saw the notebooks you left with me and couldn't believe you wrote five in three days. He wants you to write down his crazy stories and compile them into a book."

"Are you serious?" Annabel looked at her friend in surprise, who nodded. "That would make such an enjoyable read."

"He doesn't want the stories to be lost when he's gone, and my memory isn't good enough to pass them down verbally," Bettina laughed. "I know some of them, but there are dozens more. There are too many to remember and still have space for fish recipes and poetry."

"Different categories, too," Annabel mused. "Fables, horror, comedies, children's stories. I could write several books for him."

"Would you do it?" Bettina asked. "You don't have to. It would take hours."

"Then I better charge a hefty amount of dried fish for my troubles," Annabel laughed. "I have something else to tell you as well." She filled Bettina in on the playwright contest with the prize money, Kunal posing as Daegal, making peace with her mother, and her new writing lessons.

Bettina shook her head in admiration. "I'm starting to see why you want to stay. It's challenging, but there are more opportunities than you had back home."

"Exactly," Annabel agreed, smiling at her friend. "I'm not saying I wouldn't make changes. But I think I'm going to achieve something significant from this experience. Something life-changing."

Annabel reached the river and secured the netted bag to a stone while Bettina took hold of both horses' reins. "There," Annabel said. "Shall we ride back together or ride to the marketplace?"

"Let's do the latter," Bettina suggested, and they mounted their horses, settling comfortably in their saddles. "I was worried you'd only have side saddles since you live in a castle. Thank goodness you have standard saddles."

Annabel laughed. "Right! I know how to ride, and it's better for my back. They wouldn't want a farmer with an aching body, that's for sure."

"Absolutely," Bettina agreed. "Who's your favorite merchant here?

"The Sutars," Annabel replied. "I can't wait to introduce you to Rupa and Kunal. And if Sarala is there, she is as well. She's the writing teacher."

Suddenly, a deafening explosion reverberated behind them, piercing the air and startling the horses into a frenzied gallop. Annabel and Bettina desperately clung to the reins, pulling and kicking to regain control, but their efforts proved futile. With a final jolt, the women were flung from their mounts, tumbling onto the mossy grass, gasping for breath.

Annabel groaned as the horses disappeared into the woods, frustration etched on her face. "God's blood! Are you alright? What was that?"

"I'm fine," Bettina assured her, hoisting herself up and extending a hand to Annabel. "Aren't these fancy horses supposed to return home when spooked? They nearly led us into the woods."

Indeed, they found themselves just at the edge of the dark forest. Annabel shivered, an uneasy feeling creeping over her. "Let's get out of here." To their surprise, three men emerged from the forest, blocking their path. Annabel blinked against the sudden brightness, her gaze falling on their masked faces, only their eyes visible. All three carried weapons—a staff, a large knife, and a pipe—resolutely barring their way. "Excuse us, gentlemen," Annabel began, her voice calm but laced with authority. "I work at Castle Rowley, and..."

"Why don't you both take a little stroll back into the woods?" growled the tallest man, his voice laden with hostility. Annabel's eyes narrowed.

"Nathaniel, is that *you*?" she asked incredulously.

"Who is Nathaniel?" Bettina whispered, her voice filled with confusion.

"One of the new stablehands we just left," Annabel muttered, recognizing him. But her hopes of finding familiarity were quickly dashed.

"No, it's not," one of the men retorted gruffly.

"Fulke?" Annabel continued, her tone marked with disbelief. She turned her attention to the third, shortest man. "And Barnaby. What are you all doing?"

"How did you bloody do that?" Fulke demanded angrily. "You don't know us."

"You live on the bloody property," Annabel shouted incredulously. "I've worked with you all in the fields. I've spoken to you many times. Barnaby clapped at a story I told of a horse and a pig."

"No matter. Get into the woods, both of you," Nathaniel snarled.

"What do you think you're going to do?" Annabel's voice turned sharp.

"Oh, I think you know," Nathaniel sneered, tearing off his mask and leering at her with a cruel glint. "No point hiding anymore. Why don't you do with us what you do with Charlie?"

"What?" Annabel gasped, her face draining of color.

"If you're going to whore around at Castle Rowley, it might as well include us," he laughed, his tone dripping with malice. "Your friend here is a nice bonus we weren't expecting, but we'll enjoy her too."

"I'll say," sneered Fulke, joining in. "What's your name again, sweetheart?"

Bettina's eyes narrowed. "I'll cut off your manhood and feed it to the worms before I'll let you stick it in me."

Annabel was left momentarily speechless, her blood boiling with rage and misplaced guilt for being responsible for her friend being in this dangerous situation. She couldn't even meet Bettina's gaze without tears in her eyes.

"No," she managed, her voice stronger than she felt. "We're going back to the castle. You'll step aside and let us go on, or there will be consequences."

"How amusing you are," Nathaniel taunted, pulling out a hatchet and toying with it menacingly, inching closer to Annabel. He swung the weapon down with a sudden lunge, narrowly missing her as she jumped aside, yelping in surprise. Laughing, he raised a piece of mistletoe he had cut from an apple tree behind her. "Come on, sweetheart, give us a kiss."

Annabel cleared her throat. "I'm surprised you would do such a thing," she managed to say calmly, her voice steady. "I suppose none of you are superstitious."

"What are you talking about?" Nathaniel grumbled while Barnaby's eyes widened, a nervous sweat breaking out on his face.

"Baroness Phillippa Rowley," Annabel shrugged. "I sleep above the dungeon and am visited by her spirit regularly. You know it's haunted. If you assault Bettina and me, I'll have the ghost of the Baroness avenge us."

A shiver ran through Barnaby. "Baroness Rowley didn't care about peasants, only artists, and her family," he murmured. "She wouldn't help you, even in death." But Annabel could see the sweat glistening on his face.

"We were riding her horses, after all. Didn't you notice?" Annabel said mildly, her gaze fixed on Fulke. "She loved them dearly, and I'm sure she'd be devastated to see the role you forced them to play in this madness. She certainly considered them family." She lowered her voice. "Would you like to wonder, every time you're working late, if the noise you hear is her ghost coming to strangle you to death?"

Fulke rolled his eyes. "I don't bloody care."

But Barnaby dropped the pipe he had been carrying, nervously wiping his hands on his breeches. "I'm out, mates."

"What?!" Nathaniel exploded, looking at him incredulously.

The shorter man shook his head stubbornly. "I was on the fence about this from the start, and I only did it because you paid me—you can have your money back. I won't risk being haunted by that crazy Baroness ghost."

"She's bloody lying, you idiot," Nathaniel groaned. "She doesn't talk to any ghosts. How bloody stupid can you be?"

"Pretty bloody stupid," a voice rang out from the side of the woods, and Charlie emerged. "What do you fools think you're doing?"

"Nothing," said Fulke. "Move along, Charlie."

"They spooked our horses to ambush us in the woods and threatened to rape us both," called Annabel.

"Oh hell," muttered Barnaby. "Why did I let you two talk me into this? I wasn't going to do anything, Charlie, I swear. Truly, I wasn't." He looked forlornly at Bettina and Annabel. "Tell him! Please?"

"No need. I heard." Charlie surveyed the three men in front of him with incredulity. His gaze avoided Annabel, but she could see the fury simmering in his eyes.

Nathaniel, the leader of the trio, shrugged dismissively. "Come on, why don't you take your girl back and leave her friend behind so we can still have fun? That's more than fair. You don't even know this other one."

"May the heavens forget your name, as you have forgotten decency," Annabel spat. "That's not happening. I'm also carrying a weapon, and you will not force yourselves upon either of us unscathed."

Charlie's voice dripped with contempt as he addressed the group. "I've warned all of you before about this. So has Frederick. It's not your first time trying to force yourself on a woman."

Amidst mocking laughter, Fulke, one of Nathaniel's companions, sneered, "What can you do to us? Your new best mate, Fancy Freddy Rowley isn't here, and I could filet you like a fish. Do you even have a weapon?" He spun a knife casually in his hand, the threat clear.

"I do," Charlie said calmly. "But I'm not going to go for it and give you the chance to jump me while I do so."

Pointing towards the castle, Nathaniel growled, "Charlie, I said get out of here. I'm not going through all of this not to get something out of it."

Charlie's voice turned colder as he responded. "I could get you both blacklisted from betting on the fights. I'll do it as soon as I get back. You'll never gamble at the castle again."

The words hung heavy in the air, causing their eyes to widen with fear. Fulke stuttered, "I'm sorry... this was clearly a mistake. Let's forget this whole thing and go about our separate ways."

"Don't apologize to *me*," Charlie spat, crossing his arms. "Apologize to Annabel and Bettina, both of whom you tried to assault."

"You what?" Nathaniel laughed derisively. "I will not apologize to a *woman*."

"I get enough lip from Edith," Fulke nodded in agreement. "I'm not apologizing to them either. There's no need. We didn't touch them, anyway."

Barnaby dropped to his knees, his voice filled with remorse. "I'm sorry, Annabel and Bettina, I'm very sorry to both of you, and I beg your forgiveness. I'll do anything."

Bettina exhaled audibly in a silent laugh. Crossing her arms, she exchanged a look with Annabel. "I can't believe this day we're having." Barnaby clasped his hands together, his desperation evident. "Have you ever made a mistake you didn't want to make in the first place and truly regretted it? They paid me. I was desperate. Anything I can do to repay this, please say the word."

"Coward," muttered Fulke.

Annabel and Bettina exchanged glances, and the silence hung anxiously.

"Ten shillings," Bettina blurted.

"What?" Barnaby gaped, his eyes darting between the group. He looked at Charlie, who remained silent and turned his gaze away.

"Don't look at him," Bettina snapped, her voice sharp. "Look at me. Ten shillings to forget all about this." She held out her hand, and Barnaby slowly reached into his vest, retrieving a clinking pouch. He counted out ten shillings and dropped them into her waiting hand. Bettina slipped the coins into her skirt pocket. "Annabel?" She turned to her friend.

"You're now my spy, Barnaby," Annabel said thoughtfully. "You are to tell me everything interesting that you overhear the Baron and his men say, plus anything else odd you hear about around the castle." She smiled. "And I'll bade the Baroness leave you be."

"Of course." Barnaby nodded fearfully. "Thank you. Thank you so much."

Charlie stepped forward, his voice firm and commanding. "Nathaniel, Fulke? One more chance."

Nathaniel's fingers tightened around the staff he was carrying, his defiance undimmed. "What's to stop us from killing you and having our way with the women anyway? You can't call in your favors if you're dead."

"Bold of you to assume so." With a calm demeanor, Charlie nodded at them while Barnaby shuddered. "So, you're not going to apologize, the pair of you?"

They shook their heads stubbornly and advanced on Charlie, but before anything could escalate further, Frederick stomped noisily into the clearing, a deep frown etched on his face. "Fulke and Nathaniel, you incompetent donkeys," he muttered. "Can't my father even go on vacation without the hired help mucking about with rape and murder? Stand down, Barnaby. I heard you apologize."

"We wouldn't have killed him," muttered Nathaniel, fidgeting with the piece of mistletoe he still held. He stretched and twisted it absent-mindedly. "Hurt him, maybe. He's been unreasonable."

Frederick's eyes widened as he noticed the plant in the taller man's hands. "Is that mistletoe?" he suddenly shrieked, his voice echoing through the clearing.

Nathaniel dropped the plant in surprise, and Frederick demanded, "Is that the mistletoe my mother placed on my father's apple tree? Have you bloody *hacked* at it?" He sucked in his breath, shook his head, and ran his fingers slowly down the exposed branch, his gaze filled with rage as he looked at Nathaniel. "I should have your bloody head."

Nathaniel stammered, "I—it—it will grow back in time, my lord. It's just a plant…"

"You're just an animal. Shall I take some of your skin off?" snarled Frederick, his fury mounting. "And see how long it takes to grow back?"

With sudden confidence, Nathaniel stood balling his fist, looking down at the teenager. "What's to stop the three of us from killing you and Frederick?"

"I'm no longer a part of this." Barnaby shook his head, backing away. "It'd be the two of you."

Frederick shrugged, and Annabel's anxiety rose when she saw his hands were trembling.

"Who's to know?" dared Nathaniel. "I'll snap your neck like a twig right now. He spat insolently in the teenager's face.

Fred drew his dagger but stopped at Charlie's cough. He lowered the blade and sighed, scowling as he wiped his face. Finally, he sheathed it with a sneer and remarked, "Wert thou clean enough to spit upon."

Charlie smiled. "Good lad."

A weary voice cut through the tension, causing everyone to look up. Gregory, the enormous guard she remembered all too well from that second night at the castle, appeared unimpressed by the unfolding drama. "Oh, you idiot," he sighed. "You were right, Lord Frederick. Apologies for my lateness."

"I told you," Frederick hissed, his anger directed at the guard. "You should have come faster. They were about to kill me."

"Come on then, all three of you," the guard sighed, his exasperation evident. "Idiots. Are you going to come along quietly?"

"As if we had a choice," Fulke muttered reproachfully.

Gregory laughed. "I suppose you do, but the weapons I am carrying alone outnumber you all, and then there are the falcons and the backup that's on the way."

Charlie's voice cut through the tension, his focus on Barnaby. "Barnaby backed out of the attempted rape and never threatened Lord Frederick. He shouldn't be punished as much as the others."

The guard shrugged nonchalantly. "Sure, but since he was involved with the incident, he has to come with me and give a statement. You all do."

"Surely not the women," Frederick interjected firmly. "Haven't they been through enough?"

"As you say." Shrugging, the guard gestured towards the entrance of the clearing. "Gentlewomen, we will all escort you back to the castle, but there's no need for you to be questioned."

The three men allowed their weapons to be taken, and the guard began leading them down the path. Charlie and Frederick caught up to Annabel and Bettina. "Are you alright?" Charlie asked. "Silly question..."

"I'm fine," Annabel replied, her voice steady. Bettina nodded in agreement. "Thanks."

"Told you I'm not my father, didn't I?" Frederick grinned at Charlie, a hint of pride in his voice. "I've got self-control. I didn't hurt him—I even quoted Shakespeare. Did you hear?"

"You did," Charlie agreed. "Can you name the play?"

Frederick frowned, struggling to recall. "Bugger."

"Timon of Athens," rasped Annabel, then cleared her throat. She hugged Bettina tightly. "Betty, I'm so, so sorry you were in danger. I feel terrible that this happened when you came to visit me. Are you okay?"

Bettina hugged her friend wordlessly, finding solace in their embrace. When they broke apart, she swallowed and asked, "Annabel, do you have anything..."

"Oh, to eat?" Annabel interrupted, reaching into her skirts and pulling out a packet of dried apple slices. She handed it to Bettina, who began nibbling while sitting on a nearby log. Annabel offered some to Charlie and Frederick, who each took a piece.

Frederick cleared his throat. "I apologize to both of you, and I'm happy to offer you further coin as recompense for this dreadful event."

Bettina let out a laugh. "Really." She glanced at Charlie. "How did you know we were here, anyway? Last we saw, you were at the stables with these poor sods."

"Your horses came back," Charlie explained. "And Lise said she'd sent you on an errand to the river. When I saw them return, I got Frederick and told him to get the guards and follow me. I just followed their tracks from the river." He placed a reassuring hand on Annabel's shoulder. "Are you truly alright? I was so worried, but you certainly held your own."

"Yes," she replied, hugging him gratefully. "Thank you. You arrived just in time."

"You looked like you were doing alright for yourselves when I came along," Charlie grinned, his relief evident. "Nice touch with playing off Barnaby's superstitions, storyteller." He turned to Frederick. "Why don't we give Annabel and Bettina the horses to take to the market? Unless you want the carriage?"

Frederick shrugged, and Bettina nodded eagerly. "Sure, I'd take a carriage." She whispered to Annabel, "God's bones. Hang onto this one, yeah?"

Annabel smiled, her heart full. "Right."

Charlie blushed at the comment, and Frederick gestured towards the path. "Carriage is that way. We can walk you there so you don't run into any more hooligans." Bettina and Frederick rode ahead as they walked, conversing about the local fish market and economics. Charlie and Annabel walked side by side between the horses.

"How fortunate we were that you showed up when you did," Annabel replied, her voice filled with relief. "You were clever not to come alone and to think of bringing Frederick and the guard."

Charlie waved off the compliment. "It was the smart thing to do. Strength in numbers."

"The care you take with your decisions is very attractive," Annabel whispered, a hint of admiration in her voice.

Charlie bit his lip. "You were smart too. I'm lucky to know you."

"Oh, I do love you, Charlie," Annabel confessed, her voice filled with affection.

"I love you, Annabel," he whispered. "With all my heart, and then some."

Annabel visited Bettina's family on her next day off, immersing herself in their world, listening to stories, and gathering inspiration. She and Bettina discussed the book's structure and planned how to invest Frederick's offered compensation wisely.

She then met with the theater company on her following day off, presenting her play idea alongside Kunal. They impressed the theater director with their fully developed characters and multiple endings. Incredibly, Annabel received double the previous payment for the long-form play and a "year's supply" of parchment, most of which Kunal kindly stored for her. She paid him for his time and a small percentage of her winnings. The success of her play made her feel proud and confident, a sense of accomplishment flooding her veins.

Unfortunately, the elation was short-lived when Lise mysteriously vanished without a trace–casting a dark shadow over Annabel's world.

Chapter Twenty-Six

CAUGHT OUT

It was a solemn gathering around the fire that night, with one of them missing. Annabel's joy upon seeing Charlie felt as though it were waterlogged. As she gently sat on the log beside him, Cecelia on her other side, she softly asked the man she loved, "No news?"

"None," Charlie said, his voice breaking. "I begged James for information. I bribed him. He won't tell me anything—in fact, he suggested she left me because I've been stepping out on her. I almost bloody hit him."

"Did *you* tell him?" Annabel asked Cecelia.

"Of course not." The young woman shook her head. "People have seen the pair of you go into the stables together and come out hours later with no horses."

Annabel blushed. "Do you think the Baron threw her down there as punishment for adultery?"

Charlie looked stricken. "Well, I *didn't*. Honestly, I thought maybe she left, and somehow, I missed her goodbye note saying she was running off with Agatha."

"Sorry." She frowned. "But I don't think she would just abandon you like that. You mean a lot to her."

"I'd like to think that's true." He shrugged, staring into the fire. "But I wouldn't fault her for it. All of these things are gone. There's no sign of foul play in her room. The Baron only told me she resigned last night, and he was sure she would send word to me."

She shook her head. "It sounds like she went missing right after Bettina and I saw her. I tied socks in the river, and she said she'd come down to get them later. I checked after news spread she went missing, and they were still there."

His eyes widened. "She wouldn't have left it there. Maybe you're right."

Cecelia sighed. "I'm so sorry, Charlie."

"Thanks." Sighing, Charlie rubbed his eyes. "It's been a long day."

"Did you finish making a map of all the cells you've delivered to?" Annabel asked Cecelia in a hopeful tone.

"Nearly." Cecelia nodded. "I'll get it that in a moment. First—the twins have told me about something quite peculiar." She shivered. "Have either of you ever seen a diary about the castle? It's a small, green leather book with a metal buckle. "

"Oh, yes," Annabel remembered. I saw it when I spent the night in the Baron's chamber. It's on his bookshelf. Why?"

Cecelia swallowed hard. "The twins said they remembered finding it, and a previous nurse, Elizabeth, read them a few entries. They said it was written by Phillippa—but the dates are after she died."

Annabel gasped. "Are you saying–"

"Then, after the nurse was found reading it to the twins, she was fired," sighed Cecelia. "The twins said they pretended they were asleep when their father walked in, so he didn't know they heard, but Elizabeth was gone the next thing they knew. The new nursemaid is Ellen, and she's in the Baron's back pocket."

"That reminds me…" Annabel quickly recounted what the Baron had revealed in his sleep.

"Wow," Cecelia breathed. "We have to find out if Phillippa is really down there."

"Let's hope the diary will provide some answers," Annabel said. "Could we retrieve it when he's out of town next?"

"Two weeks," sighed Charlie. "Maybe best to do it while he's hunting."

Cecelia replied thoughtfully, "My father keeps all the Baron's keys in the locked closet down the left hall. The key to that closet is on his wrist." She paused, considering. "But they also keep the excellent silver polish in there.

You could ask my father for the closet key to gain access. Then, while you're there, you can try and find the key to the diary."

"It's a plan," Annabel said, grinning.

"Onto my next news. Hattie is at Geoffrey's." Cecelia delivered this news casually, but her companions gasped. "Yes. The twins had just returned from visiting, and Talon said he saw 'the coal scuttle girl' there that I'd said was missing. He was delighted to prove me wrong, the little man. I asked my father, and he confirmed."

"Well, that's one strange mystery half-solved," muttered Annabel. "You She did go missing the night we went to the play, and Colley works for Geoffrey. Maybe she just stowed away in the back of the cart?"

Charlie nodded. "You're probably right."

"There's something else," Cecelia admitted, looking at Charlie. "There's also a new inhabitant in the cell we found Agatha in."

Charlie looked up. "Who is it?"

Her voice dropped. "My father said it was a sodomite who will be punished in the fires of hell. They're going to build a controlled fire on the stage."

"Like bloody hell they are," he growled. "I can't believe this is happening again. Does the Baron just think he can pull any woman he pleases down to entertain his group of aristocratic hoodlums?"

"Do you really think it's Lise?" Annabel asked.

"I'm not waiting around to find out." Charlie stood. "I'm going down there. Neither of you have to come if you don't want to—but I *will* get my wife out of that cell. And if she's not there, James will be, and I will get real answers from him."

"Of course, we'll go," Annabel said. "Don't be daft. She's our friend, too."

Cecelia sighed. "I'm supposed to bring her a last meal of baked potatoes with salted butter and green onions."

Annabel felt a pang, and as she looked at Charlie, their eyes met and held while her thoughts returned to the trio's first night together around the fire.

Cecelia stood. "Let's go, then."

Minutes later, they were in the concealed laundry cart again, Cecelia pushing slowly as she moved the two humans under the pile of sheets and blankets, a basket of food perched atop it. There were a few unsettling moments at the dungeon entrance when it seemed they might be searched. Still, Cecelia bossily pushed on, making an excuse about needing enough time for the prisoner to eat before execution. When they stood in front of the cell, Annabel shook her head. "I was hoping not to be back here again for quite a bit more time, if at all."

"I had a bad feeling we would be," sighed Charlie. He faced the cell door and lifted the knob up, then down. Just as he turned it to the right, there was a startling gasp.

"Cecelia!" James spat. "Did *you* lead these bloody farmers down here?"

Charlie put his hand on the knife at his side, but Cecelia shook him off, walking towards her father with a look of determined confidence.

"These bloody farmers have found just one shy of all of the riddles to the lost Rowley treasure," she retorted. "If you join us, we'll share it with you."

There was a silence as James stared, opened-mouthed, at his daughter, then closed it. As he stood in the hallway, the three friends directly in front of the recessed cell door, there was a sound from the hallway.

"James? Is everything all right down there?" It was Cole, his irritated voice echoing down the corridor.

James seemed to roll his eyes for a fraction of a moment. "Yes. Yes, everything is fine. Carry on." He stepped closer to them until he was out of the view of the hallway and regarded his daughter suspiciously. "How did you find the riddles if you can't read?"

"*I* can't. They can." Cecelia pointed at Charlie and Annabel. "But I drew one out anyway. And solved another one, too. Lise is in this cell, isn't she, Pa?"

"Yes." He scowled. "The Baron enjoyed seeing *Agatha* fed to the snakes." James flicked his eyes to Annabel, who shifted nervously. "He wants to see her lover fed to the fire."

"She will not do any such thing," said Charlie. "We're releasing her now."

James tilted his head at Charlie. "Why not just leave your wife and run away with your lover? Does this not solve at least one of your endless problems, farmboy?"

Charlie's face darkened, and he advanced towards James, who flinched. "Pray listen to your words before you utter them, James."

Annabel rubbed her hands together at the cold. "It solves nothing to have one of our own locked up. We're not leaving here without her."

"And what of the show?" James demanded. "The Baron will be angry."

"Here's what's going to happen," Charlie said patiently. "We'll injure you slightly to make it look like you were knocked out. You will say an unknown assailant came upon you after you unlocked the cell, and you don't know who. We will take Lise through the tunnels and get her away from the castle tonight. This will never come back to you."

"Fine," James said quickly. He handed over his truncheon.

"Really?" Cecelia asked in amusement.

"Your mother was in this cell once," whispered James, and Annabel was shocked to see his eyes fill with tears. "Before you were born."

"Papa," whispered Cecelia, looking equally surprised.

"We wanted to leave, she and I," he whispered. "She was pregnant, and we didn't want to raise a child here. But when we petitioned the Baron, he was furious. He put her in that cell until I signed an agreement not to leave."

Charlie shook his head. "I'm so sorry, James."

"So yes, you can rescue your friend. Yes, I'm a coward, to echo what I'm sure you're all thinking," James said bitterly. "And yes, just make it look like you knocked me out before you leave, so I don't have to know what this all is about— the less I know, the better. Although if you figure out a way to leave this place in one piece, please share it with the rest of us, won't you?" This last point was said with a bit of ire.

Charlie lifted his arm with the truncheon, and Annabel held her hand. "Wait. Who is in the cell one floor down, James? I checked the blueprints in the library, and there's another dungeon cell below this one, with a lot more room than the others."

"Yes, the cell I delivered the preserved lemons, silk scarves, and oil paints to," Cecelia added.

James shook his head. "There's nothing down there. It's uninhabitable. It must have been for a decoy."

"That's not what Ma said," Cecelia wheedled. "She let it slip. It's a female prisoner. It's Philippa, isn't it?"

"No," he said quickly. "Your mother would have told me if it was."

"Really?" Cecelia asked with mock surprise. "It seems exactly like what she would keep from you to protect you. Why would the Baron tell you about a female prisoner not being fed to the underground crowd?"

"I—" He frowned. "I need to speak to your mother."

"We're running low on time," Annabel whispered.

James nodded quickly. "Fine."

After hesitating briefly, Charlie handed the truncheon to Annabel, who imparted an abrasion to the steward's forehead with the truncheon as gently as he could. James lay on the ground, stretching his arms and closing his eyes. Approaching the cell, Charlie quickly completed the knob's sequence, and the door popped open as before.

Lise was there, her hands and feet tied to a stone bench inside. He quickly cut her ropes with the knife and took her carefully into his arms as she wobbled, helping her to her feet as she clung to his neck with an iron grip, legs shaking. "Thank you, all of you," she whispered, a quaver in her usually strong voice. "I thought I was bloody done for."

"We might still be," whispered Cecelia. "Get in the cart, you and Annabel. Charlie and I will walk; we can pretend he was down already for the fighting and is walking me back out."

They nodded. As the cart moved slowly through the dark corridor of the dungeon, Annabel and Lise trying to hold still under the blankets in the cart, Cecelia said casually, "I'm pregnant, Charlie."

"What a blessing." Charlie sounded tired. "Congratulations to you and the father."

"The father was a pirate and is now deceased." She continued, "I plan to ask Frederick if he wants to claim he's the father. What do you think?" Inside the cart, Lise and Annabel stared at each other in disbelief.

Charlie coughed. "I'm *sorry?*"

Cecelia explained her reasoning. "This would grant Frederick leverage with his father—I know very well that the reason the Baron hates sodomites is because he thinks his son is one. And obviously, my child and I would have a better life than we would otherwise. We could help each other."

"That is a mad plan, that is," Charlie replied. "I don't suppose anyone can talk you out of it."

"You suppose correctly," Cecelia replied. "But do you think the Baron would be as concerned if it were Frederick's child, even if the mother is a maid?"

"You're not truly a maid," he countered. "I've certainly never seen you clean."

Lise laughed faintly, and Annabel put a finger to her lips as she noticed bruises on her friend's face. She put her hand out, and their fingers squeezed in silent reassurance.

Cecelia laughed. "Close enough. I'm just a general dogbody. My parents always found chores for me when they discovered me. Sometimes I watch the twins–but soon enough, I'll have one of my own."

"Good luck to you," Charlie sighed.

"I'm just turning a sow's ear into a silk purse," Cecelia sang cheerfully. "By the way, I've been thinking, I need a new children's story to read to the twins. They're tired of the classics. Annabel," she whispered. "Could you write a tale about two horses who are siblings? Horses are their favorites."

"Sure," Annabel whispered back with a small smile. "Will you start illustrating them?"

"I suppose so," Cecelia replied. Stopping the cart briefly, she patted Charlie on the back. "My thanks for the advice."

"That wasn't advice," he protested.

Cecelia laughed. "I really think he'll go for it. Do you remember Amos?"

Annabel whispered, "The musician from the baron's birthday feast?"

"Right. Did you know he's missing too?" Cecelia shook her head. "The twins told me. Rumor is the Baron caught them together and disinherited Frederick." She continued pushing the cart down the dark hallway until they came to a corner. "Here's our moment...the guard has just stepped away, and the new one won't remember that Charlie wasn't with us before."

Thankfully, she was right, and soon after, they were all in Annabel's farmhouse again.

Chapter Twenty-Seven

ESCAPE PLANS

"I don't know how to thank you all," Lise sighed, gratefully taking the cup of tea Annabel handed her. "I'm not injured, just shaken. A bit bruised from them throwing me in there."

"Did they say why?" Charlie asked, pacing the floor. "We've got to get out of here before they notice you're missing."

Lise cleared her throat, swallowing hard. "The Baron said he knew about who I was and wanted to wipe out the sodomites on the property—he didn't offer where he got his information identifying the so-called sodomites. I think Amos is down there, too."

"Yes," Annabel sighed. "And Frederick is disinherited."

"So there goes any chance of him helping us," sighed Lise. "What now?"

"For now, we try to hide you," said Charlie. "And then...I had a thought. After meeting Annabel's friend Bettina, whose family owns a fishery, Fred ordered a fishing boat to the river to test the route. They were trying to set up some trade."

"Oh," cried Annabel. "I didn't know that."

Lise looked at him in confusion. "That doesn't sound like young Frederick."

"He's changed a bit recently." Charlie sighed. "But the boat has a small lower deck area to store fish. I've seen it, and you'll fit in a small bag. If we steal it now, we can take the fishing boat down the river, find the Sutars, and they'll hide you." He paused. "I fear there isn't time to return to the castle to grab your things..."

"The baron burnt all my things." Lise looked down at her hands. "One by one, he had James throw everything into the fire."

"Oh, Lise," said Annabel softly. "I'm so sorry. I know it's little comfort, but I'll gather the few things of yours I have here."

"Thank you," she whispered. "That does mean quite a lot. And I'd take a bottle of barleywine if you can spare it."

"James is going to try and help us," Charlie grunted, still not entirely sounding as though he believed it. "But he gets a cut of the treasure now."

"I may be at peace with the treasure now," admitted Lise. "I'd really just like to stay alive at this point. The boat idea sounds perfect. But who would drive the boat while I ride in the compartment?"

Charlie hesitated. "I would."

"And get an arrow in your chest?" Lise retorted. "I think not."

Annabel suggested, "What about Frederick? Charlie, can I slip back to the castle and ask if he would come to meet you by the river? He could say he's testing a lunar fishing route."

Charlie's mouth twitched. "Lunar fishing."

"Yes, lunar fishing. It's a new moon—better for fish. If he leaves now, he'll be in a good position for when the fish are most active during moonrise." She laughed at the face he was making. "Make fun if you like, but Bettina swears by the practice, and it can be used for your story if you get caught."

"I believe you. And I think you're onto something; I think Fred might help," he said. "We'll head for the river when you're back."

Annabel slipped quietly through the tunnels, appearing in the cellar in Lise's old room, which had been stripped of anything that might remind one of her friends. She shivered nervously, carefully letting herself out of the room.

When she arrived at Frederick's door, she tapped lightly, holding her breath, and he quietly opened the door. Frowning, he raised his eyebrows, and she leaned forward to speak into his ear just above a whisper. "Charlie needs your help. We just rescued Lise from the dungeon and must get her out. Do you feel like taking out a fishing boat tonight with Charlie?"

Frederick stood momentarily in his nightshirt, wrinkling his forehead at her, and then he nodded curtly. "I'll change," he whispered, carefully shutting the door again. She stood nervously outside the door, listening for anyone who might happen along, but the castle was q uiet.

He reappeared quickly, dressed in oilskin breeches and tall leather boots with a small rucksack on his back. "Where are they?"

"My house," she whispered. "Come."

Following her to the farmhouse, he coughed as they approached the porch. "Thank you for fetching me."

"Don't thank me yet," she sighed. "Let's see if we can sneak Lise out of here alive first." He nodded. Inside, they quickly discussed the plan, and Annabel hugged Lise deeply. "This isn't goodbye," she whispered.

"Thank you for everything, Annabel; I mean that," Lise whispered back. "Please take care of Charlie?"

She nodded. "I promise." She handed Lise a bag with the items she had collected from around the farmhouse. Along with extra clothes, she'd packed soap, apples, nuts, a small sack of barley, a jug of barleywine, and a small sewing kit. Charlie stood as they made for the door. "Annabel…" His voice was tired.

"Yes?" She smiled.

Charlie took Annabel into his arms and embraced her, pulling her into his strong arms and squeezing her gently. "That's all."

"I love you," she whispered, smiling. She kissed him, and his lips were rough and yielding under hers. "Come back safely to me."

He grinned. "I promise."

After they'd left on the madcap river plan, Annabel thought she would lie awake, eyes wide, wondering how everything was going by the river. But she fell asleep soon after her head helped the pillow.

When the sun was just rising, there was a sharp rap on the door, and Annabel sprang out of bed. It was Cecelia. "Good morrow!"

"Good morrow," said Annabel.

"So I see you did it." Cecelia poked her head into the empty house. "She's gone. Are you going to try and leave this place with Charlie?"

Annabel shrugged. "Maybe. Do you want to come with us?" Cecelia shook her head. "I'm pregnant."

"All the more reason," said Annabel. "Do you want that child to grow up here?"

"I'd rather that than be on the run." Cecelia shrugged. "But I understand if you want to leave."

Annabel considered this for a moment. "It's tempting," she admitted. "But I won't do it unless I know we won't get killed in the process."

"You'll never know that," sighed Cecelia.

"We'll get as close as we can." Annabel shrugged. "If we have gotten Lise out of here all in one piece, that will be something to build off, perhaps."

"Isn't that the truth," sighed Cecelia. "Speaking of which—please come with me, won't you? We're going to get Frederick his inheritance back. And besides, we've got to see if you made it back to his bed so we can ask him how it went. I looked around in the stables but didn't see Charlie anywhere."

"God's bones," Annabel sighed. "What can I possibly do to help you with Frederick?"

Cecelia shrugged. "Offer moral support. I'll be too nervous otherwise to convince him of my plan."

"You, nervous?" Annabel shuddered. "This plan seems dangerous."

"But will you?" Cecelia pressed.

Sighing, Annabel reluctantly agreed.

After quickly stopping at the kitchen to snatch and eat an apple, Cecelia rapped on Frederick's door with Annabel in tow.

"Who is it?" he called out irritably. "Go away."

Cecelia nudged Annabel, who rolled her eyes. "It's Annabel and Cecelia."

There was a rustling sound, and the door opened. Frederick greeted them with a tired look. "What are the pair of you doing here so early?"

"I have a business proposition for you," Cecelia announced. "May we come in?" Annabel shot her a warning glance while Frederick raised an eyebrow.

"Fine," he grumbled, retreating to his bed where a heap of handkerchiefs and a dirty shirt lay. He began fiddling with an arrow as Cecelia closed the door.

"Did you do what you set out to last night?" Annabel asked. "Did everything go as hoped?"

"Yes." He nodded. "Charlie took us to a strange old tavern by the harbor, where he spoke to some relative of the Sutars, who fetched

Kunal, and Lise left with him. We made it back in the boat before sunrise."

"Oh, wonderful." She grinned. "Thank you, Frederick. Thank you so much."

He scowled. "You have a funny way of showing gratitude, waking me up early in the morning." Yawning, he asked, "What is it?"

Cecelia faced him and took a deep breath, smiling confidently. "I'm pregnant."

"Oh. Well done. What does that have to do with me?" Frederick yawned. "Look, I really don't have time for this," he sighed. "I've just been disinherited. I've got to figure out what to do next."

"I'm well aware," Cecelia smiled, her eyes gleaming. "I'm a good listener."

"You mean you eavesdrop," Frederick muttered. "Constantly. No one here trusts you."

"I'm willing to claim the baby is yours," Cecelia continued. "I believe your father will view both of us differently once an heir is in the picture. In his eyes, you will no longer be a sodomite but virile—something he covets."

Frederick appeared taken aback. "Would you *really* say the child is mine? Why would you do that?" He looked at her stomach and tilted his head curiously.

"My life is miserable and dull," Cecelia declared. "I turn eighteen next month, and my mother is talking about sending me away to a labor camp."

Frederick burst into laughter. "You what?" He tossed aside the arrow he had been playing with and focused on them. "Alright, this is rather entertaining, I suppose. Go on."

"Er..." Cecelia's confidence wavered, and Annabel stepped forward. Smiling patiently and patting Frederick's arm, she spoke softly, "We were... deeply disturbed, Frederick, to hear that not only did Lise go missing, but Amos as well, on account of your father?"

"Father said he just threw him down there to punish him for a fortnight. He'll be out soon enough, not that I'll ever get to see him again." Frederick scowled at her, and she glimpsed a flicker of pain in his eyes. "What can you do? The old man is a bloody psychopath who seizes those who displease him to hurt others."

"Well, that's a relief. We were ready to assist in a rescue." Delicately, she continued, "Frederick, Cecelia, and I want to help you. You're far better for the barony and the castle than your father. We all know it."

He nodded thoughtfully. "That's decent of you to say. Thank you." He sighed. "If there were a child... he might return my inheritance. Maybe I could make a difference here if my father begins to see me as a man."

Cecelia beamed. "My thoughts exactly."

Frederick regarded her with admiration. "This might actually work. If handled properly—with a willing woman to deceive the public and be the mother of my child—it could change my life."

Making his way to his desk, Frederick asserted, "Alright, then. No doubt about it, my father would be delighted to have a grandchild, even if the mother is a maid."

"I'm not really a maid," corrected Cecelia, and Annabel smiled. "Have you ever seen me clean?"

"And I wager I might trust you more than a noble's daughter," Frederick mused. "You've got more to lose. And I *do* actually know you, Cecelia. You grew up here. We used to play hide and seek sometimes."

"I remember," Cecelia mused. "Not to mention I've hidden out in every room of this castle. I've seen quite a lot of everyone here, and you may be the only person with whom I haven't seen anything I'd have a problem with."

Frederick snorted. "I find that hard to believe."

Cecelia shrugged. "I'm a bit of an oddity. But I like you. Not in that way, but I'm willing to give this farce my all." Smiling, she added with a wink, "I can even help you find a suitable wife down the line if you like. And eventually, when he's gone, you can discard your wives and mistresses and rule the barony as you please."

"You're quite something," Frederick remarked. "What do you say to that, Annabel? I'm surprised you would involve yourself in something like this, especially considering your situation with Charlie. You should be more cautious—I wouldn't enjoy seeing either of you tortured."

"To be clear, this was Cecelia's plan," Annabel explained. "I'm only here for support. It does seem like a way to reclaim your inheritance, but it carries risks. You'll have to maintain a constant web of lies."

Frederick waved his hand dismissively. "Oh, that's no problem. I'm well-practiced in that art as long as I can get what I want." Frederick's enthusiasm grew. "Let's inform Father right away."

"Now?" Annabel asked nervously.

Cecelia clapped her hands excitedly. "Absolutely!"

Taking a deep breath, Annabel followed them down the hall to the foreboding office.

Baron Henry glanced up from his desk, annoyance and disdain evident in his expression. "What is it?"

Frederick's breathing quickened beside Annabel, and she realized the depth of his fear of his father. Cecelia noticed it, too, and stepped forward to speak, impressing Annabel with her bravery. "Baron Rowley, I can no longer remain silent. I have been intimate with your son."

He laughed. "Scamper away, little mouse."

"Frederick and I," she declared. "We are pregnant."

A glimmer of hope crossed the Baron's face, swiftly replaced by a scowl. Crossing his arms, Henry replied curtly, "I don't believe you. My son, the sodomite?"

"Yes." Innocently, Cecelia retorted, "He has a strawberry birthmark on his left buttock and his manhood leans to the right."

They all stared at Cecelia in surprise, and the Baron laughed long and hard. "God and country, young lady," he said. "How did you manage to change him?"

"I suppose it was a matter of time, sir," Cecelia smiled. "We've been involved for weeks but were afraid to disclose it." She gestured towards Frederick, who nodded, his eyes wide. "However, after learning that you still believe he...well, engages in acts you believe to be unsavory, I felt compelled to speak my truth."

She moved closer to Frederick, slipped her arm under his, and affectionately squeezed his waist.

The Baron looked stunned. "Son, is this really true?" he asked Frederick.

Frederick nodded silently, looking a bit nervous. "Yes, Father."

"And she is genuinely carrying your child?" Lord Henry inquired. "Girl, would you swear to this, even in a court of law? We might have to bring in a physician."

"On my life," Cecelia promptly replied. She planted a saucy kiss on Frederick's cheek, leaving a rosy mark.

Annabel was surprised to see tears welling in the Baron's eyes. "It seems I misjudged you, Frederick," Henry admitted. "I didn't believe you were capable of change." He slapped his hand on the desk, smiling. "Annabel is a friend of yours, Cecelia?"

"Yes, my lord," Cecelia declared, grinning at Annabel. "We're writing a book together for the baby."

"Marvelous," boomed the Baron, rising from his seat. To Annabel's amazement and Frederick and Cecelia's delight, he counted several gold coins from his pouch. "Take my son shopping for a new wardrobe for his birthday feast."

"Of course, my lord," Cecelia curtsied, her hands closing around the money. She practically skipped out of the room, with a dazed Frederick trailing behind her. Before leaving, the Baron stopped them.

"Frederick!" he called out.

"Yes, Father?" Frederick responded hesitantly.

"Naturally, this means your inheritance is reinstated. Stay away from inappropriate relationships, and we can keep it that way. I'm serious, boy," the Baron warned.

"Yes, Father," Frederick assented gruffly.

"By the way, I've noticed you taking a more active interest in the castle's affairs," Henry remarked. "I'm proud of you, son."

Frederick smiled weakly before turning away. "Good day, Father."

Annabel curtsied. "Good day to you both," she said softly, and she hoped, without arousing suspicion, as she slipped away.

Chapter Twenty-Eight

HEARTBREAK

Annabel was churning butter inside, her mind wandering as she daydreamed about running away with Charlie, when there was a knock at the door. When she went to open it, Richard was there.

He smiled. "I have been released. The Baron has paid the rest of my debts." As he made a move to come in, she shook her head.

"No," she said flatly, and his eyes widened.

"Annabel, I—"

"Richard," she sighed. "To be quite honest..." She rubbed her eyes. "I'm not sure I have the capacity to deal with you anymore. I'm ready to take you up on your offer to run back to my mother, to tell you the truth—rather than having to share space with you again." She looked pointedly at his feet, just over the threshold.

"Fine, fine." Frowning, Richard backed up, and she curiously watched him sit on the porch. "No bother. I'll sit here. Will you join me? I'd just like to talk."

"Prison *has* changed you." She sighed, bringing the butter churn onto the porch, pulling her chair further away when he tried to rest a hand on her shoulder. "Do not think you have come to start your large family of sons, sir."

"Annabel," Richard sounded hurt. "I'd no idea how much you truly disliked me. I thought we got on rather well in the beginning."

"Everything you told me while we were courting was based on lies." Annabel vigorously churned the butter. "Richard, I want a divorce."

He winced. "That will be expensive for us both. It's not ideal."

"I don't care how much it costs me to be free of you. If you try to force me, I'll fight you every day until you've killed me." She said this as she continued to churn, punctuating every few words as she moved the mighty piece of wood up and down.

"Is—" Richard's voice dropped, and he sounded pained. "Is there someone else?"

She laughed. "That's a bold question for a man in your position to ask when you stayed with a harlot on our wedding night."

"Are you forever going to throw that in my face?" Richard demanded.

Annabel considered this. "You know, I really think I always will."

Shrugging off the daggers that she glared at him, he offered, "I stayed with Gwyneth on all three of my wedding nights—it wasn't just you, if that makes you feel any better."

"It doesn't," she muttered, then stopped churning and met his eye. "Imagine if you had married Gwyneth, and she abandoned you on your wedding night. How would that feel?"

His face clouded. "I have never and will never be able to marry Gwyneth."

"Right," she sighed, then smiled. "Imagine this then...imagine a seemingly nice man courted your widow *mother*. Imagine a man gave her trinkets, sweet eats, and sweet words, proposed, she fell in love, and you all imagined it was a good match."

"Well..." Richard was already looking worried. "I don't think that Mother would..."

Annabel continued smoothly, "And imagine if that man, after marrying your mother, abandoned her on her wedding night for another woman."

Her husband's mouth fell open, and she was amused to see his chin quake as he imagined the horror of such a situation. Finally, he closed his mouth and looked at Annabel. "Were you truly in *love* with me?"

Closing her eyes momentarily as she felt the old hurt return, she took a deep breath before replying. "Yes, Richard, I believe I was in love with who I thought you were. Rest assured, I'm not now."

"Then I'm sorry," he whispered. "Will you not soften your heart to give me another chance?"

"I really don't want to," she sighed. "And just for once, I'd love that to be where it ends. My desire to say no and have that be the final word. But I fear..." She stopped when Richard gasped, looking past her like he'd seen a ghost.

She turned to look, and relief spread across her face when she saw Agatha walking up to them, looking healthy and happy and wearing a confident grin Annabel had rarely seen on her outside of Lise's company. "Good morrow, husband," Agatha said brightly.

He shook his head. "Where—where have you been?"

"Are you telling me you didn't know she'd been thrown in the dungeon?" Annabel demanded.

"I knew," he whispered shamefully. "I didn't know where she'd been since she escaped."

"You *knew* she escaped?" Annabel threw up her hands.

"Let's head inside," Agatha suggested. "Do you mind, Annabel?"

"Not at all," Annabel smiled, shaking her head, trying to recover from the unsettling situation. "It's your house, after all."

"I suppose you're right," laughed Agatha.

Richard sat down at the kitchen table, his face paling. "Does the Baron know you're here?"

"Why no, he doesn't," replied Agatha. "You're welcome to trot off to him and beg him to throw me back, but perhaps you'll hear me out first."

Richard nodded quickly, and as Annabel watched him curiously, she realized he seemed afraid of Agatha. This gave her a tiny modicum of peace, and she sat in the chair closest to her new friend.

Agatha smiled. "Richard, could you pour us some ale?"

Shakily, he rose to his feet, and going to the cabinet, he withdrew three cups and plunked them down on the table. He filled each one halfway as Annabel watched in astonishment, and then he sat back down, shaking the table slightly.

"Lovely." She sipped and nodded. "Not bad. This is my vintage, isn't it? I'm impressed you haven't run through it all."

He nodded, and there were a couple minutes of silence before he blurted, "Well, what is it? What is your plan?"

"You choose." She took another sip and set her cup down. "Option one. You leave this farmhouse to us. Go be with Gwyneth. No one will tell your mother."

Shaking his head, he muttered, "Gwyneth left me."

"Smart girl. Option two: Stay here. We will help you recover from prison, but you will not tell the Baron I'm here." She looked at him for a moment. "I'd say that should take a couple of weeks. After you are recovered, when the Baron is out, you will petition Frederick to renovate the haunted farmhouse next door. When it's finished, Annabel can live in it."

"What?" Richard sputtered as Annabel's eyes widened. "Why would she live alone in a haunted farmhouse? That's ludicrous."

"Annabel is not your true wife, Richard, and therefore, she's not your concern," Agatha said soothingly, refusing to match his combative tone. "I am your wife. You may either grant me a divorce and choose a new wife to live with you after Annabel has moved out—or I will stay, and you may agree to treat me with respect; I will help you with your farmhouse upkeep, but you will also split the money hallway with me, and I will also come and go as I please. You will not only tolerate this last, but you will have no words against it and speak up f or me."

"Will you allow me to go to the harbor?" Richard asked hopefully.

At this, Agatha laughed heartily. "As often as you like, with your share of the money. But you must build me another bed, as I will not be starting yours with you."

Richard's eyebrows went up at this. "*Never?*"

"Never." She met his gaze.

Sighing, Richard looked at his hands. "Is there a third option?"

"I'm so glad you asked." Agatha smiled. "Option three: Annabel now has the ear of the Baron's son. She'll petition him to call in your mother's debts—-who I know has been relying on counterfeit coins to get by since the recoinage last year, which we both know is punishable by death."

A sharp inhale of breath from Richard made Annabel wonder how lofty the debts were. She crossed her arms and sat back in her chair, enjoying this.

"Your mother and brothers will be sent to the poorhouse, and your assets will go to the Baron's family. Annabel will leave, and I will stay and make your life miserable." Agatha drummed her fingers on the table. "It's not my favorite option, but it may be the most satisfying. Do you agree?" She directed this last at Annabel.

Annabel smiled. "I think these are all quite fair options."

Richard looked at her like he'd forgotten she was in the room. "Would you really want to live in the haunted farmhouse?"

She nodded. "It's not haunted. It just needs a bit of work."

He shook his head. "I suppose I'll go with the second option. Though it grants me no children unless you change your mind."

"Children!" Agatha laughed.

Annabel sighed. "Richard, I mean this in the nicest possible way, but perhaps you should learn to care for yourself and yours better before you aspire to have children."

"Well…" Shrugging, he sighed. "You could be right."

Agatha clapped her hands. "Then it's settled. Richard, why don't you finish your ale, then head back to the bedroom?"

Looking rattled, he nodded, yawned, pulled off his shoes, nodded to Annabel and Agatha and padded off to the bedroom, immediately slumping onto the bed. Agatha closed the door softly behind him.

Annabel laughed. "I can't quite believe what just happened." She held out her arm. "Pinch me, would you?"

"I will not!" Agatha giggled. "If it's a dream, I won't be the one who wakes us up."

Pinching herself, Annabel grinned. "I think it's real." Sweeping her eyes up and down Agatha, she nodded appreciatively. "Agatha, you look lovely. Your color's back, and you look so healthy, like you've been spending loads of time in the sun.

"I have! Working outside on a boat with plenty to eat will do that for you," Agatha replied. "I can't thank you enough for putting me in touch with the Soledads. They're wonderful folk."

"I'm so glad to hear it." Annabel drank the rest of her barley wine. "And it gave you time to develop this plan."

Agatha nodded. "I've made friends with a maid at the palace, who was able to bribe a guard to tell me when Richard was being released.

When I learned how soon it was, just yesterday, mind you—I hatched the plan. Otherwise, I would have come to you first."

"But are you still to be in hiding?" Annabel asked. "The Baron believes you to be dead."

"That's the next thing on my list," sighed Agatha. She took Annabel's hand and led her to the bench farthest from the door Richard had disappeared to by the fireplace, where the flames crackled in the wood stove. She pulled it open a crack, and the fire roared louder. Softly, she whispered to Annabel, "We must make a plan to oust the Baron."

"I agree, but..." Annabel swallowed hard. "You're talking a dangerous game, my friend."

"No more danger than you've put yourself in to rescue me, then Lise,"

Agatha replied. "Thank you for that, by the way. She's safe now."

"You're not talking about *killing* him," Annabel said nervously. "The Baron, that is? Just getting him out of the way, somehow. Bring him to justice for his crimes?"

"I don't care how we do it—whether it's exposing his corruption and kidnapping, leading him to walk off a cliff, or throwing him in his own dungeons," Agatha whispered. "But we are in a position of opportunity in having Frederick's ear threefold, with Cecelia, you, and Charlie. If we can do something about the Baron, and Fred rises up to take his place, think how much better our lives could be."

"True..." Annabel nodded. "You don't have a plan for that, do you?"

Agatha laughed. "I'm afraid I've used all my wits for this morning on intimidating Richard. But perhaps after a nap, I may come up with something this afternoon."

"Fair enough." Annabel began to pull out an extra straw mattress and a blanket. "Would you like to—"

She was interrupted by a knock at the door. Agatha quickly slipped into the closet behind a rack of wool coats, and Annabel opened the door to find Barnaby standing there.

"Barnaby, how lovely of you to call," Annabel greeted him. "Have you news for me? Come in, come in." She poured him a cup of barley wine.

Nervously, Barnaby crept over the threshold, his eyes darting around the room. "It's not really haunted in your house, is it?"

"Of course not," Annabel soothed. "That's next door. What news?"

He shivered and carefully took a sip of his drink. "The Baron is speaking to Cole and James about a lady sodomite who has escaped. He says there will be a male sodomite to take her place in the flames onstage in two days."

Annabel's face clouded. "Who?"

Barnaby frowned. "I'm trying to remember his name. It begins with an A..."

"Amos?" Annabel asked. "Is it one of the musicians? The short one with the small beard?"

"Yes, that's the one they've got." Barnaby nodded, tilting his cup back. "I should take my leave. You won't tell the Baron I've told you?"

"Of course, I won't," she reassured him. "Thank you for coming to share this news."

When she had closed and locked the door, she opened the closet. Agatha looked troubled. "He just keeps coming for all of us."

"Frederick will be sorely unhappy," Annabel realized. "Perhaps if I bring this to him, it will light a fire under him to oust the Baron himself, to rescue Amos."

"Aren't you clever?" Agatha grinned. "When will you speak to him?"

"No time like the present," Annabel remarked and began to dress. When she stepped outside, she saw Charlie working in the fields and hesitated before turning down the castle path, her heart skipping. "Good morning," she greeted him softly. "Have you heard the news? Richard is back."

"I had. My condolences," he replied wearily, avoiding eye contact.

"Actually, it's not going to be as bad as all that." She smiled. "Charlie—can we go to the stables? I want to talk to you about our next steps. We must make a plan, and I have much to tell you."

"Annabel, I have just been ordered quite firmly by the Baron to stay away from you," Charlie interjected, finally meeting her gaze but pulling away from her.

"What, just now?" She looked toward the castle, frowning.

"Yes, and I plan to heed him this time." He turned away, and she sucked in her breath sharply as she saw his shirt stuck to his back with jagged strips of crimson.

She put her hand gently on his waist. "Charlie—"

"Your husband has returned, Annabel," he sighed. "What was between us, whatever we have here, was over before it began. I will no longer see you aside from the fields."

The bottom dropped out of her world as her stomach flipped over, and she thought she might very well vomit. "Your need to avoid a married woman never stopped you before," she desperately joked. "Charlie, you can't—"

"Please," he interrupted. "I've thought about it and don't want to sneak around anymore. I did that for two years with Lise, and somehow, with you, it hurts even more." His face jerked in pain, and she felt a sob rise in her throat.

"It's not always going to be this hard," she whispered sadly. "I love you. Perhaps let us pause rather than end things completely?"

"I'll always cherish the memories we made together," Charlie said abruptly. "But it was never meant to work out, truly. I always told you to find someone better suited for your future." He shifted his gaze beyond her to the castle. "You should go home. Go back to your husband and see if you can work things out."

"By all means," she muttered bitterly, hardly believing this was happening. "Now that you've had your fun, send me packing."

"It's not like that. I have any choice." Annoyance creased his brow. "You don't understand what being here for so long is like. It changes a person. It crushes you until you realize there's no point in fighting back unless you have a death wish. The Baron can destroy lives, Annabel. I *won't* sneak around waiting for him to destroy yours."

"He already has," Annabel shook her head. "You do have a choice."

"What difference would it make?" he snapped, averting his gaze from her. "As if you would genuinely run away with someone like me."

"Why wouldn't I?" she demanded.

"Drop your act of martyrdom." He shook his head, his eyes flashing. "Pretending otherwise only insults both of us. Women like you, with obligations, families, and a future, don't marry stablehands. Frederick certainly knows that now that he's lost his inheritance."

"How *dare* you presume to know what I want," she shot back. "The only one insulting me here is you. And Frederick has regained his inheritance."

Charlie looked at her. "What? Just now?"

She crossed her arms and gazed at the sky, attempting to conceal her annoyance. "Yes. Cecelia's plan worked." She shook her head, still not quite believing the turn of events.

He whistled. "God's bones, I can't believe it. That's absurd. The castle brat and the Baron's son? It's like a Shakespearean tale."

A laugh escaped her lips, but she quickly suppressed it, refusing to be distracted. Retorting with a hint of annoyance, she said, "I can't believe you would so callously throw away what we have. Don't you love me, Charlie?"

"That's not fair." Defensively, he demanded at her indignant expression, "What do you expect me to say? It's not safe to continue as we have. Love isn't worth risking our lives."

"What did he say to you?" Annabel's heart ached. "I feel wretched he punished you, but it's more than that, right? Please tell me."

"Being whipped is enough. I don't want to argue about this. I've made up my mind," Charlie grumbled. "This was a mistake, Annabel. Leave me."

Her heart pounded in her ears. "What was a mistake?"

"Must I spell it out?" he sighed, still avoiding her gaze. "We were."

"How can you say that?" she asked, her voice filled with hurt, erupting into anger. "You bloody hypocrite. You back-tracker. You're a coward, Charlie."

"I know it." He finally looked at her. "Love is like a child that desires everything it comes across."

"Then grow up," Annabel sniffed as she turned away. Blinking back angry tears, she swiftly marched toward the castle, hoping to run into Maggie and beg for a handkerchief and a bite to eat while she hid from the world.

Outside, Frederick and Cecelia stood beside a prepared carriage. "Oh, Annabel! Come with us to the market. We need another woman's opinion while we shop for Frederick," Cecelia called out.

Clearing her throat, Annabel responded, "I'd love to." She climbed into the carriage, her hand finding the coins she had recently sewn into her inner skirt pocket. Escaping this chaotic place for a few hours would be a welcome respite.

CHAPTER TWENTY-NINE

THE OWL AND THISTLE

The journey to the market was relatively silent, save the giggles and whispers between Frederick and Cecelia as they put on a show for the driver. Annabel thought back to that first carriage ride, where she had discovered more of Charlie's past, and a flash of shame swept over her. To finally be so open with her, then to say they were a mistake—she closed her eyes and tried to push him out of her mind but only thought of him trailing hot, wanton kisses down her neck, nibbling at the tender skin under her ear —it was too much to bear, and she opened her eyes again.

She took a deep breath, and as her mind raced, she took out her notebook from her skirt and began to write. When the carriage stopped near the bustling market, Annabel quickly put the journal away and disembarked with her companions, hesitating amidst the lively crowd.

Cecelia shrugged, suggesting, "Shall we split up to shop for your clothes and then meet back here in an hour or two?"

Frederick shook his head. "Yes to the first part, no to the second. Let's make it two hours, full stop, and after shopping, let's reconvene at The Owl & Thistle for a pint and a meat pie." Annabel nodded in agreement, and the teenagers ventured away from her into the bustling marketplace, arm in arm.

Annabel strolled through the market, lost in thought. Putting off stopping at the Sutar stall, she walked until she found a stall that sold her favorite dried salmon. She purchased a generous packet and nibbled on a piece while exploring. Along the way, she bought a small drawing pad and local candy. It was a gratifying experience to have her own money from her contest winnings hot in her hands, though she intended to save most of it.

When she finally felt she had the wherewithal to approach the Sutar stall, she immediately heard a joyful voice. "Annabel!" Rupa exclaimed with delight. Annabel returned the smile and greeted her warmly, "Good morning! How's business?"

"It's wonderful. How are your lessons going?" Rupa asked.

"Better than I expected. I've already finished my homework," Annabel proudly shared. "And I started writing down thoughts on a new play on the way here."

"Good for you! Oh, that reminds me, have you been to the booksellers? It's at the end of the street, next to the stationers." Her new friend smiled as if she had a secret.

"I haven't," Annabel admitted. "I've had such little time when I've been here. And I didn't even try to go in before because I'd never be able to afford any of those books. Although maybe now..." She trailed off, swept up in longing for a moment. "Perhaps I could buy just one..."

Rupa laughed. "Regardless if you buy, you must visit. Trust me, it's a hidden gem—you mustn't miss it."

"You've convinced me." Annabel grinned. "I'll go there next."

"Also, could you give this to Charlie for me?" Rupa asked, holding out an envelope sealed with wax. "Don't worry, it's good news."

"To Charlie? Of course, I can pass it on," Annabel assured her, tucking the note away. "Although, it seems that things between us have become strained." She swallowed hard. "He ended things just before we left."

"Oh, Annabel, I'm so sorry," Rupa expressed genuine concern. "Was it too much for both of you, having to sneak around?"

Annabel felt a touch of embarrassment. "Not for me, I suppose. It must have been for him. He's the one who ended things." She shrugged. "But what can you do?"

"That's the spirit," Rupa commented, embracing Annabel unexpectedly. Annabel was taken aback but touched by the sweet gesture, even if it left a trace of sawdust on her tunic when Rupa pulled away.

Rupa took out a wooden whistle strung on a cord from her pocket. "Forget about that silly man. He's got his own complicated journey to figure out. This is for you." She motioned to put it around Annabel's neck. "This little bird of hope will remind you to keep smiling," Rupa beamed. "I carved it myself, and it works as a whistle for bird calls or makes a terrifically loud bleat."

Annabel slid her fingers over the smooth little bird, feeling cheered despite her heartache. "Thank you so much. I'll have to practice using it."

"Please do," Rupa encouraged her. "I should get back to work. It was great seeing you." With a wave, she disappeared into the crowd.

Annabel then approached Kunal. It didn't feel right to accept a gift from such a talented artisan without making a purchase of her own. She decided to buy a wooden comb and a ruler. Kunal carefully wrapped the items, and as they exchanged pleasantries, he asked, "Are you enjoying the market this day?"

"Yes, very much," Annabel replied. "I'm here with Frederick and Cecelia. We're meeting at the pub in an hour, so I've just been walking around. I'm looking forward to my next lesson next week," she added, biting her lip as she realized she was rambling. "And you?"

"I am as well." Kunal paused before suggesting, "There's a book at the bookseller's, at the end of the street, that I think you'd enjoy. It could provide you with more inspiration for your play. It's called Danse Macabre, published in 1499 in Lyon." He chuckled. "It's the first printed book to feature a picture of a print shop. That always tickled me."

"Really!" Annabel laughed at the thought. "Thank you for the recommendation. Rupa bade me go there, and with both of your words on it, I don't dare miss it." Before she left, summoning her courage,

Annabel asked, "Kunal... you're good friends with Charlie."

"Yes, we've known each other for many years, and he's always been good to me. I'd say I know him quite well," Kunal confirmed.

"He broke things off with me after the Baron bade him to do so." She shuddered. "It appeared he had been lashed on his back."

Kunal shook his head. "That's terrible. That place doesn't deserve a soul like Charlie. You know he's afraid of leaving, though?"

She nodded. "The Baron has a hold on him."

"He has a hold on everyone," Kunal sighed. "That cruel old man's got no friends in this town, that's for sure. He shorts everyone and still tries to pay us under the table with the old, chipped coins. He could get us in trouble with the law, but he doesn't care."

"Will you check in on Charlie?" Annabel asked. "I mean to stay away from him, myself, as he insisted," She swallowed hard. "But I'm sure he could use a friend right now."

"Of course," Kunal agreed.

"Please don't mention me," Annabel urged.

"He's fortunate to have you," Kunal remarked softly. "Even from afar."

"I'm nothing to him. He made that abundantly clear," Annabel muttered. "Now, I'm just trying to be a decent human being to another."

"Well, I can't speak on his behalf." Kunal smiled warmly. "And indeed, the world could use more of that. I'll check in on him. Now, go and see the bookseller."

Annabel hurried toward the end of the street with a grateful smile and was met at the door by a slightly irritable man in spectacles. She convinced him that she was shopping on behalf of Lord Frederick and was granted permission to sit down and peruse two magnificent books, including the one Kunal had recommended.

The man's daughter unexpectedly approached Annabel while her father was in the back. She inquired whether Annabel had experience with bookbinding. After a brief conversation, it became apparent that she knew Kunal and Rupa, and was involved in a bluecoat school established by a wealthy benefactor to educate and provide for poor children.

These schools aimed to teach disadvantaged children essential reading, writing, and arithmetic skills, offering them an opportunity to improve their prospects in life. Annabel promptly signed a contract on the spot to assist in repairing their dilapidated collection of books.

As she made her way to the pub, she stepped quickly when she realized her time was running short. Through the window, she spotted

Frederick and Cecelia seated, a pitcher of ale in front of them. Annabel slipped into a seat at their table, feeling a mix of apprehension and determination. Frederick immediately excitedly greeted her, exclaiming, "Annabel, I'm so glad you're here!"

"He's already drunk," Cecelia whispered to Annabel. "We've been here a half hour, and he's had three of those. I haven't had one."

"These seats are quite comfortable," Annabel remarked, running her hand over the leather upholstery.

Frederick waved his hand dismissively. "Of course they are. This is my father's booth," he proudly declared, gesturing toward a plaque bearing the Rowley name that Annabel hadn't noticed before. "Everything he possesses is high-quality, except for the house," he chuckled.

Annabel took a sip of her drink. "You don't have the best relationship with him, do you, Frederick?"

"I bloody hate him," Frederick muttered, his voice tinged with resentment. "He makes my life hell, trying to toughen me up instead of letting me be. And I know he did something with Amos."

"He means to kill him," Annabel murmured. Frederick laughed. "Father wouldn't have anyone killed at the castle because of Henrietta's ghost."

Annabel sighed. "I'm sorry—a ghost?"

He nodded. "We always used to hear a sound in our room that my mum used to say was Henrietta's ghost. We thought it was a game."

"I remember this story," whispered Cecelia. "My mum used to tell me all the time: 'Kill or be killed on castle grounds, Henrietta will take you where you can't be found.'" She stuck out her tongue. "Otherwise, I would have poisoned the Baron long ago for what he's done to Charlie."

"So Henrietta is a ghost who kills people who kill?" Annabel asked. "I admit that makes a good story. And the Baron believes it?"

"He believes it's true for him, so he's never killed anyone directly. And, the trouble is, it's come true so far," Frederick shrugged. "Martha Rush, my old nursemaid—it was known that she beat one of the servants until he died, then that candelabra fell on her the next day, and she died."

"Catherine Leeds—she rode one of the Baroness' horses so hard it expired," remembered Cecelia. "The next day, she slipped in the stable, hit her head on a beam, and died."

"Leonora Punch, the cook before Maggie," Frederick continued. "She served what she said was blessed water to a sick child, which turned out to be contaminated. She stepped on a rotted step in the larder and fell to her death the next day."

"Matthew Whit," Cecelia declared. "He beat his wife until she died for not giving him a child. Then the next day, he got drunk, wandered off the cliff, and broke his head open on the rocks."

Frederick nodded. "I've got loads more examples."

"There has been a lot of death here," Annabel sighed.

The barman had brought another glass, and Frederick poured her a drink. "I find that drowning one's sorrows helps."

Annabel took a drink and let the sparkling liquid slip down her throat, giving her a warm feeling in her toes. Emboldened, she lifted her eyes to look right at Frederick. "It helps, but it is but a bandage. Do you not wish to cure the horror at your home, not simply sustain it?"

Frederick frowned. "I am only one man."

Cecelia shrugged. "To be fair, so is Henry."

Looking down, Frederick nodded. "Why does he seem like so much more?"

"Because you're afraid of him," Annabel said. "You must turn that fear into anger. You must turn it into action." She took a deep breath. "Barnaby came to see me with news that not only is Amos in the dungeon, but he will be fed to a fire onstage tomorrow night in the underground fights. It is intended to be a spectacle to eliminate a sodomite."

Frederick sucked in his breath hard. "Tomorrow night?"

"Charlie and I have rescued Agatha from the dungeons and then Lise." Annabel leaned forward. "If you help us, we can rescue Amos."

"While we're at it, we should rescue your mother," Cecelia added.

The color drained from Frederick's face. "My mother?"

"Yes." She cleared her throat. "We've uncovered too many clues that it could be her down there, and after a bit of a breakthrough with my father—who helped us break out Lise—I learned from my mother that Philippa is in the lowest dungeon." She pressed her lips together. "They have been keeping her fed and letting her read and exercise. The Baron visits her often...but her health is worsening."

"She's been down there..." Frederick put his head in his hands. "Truly, I had no idea. I thought she had found a way out of there. I hoped she was traveling under an assumed name or had made it to America or something of the sort. Never did I imagine she was in the dungeon." He pulled out a handkerchief and blew his nose, then folded it back up and shoved it in his pocket, the tears still flowing.

Cecelia handed him a fresh handkerchief, which he gratefully accepted, swiping at his eyes. "Of course you didn't. Your father is a madman, and we're going to rescue your mother, and she will help you become a wonderful baron on your own. You will sit on the House of Lords."

He looked hopeful at this. "Wouldn't that be something?" He looked at Annabel. "Do you have a plan, then?"

She nodded. "You must arrange to sit with your father at the underground fights tomorrow night and distract him and Cole. Cecelia and I will work with James to release Amos and Philippa and get them safely. James will then come out to the stage of the fights, telling the Baron that he must come quickly, as something is wrong with the Baroness and she is dying, cannot be moved, but if he wants to say his goodbyes, he can come right away. When he comes to the cell, we lock him inside, and once the Baroness is healthy enough, she can go to the constable and turn him in. You'll be the Baron; she can do what she likes."

"Goodness," Cecelia breathed. "That's bloody perfect."

Frederick took a drink and considered this. "If we carry out this plan," he said slowly. "You and Charlie must promise to stay and help me figure it all out, not ruin off together straightaway."

"You have my word," Annabel assured him. "But you will have to ask Charlie for his. I do not speak for him; he has ended things with me."

"Oh," Frederick said in surprise. "He didn't tell me."

"It only just happened," she sighed. "Let's not talk about it."

Throwing a mischievous glance to Cecelia, Frederick teased, "Don't you go jump Charlie's bones again now that he's without a partner."

"Ha!' She stuck her tongue out at him. "That's long done. I'm yours now, sweetheart. Until you chuck me, that is."

He shrugged. "If I'm Baron, I can choose my wife. If you're carrying a child I can claim is my heir, I don't see why I wouldn't marry you."

Cecelia gasped. "You're not serious."

"I doubt I could find another lady who would accept my proclivities." Taking another drink, he nodded thoughtfully. "I'll have to think about it. What's your last name?"

"It's Rousseau," she whispered. "My family is French."

"Can you speak French?" Frederick asked in an interested tone.

She nodded. "But I can't read or write."

"Hmmm," He nodded. "That would be a problem. Do you want to learn?"

Cecelia made a face. "Not really. I suppose I might if I didn't have to clean and watch children on the time…"

Pointing at Annabel, he asked, "Can't you teach her? We could make you Cecelia's maid and you could read and write for her until she handles it."

"I think we're getting a bit ahead of ourselves," Annabel cajoled, slipping past the fact that she was sure she would never want to be Cecelia's maid, even in jest. "Let's focus on installing you as Baron first, then we'll work on what comes next."

"Agreed," Frederick toasted them both and finished his drink.

"Oh!" Annabel brought out the wares she'd bought. "There are for you." She handed Frederick the candy and Cecelia the drawing pad.

Frederick looked puzzled. "You bought me this? Why?"

She shrugged. "We're friends. I thought you would like it."

"Say, 'thank you,'" whispered Cecelia.

"Thank you," said Frederick, opening the bag and taking a piece.

"Moving right along." Cecelia rubbed her hands together. "Annabel, Frederick and I went to see his uncle Geoffrey. While they were speaking in the library, I found Hattie, and you'll never believe what she told me."

"What?" Annabel leaned forward.

"Hattie said that before she left, the Baron put his hands on her," she whispered. "She tried to fob him off as politely as she could, but it made him angry, and he threw her against the fireplace." She shuddered. "Father heard him talking about sending her down to entertain the pirates. He suggested that he'd let the pirates claim her if she didn't have him."

"That bloody monster," Annabel spat.

"Father said he gave her some money to bribe Geoffrey's carriage driver, and she stowed away in it." Cecelia grinned. "Then, once there, she applied for a job. Geoffrey liked to hire people who used to work for his brother."

"That's because he's the twins' father, hoping to learn more about them," Frederick replied dryly.

"You know?" Annabel asked in surprise.

"Of course, I know," he sighed. "Everybody knows."

"Well, all I'm saying is that once we put away the Baron, we should have Geoffrey on our side as well," Cecelia declared. "I can't believe Charlie really ended things. I really am sorry, Annabel."

Annabel nodded. "So am I. It makes it worse that Richard is back and plans to leave me be—I finally have a bit of freedom, but I'm going to be alone in it."

"You're not alone." Cecelia reached out and took her hand, squeezing it.

"Most likely, Henry threatened him, saying he'd kill you if he ever saw Charlie with you again," Frederick speculated.

"Probably," Annabel admitted. "But the fact remains that he doesn't want to try anymore. I asked if he wanted to be more discreet, but he said we were mistaken."

"Remember when Henry threatened to punish Charlie for riding Hercules?" Cecelia reminded Frederick. "He said he can clean the horses and muck out their stables; he can't take care of them, but he can't ride them."

Frederick nodded. "The old man said he'd gut him like a fish and tie him to a runaway stallion if he caught him riding any of Phillippa's horses again."

"But why?" Annabel questioned, shaking her head in disbelief."

"Because Henry despises him," Frederick shrugged. "Ever since we were young, he's had it out for Charlie."

"What kind of cruel beast harbors such animosity towards a child?" Annabel wondered aloud. "It's not Charlie's fault his father strayed."

Cecelia shrugged. "Everyone at the castle hated me when I was a child too."

"That's because you were always getting into mischief," Frederick laughed. "Charlie was years older, constantly running after trying to prevent us from injuring ourselves by jumping off the bridge into the river, among other reckless things. We were the little monsters." He sighed and signaled for another drink. "And in many ways, we still are."

Chapter Thirty

DOWN THE RIVER

Upon their return, as the carriage pulled away and they stood in the path, Frederick turned to Annabel and spoke in a low voice. "I will speak to Henry, and make sure I can be by his side during the fights tomorrow." He looked at Cecelia. "You will speak with your father?"

She nodded, and the three of them split off. Annabel checked on Richard, who was awake and eating a thick sandwich on the porch, and handed her half when she walked up.

"Thank you." She managed a smile and sat down. "Where is Agatha?"

"She's inside—her turn for the bed. I'm going to make her another one, though." He took another bite. "She's a good cook."

"She's much better than me," Annabel said through her bite. "I'll head to the fields after this and finish some work. As Agatha said, I will help you with the house and fields while we adjust to our new circumstances, and you heal from your time in the dungeon."

"My thanks." Richard finished his sandwich. "Barnaby is out there already and can use the help. I'll admit my legs have grown weak and cannot take much time out there yet." He paused. "You don't seem worried about your lack of a husband."

"I'll tell you the truth, Richard—there is no one else now." Annabel sighed. "And I am not looking."

He nodded. "Fair enough."

After several hours in the fields, the Baron summoned Annabel into his chambers. Trying to maintain an appearance of obedience and calmness, she entered and greeted him politely, saying, "How may I assist you, my lord?"

Baron Rowley smiled, revealing all his teeth in a rather alarming way, and replied, "It has come to my attention that you are taking jobs outside of the castle," he remarked in a chilling tone.

Surprised, she stammered, "I..."

Before she could finish her sentence, he slapped her. Annabel saw the blow coming and briefly considered ducking, but she realized that would likely only provoke him further. Instead, she braced herself and maintained a stoic expression as the blow shook her, refusing to give him the satisfaction of seeing her fear. Her focus shifted to survival.

"Perhaps you can begin to make up for your insolence." A smile crept across his face. "I have a task for you. I need you to thoroughly clean a boat—inside and out."

"A boat?" Annabel asked, her voice tinged with disbelief.

"Yes, my boat," Henry emphasized unnecessarily loud. "It's a small vessel that has been in my family for generations and is in a wretched state. It's docked in a quiet stretch of the river, about ten meters from Rowley Cliff. Your responsibility will be to scrub it meticulously."

"Baron Rowley, I do have barley crops to manage," Annabel asserted firmly. "I assure you, I'm not idling, sir."

His eyes narrowed, and he retorted, "I'm not making a request, my dear. With Cecelia on my son's arm, we're down a maid and need an extra hand."

Annabel's frustration grew, and she quieted it within her firmly. "I would be loathe to disappoint you, Baron Rowley. I will begin immediately." Nodding smugly, the Baron dismissed her.

Equipped with a bucket of lemon, vinegar water, soap, and a basket of brushes and rags, Annabel made her way to the unmistakably grungy boat perched on the riverbank. She started by sweeping the deck, then dropped to her knees, diligently scrubbing until the wood gleamed. Her mind wandered, alternating between daydreams and brainstorming ideas for her following books.

As Annabel descended below deck to continue her work, the door suddenly slammed shut behind her, trapping her inside.

Panic surged through her as she realized she was locked in. Annabel frantically searched for another opening but found nothing substantial enough to escape through, except for a few portholes that were too small. Her heart raced as she struggled to maintain some sense of composure and not fall to pieces.

"Hello!" she shouted, echoing through the confined space. "Is anyone there?" She quickly realized the futility of her cries against the roaring river. Determined, she climbed onto a crate to reach the hatch, desperately examining the firmly wedged door. Despite her efforts, she couldn't find anything to pry it open.

Breathing deeply, a flicker of hope suddenly sparked within her. Annabel remembered the knife she always kept in her boot and retrieved it, using its blade to loosen the door as best she could. She took a deep breath and mustered all her strength, ramming her shoulder against the door at an odd angle, causing it to budge slightly. Undeterred, she threw her other shoulder into it, but to no avail. A final upward kick with her foot, filled with frustration, only left her in pain

.

To her horror, the boat swayed, sending her into a panic. She tried to steady herself but felt the boat rock again, followed by a loud crack as it broke free from its mooring. The boat started moving, gradually picking up speed along the river.

"Oh, no," Annabel moaned, her voice filled with despair. "God's teeth. I'll bloody die in this wretched, filthy, decrepit old boat. This is how it ends."

In a panic, she suddenly began shouting at the top of her lungs, screaming for help, but her cries went unanswered amidst the roaring river. The boat bumped along the shore, carried away by the current, as Annabel felt the total weight of her helplessness.

Suddenly, the boat stopped, and she peered through a porthole. It had hit an enormous tree growing partially across the water, and she sighed in relief. It was no longer moving, so all Annabel had to do was get out before it began again. Shaking her head in desperation, she rubbed her temples, trying to conjure a new idea for escape.

His eyes lit up as she remembered the whistle Rupa had given her hanging around her neck. Annabel fumbled to retrieve it from her pocket and blew into it repeatedly with all her might, going from window to window of the boat.

After what felt like an eternity, a distant shout reached her ears, and her heart leaped with hope.

Charlie stood on the shore, a puzzled expression on his face as he observed the abandoned boat. His eyes widened when he saw Annabel at the window, and he immediately rushed down to the riverbank.

He waded into the water with determined strides, quickly reaching the boat and lifting the mooring rope. Their eyes met through the porthole, his gaze filled with relief and concern. "What happened?" Charlie yelled above the rushing river.

"The door! I can't get out!" she screamed, her voice laced with fear. "The anchor chain broke!"

Charlie glanced down, confirming the situation. His face grew stormy as he surveyed the boat's position and the river's current, then swiftly tied the mooring rope to the tree trunk. "Hang on," he shouted before disappearing from sight.

Annabel anxiously awaited his return, her heart pounding more rapidly as she wondered if this would be the end for her. Moments later, she heard a loud crash, followed by several more, as Charlie forcefully struck the door, determined to break it open. Wood splintered and rained down on the lower deck as he relentlessly hammered at the barrier.

Charlie's strong arms reached for her, and she gratefully took his hands, allowing him to pull her out. Suppressing her emotions, she said with a quivering voice, "Thank you, thank you... I'm so sorry you had to do that."

As they both collapsed on the riverbank, breathing heavily, Annabel couldn't hide her fright. "Did you see anything of what happened? I came here to clean, and then the door slammed shut, trapping me inside, and it all broke free." She shuddered.

"I only saw the boat bumping along when I heard the whistle. I was several yards down, reading." Charlie shook his head, his face etched with concern. "I'm sure you're sorry you ever came to Castle Rowley."

"Not really," she replied, her voice filled with frustration. "But this place is dehumanizing. I can't believe you've endured it for so long."

"Then leave," Charlie retorted bitterly. "What's stopping you?"

"*You* are," Annabel admitted without hesitation, then lowered her eyes, wishing she hadn't.

He sighed, his anger dissipating. "That should not be. It's over between us."

She frowned. "Yet, you still risked yourself for me."

"Well." Charlie looked away. "I'm only human, after all. I would have done that for anyone." He sniffed.

"Alright." She crossed her arms. "But there's something else you haven't told me, isn't there?"

"Yes," he sighed, a mix of remorse and determination in his eyes. "A deal I attempted to strike with the Baron."

"A deal?" Annabel's voice conveyed her disbelief. "You paid him?"

"Yes, and I am aware it was foolish." His voice was heavy with regret.

She shook her head, her frustration fading. "But you know that he's not an honorable man. Why would you do such a thing?"

"Right; I know that." Charlie explained, "But I was told you had spoken to his children about their mother and that you would face dire consequences. He planned to send James to punish you, but I offered to take your punishment instead. He agreed."

Feeling sick to her stomach, Annabel ran her fingers through her hair. "Charlie, you should *not* have done that for me."

"I have so little control here. Let me have my honor and willingness to protect those I care about," he said with resignation.

"This place is suffocating," she moaned, her voice filled with frustration. "I can't believe you've endured all this. Castle Rowley has forced you into being a martyr for those you care for, but it's not even working."

Charlie's expression hardened. "Then it's a good thing I ended things."

Annabel raised her eyebrows, surprised by his comment. "But you still took beatings for me. And he slapped me anyway and tried to kill me with this boat."

"He slapped you?" Fury flashed in his eyes. "He wasn't supposed to strike you." He paused, suddenly beholding the change in her expression. "You look upset."

"I'm not upset." She frowned, and something alarming surged within her. She narrowed her eyes and added, "I'm bloody *angry*, Charlie."

"Oh." He looked surprised. "I'm not sure I've ever seen you angry."

"Then see me now," she hissed under her breath. "You kissed me and brought me happiness when you weren't supposed to, and now you're giving up at the first sign of trouble. It's what I feared all along. Why did you kiss me in the first place if you were so quick to break it off?"

Charlie looked stricken, his voice filled with remorse. "I'm sorry. It was pure selfishness. I deeply regret it."

"Good for you," she replied bitterly, turning away to hide her tears.

"Annabel..." he whispered softly. "I didn't mean... I don't regret you. I regret my own actions."

She cleared her throat, fighting back her emotions. "Leave me. Leave me now."

"You have no idea how much I want to touch you," Charlie murmured, causing her breath to catch in her throat. "I miss you every hour. I would do anything to keep you safe and be with you simultaneously."

Annabel took a deep breath and looked at the ground, not trusting herself to look at him.

He sighed, sounding defeated. "I'm sorry. I shouldn't have confessed my feelings. I am either making things worse or harassing you. I'll leave you be."

After she heard him depart, Annabel allowed herself to break down, collapsing under a tree, her tears flowing freely. She mourned the unfairness of it all, even as she held fast to the silver lining that at least Charlie hadn't lost his desire for her. He still cared for her and wanted to protect her and her family. That counted for something, surely?

Drying her tears and pushing her sorrow aside, Annabel gathered her resolve. She stood up and returned to the now-secured boat that Charlie had anchored. Tying the top door open with a knotted rope, she continued cleaning the lower deck.

As long last, when she took the dirt path back to the castle, the darkness of night already enveloping her, Annabel's body ached from her laborious day aboard the boat. Hauling the bucket of supplies with her, she headed to the farmhouse, where she set them down by the door. When she lit a lantern and carefully opened the door, she smiled to see Agatha and Richard asleep, her friend on a newly constructed bed, and the man she used to call her husband on the old one, a screen separating them in the room. Annabel slowly pulled the door almost closed, leaving it open just a crack.

Stealing back into the kitchen, she quickly stripped down and poured a jug of healthy water into a basin, and taking a rag and a scrap of the soap Lise had left her, she scrubbed herself fiercely. With every swipe at the grime on her skin, she thought of putting the Baron away. She thought of ceasing living in fear and perhaps spending more time inside the castle and smiled. Then Charlie's face drifted back into her mind, and she felt hollow again.

Shivering in the dark, she donned clean clothes, then sat down at the table with an apple from the cupboard and a large slice of bread, thick with dates and nuts. She ate it slowly, wondering how she would ever sleep that night.

When she'd finished, she looked first at the door, then at the cot Agatha had set up for her a few feet from the fire, with a freshly stuffed mattress, embroidered pillows, and a thick quilt. After much thought, she shook her head and pulled on her coat. She had to clear her head with a walk before she could sleep, no doubt about it. The moon was low in the sky as she ambled along the path with her lantern held aloft and her mind wandering. Ahead, she heard a twig snap, and her eyes widened. She stopped, wondering if she should head back.

A shadowy figure came into view, and she sighed with relief when she realized it was Charlie. Both surprised at the other's presence, they locked eyes.

Annabel could make out his familiar freckles in the faint moonlight, his strong jaw, the worried look on his brow, and joy tugged relentlessly at her heartstrings. Annoyed, she tried to bat the feeling away.

Charlie's gaze fell upon her glistening wet hair and skin, the buxom chest heaving with relief under her rumpled clothes. Annabel's soft, hopeful eyes shimmered, and her lips trembled as she blinked back the feelings that threatened to flow.

After a seemingly endless pause, they fell into each other's arms. Charlie kissed Annabel passionately, holding her close to him, his touch filled with sweetness and hunger, and she responded with equal fervor. Her hands found their way under his shirt, caressing his chest, strong as a tree trunk, while he held her waist to his, pulling her closer as if he wanted to be one with her. Everything else faded away at that moment.

Taking refuge amidst the tall grass and seeking shelter beneath the expansive canopy of a majestic tree, the two lovers swiftly descended into the ground, their desire igniting an unstoppable flame that consumed them both.

Their lips melded together with an intensity that rendered their mouths sore and bruised as they feared relinquishing their connection. Annabel's fingers entwined in Charlie's hair as he lowered his head, planting fervent kisses on her tender neck and bosom, awakening a vibrant, wicked sensation within her chest.

"I've missed you so much," he said softly into her ear, his words a gentle caress. "I'm so sorry. Frederick told me of your plans, and they're brilliant. I want to help, and I swear I'll never let you go again."

"You bloody better not," she whispered. Her voice, laced with desire, barely a whisper, trembled, "I ache for you." His gaze turned lascivious, a departure from the stoicism she'd been receiving from him, and her heart leaped at the familiar joy. At that moment, he appeared untamed, like a primal beast driven by desire. Charlie lowered his head again to run his tongue so slowly around her soft nipples, causing her to moan with pleasure. Looking down at the top of his head as he pleasured her gave her a thrill, unlike anything she could describe. And then he was licking downwards; he was skipping over her dress, and at her hips now, his tongue was opening her up, making her clench and release, and she moaned softly. The sheer enjoyment of this experience would have been enough on its own, like the best of hot baths. However, as

Annabel relaxed into the mouth of the man she loved, his movements flowing, her body yielding, the pleasure building...she finally exploded with a shudder. Soon after, Charlie kissed her slowly up her body, along her inner thighs and belly, swept her dress back down, and kissed softly between her breasts...then when they faced each other again, she slipped on top of him. He raised his eyebrows in surprise as Annabel grinned, and then she kissed down his chest and stomach and tugged off his suspenders. He groaned in pleasure as she pleasured him, and she kissed up the length of him slowly, taking it in her mouth. As her calloused, wandering hands massaged his thighs, and her soft lips worked below his belt, he grasped at her shoulders, biting his lip as he attempted to prolong the pleasure.

Looking up at his beautiful half-naked body in the moonlight, Annabel hungered for him in an almost primal way. She wanted to have his scent on her, for him to feel her every time he was away. Her heart danced as she realized it would take much more than their current circumstances to stop loving this man who was always so quick to bury himself between her legs and taste her while she screamed and pulled his hair.

Grasping him tightly, she churned her lips around him, enjoying the moment's intimacy, occasionally breaking away to lick his stomach and thighs, devouring his pleasure in a mad, wild dance. Her nails scratched at his firm, muscular thighs in the heat of passion. He didn't last long, and as he choked out a warning that he was about to come, she slipped her face up to his and grasped him carnally with both hands, feeling wanton and wonderful and wishing she could have him completely, right now.

They nestled into each other's embrace then, their breaths heavy and labored, and Annabel gazed up at the face she adored—his countenance clever and sweet, the intriguing man she had fallen for.

When Charlie opened his eyes, marveling at her presence beside him, she smiled, and he drew her into the warmth of his chest. "Are you warm enough?" he asked, concerned as he tugged his breeches back on and tied them in place.

Still fully clothed, Annabel shook her head playfully. "Never." In response, he draped his long, loose, woolen jacket over them both, and she snuggled even closer, reveling in his intoxicating scent, the comforting touch of his warm skin, and the rough texture of his stubbled jawline. She marveled at how his body pressed against hers—solid, protective, and exuding a strength she had long yearned for.

With a touch of jest in her voice, she quipped, "So, have you gotten me out of your system now?" Uncertainty lingered beneath her words, the weight of unspoken thoughts and untold secrets pressing upon them. If Charlie declared this night a mistake, she would have to push him away forever, as painful as it might be. She couldn't bear the back-and-forth any longer.

To her delight, he grinned, his eyes filled with warmth and affection. "Not at all." Rising on his elbow, he leaned in, his gaze fixed on her. "Annabel, I apologize for not immediately informing you about the Baron's threats." He sighed, remorse evident in his voice. "It was a poor choice, and my execution was equally lacking."

Nodding in understanding, she admired the moonlight's caress upon his lips and the chiseled contours of his face. "You did handle it poorly, I must admit, and after you promised to be honest with me," she murmured, her fingers gently caressing the hand that held her own.

"I wouldn't blame you if you have fallen out of favor with me in the meantime," Charlie said. "You shouldn't have to put up with such lies."

"Let us attempt to communicate more with each other then, not less, and we will be much better served. "Annabel's mouth quirked. "You did save my life, so I'll forgive you this sin again. But never again, do you hear?"

"Agreed," he replied, his touch tenderly brushing against her hair. "Are you saying you will have me back, then?"

"Is that what you're saying?" Annabel quipped. "You are the one who broke things off, so I dare say you must be the one who mends them."

"Mend them, I will," Charlie promised. "I'll spend the rest of my life trying to mend them. As long as you haven't grown too weary of my ill-advised decisions."

"Oh, I bloody well have, so cease them," she laughed. "Why were you out on the path tonight, anyway? Don't tell me you were coming to see me."

"I was." Charlie let out a weary sigh. "When I saw you trapped in that boat on the river...I remember you said you couldn't swim. I thought it would capsize and feared losing you forever." He absent-mindedly rubbed a scar forming on his neck, and Annabel winced when she realized it was from the Baron's lashings. "In the face of the possibility of never seeing you again, all the rationalizations for pro-tecting you and my self-preservation lost their meaning. After much thought, I've realized that standing alongside you as partners may be better than placing you on a pedestal."

"I wholeheartedly agree," she affirmed. Curiosity sparked within her, and he inquired, "How was your lunch with Fred and Cecelia?"

"Informative," she replied, filling him in on the details. "What are your thoughts?"

"I'm ready to help distract the Baron with a loud, long fight while you rescue Amos and Philippa," he declared. Glancing at her, his gaze filled with tenderness, he added, "Annabel, you're like a ray of sunshine in this clouded world."

She laughed. "How I've missed you."

Their bodies aglow with contentment, they gazed up at the shim-mering stars.

"Oh," Charlie exhaled sharply. "I found the riddle, the one about the dungeon. It was in the dungeon."

"What?" Annabel gasped, turning to him with wide eyes, a delight-ed smile spreading across her face. "How did you...what is it? Where was it?"

"I've been down there looking in between the fights whenever I've had a chance." He laughed. "It's on the ceiling of the cell we found

Lise and Agatha is in, which stands empty, but the way. Do we know where Amos is being held?"

"Cecelia says she knows." Annabel nodded impatiently. "Charlie! What is the final riddle?"

He closed his eyes and recited,

Hid under half an immortal throne, my secret treasure lies,

Go deeper than you think, and look with both your eyes.

Congratulations, seeker, you've found your great reward,

Guard it well, enjoy it now...but keep it from the lord.

"Sorry, Charlie," Annabel whispered, perplexed. "I'm stumped. It sounds like the treasure room is underground through a hidden door. I fear that could be anywhere. And the immortal throne..."

Charlie kissed her neck. "I don't care if we ever find it, just as long as I never lose you again." He slipped his hand into hers.

She smiled and kissed him back. "You said you read those stories about the Greek immortals, didn't you? What were their names?"

He groaned. "There are so many. Too many."

"I remember Zeus, Hermes, Hercules, and Athena," she mused, kissing a freckle on his neck. "Mmmm..."

"Hercules was only half-immortal," muttered Charlie. "He was Zeus' son, but he had a human mother."

"Well, then he's half-immortal, then," Annabel laughed. "His throne is his stall, isn't it?"

"Oh, God's heart," Charlie exclaimed. "Yes. I'm a fool. I clean those horses almost every day, and it never occurred to me."

Annabel grinned. "Let's go." With newfound clarity, now that they knew what they were looking for, the two quickly pried up many thick, rotting boards and found the hidden trapdoor beneath them, revealing a staircase thick with cobwebs leading into the depths below.

Excitement in their hearts, Annabel and Charlie descended the narrow stone steps, their lanterns casting enchanting shadows on the walls. Annabel's eyes widened in awe as they reached the treasure-filled chamber and Charlie's face glowed with wonder.

It was a room out of their wildest dreams, filled with glittering jewels, exquisite gilded trinkets, and delicate tapestries draped along the stone walls. Annabel was immediately drawn to the books with ornate leather covers lining dusty shelves, and precious antique vases stood atop wooden pedestals. Charlie marveled at a delicate silver necklace adorned with sapphires, its beauty reflecting the soft light.

Annabel moved closer to inspect a nearby painting, its canvas worn with age but still revealing the vibrant colors of a majestic landscape. "These are heirlooms from generations past," she said, her voice filled with wonder.

"They hold priceless history and stories." Charlie set down the necklace where it had been. "We could leave this place, you know. We could carry out this plan, wait until the Baron is in the dungeon, then take what we can carry from this room and leave. Frederick wouldn't fault us, I'm sure. We can leave any time you want. I'll go where you go." He kissed her hand.

She watched his face. "Do you want to leave?"

"That's a complicated question for me." He took her hand. "I want to be where you are and to make you happy."

"I always assumed you didn't want to leave because of what the Baron threatened he'd do if you escaped, but you do want to stay, don't you?" Annabel asked curiously.

He looked at her and laughed. "How do you read me so easily?"

"I want to stay as well." She smiled. "I as much as promised Frederick I would stay for a while and help him settle into being the Baron. He and Cecelia want my help, and I'd like to give it, at least for a while, until we figure out our next steps." She kissed him. "Are you certain you want to remain after all the trouble this place has given you?"

"It's the Baron and his orders that have given me trouble. Truth be told, I've always dreamed that perhaps the old man would die in an accident, and I'd be allowed to move back into my parent's house and restore it, make it livable again," Charlie said wistfully. "It's by the river. It's lovely, or it was twenty years ago—and most of my childhood memories live there. And it's only a twenty-minute walk to the castle." He sighed. "I wouldn't mind getting to know my brother better when things are all said and done."

"Well, Frederick may give you the money to restore your childhood home and more." Annabel grinned. "You've got friends in high places, now."

Charlie smiled down at her. "I think you may be right." He bent to kiss her. "Life is about to be almost perfect."

REVENGE

Chapter 31: Revenge

The dimly lit dungeon reverberated with muffled cheers, an eerie symphony of despair and hope intermingling in the air. Annabel and Charlie stood in the shadows, his identity concealed by a fresh pirate disguise, perhaps not quite as remarkably effective as one from Lise, but a disguise nonetheless. As they peered through a gap in the curtain, the audience gathered and mumbled in hushed anticipation, unaware of the audacious mission about to unfold.

Annabel's voice, barely audible amidst the growing crowd, whispered to Charlie, "Are you nervous?" Her gaze met his, her heart heavy with the burden of the night's mission.

Shaking his head and stepping away from the curtain to lean against the wall, Charlie's false beard wobbled. "Perhaps a bit." He swallowed hard.

"I don't blame you, but worry not," she reassured him. "There's a lot of potential happiness riding on tonight, and we will make it happen."

"And tomorrow." Charlie grinned. "I wasn't sure until today, but Lise plans to return in the morning, and she has our annulment papers."

Annabel's mouth fell open. "You're not serious. How on earth did you get an annulment? Doesn't it take a long time with lawyers and the like?"

"A friend helped with birth papers showing Lise and I were related," he explained. The castle chapel priest wrote a letter of recommendation, and he has a friend at the ecclesiastical court. They have granted a decree of nullity, which Lise is obtaining today and will bring tomorrow to submit to the priest. All it cost us was the initial bribe to forge the birth records."

She smiled and shook her head. "I can't believe you did all that."

In the tender moment, he kissed her, his strong hands grasping her waist as he pulled her closer. "After this, our life could finally be our own. If we survive tonight, that is." He smiled teasingly. "Just in case, kiss me one last time."

"Don't joke about that," Annabel chided, kissing him soundly. "It's going to work. It will. All the pieces are in place."

Nodding, Charlie's eyes darted around the room. "I'm ready. How many others will go before me?"

"Three," Annabel reminded him. "Everyone is seated, Frederick next to Henry. Gregory is on guard duty, and James has instructed him to leave his post outside the dungeon in five minutes. James will take Cecelia and me to Philippa's cell, and we'll bring her up in a cloak to the second guest bedroom and brief her on the plan. Then we go down and do the same with Amos. We come back down the third time; your fight should be happening. The other pirate will seem to kill you with your retractable dagger, and you'll fall through the stage. While the Baron is gloating, James will come out wailing about Philippa, the Baron follows him, and we lock him in the cell."

"Right, thank you. I think I've got it now. I'll be ready to distract him." Charlie nodded. "Godspeed, my love."

A bell's sudden ring echoed through the space, causing everyone to startle. "Showtime," Charlie whispered, his voice barely audible. He squeezed Annabel's cold hand, bringing it to his face and tenderly kissing her fingertips. She embraced him tightly, worrying silently about the night ahead. As she slipped from backstage and into the hallway to meet Cecelia, she heard the drunken crowd cheer for the first figh t.

In the dimly lit dungeon below the stage, minutes later, James, Annabel, and Cecelia moved with caution, their hearts pounding with fear and determination. The flickering torches cast eerie shadows as they navigated the maze of cells, each step thankfully masked by the soft echoes of laughter and revelry above.

"We must be quick and quiet," Cecelia whispered, her voice barely audible.

At last, they arrived at the door of a minor, dimly lit cell. The silence within was palpable, and James' hand trembled slightly as he inserted the key into the lock. Despite all their conjectures and what they had uncovered, Annabel still wavered inwardly when she wondered if their search would come to fruition. And now, as she seemed to hear the distant fight grow more ravenous, her heart pounded in her ears, and she realized how much she yearned to find the Baroness alive inside.

The door creaked open, and there, in the corner of the cell, sat a frail figure, her eyes hollow, sitting on an oversized plush chair, the piece of furniture practically swallowing her. Auburn hair was pulled up in a loose chignon, and a tiny mole on her lip trembled. The smell of preserved lemons was thick in the air.

Cecelia gasped, "Phillippa. It's really you."

"Is it truly she?" whispered Annabel in excitement. "Are you sure?"

Phillippa, the Baroness herself, looked at them in confusion, her eyes hollow from years of suffering. Annabel's heart ached at the sight of the proud woman from the painting, and she couldn't help but feel suddenly exhausted at the weight of the night's events. Raising her head, eyes widening in disbelief at the sight of the cloaked figures standing before her, Philippa blinked in the sudden light. "Who... who are you?" she whispered, her voice barely audible.

"We are friends," Cecelia spoke gently, tears in her eyes. "We've come to free you."

"Is Henry dead?" The woman gasped. "Please tell me he's dead."

"He's not dead." Annabel gently shook her head. "He's distracted. We're trying to get you out of here, then throw Henry in this cell himself. You and your son can decide when to bring him before the constable for his crimes."

Phillippa's eyes filled with tears, her voice trembling as she spoke, "You... you shouldn't be here. He'll punish you for this. You'll be thrown in here with me. If he's not dead, then he'll kill you." She balled her hands into fists. "He's a monster. He's kept me down here for years, trying to put a child in me."

"It's been six years," Cecelia told her.

Philippa's shoulders slumped. "He kept feeding me, allowing me to walk this floor at night on a leash, giving me all my favorite things, telling me he'd let me leave as soon as I became with child." She shook her head. "The man is infertile. I could be down here for the rest of my short life."

Annabel shivered at the familiar words, her heart pounding like a drum in the hazy aftermath of chaos and despair. Her eyes met

Phillippa's, and in that unspoken connection, they knew that their lives had irrevocably changed that night.

"You'll never have to go through that again," Cecelia declared, her voice strong with conviction. "Get up, and quickly. You're not spending another minute in this cell."

Phillippa's voice, though strained, carried the weight of authority and a determination that hadn't been seen in her for years. "You're Cecelia," she whispered. "Bridgette's child. Henry put your mother down here once."

"And you're the Baroness," confirmed Cecelia with a glint in her eye. "I hope you owe us a favor now."

Phillippa's eyes locked onto theirs, and a deep understanding passed between them. The Baroness nodded, a glimmer of hope returning to her haunted gaze.

James whispered, "My lady, the servants will be on your side, I assure you. Can I help you to your chambers? They have been prepared for you—you should have a bath and rest. The doctor can see to you."

"While you are putting my husband away?" She laughed. "I'm not going to stand by and do nothing." She stood at last and stumbled.

"You're not strong enough, my lady," James insisted. "Let us bring you out of here, out of reach of the Baron, and allow you to heal."

Philippa sighed, looking years older than she was. "Fine. But the both of you, come up with me. I don't want anyone to see me yet." She gestured to James and Cecelia. "Please?"

"Go ahead." Annabel nodded. "Give me the keys, James—I'll free Amos and bring him up, then meet you back down here."

Shakily, James handed over the ring of keys, and Cecelia took a small hand-drawn map out of her pocket. "Here is where we are." She pointed.

"And here is where Amos' cell is. Right?" She looked at her father, who nodded quickly, and they set off. Annabel quickly took off toward the cell, following the map. When she finally stopped and lowered the map, her heart sank to see that the cell was empty, the door ajar

.

Quickly, she ran back to the stage as the sounds of fights and revelry grew louder. The air was tense, and Annabel could feel the weight of every step. Her heart pounded with fear and anticipation as she witnessed the unfolding spectacle, stopping short to see Amos already on the stage.

Panicking, her eyes flicked to Frederick in the crowd. His face was pale, and he was breathing heavily, his brows knitted and his knuckles gripping his knees. Beside him, Henry laughed uproariously. "Let's see the sodomite burn! Set him afire!" He nudged Cole, who sat on his other side. "Go up there and set his clothes afire. I want to see him consumed."

Blood already spattered the walls, and the pirates onstage were in disarray, among them Charlie, who stepped forward as Cole slowly made his way to the stage with a grim expression, carrying a torch.

Clearing his throat, Charlie shouted with a brogue to his voice, "I'm afraid that I must slash your fiery satisfaction, Baron Rowley." He pulled out the dagger Annabel recognized as his false one and appeared to plunge it into the neck of a shaky, tied Amos, blood erupting from his side. Annabel smiled weakly as she spotted the telltale extra blood around Charlie's sleeve that suggested it was not Amos' own wound that poured. With a crow of glee at the fury upon the Baron's face, Charlie picked up Amos and tossed him over his shoulder. As he pressed the other man's face into the side of his own, Annabel just barely saw Charlie whisper something to Amos, then he threw the other man into the trap door, where he soon disappeared.

Rolling his eyes, Cole set the torch back in its sheath on the wall. Annabel slipped away from the crowd and below the stage, where she quickly untied Amos, ignoring the surprised guard on duty. With an annoyed tone, he hissed above her, "What do you think you're doing?" She looked up to see Gregory and whispered, "We're trying to oust the Baron and reinstall the Baroness. We've just freed her, and we're coming for Henry. Are you with us or not?"

He gaped at her silently and finally nodded, and her heart soared. "Good. Follow me." Quickly, she rushed back to the stage just as Cecelia arrived, her eyes wide. Charlie shouted aloud as his crazed pirate character fought another man with a staff.

Although she knew it was planned, Annabel still winced as the staff swung through the air and connected with Charlie. He staggered forward, and the other man took the opportunity to tie him to a pulley coming down from the ceiling.

Her heart lurched as she watched the pivotal moment he was hoisted up. Her mind raced. It had gone well in practice—the other pirate was supposed to pull Charlie a few feet up, then pretend to kill him with a false dagger. The pirate would be escorted off the stage by guards, and Charlie would be pulled up out of sight, out of mind, free to follow the Baron after and help them imprison him in the cell.

Suddenly, there was laughter. A loud, ringing, familiar cacophony echoed throughout the room and caused everyone else in the vicinity to wonder. Henry paused in his mirth to shout, "Halt!" He stood, a cruel, strange look on his face.

Frederick called up to the imposing Baron, finally regaining his composure, "Father? What are you doing?" He smiled weakly. "Come back to your seat; the fun's just starting."

"Do you take me for a fool?" demanded Henry. "I know what this is." He pointed a giant finger at the stage. "I know that's your little friend. I know you've been conspiring against me."

Looking stricken, Frederick shook his head quickly. "No, Father, that's not—"

"I am not even your *father*!" Henry screamed, and with a mighty paw, he clubbed Frederick over the head. Cecelia gasped across the room, then clapped a hand over her mouth. She ran towards Frederick, and the Baron held up his other hand. "I'll deal with you in a moment, little mouse. Stay where you are—that bastard in your belly is no relation of mine."

Cecelia froze, her face paling, and her anxious gaze swept to Annabel. Henry advanced toward the stage, where Charlie was still halfway up the wall attached to the pulley. The other pirates were nowhere to be seen. Desperate, Annabel tried to signal a stagehand to lift her love out of harm's way, but they were nowhere to be found. Before she could intervene, a hand yanked her back, and she found herself face-to-face with Cole, who wielded a heavy truncheon.

"Don't you *dare* move," he warned.

Desperation took hold of her, and Annabel struggled to break free. "He's going to *die*!" she whispered, frantic to save Charlie.

"He was *always* going to die!" Cole sneered callously, his resolve firm as his grip on Annabel, as her plea turned into a scream.

The Baron's laughter echoed. "My own farmers pretending for me like a child," he sang mockingly. "I work hard all day, and if I want to see honest bloodshed in my castle, I will."

Cecelia joined them, her voice heavy with defeat. "My father is being held by a guard who won't take a bribe," she whispered.

Panic set in as Annabel understood their plan had failed, leaving them exposed and vulnerable.

"What have you *done*?" Cole demanded, his grip on Annabel tightening. "What did you *try* to do?"

Ignoring the chamberlain, Cecelia's voice cracked as she whispered to Annabel, "It's just us now. We don't have my father or Charlie. Look at Frederick. He's frozen in place with nerves. What can two women do? This was all for nothing."

The weight of despair threatened to crush Annabel, but she couldn't give in. "Not nothing," she whispered, trying to muster hope. "But we've got to get Charlie out of there." She looked desperately at Gregory, who looked to the stage in horror.

Cole sneered. "What are you doing, Gregory? Take Cecelia. These two have conspired against the Baron, and he'll have their heads tomorrow."

Uneasily, Gregory took the arm of Cecelia, who shot him a look of venom.

"I said I wanted bloodshed, and I'll make it myself if I have to." The Baron advanced on her love, and she felt him squeeze tightly in her chest, as if by a vice, as Annabel tried to twist away from Cole. "Charlie Wright. You have been a thorn in my side for years. Your parents were exactly the same; nothing but trouble."

His lip curled as he drew closer to the stage. "And despite everything I've thrown at you, you've refused to die. I'm bored of this game of cat and mouse."

Annabel's heart shattered as Charlie's fate seemed sealed, and she twisted forward again, but Cole held her back. Her eyes pleaded with him, desperate to save the man she loved.

The sadistic glee was evident in Henry's eyes as he drew a dagger; he laughed once more, then plunged it into Charlie's stomach. Her love howled, grabbing at the dagger, and his body jerked and bled as

Annabel's vision swam before her eyes, and she felt as though her heart was ripping apart.

The blood roared in her ears, and Annabel screamed louder than she ever had before, startling everyone around her, the sound growing louder and louder until it sounded like a banshee, a ghost, a demon. The room suddenly erupted into chaos as every remaining spectator fl ed.

Shaken, Cole shouted about the fray, "Stop! All of you!" It was to no avail as the group stampeded towards the no longer guarded door, and the room soon stood still, with only the castle inhabitants.

Gregory was nowhere to be seen. Annabel shook off Cole's grip and attempted again to run forward, only for him to grab hold of her arm again firmly and to find that he also had a hand locked onto Cecelia's wrist beside her. "You bloody monster," she spat. "Can't you see you're on the wrong side?"

"Baron Rowley!" A loud, mournful cry came, and Annabel's hope rose when she realized it was James. She exchanged a relieved glance with Cecelia as he shouted, "Philippa is gravely ill. You must come, my lord. She cannot be moved, and if you move swiftly, you can say goodbye to her before she dies."

"God's heart..." Henry looked shaken. "Cole and Gregory, hold these women. They cannot be allowed to escape." The Baron began to follow James down the corridor. "This can't be true. I just saw her. She was absolutely fine..."

"James is lying, my lord," spat Cole, and the Baron stopped halfway down the hall. "Mark my words; he's been helping his daughter free those you have punished."

"Really," the Baron said in a low, dangerous voice, glaring at his steward.

"*He's* the one who's lying," James said, but his voice shook. "Truly."

"I don't believe you," hissed Henry. "You've held a grudge ever since I locked up your wife. I never should have trusted you afterward...I should have stamped out your little family. I was far too soft."

"May you fester in Hades," rasped Annabel in hatred as Cecelia bit her lip.

The Baron whirled on her. "And you. My spunky little literate farmwife. What a surprise you have been. A much more boisterous mouse than I'm used to playing with."

"Shall I put her in a cell, my lord?" Cole sighed. "A small one?"

"No." A smile spread across Henry's face. "I have spent years trying to put a child in Philippa, and her coldness has endured all this time. If she is truly on her deathbed, I must move on. I must make an heir before my time is done." He chuckled softly. "Who knew the bearer of my next progeny could be a peasant?"

"No," Annabel whispered in horror, and even Cole looked surprised.

"You must not do such a thing," his chamberlain shuddered. "Baron Rowley, you are not thinking this through."

"No one need know," Henry commented, his eyes sweeping the space. "Yes, you're right. Best put her in a cell until we confirm she will be complacent. Perhaps if she is pliant, I will keep her in my chambers. Our children will be strong, sweet, and literate." He stepped forward, advancing on Annabel. "Let's give it a go, shall we?"

"Don't you bloody touch me," she screamed in horror. "I will fight you to my death or yours. I swear it."

Cole shifted uncomfortably. "My lord," he began. "Do not do this. I beg of you." Then, to her surprise, he let Annabel go, and she staggered away from them both. "This would be a great evil, Henry," he whispered. "Even for you."

Suddenly, the air filled with the aroma of burning herbs and a coughing began; then, the hallway was engulfed in a dense smoke, causing confusion and chaos. Closing her eyes as they burned from the smoke, Annabel quickly moved down the hallway with the others, away from the noxious fumes until they were against the opposite wall. As the haze cleared,

Annabel was stunned to see Phillippa's form standing tall, much taller than it should be, clad in an absolutely enormous cloak, almost seeming to float above them like an apparition.

Baron Henry looked terrified. He backed away from his wife as he gaped in horror. "Philippa," he hissed. "What are you..."

"Take my name out of your mouth. I have come to punish you," Phillippa threatened, her voice a mix of rage and resolve as she confronted her husband. "I will kill you today," she declared. "First, I will cut you into pieces and feed you to my horses. I assume you will die along the way."

"Please," Henry croaked, sounding weak. "You must not kill me here. I'll do anything."

"Yes, you *will*." Suddenly, Philippa was moving forward, but she seemed gliding too quickly for an ordinary person. She was headed straight for the Baron, picking up speed.

Annabel, James, Cecelia, Gregory, and Cole leaped to the sides, diving out of the way while the mighty form of the Baroness rushed down the hall. Annabel tilted her head in curiosity, thinking she heard a squeaking noise.

Henry chose to run directly away from his wife, screaming down the hall and through the open cell door. Upon realizing where he was, he quickly grabbed hold of the doorframe, looking fearfully towards Philippa, who crashed into him, and he fell down on his back, shouting in fear. Philippa raised her arm. Henry cringed, briefly closing his eyes, and his wife quickly threw the cloak she was wearing over his face. It was enormous, and he scraped at his face through the fabric, trying to pull it off but merely moving backward, further into the dark cell.

The figure of the Baroness suddenly moved sharply backward, and she smiled. Annabel suddenly realized she was trembling with exertion. "Close the door," Philippa rasped.

Gregory elbowed past a shocked Cole to slam the cell door, pulling an iron bolt down to secure it. James stepped forward to turn a key in the lock, and as Philippa's hand went out, he set it in her open palm. The older woman shoved the key into her pocket.

Cecelia looked up at Philippa curiously, then behind her. "Are you on a —"

The Baroness winced as she climbed down from the laundry cart, revealing a young woman below her and an older woman who had been behind her in the cart, pushing it. Immediately, Phillippa fell against

Gregory for support, her strength waning. "Help me up," she whispered. "I cannot stand that long yet. This caper has taken much out of me."

"Lise! Maggie!" Cecelia exclaimed. "What are you doing here?"

"She came to get me," Philippa said, leaning against the wall and breathing deeply. "She heard tell of a plan that had gone awry. It was said that two women couldn't possibly do anything...so we thought we'd see if three women could." The Baroness smiled. "The ghost in the laundry cart was my idea."

Lise smiled at Annabel. "It's so very, very good to see you after all that. Sorry it all went topside."

"It's good to see you as well," Annabel said, her heart aching as her lip trembled. "But Lise...oh Lise, the worst has happened."

"Don't say that! The worst is over, more like," Lise winked. "Besides, I've brought you and Charlie a present— an annulment. Would you venture a guess as to what comes next?" She winked.

"Oh, Lise." Annabel's eyes filled with tears. "The plan went awry in more ways than one."

"Henry killed Charlie," Cecelia sobbed, the tears pouring down her cheeks. "Perhaps Frederick, too. He stabbed Charlie and hit Frederick—they both went down and did not get back up. We failed."

Lise's eyes widened. "No. I don't believe it. No, I'd know if he was dead. You must be mistaken." Shaking her head, she ran back down the hall.

Annabel's heart ached with grief and anger. Lifting her skirts, she and Cecelia began silently down the hallway. As they walked back to the stage, Annabel felt numb, and she lifted her gaze back to where her love had been killed. Tears streamed down her cheeks as she thought of what they had lost, and as they blurred her vision, she blinked them back, her heart breaking.

"Annabel!" To her surprise, Charlie stepped to the edge of the stage, the picture of health, his bloodstained midsection belying his broad smile. "Did it work?"

Behind her, Cecelia fainted.

Chapter Thirty-Two

CASTLE ROWLEY

After a moment of stunned bewilderment, during which Annabel's feet seemed frozen to the floor, she ran up to the stage. "You're alive," she said in amazement. "But—"

"You didn't know?" Charlie's eyes widened. "I was waiting here until Henry was locked in the cell. I really got him riled up, yeah?" He slipped off the stage and took her in his arms as she cried in relief. "I heard your scream, but I thought you were pretending."

"No! I'm not a bloody actor," she sobbed, burying her face in his neck. "Oh, *Charlie.*"

Lise sat down on a chair, shaking her head. "God's head, you scared me."

Rubbing Annabel's back soothingly, Charlie stroked her hair. "I'm absolutely fine. Just a few bruises from it all. After all, it was a prop dagger —don't you remember? We went over it."

"But Henry *stabbed* you," she argued. "It was supposed to be the other pirate. When he went up there and plunged his own dagger into you..." She wiped her eyes on the handkerchief he handed her. "Henry didn't have a prop."

"He must have." Charlie returned to the stage and brought the dagger back to show her. "See? It retracts." He demonstrated. "I managed to cut myself down—we'll need a new pulley, though." Annabel inspected it curiously and found the retractable mechanism, looking up at him in puzzlement.

Frederick cleared his throat, shuffling nervously as he rubbed his head. "I—I switched Father's dagger. I had a hunch."

"Good man," Charlie grinned. "Thank you. You saved my bloody life, then."

"You're welcome." Frederick weakly grinned back. "Sorry I didn't get up and follow you when I awoke—I thought Henry would kill me if I did."

Phillippa had finally caught up to them, leaning on Gregory as they were trailed by James and Maggie. "My darling son. How very clever you were to band together with your friends to save me. I shall spend the rest of my life making it up to you."

"No need, no need at all." Frederick's eyes filled with tears. "I didn't know you were down here...I'm so sorry I didn't figure it out sooner, Mother."

"Now, now, sweetheart, let's look to the future, not the past." Squeezing Frederick's hand, she turned to Charlie. "Aren't you Lucas and Mara's boy?" Her smile softened. "How lucky *you're* still alive."

"Yes, my lady." Charlie nodded. "I've been able to stay out of Henry's the way only just."

Frederick cleared his throat. "Mother—we know everything. We found your letters in the attic. We know who I am and who Charlie is."

"Oh." His mother froze momentarily, her eyes sweeping the room, then composed herself. "Let's not dwell on that. It's best left unsaid just now."

"There's more." Frederick grinned. "We've solved your riddles and found your treasures. Father didn't make it to any of them."

Lise made a noise, and Charlie leaned forward to whisper in her ear. She looked discomfited but remained silent.

Phillippa put her hand to his cheek. "My little prince. My perfect boy. I'm so very proud of you, you know that, don't you?"

"Yes, Mother," Frederick whispered, his voice breaking. He swallowed hard and looked at Charlie. "It wasn't me alone...it was this lot, here. They are loyal and smart, and I aim to reward them."

"Aren't you a good man with well-chosen friends?" His mother smiled at the group. "I hid those hoping Henry was far too dense to solve the riddles and that if you needed to escape this place, they would give you a new start, and Henry would never miss them." She nodded in satisfaction. "I'm so glad it worked."

"I want to build a Rowley Museum on the property with them, Mother," Frederick said. "There are so many beautiful things that tell the rich history of this place. Things I remember you telling stories of."

"A museum..." Philippa looked surprised. "A place on castle grounds open to the public? That sounds as though you would be inviting theft."

"We could have other artists come, only those we have vetted," Frederick suggested. "We could bring back the artists in residence program."

"You don't have an artist in residence?" Philippa exclaimed.

Frederick shook his head bitterly. "Father wouldn't allow it nor a theater. But we'll bring it back—I've already got a shortlist of artists to interview. I've been preparing for this, Mother." He took a deep breath. "And know this: I'm prepared to take on the barony, or I'm happy to bend to you."

"I'm glad to hear it, and I trust you, my darling." Philippa smiled. "It's all yours." She tilted her head. "Tell me, is Geoffrey still alive? Your father said he was going to kill him."

"No, he's fine. Cecelia and I just went to see him." Frederick gestured at Cecelia, who had been standing silently with her father. "Sorry! Cecelia, come here. Mother, Cecelia is pregnant with my child."

"Oh." Philippa looked startled. "It's lovely to meet you, dear."

Cecelia nodded, looking a bit green.

Frederick took her arm and kissed her cheek. "Cecelia's a grand girl, Mother. She speaks French, minds the twins without them driving her mad, and can draw a picture of anything."

Smiling silently, Cecelia gave Frederick's hand a grateful squeeze.

"Well, that's lovely, then, isn't it?" Philippa nodded politely at Cecelia. "I daresay I need a bath and a nap. Your friends put me in my old bedroom, darling, and I aim to use it to sleep for a week." She chuckled. "Then perhaps after I regain strength, I'll visit Geoffrey for a time."

"Oh," Frederick shrugged. "So you truly don't want to stay and rule over the barony."

"No, my dear," she sighed. "I'm done with this place. Henry can rot in his cell for all I care; I've already forgotten about him. It's up to you whether you want to turn him into the constable—but Castle Rowley needs a capable ruler who is fully invested, with their heart and soul—and I simply need a break from it all." With great affection, she gazed at Frederick. "Look at you. You were just a boy when we last hugged, and now—you've planned a coup, stood up to your father, and uncovered my treasures with your friends. You're a hero to me forever, my darling." As they reached the stairs, and she leaned on her son for support, a collective sigh of relief seemed to fill the group that followed them.

When they had left the dungeon and reached the great hall, Charlie, Lise, and Annabel made their way to the cellar. Charlie began scrubbing the dried blood off himself with a bucket of water. Lise took out fresh clothes for them all and started packing a bag. "What are you doing?" Annabel asked, pulling on a fresh tunic.

"I'm going to get Agatha," Lise replied. "And take her on an adventure of our own." She shook her head at Charlie. "I had hoped to bring some of the treasure you found."

Charlie shrugged. "I've already secured some of it for you." "You have?" Annabel asked in surprise.

He nodded. "Some jewels. I asked Frederick already; he was all for it."

"Well, that's just lovely then." Lise grinned. "Thanks for looking out."

"Oh, Lise," said Charlie. "I shall always love you."

"You shall have to, my dear cousin," she grinned. "I expect a room to always be open at the castle now that your brother's in charge."

"I love you both," whispered Annabel with a grateful smile, and they embraced, giggling, and breathed deeply in relief.

There was a knock at the door, and Lise opened it to find Frederick and Cecelia standing there. "Won't you come in, Baron Rowley and his lady?" Lise invited.

"Oh, I'll never get used to that." Frederick shuddered. "I feel like I aged twenty years in the past hour." He smiled weakly at them. "I wanted to thank all of you."

"You're welcome. I was just leaving," Lise replied calmly. "But I do wish you all the best, Baron Rowley."

"You and Agatha are welcome to stay here," Frederick said casually. "Call for our carriage anytime. I'll pay the charge—a room is always open for you."

"Thanks." Surprised, she looked at him. "You know about Agatha and I?"

He shrugged sheepishly, shooting a glance at Cecelia. "Lucky for you, choosing the most prolific gossip at the castle as your companion," Lise sighed, but she smiled. "Thank you. I will be back. Thank you."

"Glad to hear it," he said, nodding. "I apologize for your imprisonment on behalf of my father." He sighed. "I apologize on his behalf for a lot of things."

"Don't spend the rest of your life apologizing for him," Lise advised. "It wasn't your fault. There's so much you can do now to compensate for it."

"Right." After she left, Frederick sighed. "May I sit?" They nodded, and he sat down on a wooden stool. "I understand if you both want to leave the castle. I'll provide enough money for you to run away, get married, and live wherever you wish."

"That's generous of you, Fred," said Charlie. "Is there a catch?"

"No catch," Frederick insisted. "Honest. But... I would beg you, on my knees, to stay."

"Why?" Charlie asked, genuinely curious, and Annabel nodded.

Frederick stood, shut the door, and returned to sit on the stool. "Because I'm terrified. I'm just a teenager. I don't really know how to run a barony." His face lit up. "But Charlie, you're smart and know how to surround yourself with intelligent people. Look at Annabel. She's the only peasant girl in the region who can read, and you've bagged her."

Annabel laughed. "Is that a compliment?"

"I won't lie that I'd like to, Frederick," said Charlie, considering the proposal. "But there's no doubt that this place has poisoned me. As much as I want to stay; a part of me itches to shake the Castle Rowley dirt from my feet." He squeezed Annabel's hand.

"Do what you like." Frederick stood. "But if you stay, I'll always respect you both and ensure you're respected. I'll give you the materials to rebuild your parent's house, start businesses with your help, and finance your woodcarving projects. I'll bring the Sutars here to be the artists in residence and start a publishing company for Annabel. My father's wealth is at your disposal as I make up for his crimes."

Annabel pondered this, fidgeting with Charlie's hand in hers as his own trembled at the idea of all this coming to pass. "You should start a theater at Castle Rowley, Frederick."

"Oh, absolutely," Frederick eagerly agreed. "You'll be an actor in it, Charlie and Annabel will be playwrights in residence. I'm going to be in charge here now; you might as well enjoy the advantage."

"That's not what I meant," she quickly clarified. "I'm just a farmer."

"Enough of that," scowled Frederick. "You can be a farmer if you like or try something else. You don't seem to need much sleep, and you don't have children yet. Might as well give yourself some time to develop your interests if you have a chance." He looked at both of them. "What do you say? Will you stay, at least for a year, before moving on?"

Charlie laughed. "We'll need some time to talk it over." He looked at Annabel, who smiled. "But I think we might be interested."

Frederick smiled thoughtfully. "I have loads of ideas to make more money off this place. That reminds me—can we go see the treasure room again?"

In the stables, Charlie used a knife to pry the panel open again to reveal the staircase below. With excitement in their hearts, the trio descended the narrow stone steps, their lanterns casting enchanting shadows on the walls. As they stood marveling at the beautiful treasures, Frederick spoke. "Our mother hid these pieces away to protect them from Henry. I remember when he took them away from her, and she found his hiding place and hid them herself." His voice broke. "For six years. What is wrong with my bloody family?"

"Nothing that was your fault." Charlie nodded thoughtfully. "These items are valuable, but they carry the weight of our past and the responsibility to preserve our family's legacy. A museum is a grand idea."

Frederick stepped closer to a painting Annabel had admired and pointed to a signature in the corner. "This one is signed by our great-great-grandmother on Philippas's side, Amelia. She was known for her love of art and poetry." He swallowed hard. "Charlie, this is my heritage. *Our* heritage, truly speaking. And it never would have been found, if not for you."

"Our heritage," Charlie echoed, his voice full. His eyes softened as he studied the painting. "We must ensure these treasures remain safeguarded for future generations."

As they continued to explore the room, Annabel couldn't help but feel grateful for the chance to witness this intimate moment between the half-brothers.

The discovery of the hidden treasure had brought them closer, unearthing not just the riches of their ancestors but also the bonds of family and love.

When Charlie excused himself to use the privy, Frederick turned to Annabel. "So, it seems I need to convince you."

She laughed. "I don't know about that."

"No, it's true," Frederick said, looking earnestly at her. "And I'm glad for it. I want my brother to be happy, and I know he's happiest with you by his side. I stand by what I said, though—if you want to leave, you can." He paused, hesitating for a moment. "But... if you were to stay..." He sighed. "I don't want to be like my father—I want to help people."

"Right," Annabel nodded encouragingly.

Emboldened, he continued, "I will start a Rowley Museum and a theater. But I'll need help, and I'd like it to be the pair of you." He smiled.

She nodded thoughtfully. "How about we stay here and assist you for six months, then you sponsor us for a holiday, and we'll return for another six months?"

Frederick grinned. "That's a bargain."

A sudden squeal pierced the air, and Annabel and Frederick looked at each other in alarm. Annabel swiftly climbed the stone steps and reached the top, where she heard a voice shouting, "Catch that pig!"

Her eyes widened as a hog charged toward her. Dodging to the side just in time as it ran past her, she suddenly recognized it and then turned back to nuzzle at her hands. "It's you!" Annabel laughed and crooned to the grunting pig, "Gavin—sweetheart, come here." She offered a treat from her pocket. "I can't believe how much you've grown. Here, come get the treat, love."

Gavin wiggled with delight and trotted over to Annabel, eagerly accepting the treat, though his collar almost slipped off.

Curiously, Annabel noticed a long rope and a piece of paper around Gavin's neck. Removing the paper, she read, "Annabel Barlow, will you..."

Startled, she looked around and saw Charlie on his knees before her. "Annabel..."

"Oh…" she whispered, comprehension dawning as she bit her lip, paper in hand.

His voice was thick. "You are the light of my dreams, Annabel. You fill my world with happiness and make me think I might do anything. I want nothing more than to spend my life with you." Charlie produced a finely carved wooden ring and extended it to her. "Will you marry me?"

"Yes!" Annabel exclaimed, tears of joy in her eyes as he slipped the ring on her finger. "Yes, of course I will."

As they gazed into each other's eyes, they basked in the warmth of their love, finally free to take a breath and live in the moment together, eyes open, traveling forward into the uncertain but remarkable future.

THE END

AUTHOR'S NOTE

Dear Reader,

First and foremost, thank you from the depths of my heart for embarking on this journey with me. I hope the pages of this book transported you to another time, one of love, adventure, and intrigue. Each reader is a unique world unto themselves, and as such, every interpretation and experience of a story differs. I would be truly honored if you could spare a few moments to share your thoughts by leaving a review.

Your feedback not only helps me grow as a writer but also helps fellow readers discover stories that they might fall in love with. Whether it's your favorite moment, a character that touched your heart, or something you felt could be improved upon, I value every word you share. In the vast universe of books, reviews are the guiding stars that help illuminate the path for others.

Thank you for being a cherished part of my writer's journey. Your support means more than words can express, and I hope you'll join me for the next book, *Treasures of Castle Rowley,* as well as the third and last installment in the Rowley Family Romance series, *Baroness of Castle Rowley*. Until our next adventure together…

Warmest wishes,

Matilda Lockwood

MANY THANKS

Acknowledgements

My wonderful beta readers, Tehniat Shuja and Yeng Cee: your wisdom and encouragement were invaluable during this journey.

Sarim Shuja, your artistic brilliance created the captivating cover and brought my dream to life. You have a true gift!

Chris, whose patience and care keep our family safe and sound every day while I'm writing and working. You're our hero.

Bailey, our little burst of creativity and joy: every day you light up our world, and my heart overflows with pride for you. You've already written many books, and I have no doubt in my mind that one day you will publish too.

To my parents and sister: your unwavering belief in me means everything. Thank you for always knowing I could do it, even when I didn't, and cheering me on.

Lastly, William Shakespeare, for his timeless works that continue to shape our understanding of love and passion.